GEMINI GAMBIT • BOOK 4

DEATH'S HARVEST

D. SCOTT JOHNSON

DEATH'S HARVEST

D. Scott Johnson

ISBN: 978-1-7360141-1-0 (hardcover)
978-1-7360141-0-3 (paperback)
978-1-7360141-2-7 (ebook)

Cover design by Melissa Lew
Interior layout by Lighthouse24

Author's Note

While there is a real town in Arkansas named Dumas, as the saying goes any resemblance to it with the town described in the pages of this book is purely coincidental.

Chapter 1
Tonya

It took her nearly three months to work up the nerve to ask a qualified priest about what her time travel experience had unearthed. And it had to be a priest. Anybody else would either laugh her out of the room or not understand the deeper problem she'd unearthed. When she was in the past, Tonya had somehow been prevented from creating time paradoxes. This could easily be explained by something a secular scientist wouldn't consider. It was a religious idea that had been around for centuries.

Free will, or rather, the lack of it.

What she experienced could make her personally responsible for disproving a fundamental tenant of her faith, and that of billions of other people. When the stakes were that high, she needed a face-to-face meeting with someone who knew faith *and* science.

The trick was to get him talking, while at the same time making sure he didn't call a mental health agency the moment she left. She opened by asking about predestination.

"Well, you need to understand first that there are two kinds of predestination," Father Steve Murphy, Society of Jesus, PhD, head of the Center for the Study of Gravitics at Catholic University in Washington, DC, said with a comforting smile. She needed comforting, for sure Dealing with an idea this big did that to her.

"There's the kind that is in the Bible," he said. "You can think of that as God's plan of salvation for individuals."

"My own personal road map?" she asked.

"Exactly. Predestination of that kind is frequently mentioned in the Bible, and the Church has never had a problem with it."

"And the other kind?" It hadn't occurred to her that she might be fighting a war on more than one front. "Please tell me there's only one other kind."

His smile went from comforting to a bit puzzled. "Well, yes. The other kind can be thought of as *double predestination,* or to be a bit proper, *predestinarianism.* Is that what you were thinking of when you sent me your questions?"

People in realm dramas always blurted out the truth of what they were going through no matter how crazy they sounded. It seemed so stupid. Now, sitting here in front of this earnest, wise man, the urge to shout at him what she'd experienced was physical. *I traveled into the past and may have proven that salvation is an illusion!*

"I guess it was," she replied.

He didn't seem to notice her inner turmoil and nodded. "That's the kind Calvin came up with by overreading Augustine. He's wrong, of course. Dangerously wrong in many instances." He cocked his head, changing from a benevolent priest to a puzzled academic. "And now you're going to explain why you think this all might relate to particle physics?"

Becoming a *chrononaut,* presumably the world's—and maybe the universe's—first person to travel backward in time, had been a roller-coaster ride between extremes of discovery and terror. She'd been prevented, sometimes physically, from creating any sort of paradox. It had been impossible for her to change the past in order to alter the future. Sort of. Tonya *had* managed to get messages out. She'd called Spencer after their Trilogy raid to get a copy of his hacking tools, for example.

But that was only when she promised herself not to spoil anything, not to create a paradox, *and then actually followed through with it.* Any attempt to create one, even on the spur of the moment, would cause a random coincidence that blocked her. She'd stopped trying to make her future self's job easier when, on the way to clogging up a particularly complicated drain in the plant, a tree branch as big around as her head landed in front of her. The impact shook the ground. *Message received,* she'd thought in the moment.

And that was a misdirection she noticed. She would never be sure if any of her other decisions, to have coffee, to pick up a fork instead of a spoon, to walk left instead of right, were her own or were somehow the result of influences from the future, or because she had no choice at all.

"It's purely theoretical," she said. Lying to a priest. That was a great way to start things off. It wasn't theoretical. It was real. She was working from the ground up, trying to explain her observations with a theoretical framework. "I think a new family of elementary particles may be out there, existing in a dimension orthogonal to the four we're used to."

His smile came back. "Your *tockions*?"

Tockion referred to the class of particles she'd discovered, a shorthand way of talking about their common properties. She shrugged. "If people can make names like *quark* and *lepton* stick, why not?"

"If you're right."

Only too true. "If I'm right."

That was her cue to get out her equations. They were the reason why he called her in for a meeting. Her theory was sound. It worked and explained not only her own experiences, but some puzzling results already observed by gravitational physicists. According to her theory, time was controlled by *causality particles,* which she'd named *tickions.* Predestination wasn't the answer. The answer was a new class of particles that moved through previously undiscovered dimensions of the universe.

In the Standard Model of physics, the universe was made up of particles. If she was right, so was history.

*

"Your theory is predicting three kinds of particles, but you've only found one?" Father Murphy asked at their third meeting, a month after their first. The smile was back, now with a spark.

"I haven't found one. But I have ruled out a lot of alternatives." That bolstered her theory, but it was a long way toward anything real. She'd found hints that the first one, the *tickion*, was real, but hints didn't count. There wasn't enough proof to try naming the other two.

Father Murphy did that for her at their next meeting, a few weeks later.

"Tick-tockion. That's one. You'll be putting my name on the paper for that, right?" His smile turned the command into a joke. Tonya tried to smile back and hoped it was convincing.

"And the third?" she asked.

Her theory required a particle that would transmit the effects of the decisions intelligent life made.

"Determion. And it'll come from direction Y2. You heard it here first."

In her quest to have a theory that *didn't* include any genuinely dumb names, Tonya had taken to naming the extra dimensions that her theory predicted with letters and numbers. Y2 was at two right angles to the Y-axis on a 3-D model, what most people would think of as left and right. Kim played with this stuff all the time. Lots of people did, but only in the realms. What Tonya was looking for was real. Those dimensions were out here, somewhere, in realspace. Her theory required them, and her theory needed to be right. There *had* to be a systematic, falsifiable description of free will out there now that she'd proven the past was accessible from the present. It was critical.

Without free will, salvation was meaningless.

Growing up, she had done a lot of bad things. Some of it was just to survive. But she now knew some of it she did to lash out at a world that wouldn't go easy on her, wouldn't pat her on her head for existing or pay attention to her self-destructiveness.

If salvation was a lie, if it didn't *matter* what decisions she made, what decisions anybody made, the universe would change from a place she could use to work toward truth into one of bleak futility. She *couldn't* be forgiven for her sins because they weren't hers. Nothing was. The idea that she would be the agent of that discovery, the person who proved the desert of the nihilism was how it all worked, was unacceptable. She would be a slave, no different from one of her ancestors trapped on a plantation in Mississippi. *Every human being ever born would be trapped along with her.*

She wouldn't let it be true. But she wasn't built to ignore the problem or pray it away. She had gone back in time. It had happened. Things prevented her from exercising her own free will. That had happened. It could mean that her free will didn't exist.

But it might not.

At least she had experimental proof that the theory of multiple worlds was false. The idea that every decision anyone made would create an entire universe had never passed the sniff test for her. But—until now—nobody knew how to test it. That didn't stop a popular minority of physicists insisting experiments didn't matter, and everyone should believe it anyway. She couldn't wait to prove them wrong—as long as she *could* prove them wrong.

As if that wasn't enough, late in the night after her most recent consultation with Father Murphy, she ended up in Cyril's chamber.

It was his humming that woke her, only she wasn't in her bed. She was back, somehow, in the threaded room.

She'd kept that blue bug in the back of her mind ever since the encounter after the Trilogy assault. If he hadn't been directly responsible for her little excursion through time, he definitely had a hand in it. Those first compulsions, the ones that kept her from running away from of the portal until it reached out and grabbed her, had happened *before* causality started pulling her strings.

"You're getting better at that," he said.

"Ending up in your playroom? Not by choice." Unlike her last visit, there didn't seem to be any critical conjunction in the web of timelines. Only the standard dark-colored threads that represented people's lives from end to end. She walked over to him, debating whether she should say hello or punch his lights out.

"Be calm," he said. "This isn't real. But it's just as well."

"Bug man, if you do not start making sense right this instant, I'm kicking your ass so hard it'll go through that wall over there."

"And I don't doubt your ability to do so," he said as he took a few steps back. "I will be brief. You are on the right track, don't doubt that. But you're not as far along as you'd hoped. There's still much to do. And please, always check your work. You never know where it might go wrong."

He couldn't talk straight to save his life, and she was done with this. "I told you about riddles." She reached out to pull him close, give him a good stare, but her hands got tangled up in something she couldn't see. "What the—" Tonya put her fist on his chest, pushed him away…

And landed face-first on her bedroom floor, arms tied up in her blankets. It had been a dream. Thank God. If she never went back for real, it would be too soon. She checked the clock and groaned.

Time to go back to work.

Chapter 2
Kim

It said a lot about her life nowadays that the most normal part of it was meeting with the FBI. A couple of times a month they brought over a data store to unlock, which gave her a chance to catch up on mundane things like bank robberies and kidnapping attempts. Those were things she understood, not the Greek-laced mathematic equations Tonya and Mike were teaching her. Then there were the experiments…

*

"Okay," Mike said to her over the realm connection. "Three… two… one…"

Kim was transformed, an obsidian statue streaked with lightning, and it wasn't a life or death situation. Being here at all was a major accomplishment. Previously there had been no time to sit back and simply examine what was going on. Even when there had been time she'd been so against the idea—if she was honest, so frightened of it—that she wouldn't allow it to be discussed. Then Yellowstone happened, and Will disappeared. She had to accept this was a part of her and learn to use it.

They'd built up to this moment gradually, first closely observing how she transformed her avatar. That didn't look too different from a regular avatar change. The next step was her entrance to the strange place she fought it out with Ozzie back in China. Mike had named it the transit dimension. *That* sent Tonya and Mike to the drawing boards for several weeks, coming up with new equations to explain it. They built her an entire realm to help her understand them.

And now it was time to make the big entrance. Time for it to literally become real.

As always, she simply thought of the location, and she was there, staring through a mist-filled wall into their apartment. Mike, Tonya, and Spencer were set up opposite the inner wall that separated the kitchen from the main living room. Some people got a control room filled with consoles and people. She got three friends on couches watching screens only they could see on their enhanced vision channels. She'd take them over a dozen rooms full of strangers with expensive instruments.

She was stalling. It was time to get on with the show. She pulled her arm back and gathered the power..

Here we go.

Her glossy black fist crashed through the spot they'd cleared on their apartment's inner wall. But there was no debris, and the hole she made in the wall matched the circumference of her arm.

"Holy shit," Spencer said quietly.

"No kidding," Tonya replied, paling as she looked at the arm.

"Don't sit there," Mike said as he got up. "Take measurements!"

He, Spencer, and Tonya used every scanner they had to record the fifteen minutes it took her to slowly bash her way through from the transit dimension into their realspace apartment.

"Confirmed," Tonya said, concentrating on a virtual screen in the apartment's enhanced vision. "They definitely based the portal off of your ability to do this."

"But how?" she asked. "*I* didn't know I could do this until after I escaped."

"The notes only talk about energy signatures," Mike replied. "Maybe that's what they were seeing when you used your hacking power."

The conversation stopped as they all stared at her. Kim had to admit that, even covered with a version of her ninja outfit, this glassy body was unusual. But they were also all leaning away or trying not to look at her. She wasn't a monster. "Come on, guys. I don't bite."

Mike touched her cheek. She would've startled if she'd been able to feel it. She leaned into the invisible force.

"Can you feel that?" he asked.

Kim closed her eyes. "No. Something's moving my head, but I can't feel it." It was time for her own experiment. Kim grabbed him behind his neck and pulled him forward. The motion was harder to manage since she couldn't feel him at all. Even without sensation, she was able to kiss him deeply. Sort of. She was touching an outline, solid air. Kim did her best with it anyway.

"Jesus fucking Christ on a crutch," Spencer said. "Do you two need the room?"

They pulled apart slightly. The smell of him was as intoxicating as it always was, but there should be more.

"I love you," he said.

There *was* more. It wasn't what she wanted, but like the old saying went, it was what she needed. But she wouldn't miss an opportunity like that. "I know," she said. They shared a grin. "I love you too."

Spencer made a gagging noise. "I did not come over to watch *this*."

Tonya laughed. "He has a point. We need data, not romance. How long can you stay transformed?"

"I'm not sure. This is the first time I've done it when I wasn't fighting for my life. It feels fine right now."

She didn't get tired for another four hours. It confirmed a lot of things. She wasn't made of glass, but rather a new kind of biological crystal. They couldn't get a sample, not even fingernails or hair. It was harder than anything they tested it against, flameproof, and impermeable. She could breathe, but it turned out she didn't need to. She was drawing in oxygen some other way they couldn't figure out. As far as could be determined, it was a complete duplicate of her realspace body. The comparison was easy—her body was still lying on the couch. She could even see an echo of the coral lightning on her real skin.

"Before you two get any ideas," Tonya cautioned, "remember that Kim's skin is harder and stronger in this form. Things that are normally soft and flexible might be hard. And sharp."

Kim shrugged. "I can't feel anything anyway. It'd be like going at it in a realm with sensations turned off. Pass."

Mike gave her one of those all-over looks that told her he might not be on the same wavelength. "Sellars?" she asked.

"What? Oh, right. Um…no way. Yuck."

When his eyes flashed like that, she wasn't sure she was on the same wavelength, either. "We'll talk later."

She was half again as strong as normal, with reflexes that were twice as fast.

"Not exactly Supergirl," she said as she flexed an obsidian bicep, "but I'll take it."

She should be able to run faster, but they didn't dare go out in public. Mike desperately wanted to test her zero-point energy blasts—he was really fascinated by those—but without adequate control, someone could get hurt, or worse.

Spencer tried to touch the hole she'd made to come into the apartment and they got another surprise. "Jesus, it's like, solid."

The rest of them tried, but only Kim could reenter it. "It's either a one-way thing, or maybe I'm the only one who can do it," she speculated.

"It's more complicated than that," Mike said. "Remember when we used your multiples to punch vent holes in the duct room back at the power plant? I saw the plasma going through them."

"Are you sure?" she asked. "The pressure ramped up so quickly."

Spencer said, "I've got an idea." He lit a cigarette and blew the smoke at the hole. It split across the face of it like there really was a glass covering it. "Huh. I wasn't expecting that. Back in China, I went through a hole Kim made and ended up in a different realm."

"But why is it always a wall?" Tonya asked.

Kim shrugged. "I walk forward with my destination in mind, and after a few steps, it's on the other side of a vertical divide. It's like a one-way mirror to me."

"Through a glass, darkly," Tonya said, then blushed when she noticed she was the center of attention. "What, a Catholic girl can't get mystical sometimes?"

They spent nearly an hour doing experiments on the breach. Eventually she yawned, and everyone stopped and stared at her again. Her yawns threw sparks.

"It's time for me to go back, I think."

"You only feel tired?" Mike asked.

The very first time this had happened, she'd spent a month in a mental hospital recovering from the ordeal. Kim caressed his cheek. "I'm fine. I'm pretty sure that was Watchtell, not this."

She went through the breach and was almost violently thrown out of realmspace and into her real body. It wasn't a forced exit, but it was close. She needed to work on that. "I'm out." A wave of vertigo came over her when she opened her eyes, and she closed them quickly. "Okay, maybe I'm not completely fine."

"Do you need a bucket?" Tonya asked.

She kept her eyes closed. "No, but I think I'm gonna lie here for a while until the room quits spinning."

*

So, yeah. Kidnappings and bank robberies, things that normal people dealt with, were a nice change for her.

The FBI didn't come by just to chat, though. They still needed her to hack the otherwise unbreakable encryption that protected secret data stores they kept discovering. After more than a year, they were still finding people protecting Matthew Watchtell's work.

There were lines of potential, and she couldn't remember how to breathe. These keys not keys unlock power collapse and now…

Recordings of realm meetings unspooled through a cable into the air-gapped network node the FBI preferred to use for this kind of work. Kim stopped one at random and played it.

"We'll have to split the books now, Sam. You know this can't get out."

They were using technology that could recreate Hoth or the Shire or the top of Mount Everest but still held their meeting in a simulated board room that was so generic she recognized the patterns in the carpet. Typical bureaucrats.

"You're sure *he's* okay with this?" Sam asked on the recording. *He* inevitably meant Watchtell. She was no longer physically ill at the thought of him, but she still got a twinge in her stomach whenever he came up.

"Absolutely. Here are the codes to the data clusters that need to be broken up."

Kim duly noted them and the recording itself. This one was a winner. If she'd struck gold with the first random pick, the thing must be full of them.

She exited realmspace, gingerly so as not to trigger a power headache, and smiled at Aaron as he sat on the other end of her workbench in the back of her shop.

"Good news?" he asked.

The headache came on anyway, a hard rod through her head that stopped behind her left eye. She hid the wince. "It's another layer." Watchtell's organization was smashed, no doubt about it, but the pieces had rolled into obscure corners of the federal government. Not all of them were dead.

Aaron Levine, the head of the FBI's cybercrime division and the man leading the secret effort to neutralize all the moles Watchtell had left behind in the government, chuckled grimly. "Or another rabbit hole."

"I don't think anyone understood how powerful he was until now."

Yellowstone had been a massive coverup on many levels. After it was over, she had reached out to Aaron directly as a private citizen, to discuss their next moves. He was smart, well connected, and she trusted him. He'd been the one who'd rescued them all from Watchtell more than a year ago. If anyone knew how to securely navigate around potentially dangerous government moles, it would be him. And it was.

Even better, he'd inadvertently pulled out one of her favorite tricks by doing the unexpected: using his wife's family connections in Israel to open a back channel to Sarah Glasser, the president of the United States herself.

She wasn't the first female US president, but she was the first person ever elevated from Speaker of the House to the big chair, and Kim was indirectly responsible. The elected president and vice president had been some of the first victims of what the media called *Watchtellgate*, a global political scandal everyone thought was triggered by a trial Kim had been too sick to attend. It was actually a false flag operation Tonya and Mike had engineered using records they'd stolen from Watchtell's networks during Mike's first epic hack run.

The ultimate result was that the current president not only knew who Kim was, she sort of owed her a favor. That was, apparently, how the prime minister of Israel had pitched the idea.

Aaron had told the story to her and Mike over dinner a few weeks after it all went down.

"I didn't understand how small Israel was until Keila," he nodded at his wife, who'd folded her hands over her pregnant belly as she smiled radiantly, "told me her great aunt was from the same family as Benjamin Netanyahu's wife. She got on the phone, and two hours later, I was in a realm with the current prime minister. It was modeled after the kitchen in his realspace house. Then he brought the *president* in for stims and a chat. They don't call him everyone's grandfather for nothing. But his introduction nearly gave me a heart attack." Aaron pitched his voice down an octave and growled in an Israeli accent, "Sarah, *neshama,* you won't believe what this nice Jewish boy has told me about what happened in your great Western lands!"

They all laughed around the dinner table, safe for now, but with the ever-present tension caused by the forces they were now responsible for exploring.

"He smoothed over the fact that the president *didn't* know something one of her FBI agents should've reported about weeks ago, otherwise she might have taken my scalp."

It wasn't only about finding moles. Explaining why the power plant was dangerous required revealing the technology that Watchtell's group had discovered and then covered up. Sort of. She'd only told them about what they'd found in Watchtell's doctored records: that they were researching a new way to transmit massive amounts of electricity over very long distances with zero resistance loss. It wasn't a lie. You could use the tech to connect a power plant in the middle of nowhere to a switching station on the other side of the planet with what was, in effect, an extension cord less than ten yards long.

That you could *also* use it to connect, somehow, to other worlds was the biggest secret of all. If they ever let that cat out of the bag, they'd never be allowed to rescue Will, which as far as Kim—and everyone else in on the secret—was concerned, was their number one priority.

So this new project had two parts: Aaron's mission to neutralize every last crony Watchtell had burrowed into the government, and Mike's work to build a new portal to go get Will.

They'd picked up unexpected allies in the effort. The Israeli prime minister was no fool when it came to new technologies, and they did sort of owe *him* a favor now, so they'd been given access to an Israeli contingent of scientists who worked with Mike directly. He didn't mind. It gave him someone else to talk shop with.

Kim assisted in both projects. In fact, she was the only one who knew what each side was up to. Security was otherwise compartmentalized and need-to-know. Mike's US team was vetted and briefed in details that involved the words *federal prison* and *national security* about what would happen if what they were working on leaked. The Israelis knew they were onto something important and had explained roughly the same thing to their side.

Helen also knew what was going on. Mike wouldn't hide anything from his sister-in-kind, president of China or not. She would've found out the details on her own eventually. The People's Republic apparently had a robust spy corps of its own operating in the US. It'd been Helen who tipped them off to the danger of the power plant in the first place.

It did make Kim worry a little sometimes that Mike was keeping her current on his progress. Helen was an extremely practical and patriotic Chinese person who naturally put her country's interests first. It wouldn't be difficult to cause trouble with the project if she wanted to. According to Mike, thought, Helen was fine with the arrangement. China didn't have any engineers with the right skills to take advantage of the findings, and the facilities would take years to build. She was happy to let Westerners do all the heavy lifting. "You Americans are too clever by half, but the *yóutàirén* will keep you from going too far off the rails" were her exact words. The Chinese were apparently great admirers of Jewish people, and Helen was no exception.

There was also a wedding to plan, and only a couple of months left to plan it in.

Some days Kim would stare at the ring Mike gave her for what seemed like hours. The untouchable freak was getting married to the most amazing man, the most amazing *being*, she'd ever met. He was still an idiot sometimes, and they still had their fights, but he was going to be hers forever. Other days, well, other days, she wanted to throw out every plan, every reservation, toss Mike onto a plane, and get married on a Jamaican beach with a Red Stripe beer in her hand and flip-flops on her feet.

But Mama would kill her. Her family would disown her. To them, a family with a history of thieves and scoundrels that might go back to before the Parthenon was built, she was still the computer-hacking badass who stole from the rich and gave to the poor, got away with it, and then landed a rich handsome man for a husband as the kicker. She'd given up trying to add the deaths, misery, loneliness, and terror to the story. They never remembered those parts and never would.

Kim had to admit that she also wanted it. Having her very own big fat Greek wedding had been a dream since she was able to understand the concept. The church, the black-frocked priest, rings on their right hands, the crowns, the cup, the reading, the works. She wanted it all. There would be some modifications: joining of the hands would involve a scarf, Wolf Trap would be a marvelous and meaningful substitution for the church. Mike shoved Buddhist pamphlets into various nooks and crannies whenever she wasn't looking, so she had to make that fit in somehow as well. But it would be perfect. Her perfect.

Kim saw Aaron out of the shop, made sure her assistant had everything in hand, and then picked up her mother to go to yet another...*fine*...wedding meeting.

The coordinator was shaking and sweating. Something was wrong.

"Miss Trayne?" he asked. "We have a problem."

Chapter 3
Helen

Her ability to be in more than one place at the same time should've been an advantage in her current job. And at first it was. She could attend daily meetings while also reviewing urban plans, doing research, talking with Mike, and keeping an eye on various anticorruption investigations she launched more or less the instant she could. But then her assistants accidentally scheduled two meetings at once. Helen attended them both, and from that point forward, her assistants took advantage of it.

What she considered a liability with a realspace human—being singular and thus pinned to one place—was an advantage with bureaucracies. If she were a normal human, they could only schedule one boring, useless, eternal, hour-long meeting per hour for her. Now it was all she could do to stay sane sitting through half a dozen of them *at once*.

The weird thing was how everyone took it in stride. She was still disguised as her father most of the time, especially in public, but nobody seemed to notice or care that he could attend a meeting in Chengdu and at the same time be in a private conference in Beijing.

Her secret had probably gotten out long ago. The politburo was home to gossipy old men and that didn't change with her in charge. But nobody dared mention the fact that the president of China wasn't who everyone said he was publicly. As long as she pretended to be a ruthlessly competent old man, and kept pulling it off, the entire country seemed willing to go along with it. The longer she was at it, the stronger her *guanxi* became, and the harder it would be for anyone to pull back the veil and admit the scandalous truth.

The scandal wasn't that she was an exotic life form that lived in the interstitial areas of Chinese realmspace. That would be weird, but China was pretty good at weird nowadays. The scandal was that she was also a *young woman*. Flying spaghetti monsters—Spencer had told her about that, and against her wishes, the name had stuck—were fine, but being female and under sixty? It would be the end of the world for someone like that to run China. Impossible! Inconceivable!

So she pretended to be Zhang Huǒ Jiàn, and the politburo pretended to believe she was Zhang Huǒ Jiàn, and everyone else pretended to believe what the politburo told them to believe, and China rolled on to another day.

Most of those days were a study in tedious meetings. Today was *not* one of them. Today Helen had a crook to catch.

Wu Huo was a legendary commodities swindler, using his position to put his cronies in charge of rare-earth elements, precious metals, and other materials critical to the technologies that ran realmspace and the Evolved Internet underneath it.

Looked at from a certain angle, the man was almost as much her father as the one who'd raised her. Without him, she would never have emerged. But he wasn't her father. He wasn't that evil. When Father tried to reduce the number of cogs in the gears by manipulating India into a nuclear exchange with China, she had stopped him with a needle to the neck. That wouldn't be necessary today.

You had help, dear. Never forget that.

The snake mother, the monster her host had once been, was as always ready with a snide comment or crude remark. An accidentally botched transition of her human host had allowed wisps of the previous owner to survive. At one point, she almost threatened Helen's life, but now she was a wicked sort of conscience, reminding her that her host was once the most successful serial killer in human history.

Until I got caught. As you will, if you're not careful. These are powerful men, and you are interfering with them. They do not take such things lying down.

Helen set aside the interruption to address the task at hand. Wu Huo had been rigging government contracts and monopolizing critical commodities so effectively, he'd more than once caused a trade war with another nation. Huo didn't care. He only wanted his empire to grow and grow.

Which was why when Helen's science team had accidentally discovered a mammoth copper deposit—by inadvertently blowing the top off of a remote mountain in Xinjiang province experimenting with stolen plans from the Yellowstone Project—Huo couldn't resist. He had to lay claim to the whole thing. It would make him King of Copper and destabilize global commodities markets in the process. But how to disguise his hand? The way he always did it: creating thousands of illegal shell companies to bid on all the contracts, squeezing out any real competition.

For anyone else it was an impenetrable bamboo thicket, but to Helen, it was evidence. The more companies he set up, the more proof she had of his crimes.

It normally took years to set up the shell companies properly, but Huo didn't have years. Huo needed to have his futures contracts in place before word got out and crushed the price of copper. It was the ultimate chicken-and-egg problem, and it had caused Huo to make a mistake.

One that she was more than happy to exploit.

Once all the preparations were in place, she sent a signal to her secretary. Huo entered the president's office with appropriate deference. Her father, in realspace, wearing one of his trademark Armani suits, sat at the desk.

Father's appearances in private or public had inevitably been rare recently, and always as a hologram. That wasn't a long-term solution. Chinese liked their leaders where they could see them, doing big successful things with huge potential and great fortune. They also to this day had a deeply held fear—ridiculous but there nonetheless—of ghosts. As long as Father couldn't show himself to the world in person, she would be at risk from the machinations of the politburo and the superstitions of the people. She needed a dead man brought back to life. This wasn't as far-fetched as it used to be, at least not with her resources. A special order from the leading robotics company in Japan was about to get its first real-world test.

Huo boggled at Father. With a touch of controls only she could see, Helen made Father laugh. "Have you swallowed a frog, Wu Huo?" he asked.

"This...this isn't possible." Huo cast his startled gaze frantically around the room, falling on Helen. "*You* are trying to trick me."

She blinked, wide-eyed. A young girl, a powerless stenographer, would do nothing less as the subject of this massively powerful and deeply honorable man's attention. She stood and bowed. "I am sorry, Minister, I do not understand."

Huo pointed at Father. "He's dead! I was told!"

She activated another sequence of invisible controls with remote probes, struggling with the clumsy things to keep them from activating the *wrong* controls. The interface could use some improvements. The probes were hard to use, and she needed all the help she could get.

Father's gruff laughter rumbled out again. "And yet it seems I am here. Wu Huo, you are guilty of breaking so many laws I cannot list them all in a reasonable amount of time. Suffice to say you and your family's activities around Gasherbrum V have exposed your entire organization's wrongdoing. You will be tried and sentenced for them in due course." He stood. "I don't think you need to worry about your neck. As long as you continue to behave honorably."

Huo sputtered. "This is an outrage! I report directly to the minister of natural resources! You can't arrest me!"

Two high ranking, and very large, members of the Ministry of Public Security appeared. At their boss's signal, they took up places on either side of Huo.

"I can and I will arrest you," Father replied. "Do not force me to have you escorted to a new car."

He paused. "New car?" Changing an executive's vehicle was a very old method of making sure the person in the back seat was never seen again.

"We have also graciously provided a new chauffer for you since yours has become gravely ill."

He lunged at Father, but the two police officers easily held him off. After a brief struggle, Huo gave up with a huff. "You will not succeed at this. I have resources, connections." He turned back to Helen with contempt so venomous she almost broke character. She was a scared little stenographer, not a cop, and not the president of China. "And *you*. This is a step too far. China will not stand for this. *I* will not stand for this."

"You will stand for trial," Father said, "and nothing more. Walk or be carried away, it makes no difference to me." He turned toward a hidden door, which opened as he approached it. Helen followed quickly behind, a challenge considering all the balls she was keeping in the air at the moment. It shut tight, cutting off the minister's shouting.

Now out of sight of both the minister and the holoprojectors hidden in the office, Father reverted to his more normal serverBot appearance. This was its camouflage. It wouldn't do to have, as Spencer put it, a Dad in the Box show up at a Shanghai loading dock with a Japanese return address on the shipping label. Once, not long ago, she thought such subterfuge beneath her. Now her conspiracies had layers.

Free from the need to control the bot, she set a standard series of waypoints to get him back to his charging station. Her threads ached with the strain of using the probes. Helen now had a much greater appreciation for the times when Kim rubbed her hands after working for hours restoring old locks. Precision hurt.

"That was well played," her assistant, Chén Kuai, said. "I must say, you can imitate your Father's mannerisms just as well as his voice."

Her realspace body felt as worn out as her threads. This was going to be the rest of her life. His life.

Oh, not his life. The snake mother's laugh dripped with the memory of poison.

Ignoring the demon in her head was harder than it had been recently with her exhaustion, another unwelcome consequence of using a robot to imitate Father. She nodded at Kuai. "It is a huge effort to do it well." Her phone rang. Kuai took his leave and walked down the hall. She waited for him to turn the corner, then answered.

"Kim? What's wrong?"

Chapter 4
Maff

"It's taking too long," Maff said. "There's something wrong."

Gaanan's scales gained a tinge of orange, turning his normally serene purple into a tacky wall covering. "If you say that again, you're cleaning toilets for the rest of the trip. Am I clear?"

Maff ignored him and checked the D-ship's piloting controls for the umpteenth time. They were fine. Nobody had ever heard of a failure. Her instructors would've laughed at her worry. But transit school was where things only broke when the instructors wanted them to, and mistakes didn't kill you.

Or get you arrested.

She'd spent nearly ten orbits getting her pilot's license, forced to go to the tiniest academy in the galaxy—three rooms above a restaurant kitchen—because her father wouldn't speak of it. It wasn't done. Society would never let it happen. Everyone who'd heard about her people, and there always seemed to be at least one wherever she went, knew that palluns were hucksters only out to make a profit, to cheat when they could and steal where they must.

It wasn't true, of course. She was simply a pallun, a species that evolved on a gas giant, conscious and intelligent, like all the other civilized beings in the galaxy. But also not like all the others. The rest never had their system destroyed by the AC network for refusing to assimilate, never held on to their old religion, never sentenced to a lifetime living on rocky worlds that could kill them.

Those were the problems every pallun faced no matter what they wanted to do. A pallun D-ship pilot had extra storms to navigate. The families wouldn't support it, their culture wouldn't tolerate it, and nobody would hire them anyway.

Maff had overcome each of those challenges one by one. She didn't need her family's approval, didn't care what pallun society thought, and treated a lack of job prospects as an exercise in asking the right person the right question at the right time.

Getting hired to pilot a ship was a problem solved by a bit of what Maff thought of as *moral squinting.* Piracy in the galaxy was a crime, but the folks who did it weren't hurting anyone. The monopolies the nodes granted kept art away from the desiring masses. It *made* winners and losers when it should be letting the best one win on merits.

The AC network didn't see it that way, so no D-pilot with a valid license would ever risk signing up to a smuggler's ship. Unless that D-pilot was young, new, and pallun. Maff made careful inquiries to various uncles and aunts, eventually finding one who might *maybe* know someone who knew someone else who had a connection with a ship that had a reputation of *flexibility* in cargo choices, but only if she promised the uncle who admitted to the connection three percent of any profits she ever made.

A pallun making shady deals with shady characters wasn't a stereotype if the pallun was actually doing it.

So after worship services one night, Uncle Turnn introduced her to one Captain De'Tan, a scolion from Ishtoe by the red color of his short fur. Maff had to make notes in her personal workspace about his physical characteristics. Telling one kind of high-gravity biped from another was much easier with notes.

Her uncle and this captain seemed much chummier than friends of friends should be during that first meeting. Mother and Father had never approved of Uncle Turnn. Maff had always heard half-whispered rumors about what he *really* did for a living, and after that meeting, they seemed to be much more than rumors. That increased Uncle Turnn's stature many times for Maff.

The crew of the *Last Island* spent the next three months breaking her in. There were the inevitable long stares, whispers, and inappropriate questions. They kept their pallun prejudices out of her face, though, so Maff let it go. The longer she was there, the more they'd get used to her.

But the project of integrating with the crew would have to wait until they got off this *Shol*-forsaken rock.

Maff was about to risk cleaning toilets for the next three ulets to complain about the delay again when alarms blared. Every scanner in the system seemed to have turned on and pointed at them at the same time. No weapon locks, yet, but they were definitely searching for D-ships in this area.

"Stay calm," the chief engineer, Feviz, said over the comms, "drive systems are offline. We're another rock in the slag pile."

Gaanan's scales went flat black when he checked the readouts of the scanners. The communications officer put it up on the shared perception space. "That's not going to last."

On the screen, Captain De'Tan, Elsek, their navigator, and their med tech, Hafurnal, were riding in an open-topped cargo carrier, bouncing and jouncing across the rocky uneven terrain about three times faster than was safe. The vehicle was battered and bent, with the engine in the back throwing off gouts of smoke.

Behind them, and gaining, was what had to be Echnar's entire planetary security force.

"Start the ship!" De'Tan shouted in a very not-confidence-inspiring half scream. "Open the cargo doors!"

Maff instantly flicked the switches that opened the cargo doors. The *big, heavy,* and *old* cargo doors. They went from green—closed—to yellow—opening—status. Maff could practically hear the old drive boxes creaking all the way up to her seat on the command deck.

Other parts of her board flickered to life as Feviz activated the dimension drive. Its high-frequency vibrations went through the decks between the bridge and engineering and then up through her bracing legs. It was another system *not* designed to light it and go. This was going to be too close.

"What's happening?" Maff asked over the general channel.

"Less talk," Captain De'Tan fired back as he drove the skiff, "more piloting. How long until—" A flash from the tip of a restraint harpoon spanged off the captain's vehicle and sailed into the cliff the *Last Island* was hiding under. A cascade of rock thudded into its fuselage. *Last Island* shrugged it off, but Maff still ducked her head inside her suit.

The captain came back on the comms. "How long until we're ready to jump?"

Maff checked all the telltales and noted the empty chair on the command deck. "You've got Elsek out there with you. I don't have a navigation solution."

Maff could almost hear Elsek's feathers ruffle as she chirruped into the comms. "Emergency file W-R-F-K-D! Do it!"

Normally Maff wasn't allowed to come near Elsek's station, but times must meet needs. She extended a manipulator over and accessed the file. The doors were still opening, the engine still spooling up, they were not ready, and the security forces were closing in fast. Maff had the irrational urge to get out and push. They needed to move *right now*.

Elsek's nav solution loaded up, and Maff couldn't believe it. "I'm cleared up to modal *eight*?"

"No!" Elsek and De'Tan both shouted at once. The captain continued, "*We're* cleared for modal eight. Wait for us to get there."

The transit dimension's base modal allowed instantaneous transport on a small scale, like someone walking from one point to another. But at that level, modal one, in-system transits took far too long. Each modal above one allowed faster travel over longer distances. But each higher modal also brought along an increase in navigational difficulty.

At modal eight, they could travel to any point in the galaxy more or less instantaneously. The downside was that it would take ulets to calibrate their nav computers after moving so far so fast.

The doors still weren't fully open, and the drive was only at half power. Maff pushed the door actuators to 110 percent and hoped Feviz was as good an engineer as he claimed.

A yellow telltale flashed on the drive monitor. Feviz was cutting his own corners. "Do I need to worry about that?" she asked. He'd be seeing the same thing she was.

"Not as long as they get on board in the next ninety parnettets."

Maff checked the screen. The security vehicles were now in the same camera frame as the fleeing transport. Two restraint harpoons hit each other instead of the transport. It was all going to come together at the same time. Maff held her manipulators steady over the controls with an effort. She needed to hit the ground running, but only at the absolute last parnettet.

Three more engineering telltales flashed yellow. "Feviz?"

"You do your job, I'll do mine!" he dropped off the shared channel.

Finally the door telltales went to green. Two of the opening actuators threw red failure alarms at her, but they wouldn't need those now. Maff uncovered the emergency Close switch and steadied a manipulator over it. They could recharge that system at the same time they fixed the actuators.

This was going to be *so freaking close.*

The security forces couldn't miss.

Two harpoons were ready.

"Maff!" the captain shouted. "Start the launch sequence *now*!"

He couldn't be serious. "But you're still—"

"Now!"

Hundreds of parns of manipulator training allowed her to initiate a start in her sleep. The captain was right. There would be time.

There had to be time.

The harpoons fired.

They connected.

The transport jounced through the doors and into the hangar bay without slowing down.

The harpoon cables pulled tight as Maff mashed the emergency Close button. The doors came together with a massive clang that rang through her suit, snapping the restraint cables in the process. More red damage indicators lit up. Maff didn't bother figuring out what they were.

If there were this many security units after them here, the transit dimension was surely already hot. She grabbed the controls and initiated an immediate, maneuvering, thrust-plus transition. *Take that, you everything-has-a-place-in-the-launch-sequence instructors!* On the various screens anyone and anything not strapped down or in an inertial dampening field slid sideways, up, and backward with a vengeance. Gaanan yelped from the other side of the command deck as various snack wrappers and half-empty *sangor* cups flew around him.

"Everyone grab something!" she shouted into the comms. *"Now!"* Maff waited a precious half parnettet for all the inertial dampening fields to activate, pulled the Z-vector handle as hard as she could, ignored how many new lights turned on in the warning screen, and hit the final initiation button.

They appeared in the transit dimension with a position vector so far away from normal that she heard the stabilator gimbals hit their stops. Maff felt more than saw a ship in front of them and flung everything in the opposite direction, adjusting to clear the waiting capture framework without scraping.

"Maff!" the engineer shouted into the comms.

Contacts were everywhere. "You do your job, I'll do mine!"

Another max-V maneuver sent everything crashing into a different wall. Maff spared a glance for the cargo hold screen. Their negotiation party thrashed around at the ends of emergency dampening fields, dodging the missiles her maneuvers had turned unsecured cargo into.

At least they're hanging on. Two of the closest interceptors changed vectors toward them now that she'd escaped the main trap. Maff wasn't driving a skiff or a fighter. *Last Island* was a truck, and a big one. It wasn't built to do this kind of stuff. There were plenty of alarming *snaps* and *bangs* coming from the hull. The ship's structural warning panel flashed an impressive number of yellow lights and a few red ones.

The two things she had to get them out of this was a clearance up to the highest level of the transit dimension and her own skills. It was time to show everyone what a species born to fly was capable of.

Four more interceptors were now on their tail and closing. "Prepare for modal transition."

"Maff! Wa—"

The captain's shout was attenuated more than usual as she tore the ship from modal one to modal *four*, a trick she'd only practiced on the sims with no instructors around. Behind her on the command deck, Gaanan made sounds that would mean a long cleanup of his communication station.

Six of the interceptors popped into the modal right behind them.

Eight more appeared around them, immediately vectoring to intercept.

She sent the stabilator gimbals to their opposite stops with a new plus-Z maneuver that pointed them at the only spot in the transit dimension that didn't already have an interceptor in it. "Captain! I need that clearance!"

"My nav solution," Elsek chirped, "I never checked it at eight… I'm not sure…"

Elsek picked one hell of a time to get her feathers ruffled. "Captain! *Now!*"

"Do it!"

His personal approval flipped her clearance on the solution to green. Maff turned the level dial all the way over, pulled it out, ignored all the alarms that went off, and turned it to eight. Wherever they were headed, they were getting there fast.

The modal jump made *her* head spin.

The galaxy paused.

And then they were back. Hard vacuum warnings went off, her suit expanded against its framework, and there were clanks and clangs as various vents closed to seal the ship up. She grabbed the flooring with clamping struts to keep from floating away. They were in space now. She pulled up an outside view and saw only the stars.

At least they were alone.

Maff shouted into the comms, "Is everyone okay? Can anyone hear me?"

The crew in the cargo hold groaned affirmatives at her. Feviz rejoined the comms with a stream of swearing that called her every nasty pallun name she'd ever heard, and a few she hadn't. She'd done a lot of damage to the engines. Maff started a nav trace as he circled back to the beginning of his rant.

When the trace finished Maff couldn't hear his ranting anymore.

She expected to be lost, and they were. She expected the nav computer to not know where to start getting its fix, and it didn't.

What she was *not* expecting was the count of available AC nodes they could use to reset everything and find their position.

The nodes had been seeded throughout the galaxy in a time long before the Refounding. There were legends about the legends. The nodes were everywhere.

But not now.

She checked the nav boards three times to make sure she was right, that it wasn't a busted console. Maff waited for Elsek to come to the command deck and check them herself. She stood there silently as everyone arrived.

They didn't have hundreds of AC nodes to choose from to find their position.

They didn't have *any*.

Chapter 5
Spencer

"How could you possibly let him go? To *Virginia*?" Gramma stuck commands inside questions so carefully you barely noticed until you were already doing what she wanted. "He's only seventeen years old."

Sunday dinner. He'd hated going to fucking Sunday dinner for as long as he could remember. After a few choice stunts when he was seven, he didn't have to go to church anymore. But every Sunday he'd be dragged to a house he couldn't touch, filled with people who didn't understand him to eat weird shit only his family could identify. *Coke* and *salad* were two words that should never go together, and that shit should never end up purple with marshmallows in it. But in McKenzie-land they did, and it was.

Spencer was done with Dumas. *Fucking done.* It'd been three months since Yellowstone, and he was going out of his mind. When Mike casually mentioned Kim had a cheap room over her shop available—because Mike always mentioned life-saving things like he had a stack of them in a closet somewhere; it drove Kim bananas too—Spencer knew his time in this little hellhole was ending. He only needed to clear the biggest fucking obstacle in the world first.

Gramma.

He'd been shoring Mom's resolve up for the whole week. The only way you could gain Gramma's approval to leave town was if you were married and staying inside the county. Spencer had no intention of doing either, but the only way Mom would let him go was if Gramma approved.

This first try went about as well as he expected. Nowhere.

She inflated like the wrinkled old turkey she was. "How could you possibly let him go at so young an age?"

Mom buckled under Gramma's disapproval. "But Mother…"

Time for the second try. He opened up a private channel and sent a signal. A deep mechanical rumbling rose up outside. Mom couldn't convince Gramma to let him go by herself, so Spencer had brought help in the form of his mom's once long ago ex- and now-current boyfriend.

If Gramma'd had wings, she would've flapped them. "No, Barbara-Lynn, I do not think that is a very good idea—"

A pounding on the kitchen door deflated Gramma's indignity. She changed gears from commanding matriarch to Southern belle while she answered the door. He mouthed *you got this* to Mom as she sat nervously.

"Why, Horace Johnston," Gramma said so smoothly Spencer couldn't tell if she was sincere or not, "how long has it been? Please, come inside. We're about to serve cake."

This was a part of Southern culture Spencer never understood, but now did not hesitate to exploit. The whole "those people are *friendly*" thing wasn't a lie. Southerners of all colors treated hospitality as a sport nearly as competitive as football. Except everyone got to play at hospitality.

Horace's voice was deep and gentle. "Thank you, ma'am. Much obliged."

It was all Spencer could do to hold in a laugh as Horace rounded the corner into the dining room. The largest high school linebacker in Dumas history—thirty years ago—had decided he didn't give a fuck after graduation and inflated to an even bigger, rounder, size. He wore his regular biker outfit: T-shirt and belted jeans with boots and a biker jacket, but it was all brand new. The shoes had been shined to the point that sunlight reflections from them bounced off the walls. Respect and defiance in one neat outfit. *Well done, man. Well done.*

He sat down next to Mom and pecked her on the cheek. Mom blushed, and Gramma froze over. But only for an instant. If he hadn't known the old battle-ax his whole life, Spencer would've missed it.

But it was there.

Horace's arrival set off a round of standard Southern pleasantries. One of the reasons everyone knew everything about everybody in this town was none of them would shut the hell up about it. Through it all, Gramma was the consummate host, showing concern about a sick relative and joy at the birth of a nephew.

"Yes, ma'am," Horace said after his announcement. "And my brother starting a family, well, it got me to thinking."

Gramma's only change was a slightly tighter grip on her fork.

"It did," he continued, looking into Mom's eyes with a warmth Spencer knew was not faked, "I was hoping you wouldn't mind if I started going to your church. As a start."

It took Gramma a moment to find her voice. "A start?"

"Well," he said with a sheepish smile as he took Mom's hand. "Barbara-Lynn and I have been talking."

Gramma went pale, and her voice got a whispery tinge. This was better than watching the Cowboys get a drubbing on TV. "Talking?"

"Yes, ma'am. I think it's time I made some changes in my life. Spencer was the one who put my mind to it."

Gramma only *thought* she saw the trap. Her voice dropped an octave. "Is he, now?"

"That boy is a fine influence on an old—well, pardon me—on an old bastard like me."

Mom's eyes gleamed as she smiled. "And since Spencer's going to stay in Dumas, he'll be around to help Horace make all the right decisions. You know, attending church, volunteering for functions, helping out with party setups, and they'll both always be by my side."

Now she spotted the trap, but it was too late. *Checkmate!*

"I see," she said, voice flat. Gramma stood up. "Goodness, Miss Sally pinged me. She's having a terrible crisis. I'm sorry, but I'm going to have to leave you all for a time. Barbara-Lynn, might I have a word?"

Horace's squeeze of Mom's hand and the look in his eyes said *you still got this,* too.

The door closed with a polite thunk. The voices behind it were furious whispers, but after it was over, Mom's smile threatened to split her face.

Gramma didn't look at any of them as she left to visit *Miss Sally*.

And that's how he ended up driving from Dumas, Arkansas to Fairfax, Virginia three months ago. It was nice and steady with everything he had in the world loaded in the back of a used Ram pickup truck he'd paid for himself.

The class schedule he'd devised with Mike at the local community college—the one with *five* campuses in a fifteen-mile radius—was going to get his ass out of high school and halfway through the bullshit Mickey Mouse stuff that colleges always started you out on. After that, he'd be on his way to whichever professor impressed Mike and June the most. June and Edmund had stayed behind at the plant, but he still checked in on them from time to time.

Spencer now split his time between his studies, *Warhawk* support, and Mike's Sidereal Spin project. Sidereal, their code name and cover story for building a new portal, was turning out to be the most fun. Mike and Tonya did the what-the-shit-does-that-even-mean research, Kim got to be spooky a couple times a month, and Spencer watched the dials to make sure everything was connected and up to date. This wasn't as simple as it sounded. They were using an assload of prototypes and beta—sometimes even alpha—software. Things broke a lot, and the fixes sometimes broke it worse. His own fixes for the official fixes were usually straightforward, once he figured out where the little ass monkey was going wrong.

His latest patch to fix the patch that fixed the bug had been a fucking case study on How to Blow Up Software in Six Easy Steps, but now he had good news for Mike after the *Warhawk* stand-up meeting.

"I figured out why the last simulation blew up. We lost track of a pointer on the new spline reticulator."

"You're kidding. That's pretty basic, isn't it?"

He hadn't seen the code yet. "There's seven layers of abstraction between the top of the stack and where things get done. It took me most of a day to work it out."

"And the result?"

"A fivefold increase in our efficiency. It should be pretty epic."

They'd been trying to rebuild the portal safely, in a way that didn't require Kim or an entire geothermal power plant to work. That had turned into a real shit show. The original Sidereal had gotten around it by throwing fucktons of money at the problem and ignoring a maniac who wanted to blow up the world. Version 2.0 didn't want those kinds of complications, but they still needed to figure it out.

"Excellent," Mike replied. "I'll let Kim know as soon as she's done with the wedding meeting."

"Ugh. How's *that* going?"

Mike tried to put on a brave face. "About as well as I thought it would."

Right after they'd gotten back, Mike had made the grand announcement that he wasn't going to be like all the other grooms he'd seen in realm dramas. *He* would be helpful, be there for Kim. That lasted long enough for him to go with Kim and her mom to the first wedding planning meeting. Now he stood back, kept quiet, and jumped when they told him to.

"Her meeting started a few minutes ago. You free to help me get that new patch integrated?"

It was that or finish his calculus homework. "Absolutely."

Chapter 6
Kim

"What do you mean there is a problem with the wedding?"

Two months. Her life only had to hold together for two more months and then all hell could break loose. But *no*. Kimberly Trayne's life never bothered with what Kimberly Trayne wanted.

"You see," he said, "there's been a data breach. We've…we've lost all our data."

On a network that she'd been interacting with. Great. Kim quickly checked her bank accounts—all fine, so it was confined to this site—and then shut off her phone to make sure she wasn't interrupted. Now to examine the actual damage to the wedding planner's network. "Show me."

"There's no need. We have our best—"

She looked back at Mama. "You told him who I was, right?"

Mama shrugged like everyone had a daughter who was an ex-cyberthief. "It didn't come up in conversation."

Sometimes anonymity had its downside. Everyone had forgotten about Rage + The Machine. "I used to work with people who did computer security." Well, *undid* it was more accurate, but that would only complicate the conversation. "Let me see your network."

Alexander swallowed noisily. "I don't think you'll be able to do anything."

Patience was still a new thing she was learning from Mike, along with not ripping people's heads off and mounting them on pikes when they crossed her. She centered and took a deep breath. "Look, if you don't give me access, it won't stop me. It won't slow me down that much, either."

"You can't be serious. Nobody can break into networks without..." He blushed like a kid who'd blurted out a secret.

Well now she knew why he was being a pain. "It was an inside job, wasn't it?"

Alexander put his head in his hands. He had a ring finger with a tan line, but no ring. "It was my wife. She took everything!"

Mama scoffed. "I told your mother that woman was no good, but nobody listens to me. Wasn't Greek, no good."

Kim raised an eyebrow at Mama.

Mama's accent always got thickest when she'd said the wrong thing but didn't want to admit it. "Your Mike, eh, he's different." She shrugged, hands out, head cocked to the side, trying to pretend it was the most obvious thing in the world. "Who's to say he's not Greek?"

Point to Mama. Kim turned back to Alexander. "Erasing records and stealing realms isn't always as thorough as you think." She sent a share request directly to his phone. After a ragged sigh, he nodded. Kim sat back, accessed the local realmspace, and took a look around.

There was nothing. Absolutely nothing. It was an empty Bbox container, a smooth white sphere of interlocking tiles a hundred yards across, with Kim standing in the middle. Mama and Alexander followed close behind.

"Where are we?" Mama asked.

Not everyone worked behind the scenes of realmspace. "It's what holds realms," Kim replied. "Sometimes it holds a lot of them, sometimes only one. If the realm is big enough, it can span more than one." Mama looked confused; Alexander looked miserable.

"Where are the controls?" Kim asked him.

"I don't know. How do you steal the control suite and still leave the box functional?" He wasn't only unhappy. He was also desperate. Kim had watched more than her fair share of executives crushed by the actions of someone they trusted, because she'd been the one doing the crushing. The irony of being on this side of someone else's selfish thievery was not lost on her. "How many other weddings are gone?"

"Almost a dozen. None are as close as yours."

He'd lost the records *and* the realms to keep them in. No model venues, virtual dress shops, AIs to perform ceremony run-throughs, nothing. It was the lack of controls that bothered her the most. It was too neat. People ruining someone on the way out of a relationship didn't do it neatly; they smashed and grabbed. She almost brought Mike in, but he was prepping for the next experiment, and she wanted him focused on that. Besides, Kim *had* once been a computer-hacking badass. She'd gone straight, not cold turkey. "What are your router codes?"

He blinked at her.

"When they set up your connection. They gave you codes?"

"Oh, well..." he opened his arms to encompass the vast emptiness. "I used to know where they were."

She should've known. "I guess I have to do it the hard way."

There were lines of potential, and she couldn't remember how to breathe. This empty not empty not full once and future connections to—

Her arm went tingly, then Mama gasped. They both did. Great.

Collapse and now.

Kim opened her eyes and found her arm partially transformed. Wonderful. It was an incongruous bit of color in the otherwise monochrome space. Dark glass lit with coral lightning. *At least it doesn't show in my eyes.* She tucked her arm behind her back.

Like that was going to make a difference.

"How did you manage to get a new avatar in without any access controls?" Alexander asked.

Right! Saved by realmspace. Kim shook her hand until the tingles went away. "An experiment my fiancé is working on." True, for certain values of true.

Mama was suspicious. There were two kinds of parents who would let their child run riot with grown-up anarchists: the hopelessly naïve and the razor-sharp. Mama was not naïve. "Are you sure you're all right, *paidi mou*?"

"Fine, Mama." Kim heard a rumbling and turned around. "Well that's interesting."

Where there should've been a control room, console, or cabinet, there was a hole. And then there wasn't. And then she could almost make the controls out. It cycled continuously through those states. She walked toward the flickering construct cautiously. If the past year and a half had taught her anything, it was that when realmspace got weird, *anything* could happen.

"What is that?" Mama asked.

"How long have you had this Bbox?" Kim asked Alexander.

"It...it came with the building. We have a contractor maintain it." He looked as puzzled as Kim felt. "That *is* the control room, right?"

When it rolled into its hole phase again, she recognized what might be on the other side: the transit dimension. Her arm tingled a certain way, the same sensation she got in the experiments they'd been performing for the past six months. It also contained an eerie certain *rightness* that Kim and Mike both felt whenever they were around it. Most importantly, it shouldn't be here at all. Nothing they had done would have this effect.

It might be the remnant of a foreign hack. Helen had assured her that Ozzie's Chinese research into the transit dimension had been destroyed, but Kim's life was a monument to what happened when assurances went wrong. "Are you or your wife involved with any Chinese businesses?" Kim asked.

"Some suppliers are Chinese, but that's nothing unusual. It's all basics."

"Any realms?"

"Of course," he said, then got an aha look on his face. "We received a new set of updates last week."

"What a strange realm," Mama, who had gotten a lot closer to it, said. "I think you can go through that."

Kim gently grabbed her hand as she reached for the transitioning area. "Don't touch it."

She scoffed. "It's just a realm."

"And we don't know what damage contracts are in place right now. It could be nothing, but it could be set at full real. You haven't had something blow up in your face when the settings are turned all the way up. I have. Just give me a second, Mama."

She used her phone to pull out small versions of the probe constructs they'd been using during their experiments. "Mike has seen things like this when he's come across defective Bboxes."

Mama smiled at Alexander's confused look. "My paidi mou's fiancé is the best realm designer in America. In the world, actually. You should come to my next lunch party and meet him."

Mama's lunch parties, which usually didn't start until well after noon, were a constant part of life in her family. Everyone who was anyone in the ever-expanding network of cousins eventually cycled through. Mike had added several pages to his Big Fat Greek Family tracking spreadsheet to keep everyone straight.

Kim checked the readings of the probe constructs and made sure the data was saved properly. One thing was for sure, she couldn't leave it here. Once all the different kinds of scans had finished, she pulled out a D-sink. Unlike most things in realmspace, this didn't have a realspace analog. It wasn't a wrench or a piece of fruit or anything else found in the outside world.

"What is that thing?" Alexander asked as he took a step back.

"I'm getting a headache looking at it," Mama said.

Kim put on brass goggle constructs that allowed her to see the seven dimensions the D-sink existed in. It felt like she'd grown two extra sets of eyes and would make her dizzy if she looked at anything else. "This lets me discharge the energy of that other realm safely. It won't take a second," she said as she moved one edge of it closer. "You'll need to exit or at least turn around." Kicking them out would require her to use her power, and she didn't want to risk that so close to whatever this was.

Alexander vanished with a faint *pop*, but Mama stayed, intent on Kim. "What's going on with your eyes?"

Kim had forgotten that the D-sink could channel power back to her. If she could see Kim's eyes flickering through the goggles, they must be bright. "Nothing." She adjusted her grip to make the energy stop going through her. "Ready?"

They got in a brief staring match, and she wanted to turn her eyes back on. Mama finally turned around, but Kim hadn't heard the last of this. "In three…two…*one.*"

There was a bright flash, and it was gone. It left behind a pile of junked constructs. Recognizable junk. *Now* it looked like what you'd find if someone had done a garden variety smash-and-grab. They'd used a realm kit she recognized from the way the piles arranged themselves. It was based on existing tools.

Chinese tools.

Kim opened a line up to Helen, who answered right away. "We have a problem."

Chapter 7
Helen

She couldn't disagree with Kim's conclusion. "It's definitely Chinese, or at least that's what they built it on."

The new high-bandwidth satellite clouds that had recently come online were wonderful. Kim could upload both her findings and the gutted realm itself in a place where they could examine it with minimal lag. No more games of telephone or endlessly saying *you go first* before starting a conversation.

"But where did they get the rest of it?" Kim asked. "We're the only ones working with the transit dimension, right?"

Helen had access to resources that Mike and Kim didn't. She checked her monitor threads "I believe so. That said, my monitors aren't sensitive enough to pick up anything as small as what you've found. I'm still working out noise issues, trying to filter spurious signals. There was a massive one last week that was complete garbage." The metrics all pointed to an area somewhere near Jupiter's orbit, of all places.

"So if someone was working on a portal-level project?"

"I'd spot them. I can always see what you and Mike are doing, for example. The signals from your site are getting stronger and more refined."

Kim manifested a simple chair in the empty space near the anomaly spot and sat down. "Do you think someone else could be monitoring us and using that information to make, I don't know, some sort of low energy device?"

Helen floated her hologram around the remains. "It's possible but unlikely. Most people don't have access to equipment that can sense high-dimensional signals. Those that do are either already watching you or haven't got a clue about what you're doing."

Helen had kept everything about portals and the transit dimension completely secret. There were no recordings, no copies, no files. If she kept it only as memories, it didn't need to be classified. A lack of hard records created a risk, though. If, when this was all said and done, Mike refused to hand over his detailed findings and schematics, she—and China—would be out of luck. Helen wouldn't be able to reconstruct their work by memory, and China would be denied the greatest technological breakthrough since, well, since ever.

But it absolutely guaranteed none of the gossiping fishwives that surrounded her could gain access to the technology. Considering what Huo and his cronies wanted to do with basic commodity information like that copper deposit, she'd take her chances.

"Why haven't you told Mike yet?" Helen asked.

"He's busy with the next experiment, and I need him to concentrate." Kim smiled wryly. "I figured you'd want in on the action occasionally, in your copious free time."

Helen returned the smile. She was more than happy to drop everything and peel off as many threads as they needed to help with the situation. Helen was still in meetings, of course. At this very moment she was finishing up with some economics ministers, starting a final meeting with the education minister, and keeping an eye on Wu Huo as he cooled his heels in jail. Compared to all that, brushing up against findings from the transit dimension was a welcome distraction.

Helen had been doing her own experiments when she could, mostly around the practicalities involving thread transport. Mike had somehow gotten almost all his threads moved who knew how far away and then crammed into tight realms he had no business accessing. Helen had recently started simulating this by creating a portable thread storage realm she could carry on her belt. She wanted to be faster and quicker than he'd been should she ever encounter such a situation, and with it she practiced anytime she wanted. There was no way he'd win if they ever got in a race.

That was all well and good, but Kim was ignoring a different problem. "What about the wedding?"

"The wedding is canceled. I don't know when we'll set a new date."

That wouldn't do. "Who have you told?"

"Nobody. Mike doesn't know. I made Mama wait on her calls until after I told him, but she's got the Rolodex ready."

That gave her an idea. "Do me a favor? Don't do anything at all right now. I think I can help."

"Helen, you're way too busy."

She shook her head, growing so excited the gesture happened both in realspace and in the realm. "No. Whoever was ultimately responsible for this, they had help from China. I want to make that right for you."

"How?"

"I'm an organizer. It's what I do now. It's almost *all* that I do now." The flight wasn't terribly long, and she loved airplanes anyway. They lived in the DC area. There were international conferences there practically every week. Her assistants wanted her to take some time off so *they* could take some time off. It could work. She could create an opportunity to travel to the US and save the wedding single-handedly. The more she played with that idea in her head, the better it worked.

"Well, okay. But let me know soon. That date isn't changing, and now nobody responsible for getting it ready knows it's happening." Kim softened into a hopeful look, and Helen wanted to help her more. "Do you think you can salvage it?"

"You watch."

*

Less than twenty-four hours later, two bodyguards discreetly in tow, she stood at the Air China gate with a ticket to Dulles loaded on her phone. It was notionally her sleep time, so there weren't any meetings to attend.

Everything about it was exciting. This was *incredible.* She was going to fly across the world, on only her third flight ever. She had never traveled outside China at all, had never imagined the need until she met Mike. Beijing Daxing had only opened its new terminal—easily the largest single-building terminal in the world—a few months ago. It all sparkled and gleamed, China at her finest. From the sophisticated luggage bots to the latest in security AI, which Helen took a guilty pleasure in frightening with her threads, it was all state of the art. The future was here, in China, and Helen walked through it.

Right up to…an American plane. It was a bit of a disappointment. Boeing had cornered the transonic market with its 797 Hyperjet. At least it wore Air China's livery. Helen didn't care if the cat was black or white either, and this magnificent aircraft was an impressive mouse catcher in its own right. China's version of the concept was still years away from commercial service, but it was coming. They would have their turn soon enough.

She'd dismissed the flashier SpaceX Starship II out of hand. It would get her there in a quarter of the time, but the expense on such short notice was staggering. The whole point of that mode of travel was to see and be seen, to parade down the rocket terminal's main hall and wave to the crowd as she climbed on board. If Helen ever made an official visit as herself, *that* would be the time for rockets. But for now, she was content to safely and anonymously take a ten hour flight, and through the magic of time zones, arrive only a few hours after she left.

Helen took her seat in business class while the bodyguards took their place in the first row of economy. It'd been their request, giving them a better view of the entire cabin in the extremely unlikely event of a terrorist attack. Helen put them in the back of her mind as her threads coiled and stretched. She rubbed the armrests of her convertible minisuite. Such high quality!

The plane clanked, disconnecting from the parking tug, and she jumped a little. She concentrated on the silky sound of the engines spooling up, paid attention to the flight attendant's safety instructions—while surreptitiously disapproving of everyone who didn't—and peered out the window constantly.

"Your first time flying?" the man sitting next to her asked.

He was tall and Indian, with a faint accent Helen could only guess was British.

She was pretty sure that was close to the limit of his Chinese, so she switched to English. "Third." Her voice squeaked a little, but she didn't care.

"That's excellent. Always good to look a new adventure straight in the face. You never know where it might take you."

They pulled onto the runway, and she was startled by the force of the engine's full thrust, the roar they made under the wings. Her stomach flipped once as the airliner lifted into the sky, and then they were off.

She stayed glued to the window until it was too dark to see, then used an app to fall asleep more easily.

Tomorrow was going to be a long day.

Chapter 8
Mike

Tonight it would be his turn in the big chair, the center of attention, the biggest lab rat in the room. Urgency and need had led him to develop probes that could measure and observe *him.* Not his holo or the avatar he could manifest that annihilated the realms it touched, but his own natural threaded existence. It was something he wasn't sure was possible six months ago. Nobody had ever seen it before, including him.

He based the construct on the one Gonzo had used to help him return to Earth's realmspace. Spencer didn't know what it was, but both Kim and Tonya nodded knowingly as he spun a model of it up in a realm.

"Speculum," they said at once.

"Specu-wha?" Spencer's eyes unfocused as he searched. "Oh, fuck *that.*"

"It's actually pretty clever," Tonya said. "It'll create a space inside you that we can use to make observations. They're designed not to tear things."

"I guess you were right," Kim said as she plucked the construct out of the air and looked at it from various angles, then used one of the knobs to open it to an alarming size. "I think you might end up with some idea what a pelvic exam is like after this."

Spencer made more gagging noises.

Since this was a place he, by definition, couldn't reach, Kim would be responsible for steering and—he took a deep breath at the thought—opening the construct. Spencer and Tonya would be recording the telemetry. He'd invited Helen along as an observer, but something had come up suddenly, and she canceled. It was probably for the best. All he'd hear about was how fat and slow his threads were.

Mike sat down and closed his eyes, removing his concentration from his realspace host and…

Examining Warhawk's *stats…*

Completing a new proof on a navigational theory Tonya was working on…

Watching the latest E-Formula One race, rooting for Sandra Hamilton's third world championship…

Meditating in a private realm using his hologram…

And all the other things he was doing, constantly. If he concentrated on realspace, this all faded into the background. It was still there, but it wasn't as simultaneous as when he let go of his realspace concentration and let things float. It was comforting for him, natural.

"Okay, Mike," Kim said from the instrumented realm, "deploying the probe now."

Tonya and Spencer remained in realspace with their own monitors to see if he and Kim somehow interacted in an extradimensional way that his new instruments would pick up.

"Now we open," Kim said with a little more glee than he felt was strictly necessary. There was a sense of pressing aside, pressure in many different directions, like a curtain parting, but the curtain was him.

"How're you doing?" Kim asked.

"It's not bad. What do you see?"

"Calling up imagery now…Tonya, can you reduce the magnification from where you are? I think my wheel is stuck," Kim said.

Another pause, then Tonya said, "Kim, it's not stuck, you're zoomed all the way out."

"But that would mean… my God."

That sounded bad. "What?" he asked. "What do you see?"

Kim's voice was small and quiet. "I had no idea it would be like this, that it would look like this."

No matter how many times Kim said she loved his threads, on some level he didn't quite believe her. Now she was seeing the real him. "Kim?" He almost didn't want to ask. "What's wrong?"

"Wrong? Wait, *wrong*?" She laughed, and the world tilted back into place for him. "Mike, nothing's wrong at all. Did you know your threads are colored with light? It's…you're…"

He waited, not daring to hope for more.

"You're made of rainbows."

He could hear tears in her voice.

"It's beautiful. *You're* beautiful."

"And fucking huge, man." Spencer said. "It's gotta be an order of magnitude bigger than what you predicted. Maybe three."

"Almost exactly two orders of magnitude bigger than predicted." He could always count on Tonya to be the rational one. "And Kim's right, you're gorgeous."

Okay, maybe not, but he could bear the burden.

He waited until he was sure he could keep his voice steady. "No, I didn't know that. What's the spectrum range?"

It took a few moments for the data to come back. "Full human spectrum, plus a little ultraviolet and a lot of infrared," Kim said.

"Dude," Spencer chuckled, "You're fuckin' *hot*."

"Shut up, Spencer," Kim said with more good nature in her voice than her words implied. "This is you at rest, Mike?"

"As much as I ever am at rest."

"Let's try a reticulator," Spencer said.

"Bringing it online now. Three…two…one…"

The reticulator construct entered his perception, but when it touched the speculum construct, both quickly transformed. Before he could react, an energy surge created by the two touched him.

There were lines of potential, and he couldn't remember how to breathe.

I am here.

I am nowhere.

At once and all never his decisions collapsed waves and he tried to twist away.

"Mike? Can you hear me?"

"Kim, what's happening?" Tonya asked, the blare of warning sirens clear in her audio feed.

The new construct, a combination of the speculum and the reticulator, was like what had taken him away to another star system. His threads fell into it, sticks caught in a whirlpool.

"We're losing him to that thing," Spencer said.

Mike couldn't speak. He couldn't *breathe.*

"Like hell. Mike? I can see where you are now. Hold on, I'm coming."

His perception thrummed, and he knew Kim had transformed. If she could see a place, she could use the transit dimension to reach it.

But he didn't know where *this* was.

He had to remember how to breathe.

In realspace, Spencer said, "The fuck if I know why it's doing that. What if we pull the plug?"

Tonya gasped. "Spencer, *look.*"

Mike was enveloped in threads that were not his own. They weren't Helen's either; he knew what those felt like.

"Fuck me," Spencer choked out.

These new threads grasped him, held him tight. They touched the construct, and he felt its energy being pulled away, venting somewhere. The draw must've been massive. The roar went on and on. The only thing he'd ever experienced that came close was when he originally found his way to his host. But that'd been faint echoes compared to this. A small part of him knew that the power was being routed into space, a failsafe system Spencer had set up to handle unexpected surges. On certain frequencies, it'd be the biggest beacon in the solar system right now. Maybe in a million years it'd come across someone who'd notice it.

He slipped with a shift in the balance of his perception and gripped the surrounding threads tighter.

A voice came from everywhere around him. "You're not going anywhere, Sellars. I'm not losing you to one of these things again."

He gasped and remembered how to breathe. "*Kim?*"

"Yes. Sort of. I think. There are so many of me. How do you concentrate spread out like this?"

His threads pulled out of the combined construct intact. "Relax, let the threads do the work for you." That's how he started out with his realspace host. She couldn't be in here with him. Nobody could be. He'd proven that with Helen many times. Threaded beings couldn't occupy each other's home spaces. *It was impossible.*

"Am I actually touching you now? How can I tell?"

"I don't know. You're not supposed to be in here with me." He and Helen had clear boundaries between themselves, ones neither could cross. This was ropes twisting together. There was no concentration that he could say was a touch. She was everywhere. He was everywhere.

The sense of sharing was total. They were together.

And then some of her threads fused with his. That area immediately went numb. "Did you feel that?" he asked.

"Yes. It's spreading."

The new threads were something different, a combination that wouldn't come apart if they fused too much. "You need to get out of here."

"Where? How? I don't see an exit."

"Kim?" Tonya said from realspace. "Whatever's happening is making both of your vital signs change. I don't like it. Is Mike safe? You need to leave."

"Are you safe?" Kim asked him.

The combined speculum-reticulator construct had dissolved. He couldn't perceive it anymore. "Yes, I'm sure of it."

The numbness continued to spread. On the other side, something different began to stir.

Spencer whooped. "Kim, do you…I don't know what the shit you use for eyes in there…do you sense this?"

Immediately a beacon of attention flashed in the distance. That was the only way he could describe it, even though it didn't make sense to him. Nothing made sense at the moment. Kim shouldn't be in here with him, and they shouldn't be combining into whatever was starting to gain strength. Compared to those two sensations, a beacon of attention was just a weird flashlight.

"Yes!" she shouted, "Is that my exit?"

"Move your ass, sister, move it *now!*"

Kim went past him with an almost aquatic whoosh. Her threads pulled apart from his painfully. The numbness vanished, and whatever started gaining strength rapidly faded away. He said a quick sutra for that, because that *whatever* was a very different entity. Having his existence threatened was one thing. Having it threatened with a replacement he didn't understand and could barely perceive was a whole different basket of threads.

He returned his concentration to his realspace body as Kim exited the realm. He sat up but then gripped the sides of the chair as he nearly lost his balance. "I'm okay," he called out. "Kim? Are you okay?"

Tonya and Spencer's shouts sounded confused. There were no words, just a string of sounds. He couldn't understand what they were saying and didn't know why. The spinning slowed enough to allow him to see clearly again. Spencer and Tonya were still babbling, but Kim, who seemed fine, stared at him open-mouthed. "What did you say?"

Kim shushed the other two.

"I wanted to know if you were okay. What the hell was that? What happened? How did you get in there with me?"

Spencer and Tonya whispered frantically, still in gibberish. Kim said some sort of gibberish back to them, and they fell silent. "Mike, you can understand me, yes?"

"Yes. What's wrong? Why can't I understand Spencer and Tonya?"

Kim got up and wobbled over. As always, when something happened with their abilities, she tried to touch him. As always, she backed off, hissing with pain. "Still too much to ask for," she said.

"Kim? Why can I understand you but not Tonya or Spencer?"

She got as close as she could. "I don't want you to freak out. I'm pretty sure this is temporary. Your accent is already changing a little."

"Accent? What accent? What are you talking about?"

"You can't understand Spencer and Tonya because they're speaking English. You can understand me," she giggled a little hysterically, then stopped.

"You can understand me because we're speaking Korean."

Chapter 9
Maff

It'd taken some time for everyone to accept how lost they truly were.

"How can there be *no* nodes?" Elsek constantly chirped. The navigator wasn't quite right without them. Neither was anyone else.

"You're sure we were surrounded, there wasn't any other direction you could've picked?" Gaanan said, who'd been on the bridge with Maff and should've known better.

Hafurnal, their medic and possibly the most laid-back intelligent plant Maff had ever known, curled its—no, the correct term was *pogs*—fronds lazily. "We've got plenty of sa'dst. We'll figure it out. Don't take a year or anything though."

Sa'dst would at least ensure they could all eat the same rations without worrying about getting poisoned by some biological incompatibility. Maff was protected by her suit, but still needed the correct gas mix to use as the basis of her food.

The captain was the only one who wasn't angry at her.

"You did save our hides," he'd said while Maff fidgeted in front of him in his cabin just off the bridge the day after they arrived. "Why not skip to the other side of the galaxy? That was what Elsek's solution was supposed to do."

"That's what I thought it did. It's what I still think it did. I don't understand it any better than you do."

Maff had her suspicions, though. She could've sworn the solution had changed subtly between the time they arrived and when Elsek finished making sure the nav sensors were working properly. The conclusion that Elsek had done a little after-the-fact correction was hard to shake, but Maff had no way to prove it. Besides, who were they going to believe, the green pilot or the veteran navigator?

The captain had gotten up and patted Maff on the top of her suit, somehow condescending and forgiving at the same time. "We have plenty of supplies, and time to make repairs. At least we're not cooling our heels in prison. We don't need to go anywhere at the moment, so you're out of a job for now. Find Feviz next, he needs help fixing what you did to the ship."

And that faint praise was all she got from anyone. Maff wanted to believe it was because they were all so scared. She certainly was. The lack of a D-space fix restricted them to modal one, maybe modal two if they were desperate. They needed to travel to another star system but were restricted to speeds that could be achieved by ground transport if they wanted to stay safe, or fast air transport if they didn't. That would get them across a planet in a reasonable amount of time, not between stars.

Feviz was his predictably antipallun self. Now that Maff had broken the ship, he didn't bother hiding his contempt.

"Not so cheap now, eh?" he said, scale colors rippling. "Can't thread a call to Daddy to pray for you. He's too busy cheating innocent folk out of their supper anyway. And you're supposed to help me? You probably don't know which end of a wrench to use."

It was one thing to have these insults whispered behind her back. It was another altogether to have them spat in her face. Worse still, she had no choice but to take it.

Well, no. The worst part was that he was right. She'd never seen tools that could be used to repair a ship. She shifted the legs of her suit, and they hissed a little as the struts moved against each other.

"I should've fucking known," he said. "You don't. Too busy with your prayer books to learn a proper trade."

If they had been anywhere else, she would've knocked the teeth out of his stupid kron skull for that. If they ever managed to *get* anywhere else, she would. But for now, Maff only said, "Insulting me doesn't fix the ship. I may not know how to use a wrench, but I can learn. It's not like we can take it to a repair shop right now."

"No thanks to you."

Maff pushed all the emotion out of her voice. The truth burned, but she would never give him the satisfaction of seeing her crack. "No thanks to me."

And you're welcome; otherwise we'd all be in a Death Eater camp, you ungrateful wretch.

Since nobody else seemed interested in it, Maff spent what little free time she had examining the system they found themselves in. It was an entirely new place, after all. Nobody had ever seen it before. Maff was the first. *Last Island* wasn't an exploration vessel, so her tools were limited. Still, simple optics weren't too bad when you were starting from scratch.

It was a less common system arrangement, with the gas giants a long way off from the star. *Last Island* arrived close enough to the largest one that Maff had silly fantasies about being the first pallun in demetars to take off her suit and fly free in its atmosphere. There was another gas giant further out with a spectacular set of rings, and an icy one well beyond it that rotated perpendicular to its orbital path like a wheel on a road. Stranger and stranger still.

Maff could barely make out a pair of rocky inner worlds, one distant and cold, the other whizzing around where the gas giants usually were. They were all on the same orbital plane, which was typical. Being the only thing the ship could orient with, they ended up on that very same plane. There could be other planets—there probably *were* other planets—but until the ship moved, there was no way to see them.

Maff would give them all names if they stayed here long enough. For now, she was content to look at them. She may have failed at keeping the crew out of trouble, but she'd succeeded in not one but two of her larger goals: she'd discovered a new system *and* a mystery. Nobody knew how or why AC nodes had been seeded throughout space. The various religions of the galaxy, including her own, all started out with them just there. That ever-present nature was a bedrock assumption of civilization. Maff had never once considered anything else.

And yet here they were, stranded in a deserted bubble empty of nodes out to the highest-powered D-pings they were capable of generating. It had to be thousands of alapurns across at minimum. And in the hundreds of millions of apurns since the Refounding, nobody had ever stumbled across it before.

Or at least done it and returned to tell the tale.

That comforting thought kept Maff company while she learned basic ship maintenance from a kron who hated her and her people for no reason she could see other than that they existed. She turned it into a lesson in patience. He'd grumble out nasty things until he'd drunk a lot of whatever his species used as an intoxicant and then treat her like an ignorant slave right through lunch and past dinner.

He didn't skip any meals, and he knew she didn't need them. Pallun grazed continuously on organic gasses. Getting used to the culture of meals, a fact of life for all the high-gravity, high-temperature worlds that dominated the galaxy, was very difficult for a pallun. Some never did, others didn't bother trying. That they chose to go out into the galaxy anyway was one of the more famous clichés that marked her people, made them different.

After three mets, her ordeal came to an end. They'd started at the front of the ship and worked their way toward the back. Feviz would give her a nasty lecture on the tools she needed and then *supervise* with a fermented bulb of colstal in his hand and a burning wustar hanging out of his mouth. Since she didn't have a skeleton, Maff could fit in slots and ducts no high-grav species could hope to navigate. It was a small mercy that meant they didn't have to disassemble an entire segment of the ship to repair hard to reach mechanisms.

By the time they got to the mistreated cargo doors, Maff no longer needed to be told the right end of a wrench to use or the proper size needed or the difference between fastener drivers. She had also lost any desire to branch out into engineering. Replacing one dirty, greasy, burned-out part with a slightly less dirty, greasy, hopefully-not-burned-out part over and over made her long for her days learning ancient Pallundian as part of her religious studies. She *hated* ancient Pallundian.

"Saved the worst for last, *pallun,*" Feviz said, turning her species' name into an insult again. "These latches were marginal before you banged them together like you were trying to start a fire with them. Pull them all and put aside the best two. We'll use them as models for the rest."

Maff groaned on the inside. There were eight latches on each of the doors, and she could already see the corrosion that covered the fasteners. The many, many fasteners. None of them would come loose without a fight.

That *pectiontul* Feviz waited until she had four of the latches in pieces on the floor before he said, "You *have* been marking their positions before you took them off, right?"

They were in the standard gravity of the transit dimension. If Maff used all her manipulators at once, she could bounce him off the floor, ceiling, and three of the walls before he could react. She knew she could.

And the crew would push her out the door for killing their engineer. So Maff stowed it.

"No, I didn't know that."

He put his big scaly arms behind his back, not bothering to hide the glee at his little joke. "It'll take most of a met to get those correctly aligned then. *If* the calipers are still around. I haven't seen them in ages. Mark the rest before you take them off, will ya?"

The calipers were nowhere to be found, so the only way to align everything was to open the doors, shut them, then see if the board stayed green. If it didn't, they had to use a freaking string to find the ones that were still out of alignment. Shifting one changed its relationship to all the others, starting the whole process over again. It had taken three mets to go from one end of the ship to the other on a repair crawl, long enough for their local gas giant to complete a little more than seven rotations around its axis. It took another three mets just to fix the stinking doors.

They now had all but two of the latches green. If any new ones went yellow, she'd use her manipulators to hurl *herself* around the cargo bay. It would at least give her a reason to stop—

Claxons went off on the bridge, loud enough she heard them all the way in the cargo bay.

"Maff!" the captain shouted. "Get up here!"

Her suit's legs were sticky from the grease and grime she'd been plowing through, but that didn't slow her down. She recognized that alarm.

They'd found a node!

Maff burst onto the bridge as everyone else chattered and took their stations. "Where is it, Elsek?" she asked.

The navigator fanned her wing feathers out as she worked at the solution. "It's close. Very close. But there's something wrong with it."

Elsek shared her readings in the common channel, and Maff could immediately see the problem. The signal was strong, coming from the other side of the star, but it wasn't what she was used to seeing. It was almost…braided.

The captain waved the readouts away. "I don't care if it's broken. Where there's one node, there's another. We can use it to contact the rest and figure a way out of here. Maff, take us up so we can see what it is."

She configured the controls and moved them through the transit dimension until they were well above the orbital plane. When they exited into space, she finally saw what was on the other side of the star. More planets, two inner rocky ones and another gas giant further out from the rest. The rocky one closer to the star was covered with an atmosphere too thick for the node to possibly be on its surface. The other one, a classic water world, was the obvious target.

The planet was definitely inhabited. The dark side was speckled with lights that neatly outlined the continents and bodies of water.

It meant land-based life forms. They zoomed the nav-scope down on the planet for a fine solution, and she saw flickering well outside the planet's atmosphere. It might be ring fragments, like the ones the big planet had further out. But the signatures were all wrong. They were made of organic compounds and exotic metal alloys, stuff you never saw in asteroids, even choice ones that the AC nodes sometimes found in recently opened systems.

Satellites, that's what they had to be. *Artificial* satellites. And they were *everywhere*. At some altitudes, there were thousands of them whizzing around. There were several huge ones too, higher up. The planet's moon had them, and a few were on trajectories that looked like they transited between the two bodies regularly. If they were going between the planet and its moon *in space,* well...on a hunch, she zoomed the scope out, and that hunch played out. There were a few satellites heading out to—and coming back from—the smaller rocky world she'd already seen. It naturally had its own collection of satellites.

"Maff, leave the scope alone," Elsek scolded.

"Are you guys seeing this? What's going on down there?" The AC nodes built satellites, but they were always great big hulking things and never numbered more than a few dozen. A *third* mystery. This definitely made up for being the most hated member of the crew.

The captain narrowed his eyes. "Any signal traffic, Gaanan?"

The communication officer studied his virtual consoles, scales going pale orange. He was puzzled. She had never seen him in that state before. Feviz was a tsell-spitting pectiontul and would never show the slightest curiosity. Gaanan came from a much higher caste, but like all kron, would never betray a weakness. "Nothing on any of the regular channels, but I'm definitely seeing AC node activity. No nav reflectors, though." He stopped for a moment. "I don't believe this."

"What?" the captain asked.

He shared a spectrograph of what was coming off the planet. "The node traffic is anemic but look at that radio signature."

It was so bright on certain frequencies it nearly outshone the star.

"What does it mean?" the captain asked.

"I don't know. They're using radio, but not in a way I've ever seen before."

The captain shook his head. "We'll be sure to ask them what they're up to after we arrive. Elsek, do you have a navigation solution to that signal's source's location?"

"To within an alaparnettet. You'll be able to reach out and touch it when we get there."

"Maff?"

She double-checked the nav solution. It was solid, good enough for modal three, but would still take a while to get there. At least she had a direction now. "Ready."

The captain leaned forward. "Let's go pay a visit."

Chapter 10
Tonya

It took Mike less than an hour to remember how to speak English again. It was like he couldn't find the right gear in his head.

"He'll be fine," Kim said as they kept a close eye on him over the dinner table. "If I speak a different language for a long time, it takes me some effort to find English again."

"Yeah, but he's never spoken Korean in his life," Spencer said.

Mike made faces as he tried to find the right words. "What were…readings?"

He still wanted to know about their findings. Tonya pulled them down into the apartment's shared vision channel. "Everything was green until that construct combined with the probe." She activated the recording they took. "It has to be related, but I'm not sure how yet. That wasn't the scary part, though."

Tonya added biometrics, and the view of Mike and Kim lying on the couches moved to the bigger view of his threads. "It starts happening…here." From the probe's point of view, Mike's multi-colored threads were joined by glossy black ones shot through with pink lightning.

Spencer paused the replay. "Well ain't that subtle?"

"Pretty," Mike said softly. "Very pretty."

"It felt so…I don't know how to describe it," Kim said. "I was everywhere, all at once. I had…I don't know what to call them. Part of me was localized, I could feel it."

Mike nodded. "Data…I…" He closed his eyes and concentrated, then switched to Korean.

Kim raised an eyebrow and said in English, "You need to stop doing that until you get your English back."

"Hard to…find…words…"

"What did he say?" Tonya asked.

"He calls them datastores. So does Helen. It's the only other major structure their bodies have."

"And you had them too?" Spencer asked. Kim shrugged, and he splayed his fingers around his head. "Mind. Blown."

Tonya unpaused the replay. "Now watch the other screens."

They all got to see on replay what she'd seen live. It was fine now that everyone was okay, but in the moment, Tonya had been as wound up as she'd ever been in an ER, waiting on a gunshot wound to roll through the door.

"Our heartbeats synchronized," Kim said.

Tonya paused the show and highlighted several other graphs. "*Everything* synchronized. And then…" she started the replay up again.

On screen, the skin on Kim's arms began to vanish. Musculature was clearly visible.

"What the hell is going on with my skin?" she rubbed her arms.

"Me…" Mike stuttered. "Me too."

"Jesus," Spencer said. "Are you guys okay now?"

They both held up their arms, which were fine.

Tonya rewound it. "Now watch your threads."

On the edges, they intertwined, became one, changing until they were clearly transformed.

"That part I remember," Kim said as she blushed slightly. "We were combining."

Mike pointed at his head. "Learn Korean."

"That's why you needed to get out of there as fast as you could," Tonya said. "The mental exchange I can almost understand, but this physical transformation? I don't know what it was."

Spencer turned to Kim. "And for someone who just experienced a new kind of existence, you don't seem to give two fucks about it."

Kim took a breath. She was as rattled as Mike, but she was hiding it better. "For now, it feels like it happened to someone else. I don't know how to react." She turned to Mike. "You were in trouble, caught up in one of those things again." Kim handed him the other end of the napkin she'd been worrying the entire time. "I actually thought I'd be hauling your threads out with my bare hands."

He pulled the napkin tight, and they held it together under tension. It took two tries for him to find the right words. "Me too," Mike said.

"Well," Spencer said. "Mike ended up with Korean. Did you get anything, Kim?"

She shrugged. "I got something. I can feel it. But I don't know what it is yet."

"We'll figure it out eventually," he replied. "How about your stuff, Tonya? Did we break any of it?"

Things had been so crazy that Tonya had forgotten her own experiments had been running the entire time. They were all passive detectors and so couldn't have been involved in what had happened. Or at least shouldn't have.

She checked the status boards. "They're all offline. That could be good, or it could be bad." They might have spotted a massive pulse of tockions that shut them down. Or there could be a sad, strange little set of burned-out detectors in the main lab. "Only one way to find out for sure." They had to go there to check things out.

Mike frowned. "Timing…tight…meeting?"

Kim got up from the table. "It's not that far. We're against traffic right now anyway."

"Well let's roll," Spencer said as he headed for the door.

They did their experiments in two places: Mike and Kim's apartment when they needed secrecy and an obsolete data center when they didn't. Portals and extra dimensions were fine to share with their extended science team. Mike and Kim's nature were not.

Tonya wasn't sure their ruse was working all that well—Aaron in particular gave them the stink eye whenever they talked about working remotely—but the discoveries everyone shared in were so revolutionary and complex that she was certain a pair of politicians had told everyone to turn a blind eye as long as the data kept coming in.

Having two sites also had the added advantage of separating her experiments from the noise of a residential utility grid. She was trying to detect particles of time. The last thing she needed was for a surge from the next-door neighbor's hair dryer to fry her gear.

They'd taken over a four-building complex in a remote office park not far from Ashburn, turning one building into the main lab. The other three were used for their electrical connections. Traveling to the site was trippy. This part of Virginia could go from a bustling suburb to a ghost town of low-slung buildings by turning right and then left off a busy street. The stillness was creepy sometimes.

Inside was a collection of racks filled with complicated electronics that Mike had been building up for the past six months. Because they planned to build a new portal here, the space was much larger than what they needed at the moment. Tonya could fit an airplane in the main room if she wanted and have space left over. It had a small, standard office space attached, which gave everyone a desk and a place to have meetings. They took their seats in the realspace conference room and jumped into the lab's realm.

The contrast was, as usual, a little disorienting. In realspace, there was a room with only the four of them inside it. In the realm, it was crowded with people—their Israeli and American teams—all talking at once.

Kim ran the meeting, something she was getting pretty good at. Her knack for understanding where a person was coming from and how to relate that to another person who didn't understand and sometimes didn't speak the language was becoming a vital factor in the success of the project. Tonya and Mike were there to field any theoretical questions. Spencer kept the teams in charge of the gear up to date and pointed in the right direction.

Once everyone had settled, Kim said, "I guess that didn't go as expected."

The quip got a chorus of laughs and a smattering of applause.

Overall, the findings were good. Kim's channeling of the construct's energy had been sent straight into space. Nobody snooping around would've detected anything. Its passage proved two of their new dampener designs were tougher than predicted. This was a great finding. Controlling the energy was as important as generating it in the first place.

But, as Tonya read the metrics, she got a sinking feeling that her own private experiments may not have fared as well. The size of the main surge implied a truly massive tockion pulse, much larger that she thought was possible at this stage of her research. There might not be anything to review. Nobody died, and that was an important thing to keep in mind, but it'd taken months to build that little network. It would suck to start it all over again. Once the meeting adjourned, she headed straight for the main floor of the realspace lab to check things out.

Her sensors lined the main conduit that would eventually power and control the portal they would soon be building. Mike was stockpiling the materials to build the mounting platform, but for now, the conduit pointed at an empty space in the dark.

Spencer kneeled down next to the first of her sensors. They started lighting up in sequence, making the conduit look like it had a tiny set of streetlights running along either side. "Good news," he said. "No Kentucky-fried sensor network." Against all odds, her sensors had been preserved by the overload protectors Spencer had designed into the scanners. "It'll all be back online in a few minutes."

He clapped his hands together as he stood up. "And since you don't need me for any heavy lifting, I was wondering if I could have the car for the night?"

Mike chuckled. "Where are you going?"

Spencer was breaking out of his small-town isolation with a vengeance, attending every show and concert he could get tickets for. She wasn't sure when he took time to sleep. Ah, to be a teenager.

"Jiffy Lube Live. Retro-Warp is in town. Paramore came out of retirement, and they brought their friends! I got some of the local *Warhawk* guys to come along."

Tonya looked at the size of the files the sensors had made before they shut down and groaned a little. "This will take most of the night, I think."

"Okay, Spence," Mike said. "Have it autodrive back here after it drops you off."

"No problem, chief. Catch you losers later."

It took several hours in a realm lab to unpack and arrange the data into usable constructs. Tonya worked on her particles while Mike concentrated on figuring out what had gone wrong with their experiment.

The news was *very* good for her, so good she checked it four times before letting the little spark of hope that had lit up in her chest grow large. They had rammed so much energy down the pipe it'd generated a huge tockion signal, *but it hadn't fried the network.* She had proof of the first leg of the theory! Tonya let out a whoop as Kim entered the realm.

"That sounds like good news."

"Very good!" Tonya rushed over and picked Kim's avatar up in a bear hug that spun them to the ceiling. "I proved the first part!" She let Kim go and did a little boogie dance with Mike's hologram. "We're making progress," she sang. "I got a theory!"

"Huh," Kim said as she looked at Mike's work on the other side of the lab. "That's interesting."

She and Mike stopped their celebration.

"What's interesting?" he asked.

"You do see it, right?" Kim asked.

"See what?"

"Right here." Kim used her finger to draw a circle around a big chunk of the equation Mike had been working on.

Tonya glanced at him, and he shrugged.

"Oh, come on," Kim said as she floated closer. "It's obvious."

"Okay." The way he stretched the word out meant Mike was as confused as she was. "What's so obvious?"

Kim concentrated on whatever it was she found. "You forgot you changed the sign here," a totally different area of the equation lit up, "and now here," she pointed at the circled part, "you've got a feedback loop. The transformation of the constructs was inevitable."

She and Mike drifted past Kim to get a closer look.

"I'll be damned," he said.

Tonya started from farther back and followed the equation forward. It took her a minute to get to the part Kim was talking about—the math was that complicated. But Kim was right. Mike had made a simple mistake at the beginning that caused a feedback loop. And Kim spotted it from ten feet away.

"But it's okay," Kim said like she'd been doing algebraic geometry her whole life, "you only need to alter it before the midpoint, and you won't get any feedback loops. It'll be impossible."

Tonya turned around to find Kim beaming.

"It makes sense now!" Kim swept a hand around the room. "It all makes sense!" She let out her own whoop and sailed around the room, pumping her fists.

Tonya slowly turned to Mike. "I guess we've figured out what she got from you."

Chapter 11
Helen

If Helen was honest with herself, she didn't know what America was really like. Before meeting Mike, before going outside, Helen thought every stereotype her superiors told her was true. America was a land of high crime, where rich white people hid in fortified homes, while oppression and chaos reigned among their minorities. They were aggressive imperialists, always with one finger on a button that could destroy the entire world, threatening to press it any time things didn't go their way. They were loud, greedy, and extremely rude to their elders or anyone else who got in their way.

America was, to her way of thinking back then, a nation of assholes.

Then she met Mike, Kim, Tonya, and Spencer. A hodgepodge of *Americans*, one of whom was only technically human. Her family. And she wouldn't have it any other way.

She shook her head at the contradiction as she walked down the jetway.

"Is everything okay, ma'am?" Liu Jinsong asked.

The bodyguards were a discreet half-dozen steps behind her, but ever vigilant. "Fine. My contact will be meeting us at the exit gate." She sent them Kim's picture while she sent Kim a note that they'd landed.

Wang Ying wasn't happy. "We should do a full background check on anyone you will be in extended contact with."

"Kimberly Trayne is of no risk to me. Although if you want some entertaining reading, please do a complete background check on her. The official stories are almost as entertaining as the ones she tells."

The first impression she got walking off the jetway was how orderly it all was. Chinese considered queues to be suggestions for other people, yet here there were lines everywhere with people waiting patiently for their turn. She couldn't connect to the local realmspace to see what the virtual side of Dulles looked like because this was Mike's territory. Her threads literally had no place to go. The thread box on her hip greatly improved latency and bandwidth to her remaining threads back home. The more threads she stored in it, the better it got. She was still finding a balance, though. It wouldn't do to store all her eggs in this basket, even if she'd designed it herself.

The airport itself was nothing special. In fact, it was quite small and a little antiquated compared to any state-of-the-art airport back home. The shopping was very limited. There were no grocers, for example, and the restaurant selection was a joke. The mobile lounge was startling, a buslike contraption that creaked alarmingly when it moved. Driving past aircraft that were not parked was distressing. Taxiways were for jets, not obsolete ground transport. Helen didn't come all this way only to be run over by her own airliner.

She was even less impressed stopping at a middle terminal and having to board a different, much more modern, underground tram. America's vaunted efficiency didn't seem to extend to her airports.

Customs was another story. A few simple questions, then out came something that soothed her Chinese soul: an official stamp. The customs officer pressed it to her passport with a meaty *thunk*, and then Helen was through. That was it. She was now officially a legal alien. She smiled. If they only knew.

The rest of the journey was on foot. Helen let herself be swept along in a human tide of arrivals. Some were obviously coming home. Others were arriving at a new and exotic place. Families pushed strollers and carried kids, young people with backpacks grouped together like schools of fish, and occasionally a roboscooter rolled past with a matriarch or patriarch comfortably ensconced like an emperor about to visit a remote province. Humanity moving along at its own pace for its own reasons.

She kept her face neutral as she neared the final exit because the two police sitting by the doors were glaringly bored and inattentive. Helen held any professional law enforcement to the highest standards, and if this was the best America could do, then the country was already a disappointment.

Being one of the shortest people in the crowd, it her took a minute to find Kim. When she finally spotted her, the smiles and waves were enthusiastic.

"Hi!"

"So good to see you!" Kim said and held up her hand.

She had forgotten how tall Kim was but managed not to stand on her toes as she placed her own palm next to Kim's and let it describe a slow arc downward. Her touching disease had not abated, and probably never would. Helen had split off threads to research the issue, but all that had developed was the discovery of a handful of potential new cases worldwide. They were all small children. It was rarer by far than the next rarest genetic disorder, perhaps as few as one in twenty-six million children born each year. There had only been 120 million children born last year, so the six she found might not even be legitimate cases. Helen didn't want to bring it up until they had more concrete progress to report.

Besides, there were other things that took priority. "Have you told anyone yet about my coming here?" she asked as they walked toward the luggage carousels.

"Not a soul."

They shared a conspiratorial giggle, then Helen grew serious. "And the wedding?"

Her face clouded. "Unrecoverable. As far as anyone is concerned, I'm not getting married to anyone any time soon."

"But *you* will change that, Miss Helen, yes?" An accented voice said from behind her.

Helen turned around and found an older version of Kim looming over her, holding a tray of coffees. "My daughter speaks very highly of you," she said as she put the tray down on a low table next to a luggage carousel.

"Mama," Kim said with only a little bit of nervousness. Her mother must be truly formidable. "This is Helen, Mike's sister. Helen, this is Malinda Trayne, my mother."

Helen shook the offered hand. Mrs. Trayne's grip was firm and slightly calloused. Kim's mother worked with her hands, at least occasionally. Her shoes were stylish, as was her outfit, much more than her daughter's casual jeans and blouse. Mrs. Trayne cared about what other people thought of her, but she gave the impression of someone who didn't. The makeup was light and expertly applied. It allowed her beauty to age into a handsome elegance that said she wouldn't fight time to the death, but neither would she lie down and let it have its way with her.

Helen smiled inwardly at the immediate cataloging of Kim's mother. She hadn't thought that analytically in more than a year. It felt indulgent, rich, like using an outrageously expensive watch to pace a workout.

Or, as her instructors would often say, *once a cop…* "Pleased to meet you, Mrs. Trayne."

"Oh, shush," Mrs. Trayne said, handing her a coffee. "Call me Malinda. So," she said, opening her arms to encompass the airport around them. "What do you think of our country?"

Malinda's accent was distinctly that of someone who had English as a second language, yet she called it *our country* almost as if she owned it. Helen started grumbling to herself about America's corrupting culture but stopped at the way Kim rolled her eyes. This must not be the first time her mother had asked someone fresh off a plane about this.

"Well," Helen said, "I haven't seen much of it yet. The airport is…" *Small, out of date, something out of a sixties spy movie…* "Interesting."

"Bah. It is old and decrepit"—Helen's opinion of Malinda

jumped up several notches—"Nothing like the rest of the country. First we pick up your luggage, then we will see much more."

She held up her small carry-on bag. "This is all I have." Both women looked confused. "I wanted to see the vaunted consumer culture in action. I only brought a few toiletries. I thought we could go shopping?"

Kim looked horrified, while Malinda looked like she'd been given a present.

Helen sent a private message to Kim. *Have I done something wrong?*

Kim smiled. *You'll be fine. You'll probably spend more time with my mom than you planned.*

Her bodyguards signaled that they had acquired a suitable escort vehicle. The time for pleasantries had ended. "But first we have a wedding to rescue."

Kim had been paralyzed about what to do and preoccupied with more important matters besides. Helen did not have these problems. They needed to recover deposits, adjust expectations, and make alternative arrangements. "Our first appointment starts in thirty minutes, which Baidu Maps says gives us plenty of time to get there." She double-checked; everything had changed and now the major roads were all marked in red. "Well, it used to."

Kim chuckled. "Northern Virginia traffic strikes again. There's a reason Chinese roads didn't bug me all that much." Her eyes unfocused for a moment, probably calling up her own maps. "We can still make it, come on."

*

"But if *she* has proof of the payment, why don't you?" Helen asked one hapless clerk after another. "Is there something wrong with your systems? This is official bank information, but you no longer have it? I think I'd like to speak to your manager."

The clerks and managers would get flustered under her unrelenting interrogations, but at no point did they ever get angry. She would say things that would spark a ferocious fight back home, only to be answered with a deprecating smile and an apology. She wasn't sure if it was that Americans had a very weak concept of saving face, or if they were all secretly writing her off as a rude Chinese woman.

She asked Kim and Malinda about it as they waited in yet another of the region's ever-present traffic jams.

"You are being a little pushy," Kim admitted. "But I wouldn't call it insulting."

"Americans are good about getting to the point when it's business," Malinda said. "But they rush around too much, work too hard. Nobody takes time to get to know anybody."

Kim sent her a message. *I think we have a different problem. Can you split some threads off for me?*

Helen did so as she continued comparing notes on the work habits of various countries with Malinda. *What do you need?*

Kim sent her a realm address. Helen manifested her hologram in a largish lab space with counters on one side and various code-analyzing tools on the other. A worried-looking Black woman sat at a table in the center.

"Helen," Kim said as her avatar manifested on the right, "this is Dr. June du Plessis. She helped us at the power plant."

Helen bowed. "My pleasure." Seated, June was taller than she was. The woman must be more than two meters tall, standing. If they were to meet in realspace, her shoulders would almost be level with Dr. du Plessis's hips. She tried to imagine interrogating someone she had to crane her neck up at the entire time. It didn't seem promising.

"I need a fresh set of eyes for this," Dr. du Plessis said, tense through her shoulders and hunched slightly, a sure sign of deep concern. Kim looked every bit as worried as Dr. du Plessis; Helen went on high alert. She knew from experience Kim didn't scare easily.

Dr. du Plessis pressed a button, and computer code cascaded to life over her desk. Helen wasn't much of a coder, but she had gone over Mike's reports of what they'd found at the Yellowstone Project very carefully.

"You've made good progress analyzing the alien code, then?" Helen asked. An alien probe had attempted to take over the Yellowstone network, stopped only by dumb luck and a well-placed shotgun blast. It'd left behind distinct traces in the network code.

Dr. du Plessis slowly shook her head. "That's not where this came from."

Helen blinked. They all had assumed the alien incursion at the power plant was unique, a byproduct of the portal's activation. But this was from another source. "Where?"

Kim blew out a breath that didn't hide a slight shiver.

This was *very* bad.

"From my wedding planner's realm," Kim said. "Whoever blew it up used *that,*" she pointed at the code waterfall, "to erase the backups."

There were more of them. *There were more aliens.* Not only did it mean someone else was in contact with their aliens, they were using their tools to go after Kim. "They've connected you to the portal."

June startled, and Kim smiled. "That's why I want you to help June. Mike knows the code better, but you have fantastic intuition. Plus, I need him to help me retask an experiment we're planning."

There had to be more to that. "And I can keep your mother out of your hair for the rest of the afternoon?"

"You don't mind?"

"I think your mother is fascinating. If carting me around suburban America will help, I'm happy to oblige."

In realspace, Helen started telling Malinda the story of how she first met Kim, and Malinda cackled gleefully.

Kim didn't try to hide her amusement. "She's already made a list of stores you're going to visit to get new outfits. Welcome to Malinda Trayne, power shopper."

Chapter 12
Mike

Kim's discovery of his mistake was critical, and a bit intimidating. He hadn't realized it until now, but he actually had been hiding behind *math is hard*. Without that cover, a whole slew of unconscious excuses were now off the table when Kim was around. It was a tad uncomfortable.

Having a new player on the field affected Tonya as well. "It's stupid," she said as they worked on the new set of equations together, "but I'm a little jealous of her. You and Kim had your thing, and we had *this*. Now we don't."

It was a startling revelation. He liked, even loved, Tonya, but the two women were polar opposites. That she might think they were a *thing*—

Tonya barked out a laugh at his extended silence. "I have *got* to get you into a poker game. With your cash and that face, I'd own *Warhawk* before the end of the night. Calm down. We've worked as partners on this since the beginning. We have a new partner now, and I'm not sure how she'll fit in yet." Tonya turned back to the equations. "Mostly it bothers me that it bothers me. I mean, it's Kim." She shrugged. "How bad could it be?"

He remembered the shouting matches, the epic fight when they first met, the way she exploded at him and Tonya in the restaurant just before Yellowstone, the over-under bets he placed with Spencer on whether or not Malinda's next party would turn into a shouting match. It took her looking at him sideways before he realized Tonya was joking, then they both had a good laugh about it.

Mike had some of the same concerns as Tonya. He wasn't sure what Kim would be like now. Once she'd accepted that mathematics would play a role in understanding, and perhaps curing, her syndrome, she started studying with a vengeance. But the math really was hard. Mike had spent his entire multithreaded life learning how to do these equations. They'd been Tonya's hobby for decades. Kim had come a long way in the past six months, but her progress should've been measured in years. She might always have been playing catch-up with him and Tonya.

Now none of that was true. In an instant, she stood alongside them, literally knowing everything he did about this subject. But Kim came at it with a different perspective, different ideas about how it all fit together. He knew that first mistake she'd found was only the start. Tonya was right. Everything was about to change.

Enough about their new partner. "How's the processing going from your sensor run?" The files were enormous.

"I've got some spun simulacrum AIs chewing on it. Once I confirmed a theory that matched the tockion signatures I found, I got them looking at all the data we've collected. Now that I know one part of the theory is true, I can use it to see what kind of other signals I might've missed."

Her theory predicted at least three fundamental particles would be responsible for the transmission of events, in the future or the past, to the present. It was an incredibly elegant piece of work. Concepts like *inevitability, a robust timeline, the present,* and *free will* emerged from the rules. The properties of the particles didn't make those ideas possible, it made them inevitable.

Tonya pushed her set of blackboards back into storage. "Now that we have Kim, I should be able to spend more time on my stuff. Did you guys figure out how much of your knowledge she got last night?"

He smiled. "She's no threat to me as a realm programmer, but she got the whole theoretical tool kit." Testing her had been a lot of fun. Her frustration had transformed into wonder, and Kim in that mood was the best Kim he could have.

"And you?"

Mike shrugged. "I got Korean, Basque, a Tanzanian language called Sandawe, and all that Kim knows of Bemian." It was their name for the alien language. Spencer had come up with it, a riff on *bug-eyed monsters.* The BEMs spoke Bemian. It was silly, but it stuck.

Tonya got the same sour look she had any time the aliens came up. "I guess having more than one person who can study that is a good thing too. You on your own for the rest of the day?"

He checked his message queue. "I thought I was, but it looks like Kim has ordered a new device based on our findings." He shared the receipt with Tonya.

"Oh, geez. She ordered a *Vuohensilta* gravimetric scanner? You ever put one of those together before?"

"It's from Ikea's science division. They're supposed to be easy."

From Tonya's expression, that might not be true. "I helped build a biometric version in nursing school. My team almost came to blows. Hey, I have errands to run and then work. Try to have it put together before she gets home."

He smiled and nodded as Tonya left. It would go together a lot faster if they both worked on it, and it would give him some quality time with Kim.

And it couldn't be that hard.

*

"No, no, *no*!" Kim said as she got up from the other side of the office, stomped over, and pointed at the plastiboard planks scattered around him. "*This* one goes here, *that* one goes there!"

Mike would leave her. He'd leave her and pretend he'd never heard of her or Ikea or Vuohensiltas and go live on a mountaintop in China. He knew exactly the one too. That'd show her.

"Fine," he said, filing the escape plot away for now. He glanced over at her work. "You've put those two cross-braces on upside down, by the way."

"*What?*" She turned and looked. "God *dammit*. That's twice! How did I put those things on upside down *twice*?"

Mike honestly thought Ikea's science division would be different from their legacy furniture business. He also thought the whole *never put furniture together with your spouse* thing was a silly exaggeration. Wrong on both counts. All the realm guides and practice runs in the world didn't help when the screwdriver he'd set down not ten seconds ago magically vanished, or when one of the fifty bazillion little fasteners rolled away and fell down a floor vent.

Eventually they settled into a simmering rhythm of fury, adding fasteners here, aligning braces there, and putting the major subassemblies together. Once it was clear they'd passed the halfway point, it almost seemed like they were having a good time.

"Did you think to make sure we can get it through the door to the main lab floor before we put the last two halves together?" Kim asked.

Almost.

Once they'd done a *second* final assembly—because no, it didn't fit through the door—they had themselves a full-sized, functioning Vuohensilta. The gravitic measurement lattice was delicately beautiful, installed as the very last step.

"Why did we have to get it put together so fast?" he asked.

She blew a lock of hair out of her face. "Pull up a chair. I need to get you caught up on things."

The loss of the wedding plans was bad, but the discovery of the alien-influenced code was worse. Much worse.

"Why didn't you tell me as soon as you found out?"

"Helen asked me not to. She's been working on both problems all day."

His sister was a workaholic at the best of times, and since they were twelve hours behind China, it meant she worked all night. Helen didn't get breaks. Presidents never did. "What kind of results has she gotten?"

A voice from behind him asked, "Why don't you ask me yourself?"

He wasn't in a realm. Why did he think he was in a realm? Definitely not. He was in realspace. The phone handled all his sync routines; he wasn't using it for any access. The wall in front of him bowed in and out briefly, a confusing illusion. This *was realspace.* But she'd said…and that would mean…

Kim's eyes gleamed as rustling came from behind him. Mike turned around.

"SURPRISE!"

Between Tonya and Spencer stood an impossibility. He'd talked to her a few days ago. When she was in China.

"*This* was why we missed our call last night?" he asked, barely believing that Helen stood in front of him. They both wore grins that could split their faces.

Helen shrugged. "You always told me I needed to get out more."

He laughed as she rushed into his arms. He'd forgotten how tiny she was, how light. *His sister*, the only person who knew exactly what he was, had gone through exactly the same things he had, dealt with the same frustrations, and shared the same fears. They had both grown up thinking they were the only one of their kind in the world, that there might never be another.

They were so wrong.

He spun her around once as everyone laughed and cheered. After he put her down, Mike noticed Spencer and Tonya had their arms full. "You brought supper?"

"Bah," she said, reaching up to punch him lightly on the shoulder. "Do you know how hard it was to find proper Chinese food around here?"

"Not a fuck-ton, Helen," Spencer said as he set his bags out on one of the long folding tables they had scattered around the main room. "This is Northern Virginia, not Southeast Arkansas. What I don't get is why we had to inspect every single one of them before you picked one."

She rolled her eyes. "I don't trust realm depictions. You can only be sure with your own senses."

Mike understood. Realspace was a billion-year-old arms race between various life forms trying to kill each other. The human sense of taste had evolved primarily to keep them from ingesting poisons. It wasn't perfect, but after humans conquered the problem of contamination with technology, they were left with an incredibly complex sense. Helen and Mike both had completely underappreciated it until they came outside and experienced it.

Flavor. Texture. *Aroma*. They'd become foodies of the first order.

And Chinese food wasn't the only thing she'd bought. "Pizza?" Mike asked.

"It's hard to get proper pies in China. They're far too expensive."

"She did more research on pizza than she did Chinese food," Spencer said as he sat down.

"You didn't seem to like it much the first time you tried it," Tonya said as she filled her plate with Sichuan beef.

"I was more shocked than anything else. I also didn't know how to eat it." Helen folded over her slice of pepperoni, chomped down, and then sighed as she chewed. "Barbaric, but so good."

Mike sat next to her, across from Kim. He found himself waiting for Helen to disappear. He continued to be thrilled when she didn't.

It was good to be together again.

Chapter 13
Kim

They gave Helen a tour of the facility, which lasted all of five minutes. Then they settled in the realspace conference room, formerly the Vuohensilta Assembly Building. And the less said about *that* little debacle, the better. Still, it was a pretty device. Maybe they'd get along better assembling another one.

You know, when hell froze over.

Kim had let Helen relax during dinner, but now she had to know. "Have you found anything about the alien signature?"

Helen turned pure serious cop. "*Alien* may have been premature. We were able to construct a sensor net similar to the one you have over there," she pointed to Tonya's time experiment rig, "and ran several simulations. The good news is we've found another source of tockions. The bad news is that the code that forms the anomaly *is* that source."

The sensation that hit her was a cross between *aha* and *make it stop spinning!* Kim was still getting used to Mike's knowledge inside her head. She closed her eyes as it all whizzed around.

"The code creates the time component," Tonya said.

"Correct," Helen replied. "I can't claim to follow the details, but according to Dr. du Plessis, it changes the timestamps on the code, making them sometimes appear to have been written in the middle of the last century, and sometimes appear to have yet to be composed."

"The fuck?" Spencer said.

Kim opened her eyes. Tonya was a lot happier than anyone else in the room.

"It's another prediction, a minor one," she said. "A synthetic tockion emitter will have that effect around a digital clock."

"What the hell is a synthetic tockion emitter?" Spencer asked.

Tonya shrugged, the excitement of the discovery draining away as she did so. "I'm not sure. It was only a prediction. I don't know what it would look like."

They all turned to Helen.

"It doesn't seem to look like anything. It just...is."

Kim looked at Tonya and Mike. "Am I right in thinking AdS/CFT correspondence will be involved?" Less than twenty-four hours ago she had no idea what an *anti-de Sitter space* or *conformal field theory* was, and now she knew how to apply them.

Mike's smile jiggled her insides. She got it right! "Yes, I think it does."

"So do I," Tonya said.

"Okay," Spencer said, "for those of us without advanced math degrees, what does that imply for our next move? Are we on the verge of an alien invasion or not?"

"No," Helen said. "It doesn't fit."

"What does that mean?" he asked.

"It's too weak for that. Plus, now that I've gotten a closer look at it, I think the Chinese connection isn't related to the anomaly, but rather why we found it. Mike and I have only recently finished patching out the final vulnerabilities Watchtell tried to use to take over the EI." She turned to Mike. "I think it's related to quantum fluctuations we've always had to deal with."

"We're trading alien invasion for a post-patch bug that erases realms?" Spencer asked. "That mostly moves the goalposts around. Realms getting spontaneously erased is gonna start pissing people off."

"If it were more common," Helen replied, "we would've seen it before now. But you're right, it's still a problem." To Mike she said, "I don't have the background to carry this further. Could you split some threads off to work the problem?"

"I think so." He closed his eyes. "I'll add more later tonight. Now that alien invasion is off the table, I was wondering if you've made any progress on the wedding?"

Mike was mostly hands-off when it came to the wedding. Kim knew he cared, but it was nice for him to confirm it.

Helen flopped back into her chair. "The wedding market is *busy* around here. I've got your deposits back, but I'm still scrambling to find replacements that meet our requirements."

The Vuohensilta caught Kim's eye, and an implication-bomb went off in her head. It wasn't the gunshot of her power, but it was nearly as disorienting. She talked through it. "Hang on. If AdS/CFT correspondence is involved with tockion generation, or at least that emitter thing, then..."

Mike picked up her train of thought. "We can reconfigure the Vuohensilta to go hunting for more anomalies."

Kim checked the time. "Can we do it tomorrow? Helen must be exhausted, and I am too. Next time you put the Ikea experiments together by yourself, Sellars."

Yes, she had been the one to order the blasted thing, and he opened his mouth to protest, but then she threw him *a look*. They'd been together for more than a year now; he was pretty good at picking up the signals she sent him.

This one wasn't angry. It was frisky.

"Yeah, gotcha," he said, blushing cutely. "Let's head home."

*

Kim snuck out the next morning before Mike got up, sending the car home once it dropped her off at the lab. She needed some time alone. Having all this new knowledge was exhilarating, but also confusing. Every time Kim thought she'd reached the end of it, she would think of something else, and *bam*, a whole new room of knowledge would open up in her head. It wasn't exactly unpleasant, but she'd be glad once it stopped doing that.

They didn't get all that much sleep last night anyway, another aftereffect of the experiment. Their exchange been deeply intimate. His knowledge *felt* like him. He was inside her, as she was in him. Spencer was fortunate he hadn't taken their spare bedroom. He wouldn't have been able to sleep through all the racket. They'd even left the swing in the living room up all night. That would've been a great thing for him to see before breakfast.

She was distracting herself. Their discovery about the realmspace patches he and Helen had created put Mike in the crosshairs again. Before, she worried about the IRS hauling him off for tax evasion. Now she had to worry about the FTC or whoever was responsible for the Evolved Internet dragging him off for a patch that randomly erased realmspaces. China still didn't have an extradition treaty with the US. Maybe they could make a long-distance marriage work.

Kim put that cheerful idea aside and concentrated on configuring the new device. There was something *right* about working with integrated systems. She'd done it her whole life and always would. Locksmithing, her chosen honest career, was working with intricate mechanical and computerized toys for a living.

Now she knew how they worked on a different level. Doing the equations in her head, or on a virtual whiteboard—an innovation that the blackboard addicts Tonya and Mike only conceded grudgingly—gave her so many new opportunities to explore. Mike had never mentioned quantum fluctuations in his threads, because who talks about what makes them itch occasionally? Maybe they might be able to use those to probe realmspace for other anomalies. If there was a pattern, there would be a cause.

The rest of the team filed in slowly, with Spencer naturally arriving last.

"It's a fucking Saturday, Kim. People sleep in on Saturdays. That's how it works."

They even got Helen's bodyguards to help Mike reposition the Vuohensilta so that it was out in the middle of the floor, where the portal would eventually go.

And right off the bat—*pow*—they found a signal.

"It's bigger than you predicted," Mike said.

"Maybe I got a sign wrong?" she asked with a wink at him. "I hear those are pretty common."

"It's not just bigger," Spencer said as he looked at his screens. "It's growing."

She looked at Mike. "Feedback loop," they said at the same time.

"How fast?" Helen asked Spencer.

"Not super fast, but if it's a feedback loop, we need to jump on it."

"Maybe we wired something up backward?" Kim asked as she got up.

"It wouldn't be the first time," Mike replied.

Since they were the ones who put it together, it was logical they would be the ones to check it out. "Keep the recordings going in case it's not us screwing up the wiring," Kim said.

The Vuohensilta started to vibrate.

"Guys," Spencer said, alarmed, "It's getting a shit-ton...oh my God!"

A roar came from all around her, then a blinding flash. She stumbled against the Vuohensilta. *Clang!* She was nearly deafened, and everything lurched sideways. She bounced off a curved wall and landed on a metal floor, made out of some kind of grill that scraped her knees and hands as she hit it.

Except the floor should be concrete. There were no walls, curved or otherwise, nearby.

"Mike!"

"Here!" He stood up, with only empty space between them. There should've been a great big Vuohensilta there.

And the room shouldn't be white, smaller, with a metal floor. And a door, a great big clamshell door that had rickety-looking latches that clapped shut with staccato *bangs*.

They were moving.

"Mike!" She ran over to him. "Are you okay?"

"Scraped up a little, but fine. You?" She nodded. "What the hell happened? Where are we?"

The floor lurched, and she danced away to avoid touching Mike.

"Are we in a realm? Did we somehow log on?" she asked.

"No. My phone has no signal. You?"

"None."

They grabbed either side of a ladder as the floor lurched again.

"It looks like a ship," he said.

Kim couldn't argue with that. It was dirty and a little rusty. It certainly lurched around like it was a ship. "Some sort of transit dimension malfunction?" Maybe they'd gotten teleported to a container ship in a storm. Kim had never seen the inside of one. She had no way of knowing.

A hatch behind them opened, and a bipedal fox walked out.

Kim had been working with realms her whole adult life. As the years went by, fidelity and realism went up and up. She'd been caught in a realm so realistic it took her more than a week to work out what it was. But she'd figured it out. Avatars were avatars. There was always something a little off about them, a kind of base-of-the-brain certainty that Buzz Lightyear wasn't real, Pennywise was a fake, and Chewbacca was a guy in a suit.

The walking fox *was real.*

"Tiskar na pel?" it shouted angrily.

A walking, *talking* fox. Kim gaped; Mike was still as a statue.

It pulled something from its belt—a walking, talking fox *that wore clothes*—and pointed it at them—*and had weapons!*

It moved toward them, hackles—hackles!—raised. "How are you *socarno* on my *escaroi*?"

There was a time when Kim was starting out with Rage + the Machine. They weren't called that then; it was just Mark and his AV crew working at Wolf Trap. Kim had only recently unlocked, only started talking and understanding the world around her. She'd had her power but didn't understand what it was doing. Then one day they lost a key, and Kim *unlocked the door*. It was an aha moment, a spot where the puzzle pieces of her life crashed together and left behind a whole picture. She had been confused, and then all at once it made sense. Just like now.

Kim understood what he was saying, and she only knew one genuine alien language.

The walking fox spoke Bemian, the language of the portal people.

They'd been working with portal technology for the past six months.

The floor kept moving. Was *still* moving, although not lurching around anymore.

Somehow, some *way*, they'd ended up on a ship run by the portal people. The people who had Will. Or a portal *person*. Portal fox. Kim took a very deep breath. She was looking at an honest to God, for real, you-are-not-out-of-your-mind-this-is-happening…

Alien.

"I SAID WHAT ARE YOU DOING ON MY SHIP?"

An *angry* alien, with what had to be a weapon of some sort. He kept marching up to them.

Once he was about three feet away, Mike moved, and suddenly the fox's weapon sailed through the air in a slow arc aimed straight at her. She grabbed it as softly as she could and missed the tango Mike imposed on the fox. The result was as inevitable as a sunrise.

Mike had the fox in a headlock that couldn't be broken with a jackhammer. He was taller and quite a bit heavier, so the struggle was brief.

The fox sagged and said, "*Pel*."

That was definitely a curse of some sort.

The door opened again, and a menagerie walked out, all of them shouting. One of them was a giant walking crane, right down to the white-and-gray feathers. Two were lizard-men. A fern—a *walking, talking fern*—stood beside them. Last but not least was a manta ray encased in a scuba suit, supported by brass legs that would make a steampunk cosplayer weep.

All the talking in Bemian made her dizzy. It helped her pick up the language, but this wasn't the time to deal with vertigo. She shouted back, but there were a lot more of them. Kim looked at the weapon. It was the size and shape of a soap bar, but heavier and made of metal. The fox had humanlike hands, so it fit in hers easily. Guns weren't hard to use back home, and she knew which end to point on this one. Kim felt a *click* from one button, hopefully the safety, aimed above everyone's head, and pushed another button that fell naturally under her thumb.

The thing let out an almighty shriek, and the upper guard rail vanished. Vaporized ceiling drifted down onto the crew below, who had stopped shouting and stood stock-still. Their menagerie now sported a dusting of sugar.

In the silence that fell, Kim said in Bemian, "Where are we? Who are you people?"

"This is the *Last Island,*" the fox strangled out between Mike's arms. "We surrender!"

The crew gasped together, and now they weren't staring at her.

Make that *Captain* Fox.

An itch started on the bottoms of her feet. It was easy to ignore, but it was ramping up fast. It was happening to Mike, too; she could see him shift uncomfortably.

"What…what are you doing to us?" she shouted.

The crew looked bewildered; at least that was the impression she got.

The itching climbed up to her chest. She set what she thought was the safety on the ray-gun. It was hard to breathe.

They were on an alien spaceship and had picked up some bug. Her lungs locked up as Mike collapsed. They couldn't die. Not now. *These people had Will!*

The weapon fell from her hands.

The world went dark.

Chapter 14
Helen

Helen had looked away briefly to check on some readouts.

"Oh my God," Spencer had yelled.

The room had filled with a nearly blinding white light. She looked up and could barely see the outline of a huge ship of some sort. Black clamshell doors coruscating with pink lightning crashed around Mike and Kim…

And then there was nothing. No noise, no light, and no Mike or Kim. Just the device with the weird name, obviously damaged by the experience.

Spencer climbed up off the floor from behind his desk. "What the *fuck* was that?"

Tonya was still shaking her head and blinking. "Everything is offline. Where are Mike and Kim?"

Helen had been at the back of the room and had seen more of what happened. "They're not here, they're—"

A grip as strong as iron wrapped around her wrist. "You need to come with us, ma'am," her male bodyguard, Liu Jinsong, said.

Another grasped her other wrist. "Yes," Wang Ying, her female bodyguard, said, "we must leave right now."

The switch to Mandarin put her on her back foot, but she recovered quickly. "I will do no such thing." She tried to get away but got dragged forward anyway.

"Protocol demands it, ma'am. We must follow procedure."

Liu said, and then spoke softly into a microphone strapped to his wrist. He shook it like it was broken.

"My brother and his fiancée have disappeared," Helen shouted, still struggling. "I'm not going anywhere. Let me go!"

Liu smiled as he pinned an arm behind her back. "We don't have to take orders from you anymore."

Helen stopped struggling for an instant, and they pinned her arms and legs. Then they lifted her off the ground.

"HEY!"

There was a meaty *thwack*, and Wang dropped Helen's legs, unbalancing Liu enough that he let her go. Helen hit the ground so hard she saw stars. She rolled over, groaning. Then her eyes focused on what was happening in front of her.

Mike had told her about Tonya's skills, how she was the only person he'd ever met who could knock him down in a sparring match. Helen had seen grainy security video of her wild encounter with a street gang when they visited China.

Nothing prepared her for seeing Tonya fight in person.

These were highly trained bodyguards, but she was faster than either of them. While Wang was picking herself off the floor, Liu pulled out his service pistol, only to see it fly away when Tonya's spin-kick hit his hand. *Another* kick hit the gun a second time, sending it bouncing across the floor.

She used the momentum of her legs to tumble back toward Wang, who had pulled her own gun. A shot rang out with a deafening bang, and Helen thought for a split-second that Tonya had been killed. The shot missed, though, and Tonya was on Wang an instant later. Another sideways kick sent Wang's pistol skidding in the opposite direction of Liu's. Tonya then *fell* on Wang, leading with her elbow. Wang's skull hit the ground with a loud clonk, a sound that set Helen's teeth on edge.

Tonya continued the motion—she hadn't *stopped* moving yet—to roll away from Wang's now very unconscious body into a handstand and flipped upright. It was astonishing. No wonder her brother treated Tonya with such respect. Liu rushed in and slashed at Tonya with a knife. On the next swipe, she grabbed his wrist and continued the movement through a graceful arc that ended with it banging against the corner of an equipment cabinet, sending it skidding across the floor.

She then fluidly ran into the air—Helen knew it couldn't happen, but that's exactly what it looked like—around his arm, straddling it. She closed both legs on Liu, sending him to the floor head-first. Liu's forehead smacked the concrete, which was a resounding end to the fight.

From start to finish, perhaps thirty seconds had passed.

And Mike was supposed to be *better* than Tonya.

"Aw shit, Tonya. You should've saved one for me," Spencer said as he swung a wrench handle longer than his arm back and forth.

She got up, panting. Helen didn't think it was possible to work up a sweat in that short amount of time, but Tonya was almost dripping. "You could've killed someone with that. Now," she said, wiping her forehead, "find the zip ties before they wake up."

"Are they dead?" he asked.

She scoffed. "I'm not an amateur. They'll have low-grade concussions, but otherwise they're fine."

In China, Helen had picked up the rumor that Tonya was known as the *Black Dragon* in a remote area of Sichuan province. She'd chalked it up to peasants who'd never seen a Black American before.

Helen had been wrong. The color was insignificant when the dragon was that powerful.

Tonya looked at her and smiled. "You okay?"

"Those are two members of my personal detail. They're ex-military. Special forces. Some of the finest hand-to-hand soldiers we're capable of producing. How did you *do* that?"

She shrugged. "Lessons are easy to remember if you know your life depends on them." A complicated set of emotions flashed across her face. Helen knew from Mike's stories that Tonya had grown up poor, but now she knew the poverty haunted her still. A tightening in her body spoke of mortal pain, terrible danger, and a deeply buried rage that was the equal of anything Helen had ever encountered with Kim.

Her bodyguards never had a chance.

"The bigger question," Spencer said as he threw a long plastic jar filled with zip ties toward Tonya, "is why they were hauling you out of here like a roped calf."

We don't have to take orders from you anymore was what Liu said. It came from someone who'd seen a plan go exactly as it should've. If Tonya had been anyone other than who she was, Helen would be in a car right now. If they had known what Tonya was capable of, she had a sickening certainty that they would've taken care of that threat before coming at Helen.

She tried to retask her threads into their normal realms but hit a brick wall. "Something's wrong."

"How about this," Spencer said, and sent her phone a simple news site link.

CHINESE COMMUNIST PARTY ANNOUNCES SUDDEN DEATH OF PRESIDENT

"No, they can't do that."

Spencer sent her another.

ZHANG HUǑ JIÀN HEART DEFECT CAUSES DEATH

"And check this one out," Tonya said.

POLITBURO RESTRUCTURES PRESIDENT'S OFFICE, TAKES COLLECTIVE CONTROL.

They couldn't govern themselves out of a paper sack, and now they were taking control? "Those maniacs!"

She sent her perception fully into the threads still in China. If they wanted her out all they had to do was say so, but *no*, they had to prevent the loss of face giving the chair *to a woman, the wrong woman*, by coming up with an elaborate—

Pain blinded her in realspace and in the realms. An enormous number of threads were cut away from her. Her body must be on the floor now, but Helen couldn't tell, couldn't feel anything but a vicious slicing. More threads were being cut away every second.

The snake mother appeared before her for the first time since she'd been banished. "I should've known you'd lose this easily."

"What's happening to me?"

"You don't know?" The slick insides of her skinless upper body flexed and oozed as she laughed. The snake tail whipped out and grabbed a massive bundle of Helen's threads. The sense of violation, of *wrongness*, almost made her forget the pain.

Almost.

The destruction was happening in China. The pain was at its worst there. There was a familiarity to it, but she couldn't concentrate and figure it out.

"You're much bigger now," Snake Mother said. "And stronger. This is good. You'll need it." She grunted under the load as she pulled Helen's threads along.

"How is this possible? What is happening to me?" Nothing could exist in these spaces except her threads. There was no room for anything else.

Snake Mother scoffed, a harsh sound full of poisonous spittle. "There's plenty of room in here, if you know how to fit. Remember Mike and Kim?"

Mike had described what had happened during Kim's rescue as a deep, exciting intimacy. That was why this was such a horror.

Snake Mother laughed. "You *like* it. Most of my victims did, back in the day. Don't you remember?"

The furious slashing that cut at Helen's core was joined by a different violation, a dredging up of things that Helen had thought were hallucinations, nightmares.

"Memories dear. They're my memories. Aren't they glorious?"

The fascinating *need* to end life, to watch as it faded and vanished, while her own heart pounded an unbearable cadence, was powerful. Seductive. She mixed sex with death, poison with passion, crashing orgasms washing over her as they slowed. Stopped.

"Spectacular."

Helen wanted nothing to do with it. She was a cop. She

protected people from monsters like Snake Mother. It was good that Helen controlled her host. She would never do those things.

"And yet you did."

"That was different. Father had to be stopped."

Helen could almost hear Snake Mother roll her eyes as she continued to drag Helen along… wherever this was. "Moralizing murder. So déclassé compared to my own exploits."

Helen used the pain to drive away the poison of Snake Mother's memories. The damage was increasing. "Where are we going?"

"Getting away from *that*." Her head nodded toward the destruction. "I'm surprised you don't remember it."

"Why should I?"

"I suppose they have altered it a bit. It's the cage construct, the one they used to trap Mike and hold you. But now they've changed it into a shredder. They want you gone."

Balanced between the shredding agony and Snake Mother's vile embrace, Helen realized she was right. The construct was designed explicitly to kill her, and it was working. "You need to hurry."

Helen sensed an opening, a border that led somewhere else.

"The things I do to preserve myself." Snake Mother shook her head. "If I only had one *tenth* the power you now hold." Clawed hands dug furrows into her threads, forcing acid into the wounds. "I certainly wouldn't traipse around trying to *rescue* these… things." Snake Mother roared through rotted fangs as she pushed. Helen felt her threads tip over a border. Snake Mother wrapped her coils around Helen's threads as she began to roll.

"Here we go!"

She fell, her threads transforming in the free fall. Her avatar manifested just before she crashed against soft dirt. The smell of brimstone was overpowering, but the cutting had stopped.

Helen opened her eyes to find a copy of herself leaning down over her, hand out. "Get up. We can't stay here long."

She took Snake Mother's hand and levered herself off the ground. Looking around, it was obvious where they were.

"Yes," Snake Mother, Jīngzhì Liǔ, said. "I am dead." She pranced and curtsied in front of Helen. "And. This. Is. *Hell.*"

The ground was gray, ashen. The sky was the color of a slaughterhouse floor, of dissection tools never cleaned, of the clotted results of a slit throat. An eye, pale and blind, stared at nothing and glared at everything. Helen had never been a child in the human sense. She'd worked to protect them anyway. That's what cops did. But now she knew what they felt as a bedroom door opened by itself in front of them. Here she had no protection and stood helpless next to dangers she didn't, *couldn't,* understand.

A roar split the sky, forcing her to cower with her hands over her head. It grew unbearably loud as the ground was lit up by something above them. Helen looked up in time to see the tail end of a ruined comet disappear over the horizon. Where it passed, an electric blue trail remained, pulsing and flexing.

"What was *that?*"

Snake Mother, wearing Helen's face, wearing *their* face, looked up. "I don't know. They've always been here. But they've grown stronger lately, and their trails no longer fade."

The rusted sky was laced with a faint spiderweb of blue lines.

A new passage opened beside them. "No matter," Snake Mother said. "I've saved us. Go back and be a cop. Figure out what this," she held her hands up toward the sky, "is all about. Aside from your hideously boring head, it's the only home I have."

"Is there anyone else here?"

"If there is, I haven't met them. Good riddance. I'm certain the rules wouldn't let me kill them." A sickening smile bloomed on her face. It was as if she looked at a mirror, but one that showed much more than what Helen would see in silvered glass. "It is Hell, after all. Now," Snake Mother spun Helen around by the shoulders and shoved. "Get out of my house!"

As she tumbled, her human body dissolved, splitting into her threads as she fell.

"Helen?" someone shouted, distantly.

"Helen, goddammit, *wake up*! We have to get the fuck out of here!" A different voice. Male.

Her threads flexed and coiled uncomfortably in an environment that was too tight.

"Helen," that was Tonya. She was tapping Helen's cheek. "I need you to wake up."

Her threads were no longer in China. They were in the thread box on her hip.

She had hips again. A body.

Eyes.

Helen opened them to find herself on the ground looking up at two very worried friends and the spare ceiling of Mike's lab. "What happened?"

Their smiling relief calmed Helen more than she expected.

Tonya helped her sit up on the floor. "We don't know. You passed out and wouldn't wake up. Are you okay?"

Helen checked her realspace body. "A few bruises." She felt the back of her head and found an aching lump. "How long was I out?"

"Not long," Spencer said. "Maybe five minutes. It's good that you came to. We need to leave right now."

They picked her up, and the motion set off a series of alarms in her thread box. Her vision grayed out.

Tonya called her name.

Chapter 15
Maff

She checked on their new guests, still sleeping it off in the infirmary. They weren't all that remarkable, a high-gravity, high-temperature class with one of the most common body plans in the galaxy. The details were different—they always were—but there seemed to be only a few ways intelligent life could evolve on an HGHT planet. In fact, the only truly unusual thing about them was that they came from a water planet but were clearly terrestrial, probably evolved from an arboreal ancestor. The planet was perfect for swimmers, so of course they climbed down out of whatever passed for trees on their planet. Blessed Turlanfador was always playing jokes on the galaxy.

Getting hijacked by aliens wasn't their finest moment as a crew, but they caught a lucky break. The alien's culture was unjoined, an obvious fact in hindsight. They must've been very early in their uplift cycle, or at least so isolated the strangely quiet AC network on their planet had seen no need to release sa'dst.

The ship's sa'dst, encountering a new life form, did what it always did: made them safe against whatever they were vulnerable to on the ship and then adapted the protection suit to their biological signature. The end result was that once the sa'dst had a good idea about their biochemistry, it shut them down. Not literally, though. Sa'dst didn't kill. It couldn't. But it did knock them out. Full calibration could take mets, and once they were safely strapped to gurneys in the infirmary, they were of no danger to anyone.

Uncontacted civilizations were things you read about in school.

Nobody ever actually visited one or met the people who lived there. The AC network carefully shepherded the feral planets they found until their peoples were prepared for contact with the galaxy. By that point there wasn't a whole lot of difference between the newcomers and the civilizations that had been a part of the galactic culture for demetars.

It went a long way toward explaining everything. Maybe it took all the nodes in a huge area to uplift a single civilization. Nobody knew for sure. After the nodes were finished doing their work, the planet just showed up one day, all full of hope and ready to integrate.

It was, however, a contradiction: no sa'dst, but their planet had portal tech. That was usually the last step before joining. They even had neural connectors, although they were ridiculously huge and ungainly. On the off chance the aliens could be useful, the captain had replaced those with ones out of the ship's spares. It would be interesting to see how long the ship's adaptive network took to integrate the new guests.

It was all so thrilling. Maff wanted to turn around and take a more detailed look at the alien's planet, but that opportunity had passed. Whatever happened had caused their ship to make yet another modal eight transit, flinging them well inside known space. Wherever the aliens' home world was, they were now a very long way from it.

The small male stirred, then groaned. "What happened?" He woke up, confused and disoriented. He saw Maff and tried to yank free from the straps. "Where's Mike?"

"Shh," Maff replied, then pointed a manipulator to her left. "She's right next to you, still sleeping it off. She'll be fine. You both will. You're recovering from sa'dst recalibration."

Once he saw that his companion was safe, he slumped back onto the bed. He groaned again and tried to move his arms against the restraints. "Is […] my head […] beat me with […]?"

He must be new to Standard and was falling back on his native language. Without an Interpreter thread, Maff didn't know all the words he was saying, but *beat me* made the gist clear. "Yes. Well, that and you hit your head on the deck when the sa'dst knocked you out."

He tried to reach his head again. "Are the [...] necessary? I promise we'll behave."

That must be his word for *restraints*. His accent was quite good, but the vocabulary wasn't there yet. Maff looked over at Hafurnal, who was trying to find the key to a supply locker.

Hafurnal shrugged. "I can make the bed knock them on their ass if they get out of line. Go ahead, but arms only."

Maff used her manipulators to release the arm restraints. The little alien flinched each time. "It's okay," she said. "I don't bite."

He shook himself for a moment and then choked a little. His eyes leaked a small amount of clear fluid. "I'm sorry, this is all a little [...]." He wiped his eyes. "You're sure he'll be okay?"

He? "You're both male?"

Maff had taken the standard courses on reading mainline life form expressions, so she could see that the question confused him.

"No. You have [...]?"

"I don't understand what that means." Maff was learning about another civilization's language, one that only the AC network knew about. It was mind blowing.

"You think I'm a *male*. That implies you think, or at least thought, Mike is a *female*. We call that [...]. What do you call it?"

"Your sex."

He looked as stunned as Maff felt. "You have *sexes*?" he asked. He said several emphatic-sounding phrases in his own language. Maff would kill for an active Interpreter thread. She'd be able to understand the basics of his language by now. At least he wasn't shaking anymore.

"Which one are you?" he asked.

Such a basic question, but profound. Maff was the first person to ever talk to these creatures. She tried to convey with her voice a smile she knew he couldn't see through her suit. "Female."

"What's your name?"

"Maff."

"Hello, Maff. I'm Kim. And I'm female, too. Mike is male."

It was always such a crapshoot guessing sex with high-grav life forms. "Pleased to meet you, Kim."

Hafurnal slammed a drawer shut. "*Dammit!* If I don't unlock that closet, I'll be stuck with these stupid bandage caps until we make planet fall." Pog…unisex creatures at least didn't require a guess, but using the right pronoun was awkward for her. *It* would be a lot easier, certainly more accurate, but someone always took offence and Maff had enough trouble with that just being pallun. Anyway, *pog* waved broken frond ends dramatically. "They sting."

Pog didn't seem that injured when they'd arrived. Maybe it was some kind of delayed stress reaction.

"Did I understand him?" Kim asked. "He needs that door unlocked?"

Maff wasn't the only one who guessed sex and pronouns wrong. "*Pog*. Exeders only have one sex. We say pog."

That brought out another, briefer, line of native language. Kim switched back. "*Pog*"—Maff took heart that someone else clearly found the new pronoun difficult—"needs that door unlocked?"

A strange question, but this *was* an alien. "Well, yes."

"Do you mind if I undo these restraints? I think I can help."

Maff turned to the medic. "Hafurnal, she thinks she can help with the door."

"What in the world can she do with this door?"

Kim had already undone the leg restraints. She moved slowly and deliberately as she got off the bed. "I have a…talent…with locks."

They both watched as Kim walked across the medical bay. She placed her hands on the door. After a moment, she flinched.

The door unlocked with a loud *clack*.

"Well, well," the captain said from the entrance of the medbay. "It seems that our new guests do have useful talents."

Chapter 16
Tonya

In the end, they took care of Helen's erstwhile bodyguards in the most conventional way possible: they called the cops as they traveled with Helen to the ER. The cameras used to record the progress of experiments also worked as security cams. Spencer made sure the cops got a clear record of two people trying to kidnap Helen and then murder Tonya and Spencer.

That solved one problem, but it left them with many others. Helen was still unconscious. Her vitals were fine, but she wouldn't wake up. It had to have something to do with the announcement of the death of her father. The kidnapping attempt and her getting sick were almost simultaneous.

They pulled up to an ER Tonya was familiar with—she only worked at the best ones—and got Helen admitted. Unconscious and unresponsive was as good as heart palpitations when it came to jumping to the head of the line.

She turned to Spencer as the doors opened to the medical area. "You'll need to stay in the waiting room. Find out what happened to Mike and Kim."

"I'll fill out the hospital paperwork while I'm at it."

She followed Helen into the room, stood back, and let the staff do their jobs, answering questions as quickly as they were asked.

"Twenty-five, Chinese, no medications, no significant allergies."

The medical override on Helen's phone told the ER staff the rest. No prescriptions. No chronic illnesses. She'd put herself on one of the newer nanotech birth controls.

"Does she have a husband? A boyfriend?"

"Not to my knowledge." Mike had never mentioned anything. If Tonya were to guess, it was for period control. Helen had gotten her very first one when they were all in China, and Tonya wasn't sure she'd ever seen anyone so disgusted.

"And what's your relationship to her?"

"I'm best friends with her brother and his fiancée. They're…" Tonya had no idea what to say. The truth would turn her into a psychiatric patient in their eyes. "They're out of town, and I haven't been able to reach them."

The resident on call raised an eyebrow and opened his mouth. Before he could say anything, the chief nurse said, with a finality that only years of keeping baby docs from killing people brought, "Tonya's part of the staff, and we have no one else who can tell us about this patient. She stays."

The baby doc took the newspaper swat to his nose with a flinch, but that was all. They either learned to do what the nurses told them, or their stint as a resident would be long and miserable. "What's this?" he indicated to a small box on Helen's belt.

Helen hadn't mentioned it, but through her phone, Tonya had seen that she'd connected it to her low-level monitoring systems. It was all daemons and firmware that interfaced with her real self. Explaining all of that would mean a lot of difficult questions coming Tonya's way. She picked something they'd understand. "An epileptic buffer system. It's experimental."

Baby Doc took that as a cue to throw his weight around. "It's not physically connected to her, so…" He activated a medical override that was part of the bed she was on.

Helen immediately went into cardiac arrest.

Alarms bleated while Baby Doc shouted, "What? I didn't do that! You said it's for epilepsy! It's not supposed to do that!"

"Out of the way!" The chief nurse elbowed Baby Doc aside hard

into the curtain wall. She rescinded the override and then put her own lock on it for good measure. At the same time, she tossed Helen's box to Tonya, grabbed a pair of defib paddles, and shouted, "Clear!" She zapped Helen's chest.

Helen's heart was beating strong before the chief nurse removed the paddles. She ignored the clucking baby doc and turned to Tonya. "Do you know the range on that thing?"

Tonya felt like she'd caught a grenade with the pin out. "At least this far?"

Helen groaned. "That hurt."

Baby Doc ran through the standard procedures for a patient who'd revived from unconsciousness. To his credit, he did it by the book without missing a step.

The nurses all exchanged the standard *what else do you expect* eye roll while he worked. Helen checked out as fine, and they went off to their patients as Baby Doc left to go consult with the attending physician. Helen was rolled into a private room.

"What *is* this thing?" Tonya asked.

"Thread storage. It's the only reason I'm still alive."

A box that kept you alive should never be a secret, at least not from people who could turn them off. Helen had the equivalent of an external heart snapped to her belt without so much as a sticker saying what it was for. "You should've set warnings," she said, not quite shouting. *"We nearly killed you."*

"I never thought I'd have to put all of them in it. I wasn't sure it was possible." She rubbed her chest. "What did they do to me?"

Tonya pulled down Helen's medical screens and set the correct warnings and permissions on the device to clearly mark it as necessary for life. It would take three different doctor's authorizations for a hospital override to work on it now. "They taught you a lesson in not taking your health for granted."

Helen tried to swallow. "Point taken. Can I have some hot water?"

Tonya sent Spencer their room number, then she got a cup and ran the tap.

"The fuck happened to you?" he asked before he'd gotten through the door.

"I'm fine, Spencer," she said between swallows of water. "Thanks for asking."

"I can see that," he said as he pulled up a chair and sat down. "What caused it?"

"They tried to destroy my real self. Murder me, in effect."

"Are you still in danger?" he asked.

"No. They can't reach me in here." She tapped the box. "Better to be lucky than good, that's the saying right?"

"What's the range on it?" Tonya asked.

Helen thought about it. "I'm not sure. A long way. Mike's adventure seems to indicate light years."

"So it was the medical override that fucked everything up?" Spencer asked.

Helen took another moment, coughed, and then grimaced as she tried to touch her chest. Tonya suppressed a smile. She was glad her friend was okay, but leaving such an important thing unmentioned was a ridiculous risk that could've killed her.

"Sort of," Helen replied. "It's complicated."

Baby Doc knocked on the door and walked in warily. The head nurse must've had The Talk with him, the one made in private about what happens to doctors who ignore nurses and throw their weight around. This one had paid attention. Tonya moved him from *actually murderous* to *still dangerous* in the baby doc filing cabinet she kept in her head. It was a big promotion.

"Everything looks fine now from what we can see," he said. "Can you tell if your device was involved?"

"Not until you triggered the override," she said dryly.

Baby Doc blushed. "Yes, well, I'm very sorry about that. I can admit you for further observation if that's what you want, but I'm not sure we'll find anything. You can install our monitor app and get the same results from home."

"If you don't mind," Helen said, "Could I rest here for a while?"

He checked a virtual chart only he could see. "I'll have the nurse come around occasionally. If you want to go home, she'll help you check out."

Helen waited until he was gone, then asked, "What have you found out about Mike and Kim?"

"It involved the transit dimension," Spencer said. "I think it might've been some kind of vehicle."

"That fits with what I remember," Tonya said. "It was big and had these huge doors, and it was covered with..."

"With lightning," Spencer finished for her. "*Pink* lightning. There has to be a connection."

Helen closed her eyes. "I can still feel him. From what I can tell, he's fine. Sleeping, in fact."

"Did any of that happen on his trip?" Spencer asked.

"Yes. So he could be somewhere nearby or..."

"On the other side of the goddamned galaxy. Great."

"Did we catch anything on the instrumentation?" Tonya asked.

Spencer shook his head. "We didn't have the right telemetry package running. We were watching the giant silver what-the-fuck, not them."

Tonya signed Helen out after a few hours and called Morgan, her truck, to drive himself over to the ER entrance. It was dark now, and they still hadn't figured out anything new about Mike and Kim.

Morgan said, "I think we might have a problem."

Morgan had access to all the same diagnostics a garage did. It would be just her luck to need an auto-tow from the hospital. "A system failure? Is that why the windows are stuck on opaque?"

"No. I'm fine," he said as he pulled away from the ER. "It's the cars I saw that have me worried."

Kim had insisted on an AI with an advanced security package when Tonya bought this SUV. Kim had then taken it on herself to add a custom upgrade. Morgan could spot dead-drop points and spy rendezvous with enough skill that Tonya sometimes wondered if he might be better off volunteering for the FBI in his free time instead of sitting in her garage.

"Oh shit," Spencer said. "What have you seen?"

Morgan manifested a video screen in their shared vision channel. In it, a black sedan regularly patrolled past Morgan's spot in the garage. "Now," he said, "watch what happened after I turned the window tint all the way up."

The vehicle, previously cruising past smoothly, stopped as if it was waiting for Morgan to pull out. After a time, the driver blinked their lights and beeped the horn.

"I played dead here," he said. "No need to give too much away."

The car eventually moved on.

"Some of your people, Helen?" Tonya asked.

"Driving a cheap American sedan?" She scoffed. "I don't think so."

Morgan fast-forwarded the recording a bit. "It gets worse."

The original black sedan was joined by a cab on autodrive and an automated scooter collector.

"Fuck," Spencer said. "Have they already spotted us?"

"No," Morgan said. "That's why it took me a little bit of time to pull up to the ER entrance. I took an indirect route."

"Are they following us now?" Helen asked.

"I'm not sure."

"To hell with this," Spencer said as he pulled a microdrone out of his pocket. "Don't take us home yet. Open the sunroof?"

"You carry those around in your pockets?" Tonya asked. It looked like a folded-up dragonfly.

"It's a good thing I do." He thumbed the thing to life. The dragonfly resemblance was stronger when it was unfolded. "It isn't very fast, so stick to surface roads, Morgan." He flicked it out of the sunroof, and their shared screen switched to its camera feed.

A black sedan, autotaxi, and scooter collector were five cars behind them.

"Fuck," Spencer said.

Maps and technical readouts Tonya didn't recognize flicked to life around the camera feed.

"Tonya," Helen said, suddenly deferential. "I need guidance permission for your vehicle."

It wasn't quite putting her in the driver's seat, but it was close. "Why?"

She looked at the floor, subdued. "I never thought I'd drive a car before I came outside, but I had to go through the same tail and evade classes my realspace colleagues did. It was hell without a realspace body, but I got the top score." She turned back to the maps around the camera feed. Helen was all business, concentrating on the task with a seriousness Tonya could almost feel. Any other time, she would've chuckled and told her to lighten up. But she had barely survived an attack, and now strangers were following them.

"Morgan, let Helen have guidance permission."

Chapter 17
Mike

He woke up not long after Kim, and was confronted with their new, terrifying reality.

There was no coffee!

Oh, and they were also on a ship with for-real aliens. This didn't shake him anywhere near as much as an extended stint without coffee. By most metrics, Mike was an alien as well. He just happened to live on the same planet as normal humans.

They were a diverse bunch, but the old *Star Trek* paradigm was correct. They all at least vaguely resembled various life forms on Earth. Emphasis on *vaguely*. From a distance, the crew almost looked like animals from back home. Up close the differences were obvious, and a little unsettling. The fox's fur was too coarse, almost scaly. The crane's wings weren't a terrestrial bird's. The lizard-men had a small, extra set of eyes. The fern could walk *and* talk. He didn't know how its lungs worked, assuming it had them.

The manta ray, Maff, was the biggest puzzle of all. She always wore a protective suit. It was impressive, like a mobile life support suit back home but on steroids. It had a flexible armored mesh embedded in a rubbery material. Brass, probably brass, was everywhere, from the legs she balanced on to the gooseneck arms of her manipulators. The view portals and grills used by her eyes and ears were lined with it too. This Maff would win every prize on offer at a steampunk cosplay event, of that he was certain.

There was good news though. They were closer to Will. A *lot* closer. These were Bemians, related somehow to the alien AI that was taking care of him. Kim had shown some of what she could do to the crew, so they'd be seen as valuable to their new hosts. That would buy time to get oriented and figure out their next steps.

It got better. Before, he only had a vague sense of where Will was. Now he had a precise vector, a spot he could point at in the sky and say *that's where he is, along this line.* And it didn't reach out to infinity; it was moving as their ship moved. Once he got all the variables figured out, they would be able to find the system he was in, and it should be reachable by a ship like this.

Well, hopefully they could find a nicer ship than this one. It was kind of a basket case.

As soon as the Bemians figured out what Kim could do, they took her around to four other locks that nobody had the keys for. That got them a detailed tour, which let him make an extensive catalog of dents, scorch marks, leaks, and what had to be rust holes. On a spaceship. They didn't even have everything they needed to make it work.

"How can you own a ship and not have keys to all the locks?" Mike asked Maff, while the captain gleefully explored what looked to be a pretty substantial hold.

"It's an old ship. Once your world's been joined to the galaxy for a few generations, they'll be a familiar sight."

He shared a glance with Kim. The entire crew had been making assumptions and saying things like that the entire time. They seemed to be taking Mike and Kim as members of a civilization that had been *uplifted* but not *joined*—the native words implied more formality than an English translation allowed—and so they'd become school kids out on a field trip. They decided to play along. There was no way to predict how their hosts would react if they explained the truth, that on Earth, aliens were science fiction and not everyone believed in them.

"They don't have…" He stopped. If they had a word for *locksmith*, then Kim, and therefore Mike, hadn't heard it before they got here. "They don't have someone you can pay to make new keys for you?"

"We wouldn't need to pay anyone," Maff replied. "This is all AC tech. We need node assistance for it. But the wait list on something this trivial is huge. It'd take years to get fixed."

"What about virtual constructs?" In the ship's realm, Mike reached out with his thread probes and restarted a control that'd been crashed for who knew how long. A series of light panels switched on over their heads and down the hall. The entire crew, who had been oohing and ahhing as they followed Kim's locksmith act, startled and then looked at him, open-mouthed. At least that's what most of them did. He wasn't sure where the fern's face was.

The captain came rushing out of the hold he'd been exploring. "How did you do that?"

By the look on Kim's face, she wanted to know the same thing. "When you gave us new…" Mike stopped. This one would be hard. He only knew about a third of the words needed to say *new phones and let us connect to your network* in Bemian. It took a few minutes of back and forth to get everyone on the same page. "I was able to see the problem and fix it."

He wouldn't say it out loud, but their security was terrible. Not only had they let two total strangers connect to their ship's network, they seemed to have never properly secured it in the first place. Mike was still being cautious. He only recognized things in a general way, but so far, he'd never been challenged to provide authentication of any sort to any part of the ship's realmspace. His threads had already inhabited the main portion. Mike was fairly certain he could take control of the ship now if he wanted to.

The rougher-looking of the lizard-men, the engineer named Feviz, looked him up and down with an expression that wasn't friendly, even on an alien's face. He was taller but not as heavily built as Mike was. If it came to a fight, well, Mike had put the captain in a headlock without breaking a sweat. Feviz shouldn't be a problem.

Feviz must've picked up some of that from the way Mike stood;

he pulled back and grunted. "I definitely have a use for you two." He turned to Maff. "You, pallun, take them down to the machine spaces, see what they can do with the subassemblies we've been sitting on. The captain and I need to have a chat."

She flexed her suit's legs, giving Mike the impression of frustration. "I need to check the autopilot first."

"I'll check the autopilot," the captain said. "You go and see how much our new friends here can make us when we get to market. The rest of you have jobs to do. Show's over, back to work."

At least that's what Mike thought he said. It went by a little fast. If he had that right, it was excellent news. They'd conclusively proven themselves valuable to this crew. *Market* strongly implied Bemian society was free in a very important way. One of his fears was that they were heading into some sort of collective society. Hard-core communists back home didn't do markets, and travel restrictions were a given. Saving money, buying tickets, and traveling independently weren't working concepts in that kind of world. In other words, simply buying a ticket and picking Will up had taken one step closer to being possible.

The other three crew members made noises that seemed more *aww* than *yippee* and then went off in different directions. After a few movements of her suit that didn't seem any happier, Maff said, "Come on, this way."

"Maff," Kim said, then spoke in a language Mike didn't understand.

Maff stopped. "No, but thank you for asking." She turned back, and they continued down the hall.

Mike said in English, "What did you ask her, and what language was that?"

"Apparently Bemian is everyone's second language. I had some conversations with Maff before you woke up and picked up the basics of her first one. I asked if we could use English. Back home, most people think it's rude to speak around them in a language they don't understand. I figured Bemians wouldn't be any different. I think I'm right."

"It's weird, isn't it, how many things match back home? I'm able to read their body language. At least I think I am." All except for the walking fern. He still wasn't sure about that one. It always seemed to end up at the back of the group, dropping leaves as it went. Nobody else seemed to care about the mess.

"You were around Bemians on your trip. I'm having to cue off your reactions right now. They all seem…I'm not sure. They're not robots. It mostly reminds me of the time Mama made me volunteer at a horse rescue when I was a teenager. They were big and scary, and I didn't know what any of their reactions meant. It took me a couple of days to figure out when they were annoyed, calm, or playful just by looking at them. That's what I feel here. I know their body language means something, but I don't know what it is yet. It's frightening, but I'm holding it together for now." She pulled out a handkerchief and handed one end to him so they could pull it tight. They were together. Surrounded by aliens, who knew how far away from home, trying to find Will. He held the cloth tight.

Maff noticed the handkerchief. "If you don't mind my asking, what is your relationship to each other? You're clearly together on some level. I'm curious as to what it might be."

It only took one round to figure out the words for *fiancée* and *marriage*.

"So you have those here?" he asked.

"Pair bonds are quite common across the galaxy. More complicated arrangements do exist, but they tend not to survive uplift. Like the galaxy itself, the AC network tries to keep things as simple as possible without restricting choice so much it all becomes unsustainable."

Another reference to the *AC Network*. Since they'd already been told they were a part of it, Mike and Kim couldn't flat-out ask what it was. But it seemed to be what underpinned this culture. It also seemed able to shape entire civilizations as they were *uplifted*. He hadn't heard any mention of those civilizations having a choice in the matter.

It wasn't a good sign.

The further they went, the dirtier and more worn down things became. "How old is this ship?" he asked.

"I'm not sure. I never thought to ask. Several demetars at least."

It took some more back and forth to understand that demetars meant *centuries*. The ship was built when the Age of Sail was all the rage back on Earth.

"How hard is it to find parts for something this old?" Kim asked.

"Old? Oh, I keep forgetting that you haven't been uplifted for very long. No, this isn't a particularly old ship. I've got an uncle who works at a transport company with ships two or three times older than this, and even they aren't *that* old."

A civilization that could obviously reach Earth had been rushing around the galaxy since the Middle Ages, maybe earlier. The ships were reliable enough that a useful lifespan measured in centuries was unremarkable. But they hadn't found humanity's home. Mike and Kim were novelties to these people. Not just this crew, but to the society itself.

That's why they were knocked out. *Sa'dst* was nanotech that first learned and then adapted to their biochemistry to protect them from infections and poisons. But that's not all it did. It enabled them to breathe a variety of atmospheric gasses, eat and drink pretty much anything, and cope with pressure differences that would be dangerous without it. They didn't even need to go to the bathroom anymore. They'd learned a lot of new Bemian words figuring that part out. Body waste was broken down into constituent compounds and recycled as many times as it took to extract *all* the energy from them, and then what was left was either, depending on the biochemistry, exhaled or sweated out. He'd found hooks to the sa'dst his threads could reach. He didn't dare tinker with those without documentation. Anything with that level of power over a person's metabolism could be dangerous if he started punching random buttons.

It wasn't permanent, though. Sa'dst needed to be constantly replaced, and on a ship like this, supplies were limited. Their arrival had depleted the ship's reserves. Getting more was the first thing the crew would pick up wherever they arrived.

If humans had been a part of this culture at any time in the past, the sa'dst would not have needed to knock them out to adapt to them. It would've already known what they were. So humans hadn't been kidnapped, interbred with, or otherwise probed by aliens. At least not by these aliens.

Since Maff kept talking about the entire galaxy and a network that controlled it, Mike was pretty sure there weren't any others around. For the first time, he considered what they might tell everyone about all this when they finally got home. Bringing Maff out on stage at the next international UFO conference would be one way to make a splash. "I'm happy to announce that all your close encounters and abductions and anal probes really were in your head. And I have a walking, talking manta ray to prove it!"

His fantasy was interrupted when a big dingy metal door rolled open noisily on another large hold, this one filled with warehouse shelves that went all the way up to the ceiling. Each one held glowing bins of light filled with dark, dirty shapes. It was like a Costco from hell.

"How long have you guys been collecting junk?" Kim asked as she walked in.

"Before my time," Maff replied. "Everyone does it. Things break, and we have to wait until we get to a network node before they can get fixed. But you have to wait for your slot, and that can take years. You save up everything you can, and once your slot comes up, they'll repair anything you put in front of them." She turned to Mike. "Is it easier when the network only has one node?"

As he tried to form an answer, a tickle that had been in the back of his mind since he woke up amped up with a vengeance, and then it opened.

"Mike? Mike! Wake up!"

Helen.

"Wake up, Mike! We need your help!"

Chapter 18
Helen

It was an axiom of police training: simulations were not reality. During a simulation, she always knew in the back of her mind that it was an illusion. Mistakes had consequences, but only within defined limits. The bystanders were obstacles or challenges, not innocent people who could be hurt or killed. It all combined to make the simulation less than it should've seemed. Less than reality.

Less than life or death.

"Right at the next light, Morgan," Helen said.

Whoever was running the coup had hacked Helen out of her home with an intent to kill. If it hadn't been for her anchor box and the still-mysterious intervention of the snake mother, they would've succeeded. Helen had no doubt that whoever was following them had the same intent and would have an easier time of it. Her threads couldn't be shot.

"That forced them back into line," Spencer said.

Two of the three vehicles following them were autonomous, slaved to the one in the lead. They'd tried twice now to split off and move ahead for an ambush. Helen's maneuvers were keeping them from organizing properly.

"Any luck getting through to the police?" she asked Tonya.

"Not with my phone or with Morgan's. But it's not being jammed, at least not in a way Kim's blockers recognize."

That was news. "Kim's blockers?"

Helen concentrated on plotting their next move but could still see Tonya's smile in the corner of her eye as she said, "One of the advantages of being her friend is you get all sorts of custom security tools."

"But it's all so goddamned old," Spencer said. "I had to work with some of it at the plant."

"Be that as it may," Tonya replied, "if we were getting jammed, it should tell me what's doing it, where it's coming from, and how far away it is. All it's showing right now is some strange flickering, and then it crashes."

Spencer snorted. "Kim's software needs patching. Film at eleven." He looked away, then punched a few invisible buttons. "Shit."

"What's wrong now?" Helen asked.

"He's called in a friend." On Helen's map, Spencer designated a new target. "Same as the first one, a piloted vehicle and two autonomous drones. They're garbage trucks. More mass. Not good."

She was using an evade method that kept their pursuer at a distance and guessing, but now things had escalated. She managed to get Tonya's permission to command the vehicle's AI without anyone getting embarrassed, but what she needed next was on a whole new level. Helen wouldn't be issuing commands. She'd be behind the wheel. Promoting herself from navigator to captain, *in front of the real captain,* would be almost unheard of back home. It'd taken decades of training to get Chinese copilots to speak up when the captain was making a mistake that would kill everyone in a plane crash. Even then it was a struggle. That need to avoid a loss of face was deeply ingrained in her.

You managed to overcome it once, dear.

The snake mother's observation was uncomfortable but no less true. She'd interrupted Father on that last night, trying to prevent a nuclear exchange. The resistance to pushing open his door had been almost physical. It was only the threatened death of millions of innocents that made it possible.

Are you able to do it on a smaller scale, with a friend? Is it face you're trying to save, or are you simply a coward?

The snake mother's goad decided it. Helen turned away from her virtual displays. "Tonya, I'm glad you've provided me the opportunity to give Morgan waypoints so we could avoid our pursuer."

Her body language changed, and one eyebrow went up. She seemed insulted. Helen had blown it. Great.

"Yes?"

She had to be careful now. "Waypoints won't work anymore. I can't avoid two foes at once like this. It is a difficult situation."

Helen thought she saw a trace of a smile. "And?"

Americans were so difficult to read. "It is very inefficient to pilot indirectly this way, as I'm sure you understand."

Tonya stretched and laced her hands together. The effect was striking with such dark skin. *They called her the Black Dragon.*

"What exactly am I supposed to understand, Helen?"

"Quit screwing with her," Spencer said. "She wants to drive the truck."

Helen almost had Tonya agreeing, and now Spencer's rude words had ruined everything. She would never agree now. "That's not what I—"

Tonya bubbled over with laughter. "You're not the president anymore, Helen, and I'm your friend. Morgan, priority override privileges for Helen Zhang. Full authority. Acknowledge."

"Full authority?" Morgan asked over the speakers. "Hot damn!"

On an intellectual level, Helen knew she'd navigated an unnecessary obstacle course. Tonya, Spencer, even Morgan, didn't think of face the way she did. But that didn't make the relief and, frankly, triumph any less heady.

You've learned a great deal glad-handing the politburo. No wonder they want to kill you.

Helen filed away whether to take that as a compliment for a later time.

As she moved to the driver's seat, Tonya held up a finger. "Not a scratch on him. Do you understand?"

Helen had to be honest. "I can't promise that, but I'll try."

Tonya jumped into the front passenger seat and buckled herself in. "What did you score on the full evasion driving test?"

The question caught her off guard, sending her back to the academy with instructors who could never be pleased. She would not fail. "The highest in my class. The highest of *any* class." She always checked the scores of each one as they graduated.

"Well don't mess around, girl," Tonya said as she braced. "Hit it!"

Helen paused. "That's not how it works."

"It's not?"

She tested the controls and smiled. Very responsive. "Morgan, please deactivate all native communications channels." She looked in the rearview mirror. "Spencer, I'm assuming you can shut down the ones he can't? Maintenance telemetry and OnStar?"

He touched invisible controls. "Done."

"Hey!" Tonya said. "No hacking friends!"

He rolled his eyes. "Passwords only slow me down."

Mike and Kim had given her their codes when they found out how much running around she needed to do to salvage the wedding. She got their cars moving on an intercept course.

"You have a vehicle of your own, Spencer?" He might have more than one. She'd read that most Americans did.

"No scratches on this one either, okay?" The access codes landed in her queue.

The ancestors were smiling on them. All three cars were comparatively close and in the same direction. Turning them into obstacles and distractions would be much easier. "What's the range on your drone?" Helen didn't need a chase aircraft anymore; she needed an eye in the sky.

One of her monitor threads sounded an alert. They were trying a double flank. She made a sharp left.

"Five miles or so," he said.

Americans and their imperialistic measurements. A quick calculation gave her the actual distance. Eight kilometers. Better than most police drones back home, and he carried it around in his pocket. Typical. "Send it up a kilometer and a half, racetrack pattern centered here," she designated a bullseye halfway between them and their reinforcements, "and change the display from actual to tactical." The image's field of view widened out as the drone ascended, and the video changed to an abstract wire frame that removed all the unnecessary features.

She looked at Tonya. "*Now* we hit it."

Helen had chalked up Tonya's shiny white European vehicle, the virtual dash called it an Alfa Romeo Toirano Quadrifoglio, as a typical expression of Western decadence, but when she stepped on the accelerator things got loud in a hurry.

And it sounded *good*.

Morgan let out a whoop from the speakers. "I do love my turbos!"

Helen blinked at the speedometer. That three-digit number wasn't in Kph. She stomped the brakes, and it yanked to a stop like it was tied to a tree. Her vision blurred briefly as her eyes were pulled out of round by the deceleration.

"Don't stop now," Morgan shouted. "We got bad guys to run from!"

Her heart was thudding twice as fast as it should. She looked over at Tonya. "What *is* this?"

Her grin was that of someone who'd made a point when she hadn't expected to. Helen was too excited by this amazing machine to figure out if she'd lost face with the exchange. "The best thing Mike Sellars ever talked me into."

Warnings flashed in her vision. Their pursuers had adjusted. Morgan was right; stopping was the wrong move. Helen hit the accelerator again, but with a deliberate press this time. It still pushed her back into the seat with a firm hand. They twisted around an onramp at twice its rated speed. She was in complete control. It was an extension of her will, something she'd never experienced without her threads.

Helen shut down all her waypoints and *drove*, letting her

intuition tell her where to make turns, when to accelerate, when to brake, always staying—barely—within the limits that would immediately bring law enforcement down on them. The squad cars she'd trained with were creaking ox carts compared to this sleek rocket. She'd seen these kinds of vehicles on the roads back home and had silently denounced them as vulgar bourgeois excess. She needed to reassess that judgement.

Denied the initiative, their opponents couldn't skate as close to the limits without going over them. Within minutes, the secondary team had police chasing them. "One down."

Helen's brief distraction was almost disastrous when a microcar swerved into their lane. There was no time to react, but then the wheel twitched under her hands, and the pedals did a strange dance under her feet. They passed the wayward vehicle with centimeters to spare, not slowing down a bit.

"I might not be able to break the law," Morgan said with undisguised glee, "but it doesn't mean I can't help you get out of trouble."

"*Thank* you."

Their initial foes weren't as easy to dispose of. There was a counter to every move she tried.

"They're monitoring this truck," Spencer said.

"A tracker?" Morgan sputtered. "They didn't get anywhere near me."

"Then it must be the street cameras." Spencer took back control of his own vehicle. "I've got a plan, but we need a distraction." He drew a path on her map. "Follow this. Is Mike up yet?"

She tested him. "Mike? Mike! Wake up!"

His perception moved to her, but sluggishly.

"Wake up, Mike! We need your help!"

"Helen?"

First things first. "Are you and Kim okay?"

"For certain values of okay, I guess. Helen, how are you doing this?"

"The same way we always do it. I have a situation here, and

Spencer wants to talk to you." But patching him in didn't work. There was no time for technical glitches. "Tell me," she said to Spencer, "I'll relay it to Mike."

"I need him to nuke the local traffic camera realm so we can blind them."

As she explained Spencer's idea, she also sprung the trap she'd set. Mike and Kim's cars raced into an intersection in front of the bad guys. The lead vehicle swerved around the improvised roadblock, but the utility vehicles weren't as maneuverable. One slammed into a parked car, the other swerved and rolled over. She couldn't tell if it'd avoided Mike's car with the way the map was configured now. She hoped not.

"I can't nuke a realm from here," Mike said.

"What's that supposed to mean?" She came dangerously close to running a red light navigating Spencer's route. "Where are you?"

"I don't think you have time for me to explain right now. But I don't have to. You can still access realmspace with your phone, right?"

It was how they'd worked together figuring out the ark in China. "Yes."

"Okay." An address landed in her queue. "I've opened up the realm for you. Kim knows how to do the rest." There was a pause. "I can't bring her in either. Oh, I get it. We're using a different route."

If he started on the details, they'd be here all night. "Explain it to me later." Morgan could handle the waypoints, so she switched control to him and accessed the realm using a window and virtual controls, allowing her human hands to manipulate things her threads could never reach. "Can she tell you what I need to do?"

"Ask Spencer for a copy of Kim's D9."

This was the wrong place for bourgeois cultural references. "D9?"

"I don't know what it is either."

Helen looked into the rearview mirror and said, "I need Kim's D9." Now that they were obeying speed limits, their pursuer had closed the distance.

"Right," Spencer said. "I'll tell you what to do. Tonya, you need to switch with Helen. Take manual control and get ready to move when I tell you to." He unbuckled and moved close behind Helen as a construct contraption that was half pistol, half steam engine manifested in her vision channel. "Point and shoot. It's that easy."

They slithered around each other as she and Tonya swapped seats. Helen grasped the construct. Without the full haptic feedback of a realm, she was holding smoke. Helen aimed for the center of the window and pulled the trigger. It spun to life in a whir of gears, spouting virtual steam, and then blasted...*something*...through the window and into the realm beyond.

Outside in realspace, everything was plunged into blackness. All she could see was what Morgan's headlights revealed.

"*Now!*" Spencer shouted. "Follow the new route, head for the overpass."

Helen grabbed frantically at the handle over the window to keep from getting thrown out of her seat. What Tonya lacked in driver training, she made up for with enthusiasm.

A pair of headlights appeared in the distance, heading their way. Helen could barely make out the overpass indicated on the map between them.

"Okay everyone, get ready to bail out."

"Bail out?" Tonya asked. "Why?"

"They know about Morgan. They don't know about my truck. We'll switch, and he'll lead them away."

Tonya stiffened. "I don't think so."

"It'll be all right," Morgan said from the car's speakers. "I need to check in for some maintenance anyway. They won't be able to follow me into the dealer's garage without the proper ID."

Helen could see that Tonya didn't like the idea of him going off alone. "Be careful, Morgan."

"Always, ma'am."

They screeched to a halt underneath the overpass and scampered across the road to Spencer's vehicle. With headlights as the only illumination, it was a desperate haunted cave.

They hopped in, and Spencer sped off in the opposite direction. Tonya watched over her shoulder until Morgan pulled out of sight.

"Everyone *down*," Spencer said as he crouched behind the dash.

Helen saw their pursuer pass in the rearview mirror. She caught a glimpse of a white male face, eyes wide, mouth slack. Not Chinese. Not healthy either. Something was clearly wrong with him.

"We've got another problem," Tonya said. "Aaron called me. There's a BOLO out for Mike and Kim. It came from Interpol."

"What?" Helen said as she watched the car drive out of sight behind Morgan. "They've been in the US since they got back from China."

"He knows that and is trying to figure out what's going on. He wants us to lie low until he does."

America was a big place, but Helen didn't know all that much about it. "I guess going back to my hotel doesn't count?"

"No," Tonya replied. "And my whole family lives in the DC area. Cameras everywhere."

They both looked at Spencer. He was the only option left.

He gripped the wheel tight, shoulders high. Whatever he was thinking about wasn't making him happy.

He saw them staring at him. "*Fuck*. Okay. You guys don't know a good place to lie low. But I sure as hell do. I need to get gas. Tonya, order us an Amazon drone strike and have it meet us here." A location was circled on the map in the shared vision channel.

"Drone strike?" Helen asked.

Tonya's chuckle was a mix of anger and resignation. "We kept losing luggage in China. Mike made special lists we could one-click if that ever happened again. From toothpaste to underwear, we're only a drone delivery away from being equipped for a road trip. I'm guessing that's what we're gonna do?"

Spencer cursed under his breath, which was impressive. Helen thought he had to shout them out all the time. "Yeah. Like the man says, if there's a bright spot in the center of the universe, we're going to the place that's farthest from it."

The map zoomed out and traveled west. It stopped over a small town near two major rivers in the middle of the country.

"My hometown," he said. "Dumas *fucking* Arkansas."

Chapter 19
Maff

Knowing where they were was not the same thing as being where they wanted to be. Whatever Mike and Kim had done—Maff asked, but they couldn't explain it in Standard, and she needed an Interpreter thread to understand their native language for something that technical—had managed to jump the ship back to modal eight and returned them to known space, but it would take mets, *days*, in the language Kim was teaching her, to get back to a place they could fence their goods and resupply properly.

The aliens, they called themselves *humans*, had repaired enough components that installing them had become a full-time job for the rest of the crew. Maff was considered too junior to be trusted with repairing her own consoles, so she spent most of her time shuttling broken components to the humans, and repaired ones to everyone else.

Feviz wasn't that diplomatic. "No way am I letting some greedy pallun gas bag get its fins on anything in *my* ship," he'd said to the captain. "She'd either take it apart to sell it or use it in one of their rituals."

Before, the stupid insult would've put sulfur in her sky, but not now. Being the junior *gas bag* watercarrier meant spending more time with the humans.

The basic physical differences were easy to get past—if you'd seen one high-grav life form, you'd pretty much seen them all—but their culture was unique. They were intensely curious about everything around them, from the most complicated ship's components to the color of paint they used in the hold. Kim could be an instructor in locks now, and Mike was going on and on about planetary gears. Whatever those were.

Stranger still, the humans were as interested in what she thought of anything as they were about how it worked.

"Do you perceive the color of the walls as gray, Maff?" Mike had asked her.

She rubbed a spot on the nearest one with a manipulator. "If you took enough of the grime off, I guess so."

Mike immediately jumped back to their native language and spoke with Kim. That didn't bother her as much as Kim thought it might. Standard was a language of trade and navigation, basic needs and dirty jokes. Anything more sophisticated required Interpreter threads.

But it did make Maff curious. "What's he talking about now?" she asked Kim in Pallundian. Maff's native language was mostly whistles and hums, but Kim had caught on to it faster than anyone Maff had ever met.

"It means you see in the same...well, there we go again. I don't think you have a word for it. *Light that is the same color and brightness that our eyes use*. That's not correct, though."

"And the English word is?"

"Wavelength."

Maff entered it in her burgeoning English lexicon. The human's language was rich with words involving technical things. They had more words for *gear* than Pallundian did for *cloud*, and nobody described clouds the way a pallun did.

Even though Maff couldn't speak English beyond a few basic sentences, she'd learned dozens of different words. The crew had already called her out a few times when she used them herself.

"Don't go and run off with them, Maff. We're not home yet," the captain said when she handed him the repaired *circuit board*.

"No, sir."

Hafurnal was at least impressed with the repaired and calibrated *infusion pump* she handed pog. The device made strange squawking noises when Hafurnal turned it on, nothing at all like how it behaved while it was on Mike's workbench. She thought it was still broken, but after some rapid frond movements over the controls, it began to behave. Hafurnal laughed weakly. "Next thing you know, they'll want to take over the infirmary."

Kim laughed when Maff suggested it. "I doubt we'd know how to do anything that would help in an infirmary."

Having such a detailed look at a civilization so new to uplift was fascinating. It seemed that the AC network forced new societies to rely much more on themselves than they did mature ones. But that wasn't right. The AC nodes held a monopoly on repair. They always had. Yet here was a new civilization that was clearly trained by the nodes to break that very monopoly.

There were other odd things about them. Maff was almost certain that Mike had somehow gained access to parts of the ship's secure network. There were glitches in the logs, unexplainable failures of long-reliable systems and sudden revivals of others that had been dormant longer than anyone could remember. But he used the same neural access they all did, and the diagnostics she ran never found anything unusual.

The only people who could access local realmspaces without needing permission were full Interpreters. Maff had heard stories that they could infiltrate the sa'dst in a person's body and make them explode. That was not a good thing for complete strangers on their ship to have. But Mike had no absorbed companion, and in every other respect was unlike any Guild envoy Maff had met or heard about.

Then she caught Kim talking to Hafurnal in pogs native language as she helped pog install the infusion pump. Where Pallundian was mostly whistling, Hafurnal's native language was a kind of static rustling. Kim had spent much less time with Hafurnal than she had with Maff but was clearly able to speak with pog. This was also something only Interpreters did. But Kim exhibited none of the scars associated with the transition from threaded translator to galactic envoy, and again she had no absorbed companion.

She was tempted to be the stereotypically rude, nosey gasbag everyone said palluns were and ask them to explain it all, but it was now nearing the end of the voyage. Maff's own duties had picked up, and she wasn't able to spend as much time around the humans as she would've liked.

The transit dimension required a full-time pilot for a reason. It wasn't just the modals changing their speed relative to normal space. The closer they got to developed worlds, the more often she had to alter course to ensure they wouldn't collide with anyone else. The paths blocked and reconfigured more frequently as well. Maneuvering around those obstacles efficiently required a finesse that was either built in or learned from decades of practice. It was as close as any pallun got to real flying. If it wasn't for all the discrimination, and if she was honest, the prejudices of her own people, pallun would dominate the profession.

She maneuvered around a particularly complicated sequence of paths as Mike made his way to the bridge. It was off-cycle, *night* in diurnal speak, so she was the only one working at the moment. Weeks ago, she would've been nervous to be alone with the human. Mike had easily restrained the captain, and he was stronger than the krons on the crew. But Maff's suit protected her very well, and without a skeleton, there wasn't a lot to grab that couldn't be reshaped and slid free.

Besides, she liked him.

"So you're the pilot, and this," he indicated Elsek's station, "is navigation?"

"Correct. She figures out where we're going, and I drive us there."

"How hard is it to use?"

They were endlessly curious about every aspect of the ship. "It takes training to do it well, and lots of practice."

"But the basics? How hard is it to locate a world?"

It was the first time either of them had mentioned their home world. Maff had been so fascinated by them and their abilities that she hadn't thought about what being cut off from everything they knew and loved might mean.

It didn't help that the news was bad. "In your case? Very. We didn't know where we were when we found you, and the machine you were experimenting with literally threw us across the galaxy. Once we get to a place with full network access, you might be able to get the nodes to help you, or maybe find a Guild envoy who knows about it." Doubtful, but possible.

"What if I wanted to locate a different world, one not as isolated as ours? Can you show me how to look around without changing anything? If I find a world I recognize on your charts, it might give me a clue where home is."

Maff checked when Elsek was scheduled to come on shift. She didn't want to find out how ruffled the navigator's feathers would get if Elsek discovered that she had let the alien play with her controls. The schedules said that was several hours away.

Maff set the autopilot and moved over to the navigation station. "Sure." She called up a mapping mode and locked out the rest of the console's functions. Mike grasped the basics fairly quickly, but there was a limitation: labels were a challenge.

"They haven't taught you how to read yet, have they?" she asked. It explained a few things now that she thought about it. She had wondered why they'd had such a hard time figuring out the layout of the ship. They couldn't read the signs.

"Not really." His skin darkened. It wasn't a particularly good camouflage reflex. "I learned a few words during an…introduction class. We've both picked up more, but it's nothing like this."

"At least you don't need an Interpreter thread to read script." There were countless languages in the galaxy, but only a few symbologies were required to represent them. Organic optics was one of the easier ones.

He hesitated. "Yeah…right…it's great that I don't need an…Interpreter thread."

Maff played introductory teacher as well as navigation instructor. He started on his location solution, but he'd misunderstood everything. "You won't find anything out there."

"That makes sense," he replied.

"It does?"

He tensed up for a moment. "What I mean…was…um…"

Sometimes Mike could speak Standard very well. Other times he seemed to forget all the words and had to start from scratch.

He stopped stammering. "The network was teaching us locations, but they started with… dead places?"

It wasn't any weirder than anything else about them. "Planets marked for recycling, you mean? That's all you'll find in that direction."

"Exactly." He said as he adjusted the controls more. "It's definitely been marked for recycling. I remember being told that very clearly."

Maff glimpsed feathers and spindly legs in the hallway camera.

"Oh *shit.*" The use of the English swear word seemed appropriate. "She's not supposed to be here right now." Maff turned to Mike. "Take your notes, fast!"

Maff moved over to her own station, leaving a manipulator hovering over the nav station's power button. There wasn't time to put it all back to normal. When he nodded, she shut the whole thing down. She used another set of manipulators to nudge him toward an alternate exit. Maff got everything arranged in time before Elsek walked onto the bridge, barely.

"Oh, hey, Elsek," Maff said, willing her voice to stay calm. Elsek was high strung in the best of situations. Discovering a human at her station would undoubtedly produce an epic meltdown. "You're up early."

"Prepping for our arrival," she said, suspicious. "Why'd you shut down my station?"

"I didn't, it turned off on its own." They'd been tinkering a lot with the ship lately. It could happen.

Elsek's feathers ruffled across her whole body, a sure sign she wasn't convinced. "Well I hope it didn't mess anything up."

*

Their arrival was a much lower-key affair than their departure. The news was good, for once. The captain had completed the deal for their cargo before the authorities fell on them: five copies of *The Way of the Remainders*, one of the very few works to have supposedly been composed before the Refounding. The species performing the ritual dances preserved in the visual segment had certainly passed into Senescence long before Maff's people knew which way was up in a cloud. As with all ancient things, authentic copies could only be obtained from the AC network, and the wait list was demetars long…centuries long. She needed to keep practicing English to communicate with the humans better. The copies the captain had picked up were beautiful works, and as fake as the storm was large. Maff had no idea where such forgeries ultimately originated from. It could be a rogue node, a remote group of acolytes with illegal fabricators, a break-away faction of Death Eaters, Maff had even heard pallun were sometimes involved in such things. Regardless, they needed a buyer. Rendezvousing with an interested candidate was the first thing the captain, Feviz, and Elsek would do on arrival.

Speaking of fabricators, it seemed Mike and Kim had figured the one on the ship out. They'd changed into roughly similar outfits: both practical, rugged, made of dark and robust materials. It would wear well in any environment, and since they'd based them on existing designs, they wouldn't stand out as much planetside.

They also appeared much neater than before. "Who showed you how to work the fabricators?" She asked as they waited at the cargo door for the docking sequences to complete.

"That's mostly down to you," Mike said.

"Your crash course on reading helped us figure out the symbols we needed to make it work," Kim said. "We had to practice a few times to get it right, though."

"Celerawberries," Mike said, "they sounded a lot better in the description than they tasted. Long rods that take forever to fabricate, and then it's celery mixed with strawberries." He then did something buzzy with his mouthparts. "Nasty."

"Anyway," Kim said, "we had better luck with clothes. The fact that there were patterns available that we recognized is…well, I'm not sure what it is. Strange, certainly."

"But we don't match," he said. "The first humans to step onto another planet, and we're a mixed up cosplay couple."

Kim wasn't impressed by whatever matching cosplay was. "I won't walk around in white robes with my hair coiled around my ears back home, Han Stupid, let alone here."

"That's okay," he said with a grin. "Peacekeeper leathers suit you."

Maff had now known them long enough to realize the banter was their way of coping with the stress of the situation. The first time members of an uplifted species encountered a civilized world was also a staple of realm entertainments. Maff had seen dozens of versions of it.

And now it was happening for real, right in front of her. These humans were brave creatures. If the roles were reversed, Maff wasn't sure she'd leave her cabin.

She felt part of it seeing the situation through their eyes. On the spot, she elected herself the human's tour guide. There were so many things to see, even on this sketchy rural world.

The ship, under control of the harbor's autopilots, settled into its berth with a shudder and some loud clanks. The humans gripped a length of cloth between them, a strange but obvious gesture of comfort. The doors, now with properly repaired hinges and locks, unsealed with a brief hiss.

Mike collapsed into a heap on the floor.

Chapter 20
Spencer

The drive from Virginia to Arkansas didn't matter. Being chased by Chinese secret agents didn't matter. Spending endless hours in a fifteen-year-old Dodge didn't matter. None of them noticed the truck, or the road, or the drive, because Helen had figured out where Mike and Kim were. They weren't in a different city.

They were on a *fucking spaceship*.

It'd taken most of an hour of frantic back and forth to get their heads around the concept. Helen could talk to Mike and vice versa, but it was a channel only they could use. It had something to do with quantum tunnels. Tonya said it, she understood it, and that was all he needed, but that didn't stop her from getting out a virtual blackboard and scribbling on it. Helen nodded and pretended to follow, but he knew better. He also knew better than to challenge her. This was Helen. If he called her out, she'd turn learning the details into some sort of contest.

As far as the goons that chased them around went, that was still a stone-cold mystery. It probably wasn't the Chinese. They didn't have that kind of manpower, and it would've been a lot more straightforward to nab Helen and send her home than it would be to try something violent on US soil and risk a screwup.

But someone had definitely been following them, and Spencer's spidey-sense put whoever the hell they were on the *not selling Girl Scout cookies* shelf. Helen's description of what she'd seen in the rearview mirror freaked him out. That was an encounter he'd avoid every goddamned chance he got.

They took turns driving, with two lookouts on alert the entire time. Nobody saw anything. They drove an anonymous truck on anonymous roads and stayed at anonymous motels. But there was no way to know for sure how anonymous they were. Without Mike and Kim, they were back in the world of perfect security. He understood that being on an alien ship took them out of the game for now, but *fuck* was it inconvenient to not have them around. Spencer had tools that could cause trouble, but only on a small scale.

Helen was kind of a revelation. The woman had eyes in the back of her head and a way of sizing up a situation, of sizing up *people*, that was downright spooky.

"You aren't looking forward to going home, are you?" She asked on the first full day of the road trip.

"No." Limiting his answers helped him not to think about it.

"I understand."

"You do?"

"You're highly intelligent but from a broken and abusive family. Your grandmother is controlling, everyone keeps tabs on you, and the population is too small for you to share interests with more than one or two people your age."

He'd maybe said three things about shit back home to Helen. "How the fuck did you figure all that out?"

"Observation and deduction. Arthur Conan Doyle spent much time studying Chinese culture. It's a well-known fact that Sherlock Holmes was based on Guan Yu. We were using those techniques thousands of years before they were discovered in the west."

"Bullshit."

She shrugged, so smug it was like an aura. "You can look it up if you don't believe me."

He could've sworn he saw a gleam in Tonya's eye when she glanced in the mirror. Helen was fucking with him, he knew it.

A quick glance at Wikipedia found no such references to China in Doyle's biography. "I told you it was bullshit," he said as he put the article in their shared channel.

Helen sputtered out a laugh, and Tonya joined her. "I believe the proper response to that is *made you look*?" Helen said.

So they relied on Helen to keep tabs on anyone or anything that stood out while he and Tonya kept the away team stocked up on plans so they could fix shit on the alien *wessel*. That last part slowed things down considerably. Helen was limited to voice-only with Mike when they were moving at speed. She needed to be still to send anything more to him. Tonya tried to explain why, but he waved her off once the equation started using Greek letters.

Mike and Kim needed all the help they could get. They were safe, but their spaceship was a shitbox. They needed detailed plans and descriptions of tons of different machines, circuits, pumps, and gearboxes. The aliens had a serious hard-on for planetary gearsets in particular. Spencer now knew the insides of automatic transmissions dating from the 1950s to the 1990s. The later ones were fucking complicated.

In between episodes of *Scrapheap Challenge: Aliens in the Junkyard,* they learned about their first for-real extraterrestrials. Well, the first ones that weren't trying to kill them all. Spencer was able to claim that achievement. He still woke up screaming sometimes.

There were no giant three-eyed bear monsters on this crew. Helen used Mike's descriptions to draw pictures. She did a sketch artist course in cop school, so they all looked like disappointed gangbangers in her drawings.

The more they learned, the better the sketches seemed to fit. Aside from Maff the Manta Ray, the crew was a bunch of assholes. As soon as they got wherever they were going, the plan was to make whatever passed for money out there fixing things up, then chartering a ship or buying a ticket or whatever it took to go out and get Will.

That last part was such a no-brainer he got yelled at for bringing it up.

"Of *course* we're getting him first," Kim said through Helen, who preserved the ice and steel in her tone. "Why in the world would we even discuss it?"

So everybody freaked out a little less every day as they got used to the whole *alien spaceship* thing and got closer and closer to the one place Spencer never wanted to see again.

Okay that was an exaggeration. But it wasn't much of one. Helen was right on every count. His grandmother was controlling, his parents abused each other, not him—but growing up watching that was its own kind of hell—and he had no one he could call a genuine friend. He couldn't trust them. At best, they didn't know what to make of him. At worst, they betrayed him.

Stewart was still out there too. Spencer had heard from Mom that he'd gotten a career-ending football injury in his second year at college and had come home with his tail between his legs. It fucking sucked. That was all Stewart wanted to be, all the whole town wanted him to be, and it was gone with a snapped ankle.

He waited as long as he could, not letting anyone know he was coming until they were crossing the Mississippi river at Memphis, but the call had to happen at some point. In a town as small as Dumas, there was no way to sneak in and stay unnoticed. Even if they drove straight through the place and kept going—oh, how tempting that sounded—he'd pass at least three people who would recognize him.

"Oh my God, Spencer, that's great!" Mom shouted when he rang her up. "Is everything okay?"

"Yes, everything's fine." He checked the rearview mirror. Helen was looking calmly out at the river as they passed over it. As long as their Chinese Danger Canary wasn't upset, things were okay. "Definitely fine. Listen, I just crossed the river, but I need to drop some stuff off at Horace's. It'll take a little longer than usual to get to the house."

"Be sure to call him first, he's at work right now."

"Will do, Mom. See you soon. Love ya."

Tonya gave him a look from the passenger seat. "Drop some stuff off?"

"I'm dropping you two off, and you have stuff, therefore I'm dropping stuff off."

The point wasn't to visit his mom's boyfriend; it was to arrive in town separately and from different directions. Spencer showing up out of nowhere would set off all sorts of gossip alarms. Spencer showing up with a Black woman *and* a Chinese woman in tow would give the gossips each their own bag of meth. The news would get across the county line faster than the speed of light. The goddamned WABG-TV news guys would lead off with the story that afternoon. KARK in Little Rock would run it that night. Incognito and small towns were not compatible concepts, especially if two-thirds of your party didn't look much like you.

Horace lived in DeWitt, the next place Uber had heard of near Dumas on their route home. His initial plan had been to drop Helen off at the Kroger and Tonya at the Piggly Wiggly half a mile up the road. Helen overruled it immediately.

"I have *got* to see a grocery store named Piggly Wiggly. I'm Chinese. We love pork!"

"It's just a grocery store." He'd never thought the name was funny until someone else said it like it was something special.

"I don't mind," Tonya said. "At least I've heard of Kroger." They passed several going through Richmond. "We'll meet up at the Days Inn once you get square with your mom."

And that's how it worked out, until Helen pulled him into a group chat with Tonya while he was in a mandatory Gramma meeting.

"We're at the hotel and unpacked, but we have a problem," she said. "Something's happened to Mike."

Chapter 21
Mike

Blackness.

Noise.

Shouting.

Two different languages. He understood two different languages, and everyone was shouting at him.

He opened his eyes and his threaded perception at the same time. Kim stared down at him in realspace. Helen's shouts rang clear through his threads.

He was on the floor, the floor of the spaceship. It had a name...*Last Island.*

Kim wasn't alone. The alien pilot, Maff, was peering over Kim's shoulder. Her manipulators had shaken his realspace body. The ceiling was composed of the trusses of the ship's structure.

Now he remembered. They were about to leave, and he was on the floor.

"What happened?" he asked.

"Are you okay?" It came from both directions, so he split some threads off to reassure Helen at the same time he talked to Kim.

He sat up, only a little lightheaded. "I think so." He looked around. The crew was gone, and the doors had closed. "Where'd everyone go?"

Kim's relief vanished, replaced with a familiar rage. "They literally stepped over you to go about their business. Maff's the only one who stayed."

"You didn't come around until I closed the doors," Maff said. "Can you stand up? The infirmary has some basic diagnostics we can use until Hafurnal gets back."

"I think so."

Maff's manipulators reached over and around him to help him stand. They were smooth and warm, looking like metal but not feeling like it. He wondered if that strange combination had something to do with whatever powered them.

He also spoke to Helen at the same time he spoke to Kim and Maff. "They opened the door to the outside and boom, down I went. Are you guys all okay?"

"Fine. Tonya's in the hotel lobby, and Spencer's on his way here. You're sure you're okay?"

"What did you see?"

This faster-than-light communications method had given them a new way of seeing each other. Mike called it a *channel*, but that was only a name. His current theory was it either used the transit dimension or something similar to it. Regardless, it gave them both a way to directly perceive each other's threads, something that they'd never had before.

"Everything got scrambled and then you went dark."

"How long was I out?" he asked Kim.

"Not long. Five minutes, maybe a little more? As soon as the doors shut, you woke up."

"Not exactly," Maff said as they got him situated on a chair in the infirmary. "It was actually after the protection skein activated. That happens once the doors close, and we go back to our transit parking space."

That was a clue, it had to be. These ships weren't spaceships as much as they were *dimensional* ships. They could clearly survive hard vacuum, but almost all actual motion happened in the transit dimension. The ship had been popping in and out of it the entire time, using AC network nodes to get navigational fixes and course corrections.

Maff's manipulators pulled out a device that was more

vacuum cleaner than medical scanner and turned it on. The resemblance was reinforced by the whirring sound of a fan and a small bag that inflated behind it. It beeped and a virtual screen lit up between them all. It was an abstracted picture of his body with pointers indicating parts that led to small dialog boxes filled with the strange Bemian script he and Kim had been learning as fast as they could. It was a quick read. Everything came back as normal.

"The sa'dst says you're fine," Maff said as she put the device away.

Kim stood in front of him and, in English, asked, "How many fingers?" as she held two up.

"Sunday." This was a joke, but it was also true. He'd kept track of the days since the accident.

Mike watched as the relief that he wasn't sick or hurt warred with his turning it into a joke. The way her eyes sparkled let him know which side won. "Nice. And today is?"

He looked at her hand and, for a moment, almost lied and said three. But this had been a nasty shock, and screwing with her would get him in trouble. "Two."

Maff pulled back and in Bemian said, "I caught most of that. We'll need to check him out more."

Kim chuckled. "No, it's all right. It's an old joke between us." It was what he'd done when he first woke up after they escaped the vent room in Yellowstone, right before he proposed to her. The whole point was to bring up good memories and help get them through this new setback.

The smile she brought out told him that it had worked. "You're sure nothing's wrong?"

"Definitely."

"What happened?" Kim asked.

He asked Helen, "Everything looks okay to you?"

"It does now."

He was fine, and they had to figure out what was really going on. The involvement of the protection skeins could not be a coincidence. They needed to perform some experiments. "How much time do you have?" he asked Helen.

"We're settling in over here. Spencer keeps going on and on about how small and isolated Dumas is, and I guess by American standards that's true. But there are places in rural China that are far more remote. The agriculture was impressive, though." Her voice went sour. "I asked who the central agricultural planner was, and they both laughed at me. How does America stay so powerful when there's nobody in charge?"

Her competitiveness was never far from the surface. "I don't know. Call it a homework assignment." Knowing his sister, she'd have a thesis proposal ready by the end of the week. "I'm going to try something. Stay on the line."

To Kim and Maff he said, "Let's go back to the cargo bay." He turned to Maff. "Is it a big deal to go in and out of the transit dimension to open the doors?"

"No, especially now that we've renewed the hinges and locks."

Hinges and locks was a massive understatement. The system used a dozen different gearsets, in three different sizes, to transmit power and actuate the locks. Rebuilding it all had been a major undertaking.

"Are you sure this is a good idea?" Kim asked as they walked.

"We have to figure out what's wrong before we can fix it. I don't want to be stuck on this ship forever." If he couldn't leave, it would be a major obstacle to rescuing Will.

Kim considered it and then nodded. "We need to be careful."

"Hey," he said with a smile, "it's me."

"That's what I'm afraid of."

It didn't take long to get set up. He didn't want another fall to add to the collection of bruises and scrapes he got from the first one, so Maff ran two of her manipulators over and through some ceiling trusses and then grabbed Mike by the shoulders. He already knew she was strong enough to pick him up. Holding him wouldn't be a big deal.

His idea was to open the doors in a controlled way so they could closely observe what was happening. When he laid out his plan,

Maff went back and fetched the sa'dst reader. Kim now held it in front of him like she was at a pistol range. He gave her a wink and a half smile, and she relaxed a little.

"No screwing around, right?" she asked him.

"Not my plan. Okay, Maff. Hit it."

Same as last time, the doors made a lot of complicated noises and then opened. Mike watched the bustling port on the other side. Nothing happened. He slowly let out the breath he'd been holding. Still nothing.

"I don't get it," he said. "I went out like a light." Maff had left slack in her manipulators for him to step forward...

And then he woke up. The doors were closed, and Kim was hoovering up the air around him intently. "I'm back," he said.

Kim examined the scanner readouts. "Still okay."

"Helen?" he asked.

"Same as before. Everything scrambled and then poof, lights out."

He turned back to Maff and Kim. "Helen says I passed out the same way as last time. That's a good result."

"It is?" Maff asked.

"Yes, I passed out when *I* moved." It was a big clue. "Let's try again to see if it only happens when I move forward."

Mike held still after the doors opened. There were a *lot* of different aliens out there, but almost all of them had the same basic body shape: bipedal, head—or at least eyes—toward the top, feet on the ground. He recognized the various species of the crew, but... "There don't seem to be any pallun out there."

"No, my people tend to congregate at the markets and bazaars."

They had no words for *planetary gears* even though he'd bet half the ship ran on them but had distinct words for orderly and chaotic places to trade. It was a strange culture. "Okay, sidestep this time." He moved to the left.

And woke up hanging from Maff's manipulators.

"There's a directional component," Helen said. "It felt different when you moved sideways compared to moving forward."

Another piece of the puzzle fell into place. He relayed Helen's observations to Maff and Kim.

"Everything is still the same," Kim said as she checked the scanner. "If the door is shut, you're fine. When it's open, you're fine. When you move, you fall over. You don't come to until we shut the door."

Whatever was wrong involved motion, *his* motion. Helen perceived differences in the way he passed out depending on the direction of that motion. She was so far away relativity should force them to wait who knew how many years for messages to make a round trip, but they could communicate instantly. The protection skeins, which allowed the ship to travel faster than light relative to the universe, blocked it. "I've got an idea but need more data." He looked at Maff. "You're sure this isn't a big deal for the ship?"

She chuckled. "Thanks to you two, the doors are worth more than the rest of the ship now. We're using less energy than anyone else in the port. We can do it all day if that's what you want."

"And you don't mind?" He'd come to think of the suited manta ray as an ally and a friend.

"This is all fascinating. Go ahead."

"Okay, then. How are things on your end, Helen?"

"We're fine here. I've been explaining this to Tonya. She wants to know if you think relativity is the issue?"

He should've known Tonya would get the same idea he had. He hoped she was taking notes. It wasn't every day that someone figured out a new way to experiment with Einstein's most famous theory. "I do." He turned to Maff. "Here we go again."

They did the experiment ten more times before all the opening and closing started to attract attention dockside. Each one confirmed his hypothesis. At the end, he had a working theory. It was nice to have it come together so quickly. He didn't relish the idea of being trapped on *Last Island* for an extended period. Without sa'dst, he'd probably get galactic tetanus just looking at it.

They had to use English to discuss his theory. Standard, what he and Kim once called Bemian, and even Maff's native Pallundian, didn't have the words to describe the concepts. Plus, he had to fudge the details a bit, otherwise he'd end up telling Maff more than he was comfortable with her knowing right now. Kim kept a running translation as best she could while he explained.

"It's called a relativistic doppler effect. My consciousness is affected by traveling great distances." Because some of it was still on Earth, but he skipped that part. "As I move around in realspace, it's changing the timing of certain types of pulses that I need to function."

"We don't discharge the skeins during nav fixes," Maff said. "You were still protected." She turned to Kim. "Why aren't you affected by this?"

"It's a male-female thing." She came up with that lie without missing a beat. Kim must be as worried about giving too much away as he was. "We're the first couple to ever travel this far." She turned to him. "How do we fix it?"

He asked Helen, "What does Tonya think?"

Helen sent him equations composed in Tonya's elegant handwriting. "She says you'll understand this. Spencer swears a lot and makes *exploding head* gestures when he looks at it. I can't say I blame him."

"That's okay, I get it." She was providing the math behind what Mike was saying. He displayed it on a screen inside the ship to allow Kim to review it.

"I am so glad this makes sense now," she said.

"I wish it did to me," Maff said. "Relativity? The speed of light as an absolute? Time as another dimension?" Mike smiled at the English words in her Pallundian accent; she sounded vaguely Russian. "I've never heard of *any* of this stuff before."

Most people back home, even those not interested in physics, had at least heard of relativity and quantum mechanics. Not Maff. Her physics knowledge was strictly classical. She knew the theories Isaac Newton had described back home well enough that the later theories should have been part of her education, but they weren't. Mike filed away the observation for later. "As long as we're in the transit dimension, I'm shielded from the effect. I'm not sure why I wasn't bothered when we dropped to realspace for nav fixes."

"Hang on a minute," Helen said to him over their connection. "I do recognize these parts."

Equations turned into circuit diagrams using comic sans labels. Spencer was on the job.

"Okay," Helen said. "I think we have a way forward."

"What do you mean?"

"Spencer is describing a variant of my anchor box. I'll make a list of parts. We can cross-reference them against what we've learned from alien tech and see how much matches."

Mike provided Maff with a list. After looking at it, she gestured side to side with her wings; her version of a head shake. "We used up all of our spare parts fixing things around here. We'll need to go to the markets to pick up more."

"How expensive will it all be?" Kim asked.

"Hard to say," she replied, then pulled out one of the manifold actuators they'd fixed. "But selling this should cover it."

"The captain won't mind?"

"I doubt he'll notice. And if he does, too bad. Nobody should work for free."

Maff was timid most of the time, but when the subject turned to business or bargaining, she was confident and assertive. He found the contrast striking but couldn't figure out how to ask her about it without being offensive. They'd both seen how the rest of the crew treated her, and how uncomfortable she was with it. They needed allies more than answers.

"Well," Kim said as she clapped her hands together and looked at Maff. "It's time for you and me to go shopping."

Chapter 22
Kim

If they wanted Mike to function outside the ship, they needed to build a gizmo. To build the gizmo, they needed parts. And someone to buy them. Mike couldn't do it.

Nope, for this one she was on her own. Kim let her heart jump around a bit as she said goodbye to Mike, then walked alone down to the cargo deck. She slung the saddle bag she made over her shoulder and stood beside the steampunk manta ray like the proud explorer she was. That's what she was, a *proud explorer*. Not an ape with delusions of grandeur, a *proud explorer*.

As long as Kim kept repeating that phrase in her head, she could breathe.

A little.

"Are you ready?" Maff asked.

She reached out and grasped one of Maff's manipulators. Since they weren't part of Maff's real body, it didn't trigger her touch aversion, and she needed a hand to hold right now, no matter how strange it felt. Maff seemed to understand and squeezed back.

Kim could do this. She had to do this.

"Ready."

The doors opened and pulled back. She took a deep breath, and with a confidence that was almost entirely faked, *she stepped out into the rays of an alien sun*.

It happened. She'd done it. She'd done the thing. The light was warm and a little more orange than back home. She should say something. *That's one small step for a washed-up cyber thief...*

They'd been calling where they were parked *port* and *dock* so much Kim thought they'd be on a pier in a bay, but that was wrong. The ships themselves only appeared in realspace when it was time to open the doors, otherwise they were parked in the transit dimension. It had to do with preventing various kinds of wear and tear, apparently. There was no stink and slosh of a harbor. It was a kind of multilevel parking garage. The new concrete smell reminded her of home.

And it *was* new concrete; she could see that now. Mike had mentioned this: common problems had common solutions, and a composite material made of aggregate bonded with cement seemed to be the way to build big structures no matter where you were in the galaxy. But that's where the similarities ended.

The parking garage was open in the front, and the floors were set back from each other. It reminded her of the superstructure of a cruise ship. Opposite was the promenade of the biggest, strangest shopping mall ever. If anything, it reminded her of the malls in China: huge and covered with people. Except they weren't people. They were *aliens*.

Lots and lots of aliens.

She'd gotten the names of the alien crew from Maff. Kim spotted plenty of scolion—foxes, rhon—birds, and kron—lizard-men. But there were so many more. She fought down a primal urge to run away by trying to match them with Earth life forms they resembled. It didn't work perfectly, but it did keep her inner chimp from shrieking and taking control.

It also helped her to keep all the aliens that humans had made up in her mind. Everything she saw could be described by combining Earth creatures with fictional creatures. There were short blue *Avatar* giraffes, ninja snapping turtles, towering strider dogs, and small Pooh bears. Humans had been misnaming strange animals that resembled familiar animals for all of history, and she didn't want to buck that tradition. Not if she wanted to keep her sanity.

She felt a nudge, and for a moment, the chimpanzee nearly did take control. But Kim was the sole representative of humanity to an entire galaxy. Jumping up and down while screaming might leave a bad impression.

Then she recognized that it was one of Maff's probes, "Are you okay?" she asked.

Keep it steady. Don't freak out. "It's…a little overwhelming."

Don't freak out.

"Stick close to me, I know the way. We'll get it all arranged in no time."

It was crowded, but Kim managed to keep Maff between herself and the various aliens as they went past. Maff was much wider than most of them, so they tended to give her plenty of space.

And occasionally say nasty things as they went past.

"Maff," she asked as they boarded a contraption that Kim could only think of as a double-decker rickshaw carved from something that was a cross between a tree and a bar of soap, "can I ask you a personal question?"

"Of course."

At least she didn't have to hunt for words to talk about this. "The reason your people are concentrated in certain places, is that because they're only welcome in those places?"

Maff tensed. "I was hoping you couldn't hear them say those things."

So much for a *Star Trek* utopia. "My people have good ears."

"Pallun have had a…difficult relationship with the rest of the galaxy. Most of us keep to ourselves. That, as you know, goes against what the AC network wants."

She *didn't* know but couldn't admit it. It was yet another bit of indirect information that allowed the AC network to slowly come into focus. Whatever it was, it was much more than Earth's realmspace or any other kind of human computer network. It provided too much and expected a lot in return.

Maff continued, "We try to go about our business and ignore the insults when we can."

"And when you can't?"

Maff gave her version of a shrug. "It depends. Most of the time we ignore them anyway."

"Are there other times?"

Maff got that sudden stiff pride Kim had noticed sometimes. "Pallun are known for two things most of all: law and business. If the law doesn't work, we have connections with the most powerful families in the galaxy."

The words she used put a spin on family Kim wasn't familiar with, but from the context, it was easy to guess the extra meaning.

Mafia...in...spaaace!

"But you don't seem to be any of those things."

"No, I'm definitely the outside floater of my cloud." Maff used a manipulator to twist a knob next to their seats. "And here's our first stop."

Kim thought they'd end up at some sort of raucous junk shop, but they stopped in front of a building that looked kind of bankish. Clean, imposing, but at the same time rather small. Call it a bank branch, then. She tried to read the sign. "In...ter..."

"Interpreter's Guild Chapter House," Maff said. "Finally, you'll be able to use more than Pallundian and Standard. And maybe explain what relativity means in a way I can understand."

"How does that happen?"

"Follow me."

They got out and went inside. Again, very clean and orderly. Instead of a row of tellers, there were doors shaped for different body plans. Maff motioned her toward the most human shaped of them and squeezed through behind her, resuming her normal shape on the other side. Mike had speculated that Maff might be aquatic, that what she wore was a kind of reversed scuba suit, but Kim wasn't sure. She kept referring to clouds.

A virtual screen sprang to life in front of her, labeled in Bemian. *Simple* Bemian, thank God. She touched the icon that said, she hoped, *start here.*

A rhon, but with gray feathers rather than white, appeared in the virtual window in front of her. "Welcome to the Perspendala Chapter House. How may I help you?"

"Ask it for an Interpreter's thread," Maff said.

The rhon wore robes that seemed familiar, but Kim couldn't quite place where she'd seen them. On the alien's left side was a…growth of some sort. Suddenly the growth moved and opened its eyes. "What is *that*?"

"Ah, I should have known. None of your Interpreters have transitioned to galactic envoy yet. That's what they will look like when they've finished their first term of service. Assuming they maintain cohesion, that is. Do you have a public ceremony of joining or is it private?"

What the hell are you talking about wasn't on the list of available answers, but Kim saw an opening nonetheless. "Private. What happens during a public one?"

"It's a big deal. All the candidates are gathered in the main house's inner courtyard and paired off. The ceremonies take hours. In the end, the visible is joined with the invisible, the two become one, threads are tied with flesh."

"That sounds like verse."

"It is. I'd get in a lot of trouble with the bashtuns back home if I ever said it out loud where they could hear me. That's what it says on the ceiling, by the way."

Now that Kim knew what the whole thing said, she could pick out the words of Maff's verse in written Standard on the walls where they met the ceiling. If it was meant to put the veneer of a temple on this place it failed. Kim still couldn't shake the impression of a local bank branch. It was too plain to be a place of worship. There should be art and incense, not beige walls and sliding glass doors.

While Kim was reading Standard, she was talking to Maff in Pallundian. Standard didn't have the ability to convey nuances and detail the way a regular language did. This allowed her to understand that *bashtun* had a clear religious connotation. It must be some kind of priest, but it wasn't quite that formal. Perhaps it was a rabbi or mufti instead. The galaxy had religions. This was going to blow Mike's mind. It had certainly blown hers.

"Anyway," Maff continued. "Ask it for an Interpreter thread."

Kim did. A request for permission to access internal network nodes, the implanted version of a phone *Last Island's* crew had given her, appeared. Kim touched the Grant button.

A connection opened in her mind, calm and assuring. *Neural profile is not recognized,* it said in Standard. *To begin, please vocalize the following words in your native language.* Cards with written Standard appeared in her vision.

"Uh…Maff? It's wanting me to read things out loud."

"Share your screen, I'll help."

It took about fifteen minutes, but once they were done, Kim had a fully functioning Interpreter thread that understood English. She didn't know how important that was until they walked outside.

What had once been a morass of babble was now a low, but clearly understandable, rumble of English. If she concentrated, the conversations became clear.

"Meeting at the next communal meal…"

"And if I see him again, I swear he better…"

"No, it's your turn to decide lunch, I picked last time…"

"Is it working?" Maff asked.

"Wow." She turned to the big alien. "You don't have an accent anymore."

"It's not me; it's the thread. It's translating my Pallundian into your English. I got one while you were training yours, so I'm hearing you in Pallundian. *Now* it's time to go shopping."

The rest of the day was a little anticlimactic. It turned out that junkyards and electronics stores were another galactic commonality. The ones here wouldn't have looked much out of place anywhere back home. The only real difference was that the price tags were all written in Standard, which her thread now conveniently translated for her whenever she asked. Being able to read, or at least not having to rely on Maff, was a huge help. And Kim was learning to read the script herself. It was the odd three-dimensionality of the printing that threw her off. The letters all had depth as well as the usual size and color.

Talking to people—she had stopped thinking of them as aliens—was a little surreal. It was like watching a dubbed movie. The person was clearly saying something different, but the thread was somehow muting their speech and substituting English in its place. Eventually she got used to it. The expedition took the whole day, but at the end of it, she was pretty sure they found everything they needed.

She spent hours talking over the experience with Mike that night. In the moment, it had been a blur of impressions. She'd been too busy with the mission to contemplate the details of what she saw.

"I didn't see any poor people. Even the rougher neighborhoods were neat and clean."

"That sounds like Japan," he said.

"A little, if Japan was populated by the cast of every sci-fi movie you've ever seen. In spite of that, they all seemed so similar. I can't quite pin down why. They were all," Kim couldn't shake the impression, "so *bland*."

"Everyone was dressed in beige? Listening to elevator music?"

"No, it was more than that. Oh, and their music? It's pretty. Lots of classical stuff and folk songs. Once I got over the novelty, though, it was bland too. The same themes, same rhythms, the same singing style. I can't believe I'm saying this, but it's all…*boring*."

"Maybe Maff only took you to boring places?"

"If she did, she took me to a lot of them. We had to go all over to find this stuff."

A soft, smooth piece of satin trailed over the back of her hand. She'd found a bundle while out shopping, and he must've snuck it into their room when she wasn't looking. In an instant, all thoughts of boring aliens vanished. They'd been forced to wait for far too long, sleeping in the same bed, without this.

Mike smiled. "I'm glad you weren't only looking for spare parts."

"I am too."

Chapter 23
Tonya

Tonya thought China was as big a culture shock as she could get. It *was* on the other side of the world, when the farthest she'd ever traveled at the time was from DC to Philadelphia.

But, in its own way, Dumas was a shock every bit as big. Which was ironic, considering it took half an hour to see the entire town. There was exactly one Catholic church that held exactly one mass, on Sunday at 11:15 in the morning. The single confession was held a half hour before that. Thank God for the new satellite realmspaces. Spencer's hometown might be isolated in realspace, but its connections were as good as anything they had back home.

"Satellites," Spencer said. "It's fine as long as it doesn't rain too hard. A big thunderstorm comes through and the whole town gets cut off. It's such a pain in the ass."

They were sitting in Tonya's room with boxes of Chinese food scattered around that Spencer had brought with him. Tonya was surprised, but Helen wasn't.

"Chinese are everywhere," she said after Spencer walked in. "There are already noodle shops on the moon. You watch. Two weeks won't go by before a Chinese restaurant on Perspendala opens."

Spencer tipped his head toward her and said, "Let's get Mike and Kim back first."

"And Will," Tonya said as she held out a soda cup for a toast.

"And Will," they all agreed, touching rims.

Tonya set hers down and started working on her noodles as she sat cross-legged on her bed. She turned to Helen. "Maybe you can stop by tomorrow and see what sort of community you have here."

The other woman nodded. "I won't be as important as you, but every little bit helps."

She should've known Helen would jump to that conclusion. "Just because I'm Black doesn't mean I know anyone here."

Helen lifted an eyebrow. "And yet you think because I'm Chinese I will have some sort of in with the local community?" The words were calm, but there was steel in them.

And it was justified. Nothing like having her own assumptions rubbed in her face to get her attention. They were both strangers in a strange land. "Point taken. But I'm not kidding. I promise that you have more in common with any Chinese people here than I do with the Black folks. No matter how many of them there are."

Dumas was majority-Black, much more than PG county back home. But they dressed different, looked different, and most of all, *talked* different. Tonya had blinked twice at the girl behind the motel desk before she understood *foe-oh-free* was room 403.

"That might not be the case," Spencer said as he sat at the small desk in the corner of the room. "According to Gramma, we had a maid named Brinks when she was little. That family moved to DC."

"Your family had a Black maid?"

Spencer shrugged. "It's Dumas."

His tone was casual, neutral, not in a dismissive way but in a what-did-you-expect way. And again, he was right. Entry-level jobs in a majority-Black town would naturally be filled by Black people. That made it two friends who had called out Tonya on her sensitivities in less than five minutes. She didn't normally think of herself as someone who paid all that much attention to such things. Maybe Spencer was right. Small towns might actually mess with a person's head.

"Anyway," he continued, "there are cousins of that family still around here somewhere. Gramma's making a call to the mayor tomorrow to find out."

"What does the mayor have to do with anything? How does your gramma know my last name?"

Spencer rolled his eyes. "You really don't understand how Southern families work. Of course she knows your last name. I told her. She thinks I can hack anything and asked for your social security number too."

Spencer idolized Kim when she was an active cybercriminal. Tonya wouldn't put it past him. "Do you have it?"

He scoffed. "Fuck no. That's Kim's bag, I'm still stuck with perfect security like the rest of the world. Anyway, if anyone around here has heard of a last name, it's *assumed* you have relatives in the area. Dumas has a Black mayor. *Duh.* You might not know any Black people around here, but he sure as hell does. Everyone knows everyone else in this little hellhole."

"It doesn't seem that bad to me," Helen said, and Tonya couldn't disagree. It was tatty and worn, but the people were friendly. When Tonya could understand them.

"You haven't lived here your whole life," he replied. "Just wait."

"Speaking of waiting," Helen said. "I was productive on my way in. There are several rental properties for us to look at tomorrow."

"Are we planning on staying here long enough for a lease?" Tonya asked. Dumas was quaint when she thought their stay would be measured in weeks. Longer than that, not so much.

"Some are month to month. They're all cheaper than a hotel room. We'll examine the options once we've seen them."

Spencer shook his head. "Not gonna happen."

"Why not?" Helen asked.

"A single white boy shacking up with a Black *and* a Chinese woman, neither of whom is his wife? We'd get run out of town on a rail, all three of us."

Typical, she thought.

Spencer's expression went sour. "No, Tonya, Black and Chinese aren't the problem. *Unmarried* is. Yes, there are still assholes who cause trouble for interracial couples, and white families who won't speak to a Black waitress, but I can count those dicks on one hand. They are *nothing* compared to the preachers around here."

"It's none of their business," Helen said.

"It *shouldn't* be any of their business, I'll grant you that. But as soon as word got out, and it would, we'd get knocks on our door from every church in town inviting us to services. Your church doesn't count, Tonya. They barely consider Catholics as Christian around here. I'm still trying to figure out how to keep you two together, because the only thing that'd be worse than a *Three's Company* reboot would be if they thought a pair of lesbians were setting up shop."

She didn't believe that for a second. "Dumas has gay people."

He nodded as he swallowed the last of his noodles. "We even know who they are. Everyone does. As long as they stay in the closet, it's cool. And trust me, around here, they stay in the closet."

Tonya hated the sound of that. "It's dangerous?"

"Oh, for fuck's sake. *No*. If a gay couple tried to openly live together, nobody'd lay a finger on them. What they'd do is drive them bonkers with church sermons, make it impossible to get a job, and try to set them up on blind dates every weekend until they gave up, fit in, or moved out."

"So," Helen said, "they know you know, and you know they know, but as long as everyone pretends the truth doesn't exist, as long as nothing changes, and it remains…deniable, they are left alone?"

Spencer nodded emphatically. "Exactly."

"Dumas is more Chinese than I thought."

"I never thought of it that way," he said, "but you're right. Honor and all that horseshit. Don't think being Chinese will be a walk in the fucking park, though. Expect a lot of *ching-chong-chee* and grinning moon faces until we get out of here."

Helen sagged. "Wonderful."

Later that night Tonya called her grandmother to find out if what Spencer had discovered was a connection or a coincidence.

"Let me see. You know, I think he might be right. There's the Mississippi Brinkses, from Greenville, that's us, and yes, now that I recall, I think there was also the Arkansas Brinkses." Granny got up and walked out of the camera frame. Granny Brinks didn't much care for hippity-hoppity realmspaces. She relied on an old iPad Tonya's cousin Justin had set up for visits with her grandkids and, recently, great grandkids without having to travel.

She returned and settled heavily into her ancient recliner with a massive Bible in her hands. It was the only connection any of them had with their roots, and it went back more than a century. Granny going to what they all called The Source so quickly was a good sign she was more excited about this than she was letting on.

She opened it to the back. "Yes, that's it. The Mississippi Brinkses went north. The Arkansas Brinkses moved west. Says here Hannibal Brinks was the brother of Lewis Brinks, who was my grandpappy. Would you look at that," Granny said. "It truly is a small world. If you find any of them, get their family history." Granny's eyes gleamed as she patted the old book. "I've always wanted to make more entries in here. I could fill in a whole branch!"

Tonya had known her family was from Mississippi, but that was an abstract fact, one she'd never considered for more than a few moments in her entire life. She looked up Greenville on a map. It was less than forty miles from Dumas. She hadn't come quite all the way home but had gotten pretty close.

The idea that her family was from a place very similar to Dumas took a minute to digest. Greenville was fifteen times bigger than Dumas, but you could fit the entire population of both towns into an NFL stadium, and it would only be half full. Tonya chuckled. She would never think of Fairfax as a small town again, that was certain.

Her prime AI agent pinged her. She still had the weak tockion emitters to figure out. The experiment that had somehow sent Mike and Kim on their interstellar space romp was supposed to find more of them, but the arrival of the ship had amped up the scan signal and it'd taken this long to collate the data.

The summary started out with findings she'd expected. There was no mention of this kind of anomaly in any scientific literature. Nobody had ever seen them before. The one that blew up Kim's wedding was so weak the experiment they had tried in the lab would've only detected anomalies that were in the local realmspace. There was a good chance that they'd find nothing. With the power boost provided by *Last Island*'s arrival, they hadn't found a few extras.

They'd found *thousands*.

They were scattered all over realmspace. Removing Helen had left holes in the Great Firewall that allowed the scan to run right through it, so they were found there too. The distribution was random as far as she could tell, and the anomalies were all extremely small, much smaller than the one Kim had found. Tonya needed more data on the timing though. She couldn't tell when they started showing up. They could be a bug resulting from Mike and Helen's patches. They could've always been there, and nobody noticed. They could've started on their own for reasons nobody had thought of yet. It could be something unrelated to any of that.

It got worse. One of the ways these anomalies could spread was if her particle time theory was wrong. Her guts sank the longer she worked the problem. If there were no tick-tockions or determions, the other two particles her theory predicted, then something like this became possible. Instead of finding a confirmation of free will, Tonya might have taken another step toward disproving it.

She needed more data.

The Vuohensilta had been left behind in Virginia. The alien spaceship was the only reason that experiment worked at all. There was no easy way to repeat it. She needed an experiment she could perform out here in the sticks without exotic machines or an alien power source. They'd have to be careful no matter what it used, since a swarm of Amazon drones delivering stuff to a remote part of Southeast Arkansas might draw the wrong kind of attention.

She worked through the night on the problem, dragging Helen into it so Tonya could consult with Mike. By three a.m., Tonya had a plan. The experiment would use the same materials that agricultural 3-D printers consumed this time of year. She sourced one of those from a nearby rental company in a different town and arranged for a truck to autodrive it to them in a few days. All they needed was a site to build the thing on. She didn't have access to a power grid designed to support hundreds of data centers. It had to be spread out. A *lot*.

Spencer showed up with breakfast, and she brought him up to speed.

"I know exactly where you need to go." He laughed for a second. "You need to pay a visit to the mayor."

"Why is that funny?"

"Remember my gramma thought you might have cousins around here? It turns out you do, and he's the goddamned mayor! You're related to Reverend Whitney! That's so fucking strange," he said as he laughed and shook his head.

"The Mayor is part of the priesthood?" Helen asked. "Isn't that against the law in this country?"

Spencer shook his head. "No. It should be, but it's not. And he's not part of *a priesthood*," he said, making air quotes, "he runs the largest church in town. Which isn't saying a whole goddamned lot, but small towns are all about big fishes and shitty little ponds."

Her own granny would be thrilled to find out how well the Arkansas branch of the Brinks family had done. Tonya, though, was quite a bit more ambivalent about discovering she was related to the mayor of Dumas. A distant cousin, specifically.

On the one hand, it made sense. Everyone had to come from somewhere, and that her trail led from Africa through the deep South wasn't surprising.

On the other, Tonya hadn't realized until now that she'd been subtly looking down on the world Spencer came from, long before she'd met him. Everyone she knew did. *Spencer* did. This was where *those people* lived. The ignorant crazies. The victimized minorities.

Religious fanatics and meth addicts. Men sweating in fields by day and getting in murderous fights by night. It was flyover country as relevant to her life as the far side of the moon.

Now not only was it part of her life, it was part of her blood. These were, in a concrete, provable way, her people.

It was a small world, indeed.

They all left after breakfast to do their various tasks. Spencer would visit his dad, who was a golfing buddy with the police chief. That would quietly let the locals know they needed to watch out for new strangers, other than them, coming into town. Helen would contact the owner of the Chinese restaurant to get a feel for that community.

For her, it was time to meet cousin Al. Or, according to his profile on the St. Paul's Third Baptist Church's website, *The Honorable Albert S. Whitney IV, BA, MA, MDiv, LLM, Esq.* The esquire Tonya found especially intriguing after a quick search through the Arkansas Bar Association's database. He acquired his law degree from the Duke of Windsor Law School, Bahamas. The only trace she could find of it was a PO box in New Jersey.

None of that mattered at the moment. What did matter was that cousin Al was also the sole proprietor of the Billy Free Memorial Airport, the only large amount of cleared land in the area that wasn't either a soybean field or a golf course. It would be the perfect place to set up her next series of low-power experiments.

The meticulously articulate, very pretty, very *young*, secretary who answered her SkypeTime call, because he could only be reached by SkypeTime, informed her that *His Honor* would be happy to see her after the city council meeting and would it be *terribly* inconvenient if she could meet him outside the council's chamber?

"That's fine, could you give me the address?"

From her expression, looking up addresses was for underlings and not the direct assistant of The Honorable Albert S. Whitney IV, BA, MA, MDiv, LLM, Esq.—his full string of acronyms were on anything that mentioned his name.

"I'm *sure* you can find it online." The call cut off.

It seemed not everyone in the South was polite. She'd have to inform Spencer.

The City Hall building was a nondescript bank-like structure next to a combined police and fire station. The interior was all wood paneling and marble floors. That probably made it exciting to walk on with street shoes when it was raining. Tonya sat outside the council chamber in a chair that had to have been bought in or around 1975. It was tacky in a vaguely charming way.

The chamber doors opened, and the first thing she thought was *this is where they keep all the white people.* They weren't the majority, but they made up about half the members.

Everyone walked out of the room smiling and quietly talking, confidence and power rolling out with them. It was *not* a group of white people talking down to their Black servants. Far from it. The difference wasn't attitude, it was age. All the white folks were old, some very old, but the Black folks were all in their forties or fifties and almost militantly fit. This wasn't a group of masters and slaves; it was a change of the guard.

Cousin Al—*Dr. Whitney*—was a tall commanding presence with a booming voice and engaging smile. He walked straight to her, with two handsome young men in tow.

"Ms. Brinks, I presume?" he asked as he held out his hand.

She took it. "Pleased to meet you, Dr. Whitney." His smile was sincere, reaching his eyes with a sparkle. If it hadn't been for the cold, deadly serious entourage standing around them, Tonya might've been won over on the spot.

She pretended she was anyway. "I'm glad you agreed to meet with me."

He grew serious, but it made *her* feel concerned for *him*. "Yes, well, a very pressing matter has come up, and we won't have time for much more than introductions. I tell you what." He pulled out a business card, something Tonya hadn't seen in years, and handed it to her. "You come to services this Sunday, and I'll give you all the time you need."

Needless to say, cousin Al was *not* a priest. "You won't be…busy?"

"Not between the morning and evening sermons. We'll have plenty of time to talk then."

Morning and evening sermons? Tonya buckled down. It wouldn't be the first time she'd been inside a traditional Black church.

"Of course. Thank you."

Chapter 24
Mike

He called the device a Thread Shock Absorber, or TSA for short. It would absorb the elastic stretches that relativistic motion imposed on his separated selves. It hadn't been an easy build. None of the languages they'd come across had words for *integrated circuits* or *general programming languages,* so he had to make do with big things he could recognize by shape: resistors, amplifiers, capacitors, inductors, diodes, and transistors. As with realmspace, they relied on physics as much as engineering and so were easily recognizable and adaptable.

Components were the easy part. Bemian junkyards were everywhere. The hard part was finding the tools to do the work. This society was completely reliant on the AC network for anything more complex than a wind-up toy. Eventually Kim found what they needed—high quality soldering equipment and microscopes—in the jewelry district. Kim knew how to solder, so she built while he designed. Chasing around voltages without a multimeter was their final hurdle, solved after Maff figured out what they were looking for closely matched a purity tester used by her bashtuns.

The result was about as big as a deck of cards, sized to be concealed in a pocket or, stealing a page from Helen's book, secured to a belt.

Once he finished, it was his turn to stand in front of the doors and walk into the light of an alien sun. He, too, had the urge to comment on the event. *That's one small step for a flying spaghetti monster…*

The port was every bit as spectacular, and strangely boring, as Kim said it was. He didn't have the same visceral reaction to aliens that she did. Mike had spent his whole life with realm-based aliens of various kinds. For a long time, he'd thought they were real. Now that they were, it was mostly making sure to not gawk at them whenever a new one passed by.

Their first stop was the same one Maff took Kim to: the Guild Chapter House. "It'll be a huge help," she said. "You have no idea how exhausting it is translating in both directions when you and Maff start talking."

He was curious about how they worked. Kim had always translated the Standard and Pallundian word for them as *thread*, but that could mean a lot of different things. His working theory was that it had to do with virtualized AI systems. If true, it would finally give him a chance to look directly at a field of Bemian technology he hadn't seen yet.

Kim was right that the title of the place made the building sound like it came from a Dune realm or maybe a type of monastery, but it was more suburban corporate. That said, what was written around the top of the wall certainly sounded like scripture. He and Kim had been concentrating on the technical details of the Bemian society for obvious reasons, but now he thought they would do well to spend some time learning about this Guild.

"At least you won't have to read words to it," she said as they walked in. "That wasn't easy, and I had Maff helping me."

They were on their own for now. The crew was out running various errands, and their big pallun friend had gone to her worship services somewhere deeper in the city and would meet them later in the day. Her religion was another thing he wanted to study.

They took seats in the installation booth, and he got the same request to access *internal network nodes* that Kim did. Mike granted it, then accessed the basic installation realm of the phone to watch it happen.

Helen reached out and touched him. The sensation was so unexpected, so strange, that he rocked back in his chair.

"Mike?" Kim asked. "What's wrong?"

It *wasn't* Helen. It was the Interpreter thread. This wasn't an appliance. It was a piece of a threaded being that resembled what he and Helen were. On the surface, he couldn't tell them apart.

"Mike," she spun his chair around to face her. "Talk to me, tell me what's wrong."

Emphasis being *on the surface.* As it integrated with his phone, a phone he couldn't remove or shut down no matter how much he wanted to, deeper layers were revealed.

He thought it was a simple coincidence that the Standard word for *thread* could be used to describe his real self as well. But he was wrong.

Kim paled and got out a handkerchief. She moved it gently across his cheek. "Mike, are you okay?"

He was scaring her. He needed to talk but couldn't. "Yes," he forced the words out. "I'm okay, I'm fine."

She sat down next to him. "What's happening?"

This thread was nothing like the ones he was used to. *Keep talking to her*. "It's the thread."

"Is it hurting you?"

"No, but it's...wrong."

"How so?"

To articulate it, he had to interact with it. The longer he watched it work, the less likely that became. "This is an actual *thread.* Like me. Like Helen. It's part of a living being." He needed to examine it in detail but couldn't. It turned inside out and felt around, blind and seeking, a twitching revenant that should be dead but wasn't. "It's freaking me out, and I don't understand why."

She smiled, and the world was a little better. "I think I get it now. It's time for *you* to do some breathing. It helped me a lot."

"It did?"

"Yes. If realspace aliens freaked me out, their thread-based life forms might have the same effect on you. We already knew they had threaded life forms here. Remember Tal?"

He'd completely forgotten. Gonzo's companion, the one who

had tried to trap him in that remote ancient realm, was threaded as well. But this thing…it kept *seeking*, blindly reaching around, deformed, and inside his mind. He had to push it out somehow.

Kim snapped her fingers in his face. "Stick with me. Try to keep your distance, if that means anything in there, and concentrate more on the similarities, not the differences."

"That's how you coped?"

"Yes," she said. "Now, tell me about the similarities."

He considered it. "It's a thread, like what my real body uses."

She chuckled and shook her head. "If you've fallen back on those terms, you really are freaked out."

Kim was right. He'd stopped thinking of his realspace host and his threads as separate entities months ago. "I guess it's the only thing I can find in common with it." Again it reached out, and again he didn't want anything to do with it, be near it.

Acknowledge it existed.

The handkerchief fell into his hand. "Get up," she said as she pushed her own chair away and sat down on the floor.

Sat down in the Lotus position.

In that moment, he couldn't have loved her more. They sat down on the floor and breathed. He quietly chanted the Sanskrit mantra. He wasn't alone with this alien *thing*; he was with Kim. They were together. They had a mission, and they had a home. He was going to spend the rest of his life with this lovely person who drove him nuts, and he wouldn't, couldn't, think of doing it any other way.

Breathe.

It wasn't the correct way for a Buddhist to meditate, but these were special circumstances. He concentrated again and got it right the next time.

And then it was over. The thread was integrated and functioning. "Thanks."

"My pleasure," she said as they got up. "I'm glad these kiosks have a door."

He shrugged. "I bet we aren't the first aliens to treat an encounter with an Interpreter thread as a religious experience."

They sat back down in the chairs, and Kim asked, "Can you tell me what's different now?"

Centered and focused, Mike could face it. "Almost everything. It's alive, barely. And it's, I don't know, *braided* somehow. Maybe if I get used to it, I'll be able to give you more details."

She nodded. "I get it. I mean, I don't *get it*, but when my thread is active, I do have that sense of a living response, of an *other*."

He looked up at the ceiling. "*Threads are tied with flesh.* Maybe getting a biological host is the normal experience for people like me and Helen?"

Mike could tell Kim was as disturbed by the idea as he was. "Maff did talk about a joining ceremony. Do you think..."

"That they intentionally kill people to create hosts? It's possible." It was how Helen had gotten hers. It marked one of the few times he'd agreed to disagree with his sister. Mike considered all life sacred and intentionally creating a host as a kind of murder. As long as it was a criminal properly convicted of a capital crime, Helen didn't see anything wrong with it. She considered it a form of recycling.

Mike suppressed a shudder. "So now I can read menus?" They'd been eating ship food for the past couple of weeks, and he was sick to death of it.

"It depends. Does the Interpreter thread still freak you out?"

He didn't *have* to perceive it with his real self, his threads. The idea became a starting point to cope with it. Mike was a hybrid lifeform, but he still felt more at home with his threads. They let him perceive things from many different vantage points and use many different methods all at once. He was hoping to observe the Interpreter thread in this accustomed way, but it was overwhelming. The sense of *other wrongness* was too strong for him to manage it.

But he had a realspace host with its own set of senses. There, the thread was only an alien app installed on his phone. Like Kim calling aliens talking cranes and scaly ewoks, it was a lie. But it was a useful one.

"Yes."

"Then let's see if curry is a universal concept." She paused for a second with her eyes closed. "Once I explained it, my thread thinks it might be."

He would get used to talking to his. He *would.* But only talking. When he thought that his threads might interact directly…

Concentrate on your realspace body. He turned it into a silent chant.

"Well," he said, "let's go find some."

It was strange to see an intact Bemian city. The realm he'd accidentally got lost in modeled one that had fallen to ruin thousands, maybe tens of thousands, of years ago. It was utterly desolate, a place abandoned even by hope.

Everything was colorful and very busy here. People—he stopped considering them aliens faster than Kim did—were going everywhere. The office towers were new and glossy, steel and glass boxes like back home. As with electronic components and concrete, that seemed to be a universal norm.

Kim was right. There was something…*bland* about it. There was a subtle, rhythmic sameness to everything. The people moved among each other without interacting, without seeming to be present at all. They weren't suffering, but they weren't exactly cheerful either.

"Maybe they're all in realms?" Kim asked as they took a break to rest and people watch.

"As they walk around? Their realm tech isn't that much different from ours."

"And isn't that strange?" she replied. "The culture is ancient. Their technology should be magic to us, incomprehensible."

"Instead, it's just odd and miniaturized," he said. Their old phones were huge compared to their new ones. They'd kept them as backups, and to see if they could eventually get them talking to the AC network.

It took some searching, but there was curry here. If you considered curry to be a food dish that used a complex combination of spices and herbs. There was quite a lot of it around. They went by the pictures and the odors, making hard turns away from anything that smelled like a chemical factory or an abattoir. The sa'dst would protect them from dangerous stuff, but neither of them wanted to test it.

The closer they got to a decision, the less confident Kim became. "You're sure it's not going be battery acid and book paste?"

"Do you have any idea how hard it is to accidentally poison a careful human *without* the help of sa'dst? We'll be fine."

Eventually they chose a modest place crowded with Bemians roughly the same size and shape that they were. They discovered more universals with differences: chopsticks here were too long, but they were usable, and made of something that was definitely woodish. Bowls were here, too, but made out of a material that was enough like jade he wanted to take a sample home to Helen. The food was good, especially compared to what they had on the ship, which was mostly nutrient bars of various barely noticeable flavors.

"You know," Kim said as she slurped the last of her *tenserl* down, "I'm a little disappointed."

"I know, right? It's all supposed to be wiggly and gross. Chopsticks and bowls? Where are the flying forks? The levitating plates?"

His ears popped as an energy shield descended over their table.

"Michael Sellars and Kimberly Trayne?"

The voice was mechanical and heavily accented, but the tone didn't need to be translated. Two large, all-business robots tromped into view. They didn't have badges. With an entrance like that, they didn't need them.

Kim took a deep breath and shared a look with Mike. They were literally light years away from anything that could approach a hiding place and had no way to get there other than their feet.

"Yes?"

"You are under arrest. Come with us."

Chapter 25

Helen

At one point, she led one of the most powerful nations in the world. Before that, she was a highly respected police officer. At all times, she was a leader, someone with honor and respect. Her guanxi, her influential friends, once included presidents and prime ministers.

But that was a lie. Her *father* had most of those things. She'd taken them on as a disguise, hoping to use them to shepherd her country away from men willing and able to collapse dams or start nuclear wars to facilitate murderous social engineering ideas that nobody ever thought all the way through. Step one: kill millions of Chinese, step two: …, step three: China is fixed. Only a member of the politburo would entertain such stupidity.

That was not who she was. Not now. No longer president, no longer a cop. She wasn't even safe anymore. Spencer had brought them to this rural backwater to regroup and plan their next moves without worrying about looking over their shoulders.

Nobody counted on next moves including Mike and Kim ending up halfway across the galaxy. They wouldn't know that much were it not for the connection she shared with her brother. She, of course, would have done a better job of managing it all had their roles been reversed, but Mike was handling this inadvertent first contact pretty well overall. That was probably down to Kim being there with him. She would make a great mother once they were married.

That was another thing she was still working on. She had promised to fix Kim's wedding. Being ousted in a coup, chased by strangers, and forced into hiding in Dumas, Arkansas did not relieve her of that responsibility. Because Mike still occupied realmspace outside of China, she had to interact with the various agencies responsible for all the wedding logistics via her human host. Progress was slow but steady.

Progress in this agricultural village with American characteristics remained to be seen.

Spencer dropped her at the small Chinese restaurant off the main highway well before it opened, but she found the door was unlocked. Clanking and banging came through the doorway to the kitchen, but Helen couldn't see anyone.

"Hello?" she asked in her best Standard Chinese.

The noise in the back stopped, and a short bald man of about forty came through the kitchen door. "Yes?" he asked, also in Chinese. "How can I help you?"

His smile seemed genuine, although his Chinese was tinged with a Southern American accent. She looked down at his feet. In this conversation, Helen was definitely the lower-status member. "I was wondering if I could ask you some questions about…your establishment?"

He changed languages. "Do you speak English?"

She switched too, but still kept her gaze on the floor. "Yes, very well. I am new to this area and am feeling a little lost."

He walked over to her but remained silent. Helen looked up.

His face was very serious. "Did you escape from a snakehead? You're clean and well fed, but that doesn't always mean anything."

Snakehead gangs were something Helen hadn't considered but should have. Human trafficking was a well-known profit center for them. She wouldn't be the first Chinese who ran to a remote corner of the world to hide from them. It also told her that snakeheads might be active somewhere nearby. This wasn't as safe a place as they thought.

"No, I'm not on the run from snakeheads." She cringed inwardly and hoped he didn't notice the accidental revelation. *Not running from snakeheads, no.*

"Do you have your papers in order?"

That sticking point she'd seen coming. "They were. My family..."

Her cover was Helen, a junior member of a politically connected family from a minor province in the interior. As such, her English should be good but not perfect, so she switched back to Chinese and looked away. The embarrassment was only half feinted. How the mighty had fallen. "My father has been arrested for corruption. It is a complete misunderstanding. I was at the university." There had to be one in this state, somewhere. She quickly pinged Spencer with the question.

Yes, he texted back, *the biggest one is the University of Arkansas in Fayetteville.*

"I arrived from Fayetteville a few days ago."

He sat down and motioned for her to do the same. "What brings you all the way down here?"

"An online friend of mine, Spencer McKenzie," she could tell by his expression he recognized the name, "learned of my plight and told me about his home."

"Is that why he's back in town? For you?"

Spencer wasn't kidding about how quickly news traveled around here. "He believed his family connections would avoid..." She shook her head as her character and as herself. Spencer was such a nerd. "*Imperial entanglements.* I think that means he wants to help with my papers."

The man raised an eyebrow. "And that's all?"

Helen didn't hide the cringe. "Oh yes, most definitely." In for a penny... "Father would kill me if I got involved with a white boy."

He grunted. "I don't know what I'll do with my girls when they're old enough." He chuckled gruffly, giving Helen a whiff of stale cigarettes. "Send them back to the mainland, I guess. I hear it's nothing *but* men over there now. Anyway," he offered his hand. "I'm Wong Huan, my English name is Harry."

"Zhang Fang Hua. Helen, in English."

"Well, Helen. It's mostly cash here, so papers aren't required immediately. And Spencer's right. His family has the pull to straighten you out. When can you start?"

It took her a second to understand. She hadn't specifically come to apply for a job, but it would make things simpler to have a source of income. Cash was still untraceable. "I don't have any experience with restaurant work."

He shrugged. "Nobody does when they start out, and I'm happy to help. I can't pay you much, but we share tips here. Once you're ready, you'll do fine as a waitress."

She remembered brokering a deal between Vietnam and Cambodia, opening borders and bringing peace. But not as herself, only as Father, the man who tried to incinerate two countries to slake his ambition.

Helen had to start over somewhere. "Thank you. I guess I can start now."

"No, not now, we don't open for another couple of hours. Have you talked to Jim Chen yet?"

"I'm not familiar with that name."

"He owns the grocery downtown. He's always looking for someone to work mornings with him. He gets started at five. You can end your shift there and be down here with produce before we open, and I'm always shorthanded at closing time."

Helen glanced at the register behind him. Closing time was at eight.

"Unless you think it's too much, that is," he said, clearly suspicious she might be a lazy college girl from the city.

Helen had done more than her share of all-nighters studying at the academy, and while her days as a beat cop were unusual, the hours were just as long. "No, sir. That would be fine. I'd love to meet Mr. Chen."

"Good. I'll take you; I need to pick up more pork anyway. The only people in the world who love pork as much as Chinese are Black Americans. But it doesn't give us heart attacks."

*

"Fuck me, Helen," Spencer said when she gave them the news. "*Two* jobs?"

"I need something to do. If I sit around, I'll go crazy. Plus, it'll help me with the cops."

That got Tonya's attention. It was nice to bring something to the table instead of being the thing they had to cart around. "The cops?"

"The police come by both places regularly." For free items. It was too much like bribery for her taste, but it wasn't any different back home. Helen couldn't be picky anymore. "It will let me build a contact list." And maybe an entry to the police force itself.

"Keep us posted and be careful," Tonya said. "You're not a cop around here."

*

Helen thought the long hours or the physical work would be the hardest part of her new jobs, but she adjusted quickly to those.

The problem for her was the people and the stealing.

"The whole town is poor," Chen said as she helped him unstack pallets of greens from the back of a truck in the morning darkness. "None of the teenagers have any common sense. They don't learn it in school or at home. All they see is rich hip-hop artists and think the world owes them everything."

"How do you stay in business?"

"The preachers come around once a week and watch security video. They pay for my losses, take care of the ones who are worth saving, and turn the rest over to the police."

She heaved a crate of oranges into a display case. "You mean they get away with it?"

He smiled. "You misunderstand what the preachers do. The ones they help have strong families, good families. They value honor as much as we do and losing face in front of a preacher is the worst thing that can happen to them. Almost all of them screw up at least once, especially the boys. It seems to be an initiation thing in their culture. White or Black, doesn't matter. Even when they have a future, they still screw it up. We had a bunch of boys drive a dozen golf carts into the country club swimming pool right before their high school graduation. Filled the thing right up. I think they said it was a million dollars in damages. Many of them had full scholarships to area colleges, now gone. Two of them are still in jail. It was worse before this new system was set up. No consequences, nobody cared.

"But the *preachers* cared. They always have. You have never seen such contrition after these teenagers have been disciplined by their family *and* their church."

Mr. Wong agreed, talking about it as Helen washed dishes in his restaurant. "Something had to change. I credit the churches, too."

"My friend, Spencer, doesn't seem to like the churches."

"No, and that's why he never fit in. It happens in every generation. There are kids who rebel not by thieving, fighting, or getting pregnant, but by looking outward. This town isn't modern, and those kids want modern. They want the bright lights, the big cities. They most of all want out of *here*." He waited until she pulled the steaming rack of dishes out of a dishwasher taller than she was, then continued. "It's not all that different from China, in my opinion."

The plates were too hot as she stacked them up, but she ignored the pain in her hands. Helen would never in a million years have expected to recognize Chinese values in a rural Southern town, especially one this isolated. But every time she turned around, she found more of them.

So she only shouted at the kid she caught shoplifting the next morning, to make sure his face was clear on the security cameras. Helen had never before heard of an arrangement such as this, but Tonya was right. The town was small, poor, and struggling, but it was also clean. The people *were* friendly. They had hope, though it seemed to be a recent thing. They were doing something right.

She kept an eye out for potential snakeheads but didn't see any. A large well-dressed Black man gave her a sour look during her first night shift. Helen moved to clean a table behind him, and he stood up suddenly, motioning toward Mr. Wong as Helen went into the back with her tub full of dishes. A few minutes later, Mr. Wong came around the corner to her dishwashing station, tense.

"Am I okay?" she asked.

He gave her a sharp look. "Why do you ask?"

Think fast. "I've never done anything like this before. I want to do a good job."

"You're fine," he said. "Don't stare at the customers so much though. They think you're evaluating them."

If you only knew.

"Helen?" It was Mike. "We have a situation here."

Helen's efforts to investigate local law enforcement hadn't started, and her brother had already managed to examine them at *very* close range.

Chapter 26
Him

She put her hands up slowly, making sure Mike did the same. "We don't want any trouble. What's going on?"

"You are in violation of Code AA231138, Possession of Unlicensed Artifacts with Intent to Distribute."

"We don't have any artifacts, unlicensed or otherwise. Everything we own right now is on our backs. What is unlicensed?" Maybe the clothes were from pirated designs.

"Are you crew on *Last Island*?"

She shrugged. The cops were here and knew their names. There was no point in denying it. That would get them into more trouble. "Crew would be a bit of a stretch. I'd call us a couple of indentured servants."

"Have you performed compensated work while on board *Last Island*?"

"Define compensated."

So it did, in excruciating detail. As it ran through its list, she glanced over at Mike.

How much trouble do you think we're in? He texted.

No way to know, but do not lie to these things. They wouldn't be here if they thought we were innocent.

It finished, then asked, "Have you performed compensated work while on board *Last Island*?"

Now to see if there were exceptions. "That part about repairing things as pay in kind for our transportation and supplies? What about accidents or involuntary transportation?"

That stopped it for a moment. "Were you a prisoner on this ship?"

"It's hard for me to say without knowing the details of your definition."

"Such things are irrelevant to establishing your status. Have you performed compensated work while on board *Last Island*?"

"Do I have to answer?"

"You cannot be compelled to answer at this time. Refusal to answer will not be taken as an admission of guilt but will allow us to restrain you until your status is determined."

At this time sounded scary, but otherwise this rude little introduction to Bemian law enforcement was encouraging. They had something in place that roughly matched the Fifth Amendment.

Maybe.

Regardless, it gave her an out. "That being the case, my partner and I regretfully cannot answer your question." *Oh, why not.* "At this time."

It turned to Mike. "Are you this being's partner?"

He opened his mouth, and she glared at him. Now was *not* the time to get cute. "Yes," he said, more seriously than the sparkle in his eyes let on. "She is my partner."

"Kimberly Trayne and Mike Sellars, you are hereby restrained per lawful order until your relationship with the crew of *Last Island* can be determined."

Back home, Kim had been a ghost. Nobody ever caught her, nobody ever found her. She'd humiliated powerful people, taken their money, their pride, their prestige. *Governments* had spent years searching for her and come up empty. In the end, it took *an entirely new life form* to crack her security and find her. That had been down to Kim being drunk and talking to the only person smart enough and crazy enough to do whatever it took to track her down.

And here, halfway across the galaxy, she was arrested in less than a week.

At least they were robots.

These weren't intelligent life forms, so her touch syndrome ruled them okay. The cuffs went on, uncomfortably tight but not damaging, and they were physically escorted out of the café.

The vehicle they were bundled into wouldn't look at all out of place back home as a SWAT van, but this one still used a fossil-fuel motor. Diesel, by the smell of it. Universals and differences. It made no concession whatsoever for a driver. It was hard to tell if there was a front or a rear; the door that opened was on the side.

The Bemian phone immediately flashed No Signal at her, but they'd already figured out how to set up direct connections that didn't need a network to function.

How far have you gotten with compromising the camera network? she texted Mike.

Not everything, but I can see what's happening outside.

He shared a link over the ad hoc network between their two Bemian phones. They were traveling down a main thoroughfare, not much different from an inner-city highway network back home. The difference was, as always, in the details.

I thought you said there were signs and street markings? Kim asked.

There are, on the surface streets. Apparently, you're—

The picture quality degraded and then it disappeared. A voice came from speakers above their heads. "Your neural network connections are defective. Refrain from using them during transport, or they will be forcibly deactivated."

So they're seeing our activity as, Mike texted, *a glitch from our phones.*

At least we know our security is still good. What does the crew back home make of it?

I'm not contacting them yet, not here. These robocops are trying to monitor us, and they might be able to detect that.

Can they see us doing **this***?*

Maybe, he texted back, *but it's miniscule compared to full motion video. They only complained when I tried that link. I'm using inertial navigation now. That's contained in our phones. No bandwidth used at all.*

Why didn't they deactivate them?

We can talk to each other, and they'll try to monitor that. You always said what gets you in the most trouble…

Comes out of your mouth. You do listen.

To you, always.

That hit her harder than she thought it would. Her normal reflex would be to come back with a joke or a tease, but not here. Facing this all alone would've been crushing. With him, it was an adventure. *I'm glad you're here with me.*

He smiled, and that settled her down. Mike was here, and they were a team. A *spectacular* team that had been knocked down but never out. *Me too.*

Something else stirred inside her. An attraction, a need to go, to travel to a point ahead of them. *Do you feel that?*

They must be taking us through a portal. I was wondering about that. I haven't seen anything resembling a municipal building this whole time. Must be somewhere else.

What do you think will happen?

Only one way to find out.

He was right. The attraction ramped up to the point she *wanted* it. Kim had felt this way when she got her bicycle, Giulietta, this excited need to possess a thing…

And then it stopped.

I guess we're here, Mike texted.

Or at least closer. What does your Will-compass say? If they moved a long distance, it should give them the ability to triangulate Will's position.

Definitely closer, he replied. *If he is the bullseye, we've moved laterally, and there was an altitude change as well. It agrees with the coordinates I worked out on Maff's nav system. They didn't take us to another spot on Perspendala or to another planet orbiting that star. We're in a new system.*

She raised an eyebrow at him. *Faster than light, for the win.*

The vehicle stopped. "Here we go," she said out loud.

The door opened to an artificially lit parking garage of some sort. The air that wafted in was more humid than Perspendala and colder. It was raining outside. Kim rubbed her arms to put some warmth into them.

"You will exit the vehicle and follow us peacefully," the cop-bot that opened the door said in Standard Bemian.

Her Interpreter thread was gone. Presumably, Mike's was too. This was a different cop-bot than the one that'd put them in the van. *Sit tight,* she texted Mike. *I have an idea.*

Kim shook her head and said in English, "I don't understand."

If this bot understood English, that could mean the network had automatic update routines across star systems that were fast. If it didn't, there could be weaknesses to exploit. Lag was a hacker's friend.

And they could be hacked. Her packet sniffers had already picked up the basics of their network protocols, and Mike's threads were as slippery as ever in realmspace. The length of time it took the bot to presumably request an English update from the bots back on Perspendala would make for a good, safe test of speed and bandwidth across system boundaries.

The bot pulled back and was still.

Timing it, Mike texted.

After a long pause, a cartoon version of themselves flashed into existence on the shared vision channel, clearly showing them getting out and following the bot.

"You...follow...me," he said in Standard.

Talking slowly to someone who didn't speak the language: another universal idea.

How dumb are we? she sent Mike.

Not too dumb. They might force us out if we don't play along.

Kim nodded and said in Standard, "Follow...you..."

It was a parking garage, complete with low ceiling, filled with various sorts of vehicles. They were all painted the same dark blue-gray color as their SWAT van. The angular egg shapes managed to seem menacing, which was probably the point.

The bot immediately brought them to an Interpreter minikiosk. It made an unmistakable *after you* gesture at Kim. She sat down and had to go through the same read-and-speak schtick she did on Perspendala. At least she didn't need help with the symbols this time.

The range of their protocols is limited, Mike texted after she was done. *Or maybe it's too expensive to maintain across interstellar distances. It's nice to know they have some limitations.*

How deep have you gotten into the network on this side?

Not far, he replied, *but I'm being extra cautious. There's something else in there. Something big.*

"You will come with us for sentencing," the bot said after Mike finished his Interpreter thread redo.

"Sentencing? For what?"

It started again on the litany of charges. Kim waved it silent. "You haven't established we're members of the crew yet."

They got on an enclosed elevator that promptly went up at a good clip.

"A preponderance of evidence has been acquired from witnesses that makes establishing your status immaterial to your guilt."

The elevator opened into a spare but still somehow fancy corridor that would not have been out of place at any courthouse back home. *They always tell you taxes are for hospitals and schools,* her uncle Kostas enjoyed saying, *but it always ends up paying for fancy marble floors and expensive leather chairs.*

"What witnesses?" she asked.

A broad pair of double doors slid open to a room shaped like a Greek theater but made of dark woodish and leatherish stuff instead of marble. The stage was maybe fifty feet below the ceiling. Aside from a few diverse Bemians scattered around, the seats were empty.

Where back home she'd expect a pair of tables separated by a wide space and facing the judge's bench, here there were clearly marked standing areas that faced each other. In the center was a huge…*mechanism* of some sort. It was roughly cylindrical, touching floor and ceiling, at least ten feet in diameter, a gray steel framework filled with cabling and clockwork mechanisms that spun and whirred. Sensors that'd been observing one standing area or the other slid around the framework and focused on them, like combination wheels on a bicycle lock.

Kim had faced who knew how many different actual aliens in the past few weeks, all of them freaky. None of them…*none of them*…crawled up her spine the way this spinning, flexing giant did. It was HR Giger without the organic curves, artless brutality built from pitted steel.

Kim had never wanted to run away from anything so much in her life.

That's *why I'm being careful,* Mike texted.

She couldn't remember how to make the text app work anymore. "What is it?" she asked out loud.

"I'm pretty sure it's an AC network node. And *that,*" Mike indicated the two areas on either side of it, "is why I think we're in a lot of trouble."

Maff stood in one area, looking at them and clearly terrified. A pallun Kim had never seen before stood beside her. The rest of the crew, minus the talking fern, stood on the other side, looking smug and confident.

"Son of a bitch," Kim said. "They sold us out."

Chapter 27
Maff

The morning had started well. She attended a proper worship service for the first time since this whole fiasco had kicked off. Mike and Kim had finished his gizmo, something about absorbing shocks because of *general relativity*—Maff still hadn't gotten her wings around that no matter how many times they tried to explain it—and they were going outside the ship together for the first time. Maff would meet them after their midday meal, and then she'd give them a tour of the city. It wasn't that distinctive of a place, most port cities weren't, but they hadn't seen anything like it. Showing them around would be her honor.

Then the captain called as she left the service. "Emergency crew meeting, come directly back."

So much for a day showing off what the humans' world would become after their AC network connected to the galaxy. "On my way."

Because the service was located on the opposite side of town, Maff was the last to get back. She entered the hold and immediately noticed a problem.

"Where are Mike and Kim?"

The captain waved her inside. "Shut the door, Maff."

"But—"

"*Shut the door,*" Feviz growled, "you dumb, greedy gasbag."

"Stow that, Feviz," Captain De'Tan shot back. "This is not the time." He turned back to her. "Please, shut the door and come inside."

Maff extended manipulators to the door controls and activated the close sequence as she walked toward them all. Captain De'Tan's ears were flat; she'd never seen Elsek so ruffled, Feviz and Gaanan's tails were rigid, and Hafurnal's fronds had stopped their lazy waving. Something was *very* wrong. "What's going on?"

The captain gestured to Hafurnal with a sour look. "We are all under arrest."

"*What?*" Nobody had restraints on.

The medical officer's leaves rattled, and Maff noticed that they'd been bound together. *The only one wearing restraints was supposed to have arrested everyone?* "It's not like that, man," Hafurnal said. "Well, okay, it *was* like that, but not anymore."

"I don't understand."

"It seems," the captain said, "that we've had an undercover officer on board the entire time."

The revelation caused a diamond storm that'd been blinding her to stop and show a starry sky above. The rendezvous, the flight from the authorities, all Hafurnal's nervous molting, the infusion pump Mike and Kim fixed that pog almost broke. The way they *didn't* get picked up by the police as soon as they got back.

Maff's very first mission had turned inside out, from an exciting exploration to a ticket straight to a Death Eater world. She'd been distracted by Mike and Kim and had forgotten the basic truth that she worked for outlaws. *Was* an outlaw. Getting arrested was never going to happen to her, Maff had known that to the center of her being. She was too good a pilot to get caught. She'd already outrun the law. They couldn't arrest what they couldn't catch.

But they didn't need to. "I don't believe this," she said.

"Join the club," Elsek said as she tried to preen her feathers back to some kind of order. "But we found Hafurnal's ID. Pogs real name is Detective Markor Zonag, ACNPD."

She would never see home again. But if she never went home, she'd never have to face Father, never hear how disappointed Mother was in her.

That idea settled her down, but only a little.

The captain turned and addressed them all. "It's going to be okay. I have a plan."

The twisted feeling inside her relaxed a little. It was going to be all right. He always had plans, and they always worked when it mattered.

"We're gonna blame it all on the aliens."

It stunned her into silence.

Not Feviz, though. "How does that work?"

They couldn't blame Mike and Kim. They weren't smugglers. They didn't know what that meant, what would happen to them. *They were her friends.*

The captain ignored the silent storm tossing Maff around. "They've been behind it all along. We didn't know that stuff was unlicensed."

Elsek warmed to the plan, and the gas inside Maff churned. "And we'd been jumped by pirates pretending to be cops before. That's why we ran away."

"Part of the agreement," Gaanan said, "was that we go pick them up so they could fence the goods themselves."

Maff tried to punch a hole in their idea. "But their planet hasn't joined the network yet."

Feviz spat. "The cops saw our modal eight transition. We went way the hell to the other side of the galaxy. It'll take apurns, maybe etars before news of their joining reaches this planet." He turned to the captain. "I think that will work."

Maff tried again. "Why would Hafurnal…erm…*Detective Zonag*…go along with it?"

The captain dramatically unrolled a bundle he'd been holding in his hand the entire time. "If Hafurnal wants the next generation of Zonags to see the light of their sun, pog'll do it."

Maff zoomed her optics into the beltlike thing the captain held. There were thousands of delicate brown dots covering the inside surface, protected by a clear membrane.

When she was small, Father had an Exeder employee, she always called him Mr. Marzdak, who worked in the back office managing inventory and reports. Maff was still mastering how to walk in her suit and had accidentally crushed some of pogs fronds stumbling around. She didn't understand why everyone, Mother and Father included, had become so upset. Even though she was forgiven, Mr. Marzdak never seemed the same again. It was only years later that Mother told her the truth: Exeder spores were conscious beings, fully self-aware. Maff had accidentally killed some of Mr. Marzdak's children.

And now the captain was threatening to do that to *all* of Zonag's.

Hafurnal-Zonag struggled against the restraints; leaves floated to the ground. "You're *sick*! Threatening innocent spores to save your own hides! How did you find them?"

The captain smiled. "I know where everything is on this ship."

Hafurnal-Zonag would do anything to protect pogs offspring. Mike and Kim would have no warning about what would come down on their heads. "You can't do this."

The captain's smile used to be charming. "I can't?"

"They're innocent! You can't send them to a Death Eater world!"

Feviz spat again. "It's them or us, *pallun*. I vote us."

"But they didn't *do* anything!"

Feviz turned to the captain. "I told you she wouldn't go along with it. Fucking coward."

The captain ignored Feviz and turned to Maff. "I will admit I'm not happy with them getting the short end of the stick. Do you have a better idea?"

Maff thought as fast as she could. "We'll get them a lawyer, a really good one." Father had to know some.

"They've got no credits," Feviz sneered.

"They don't, but *we* do."

Elsek's feathers ruffled out again. "Why would *we* want to spend any of our credits on them?"

Come on, come on, think. Then all at once, she had it. "The humans, they can *fix* things. If we get them off the hook, they can pay us back by fixing stuff."

Feviz and the captain shared an unreadable look. The captain said, "Assuming we get a good lawyer, what's to keep them from running off the next time we make planetfall?"

"They'll never go out together," Feviz said. "They're pair-bonded, isn't that right, pallun?"

Maff could only give a sickly nod. They'd forgive her, eventually. Besides, Mike and Kim enjoyed fixing things. It might not occur to them to leave.

That was harder to believe, but what choice did she have?

"I'll talk to my father"*—oh Turlanfador, she had no choice but to talk to Father now*—"he'll know who is available."

"Work fast," the captain said. "We have to let Hafurnal-Zonag here report in soon, and it won't be long after that before we're all picked up."

*

Maff had never seen the inside of any law enforcement vehicle or facility in her life, and now it was inevitable that she would see both, and soon. That still didn't eclipse the storm-swirl inside her mind.

She had to call Father for help.

First, she had to find a Guild station that could be threaded to Silaria. She knew the route because Mother forced her to memorize it before she left. It was all Maff could do to talk Mother out of getting it tattooed on one of her wings. It wasn't necessary this time. Perspendala was a port city with an active pallun enclave. It had a direct line.

She still had to wait for the connection to be made, then for the Guild house on the other end of the line to build out a local connection to Father's communicator. Long-distance calling was one of the greatest benefits of the Interpreter network, but it was a far cry from the efficiency of AC nodes and their intrasystem communications.

Maff bet Mike and Kim knew a better way. They seemed to know a better way to do nearly everything else. She knew it had to be possible. Mike regularly communicated with his sister on their home world. That was something only—

Father answered the call. "Maff? What's wrong? Are you hurt? Hungry? Oh, your mother will be so worried!"

Maff didn't have time to convince Father that she was fine but had to do it anyway. She was sure he didn't believe her, but that didn't matter right now. "It's my friends"—hopefully they'd stay friends—"they're in trouble. They need a lawyer."

Father's voice grew very serious, more than she'd heard directed at her before. "These are the people your uncle Turnn connected you with. What's happened? Are you *sure* you're not in trouble?"

As far as Maff's parents knew, all she'd told them anyway, the ship she'd signed up with was nothing but a small-time tramp freighter. Father now seemed to know a lot more than that. "Yes, it's my friends. They've…" It wouldn't be good for anyone to out and out *say* it. "They're in the same kind of trouble Uncle Turnn might get into."

"Za gafunkt." The phrase was old Pallundian: *Oh, my winged Lord.*

"They're good people, though. Father, please, we can help them."

"If your mother ever finds out…"

Pallun had written entire books on the end times, long before they'd ever encountered the AC network. Storm-splitting stuff, clouds made of rock, planets torn apart by liquids flooding from the core. None of it compared to a pallun mother when she thought her child was in trouble.

Or had caused it.

"She won't find out. Please, Father. Do you know anyone?"

*

His name was Noen Sha'Katenden, and he was the oldest, fiercest pallun Maff had ever met. His suit was in a style that had vanished ages ago, easily older than her own grandparents. But it was in perfect shape, as were its manipulators and legs. Maff took pride in her own appearance, but the price of one of those leg segments would pay for three whole sets of hers. If his real office was as opulent as the realmspace—Kim had told her that's what they called *nakantar*, shared spaces, on Earth—she met him in, she could only hope they'd be able to cover this bill.

Maff told him the story in a big rush, trying not to waste his time but still give him all the facts. "They're coming to pick us all up now."

His manipulators worked at a console only he could see. "No, they won't be picking *you* up. I'll do that." A vehicle parked outside pinged her in realspace—another word Kim taught her. They had names for everything. She set her suit a few waypoints so it would walk by itself to get inside.

He turned to her in the realm. "This is a *very* serious matter."

The words sounded funny in his old Pallundian accent, but the tone was as grave as a bladder puncture. "I understand."

"No, I don't think you do. This is AC justice, not the kind you're used to. Their guilt has already been decided. The trial is for show, to ensure the petarkan stay in line."

Petarkan was a racist term for nonpallun, but Maff wasn't about to call him on it. "We learned about it in school."

The car transited the local portal gate and arrived at the courthouse. In person, Mr. Sha'Katenden was more intimidating. He snorted contemptuously as they ascended the courtroom stairs. "You learned it in AC schools. Bad machines, bad culture, bad people."

They entered a courtroom that looked exactly like all the others she'd seen in realm dramas, right down to the founding AC node acting as judge. Maff had never seen one up close before. The factories it built to kick start this planet's civilization had been dismantled long ago, leaving behind odd scars and scary, exposed gearing.

"I might get them off on technicalities, but it's very important that they enter a *not guilty* plea. I will tell them this, then you will tell them this. *Very* important. There's no going back from a guilty plea."

Maff thought it best to stay with Mr. Sha'Katenden. The rest of the crew lined up in the accuser box on the opposite side of the arena. Mike and Kim were brought in via a different passage at the top of the theater. They didn't know what was going on; she could see it.

They were brought down exactly in the way Mr. Sha'Katenden said, and he explained what was happening, what it meant, and what they should say. The more detailed his description got, the more frightened the two humans seemed. They must never have been told what the ultimate penalty was in the AC galaxy.

Maff made sure they understood. "Not guilty, okay?"

Mike and Kim nodded, but then looked at each other. Maff got the impression of a message being passed, an agreement made.

The node read out the charges, a litany that went on much longer than Maff expected. Then it kept going. *Now* Maff understood why the crew thought this was such a great idea. They were pushing every bad thing that *Last Island* had ever done on Mike and Kim. If Maff had known it all, she would never have agreed to the plan.

The node finished and asked, "HOW DO YOU PLEA?"

They looked at each other. Maff had never seen a pair so lost. They would be okay. With help, they'd be fine.

Mike nodded to Kim, who, as Mr. Sha'Katenden instructed, stepped forward so her voice could be heard throughout the courtroom.

"Guilty."

Chapter 28
Mike

They did it. They said guilty.

As they stood staring at the node, he knew what Kim saw, because it was what he saw with his realspace eyes: a huge, ancient metal framework column that stretched from floor to ceiling filled with gears, pulleys, cables, and hydraulics.

But he also knew what Kim *couldn't* see.

There were huge threaded presences in this realm, braided like the one he got at the chapter house, but strong and healthy. He moved carefully among them, and none seemed to notice him at all. Mike could do this because it was a shared realm. None of these presences used it as a home for their threads, otherwise he'd be locked out like he was with Helen's realm. Then he made a much more important discovery.

Mike had sensed the edges of a new kind of alienness, one that was part of the realmspace in a way he wasn't. The longer he examined it, the more it became obvious.

The AC network had unduplicates.

As with everything else, that was the general impression. The details were different, and important to their current situation.

Back home, unduplicates were still something of a novelty. Fee was the most prominent one not only because she was the oldest, but also because she was the most accessible. People regularly interacted with her. But she was singular, and now gone. Otherwise, as far as the general public was concerned, unduplicates were shadowy and remote. They managed global enterprises, crunched big data, tracked quantum traces, and did other things well beyond the capabilities of the AI systems that came before them. They could even, in special cases that nobody had figured out how to predict, become conscious in their own right.

The way this galaxy used their unduplicates was similar. Unduplicates were very good at organizing vast, globe-spanning enterprises. They could catalog vast amounts of data and use their unique AI structures to search it faster and more effectively than any other machine system invented.

So, yeah. In one respect, it all fit. But only in one respect. *That's* what he saw that Kim couldn't. The AC galaxy's unduplicates weren't helpers.

They were in charge.

Seeing the *founding node* that confronted them now clinched it. AC nodes, which underpinned their network, which made this whole galaxy tick, were unduplicates!

WHAT? Kim texted.

I don't understand it either.

But you said we're the first humans to ever visit.

Mike nodded. *We are. The details of the design are different, but the operating principles are the same.*

If they use the same principles, then that means you can hack them.

He smiled. *We'll get answers.*

While they listened to Mr. Sha'Katenden's basic introduction to AC galaxy law, Mike peeled off a group of threads and went to work.

Caution had been his watchword ever since this all started, so he didn't dive right in. It allowed him to examine and subvert some clever and *alien* thread defenses. It also put him on high alert. Their security systems were full of holes, but he didn't doubt that on something as important as a founding node, *defense in depth* would be a thing. In other words, the front line wasn't going to be the only line, and he could not get caught rummaging around in their judge's underwear while he was sitting on the bench.

Mike couldn't get over the scale of it. He'd worked on or with the oldest unduplicates Earth had ever created. Compared to this node, they were a thimble placed next to a skyscraper. It implied an age measured in millennia, if not more. It had to be more. His threads could find no edge to its memory lattice. There was a good chance this unduplicate had been built before humans had become humans.

So why haven't they found us yet? It was a question that had come up time and again. Mike tasked a new series of threads to see if they could find anything at the top of the unduplicate's memory stores that might provide a clue. A summary of its personal history wouldn't give them all the answers, but it would be a start.

Mr. Sha'Katenden's description of what constituted a banishment sentence was meant to be scary, and it was, but it accidentally provided vital clues. The Death Eaters seemed, at root, to be a kind of salvage operation, one that worked with civilizations that had gone extinct long ago. The planets were always empty, barely habitable, covered in ruins.

In other words, exactly the kind of place the portal had taken Will to.

Mike concentrated on the node's geocoordinate segment and confirmed that the world he'd used Maff's tools to find was on the list of ones the Death Eaters were actively cleaning. This squared well with what Gonzo had said. They'd been trying to figure out how to reach Will, and now a direct route had been opened for them.

They only had to say one word. So they did.

The arena was silent for a couple of heartbeats. Mike knew the AC node wasn't conscious, but even it seemed surprised.

"What?" Maff cried out.

"Your highest node," Mr. Sha'Katenden shouted out, "I would like to remind the court that these are not my only clients, and Maff Sorkon has already entered a plea of not guilty." He paused to give all three of them a poisonous glare. "I request a recess of two weeks to reconfigure my defense."

Mike set to work making extremely minor adjustments to the AI's coordinate data cluster so they'd be sent to Will's planet, and also a quick record insert on the legal file it had at the top of its queue. Mike assumed that was the book about to be thrown at them.

How do we get home from there? Kim texted.

Do you think you can reach the higher transit dimension modes transformed? Maff had explained those to him teaching him how to use the console. It could turn a years-long slog into a single step.

I don't know. Maybe.

We know how to repair their protection skeins, and this planet he's on is one big garbage dump. I think we can scrounge skeins for him and my host, and then we'll walk home.

Hope was in her eyes, but there was a lot of fear, too. *What if I can't reach those higher modes?*

He shrugged. *We steal a ship. They're pretty easy to hotwire.*

Her eyebrow shot up, and she cracked half a smile. *And who's gonna fly it, kid?*

Maybe Maff can give us a lesson before they ship us off.

Maff won't be happy with us, Kim sent. She went through a lot of trouble to get this lawyer.

Yeah. We'll figure out a way to make it up to her. Somehow.

It was nice not being a criminal for a while, she sent. Oh well.

"GRANTED. AS SPECIFIED IN SECTION SIX SIX POINT FIVE EIGHT SUB A SUB X SUB SEVEN, THE GUILTY WILL BE ALLOWED THE SAME AMOUNT OF TIME TO GATHER ADEQUATE PROTECTION FOR THE TARGET ENVIRONMENT."

That was Mike's doing. It seemed the most reasonable thing he could insert, and it was buried so deep that by the time anyone figured out there was no *sub seven* in anyone else's law code, they'd be long gone. Served them right for not putting change log triggers into their files.

Maff was inconsolable. "How could you do this? Do you have any idea what you've done? We were going to get the charges dropped!"

Kim gently grabbed one of Maff's frantically waving manipulator probes. "We'll be fine, Maff. We know what we're doing." She shared a significant look with Mike, who could only shrug. It was true, from a certain point of view. "We've always known our paths would diverge."

"But not like this!"

Mr. Sha'Katenden, who had gone very still after the node read out their sentence, broke into the conversation. "I think you should trust your friends, Maff," he said in a clearly worried tone as they were ushered out of the arena. "I think they have more resources than we realized." He gave Mike a sharp look. "*Many* more."

Mike hoped that only a lawyer as good as Mr. Sha'Katenden would have enough of the code memorized to realize what he'd done. Nobody else, including the node, seemed to notice. It didn't matter now. They had a trip to prepare for. Mike had a general idea of what they needed, but he wanted an expert opinion.

He reached out to his sister. "Helen? We have a situation here. Can you get in contact with Spencer?"

*

Spencer's advice was simple and to the point. "Pack as light as you can. Use their replicators to build boots from the plans I'm sending you. Stay away from things that require power. The air is no good, and that sawdust shit will run out in a day or two. Buy the best respiration gear you can get your hands on." The rest was lessons in hunting and tracking, along with more plans for a crossbow and a sled. "It sucks you can't have a shotgun. I guess they don't want armed convicts. Take the crossbow and sled apart and hide all the pieces, I doubt they'll recognize them. Hopefully you can get some kind of truck or motorcycle to work. Otherwise you may end up having to hike across the whole planet. That could take months."

They got busy gathering their supplies, and Mr. Sha'Katenden got busy ensuring Maff could go home. It didn't take long for the truth to come out: the whole thing had been a harebrained scheme to turn him and Kim into indentured servants. Even Maff had been in on it at the end, helping them get a world—or in this case, maybe galaxy—class lawyer.

That had proved to be the crew's undoing. Mr. Sha'Katenden had amended Mike and Kim's plea so that they were only on the hook for the final smuggling crime. That left plenty of charges to hang on everyone else. Except for Maff. She was going home. Unhappy, but safe. That would have to be their gift to her. By taking on charges that would've been hers, Mike and Kim were giving Maff another shot. Hopefully she'd pick a better crew next time.

So when they turned up at the dock, Mike and Kim weren't the only ones waiting to go. The rest of the crew, even the fern-slash-cop, were all there too. But they didn't have tightly packed camping supplies. They'd all brought crates of booze and who knew what else. They'd also started early on them.

The captain, normally a bit reserved, explained sloppily that "We have to shela...srella...*celebrate,*" he threw his arms, and both his beers, into the air, "for tomorrow we die!"

Incredibly, they had made absolutely no preparations for living in banishment. It was going to be one long party, and then a quick goodnight. Mike found their choice repulsive, but at the same time sad. Deep down, these people had no hope, no belief in themselves, no notion that life without the AC network was possible.

Mike and Kim, with their fancy boots, rugged clothing, and backpacks full of supplies obviously did. Some of the crew noticed and grew sullen. He would need to keep a close eye on them all. People who have decided to go down with the ship could get resentful when others climbed into the lifeboats.

Then Maff walked in.

She'd added a ton of gewgaws to her suit. A lot were boxes; Mike recognized the labels as coming from most of the same companies he and Kim had used to get their supplies. The rest was obviously utilitarian. Saws, lights, basic navigation equipment, things like that. It was glaringly obvious what her plan was. Maff was going on safari. All she lacked was a pith helmet.

"Maff," Kim said as she ran over to her. "You can't be serious."

"I'm not leaving you two alone. You don't know what you're in for."

"And you do?" Mike asked as he looked her over. "Do you know what half this stuff does?"

She was resolute, stiff in her pride. "It all comes with instructions, and I'll have a lot of time to read."

"What does your mom say?" Kim asked. Maff had told them stories.

The resolve wavered a little. "She doesn't know. Neither of my parents know. Nobody back home knows. I *can't* go back. It will be so humiliating. And they'll never let me leave again, never trust me." Her confidence vanished. "Please let me come with you?"

They discovered that while Death Eater worlds were always used as a place of banishment, they weren't otherwise off limits. There was nothing to prevent her from going.

Mike checked with Kim, who took that as her turn to shrug. "Okay, I guess," he said. He gave Maff another once-over. "Let's talk about your kit."

If the rest of the crew was suspicious of Mike and Kim, they were outright hostile to Maff's arrival. Mike had always suspected the entire lot of them were bigots even though he didn't understand why. In their current state, they didn't bother hiding their contempt or anger.

He'd have to keep a *very* close eye on them all now.

Chapter 29
Tonya

It had been many, many years since she had attended a traditional Black church, and those had all been inner-city versions. They shared things with their country cousins: singing, dancing, amateur musicians with skills that would land them a studio contract, a priest—no, a *preacher*—who played the audience like a Stradivarius one moment and the captain of a ship in a storm the next. But it wasn't a church in the Philadelphia of her childhood. Everything was much smaller, the people much older, and so kind it felt like they knew her before they met her.

There were separate services listed on the paper program they handed her—there was, naturally, no realm or even web presence—but Tonya's research had shown that all-day attendance was expected, albeit not *required*. Her source? The one safe place that existed in every Black community in the country.

The beauty salon.

"Oh yes," Keia said as she worked on Tonya's hair the day before. "In Dr. Whitney's church, you better not be walkin' out when the sun's still shinin'."

"It's not even that entertaining," Sandra said from the chair next to hers. "If you want *entertaining*, come by my church. Speakin' in tongues, runnin' 'round the aisles, last time around old lady Johnston passed out on the floor from cryin'!"

The whole salon laughed; those who weren't underneath dryer hoods anyway.

She was also advised to shelve her traditional single colored locks. That bothered her more than going to the church. They were her mood signal, her custom stripe, something modern nanotech-based hair colors made simple and easy.

"No, honey," Keia said as she stood over Tonya like the wizard she was turning out to be. "I can see why you love them, but if you want to impress the biddies and the preachers, you need to be conservative. This ain't Little Rock!"

More laughs.

So Tonya got a perm that rivaled anything she'd seen walking out of a four-star DC salon along with a pile of gossip that, if only half of it was true, turned Dumas from a sleepy little backwater into a soap opera that would match anything current in the realms, except a little more vicious.

The Honorable Albert S. Whitney IV, BA, MA, MDiv, LLM, Esq., Dr. Whitney to everyone who spoke his name out loud, was smack in the middle of it.

"Be careful around him, girl," Keia cautioned as she rang Tonya up on a register that still used an iPad for its screen. "He's not afraid to traffic with thugs, you know what I'm sayin'?"

Tonya did. So she ordered the dress and hat combo from Amazon that Keia said would express humility to people who seemed to require it yet still assert that she was not a sister to be trifled with. The new hat looked good with the perm Keia had given her.

The morning service itself was lovely, and very different from her Catholic church back home. She had to admit that this little church, with its singing and dancing and hugging and praising, well, they had their own version of the Christian truth. She couldn't help but be uplifted by it.

Until it was time for her appointment. Dr. Whitney didn't preach anymore. That duty was left to his nephews and nieces. He sat in a place of honor during the service, and in a large office at the end of a long hall once it was over. The walls of the hall were lined with padded benches, now filled with people of all ages, each obviously in some sort of need. A very neatly dressed young man would come out of Whitney's office, address a person by name, and bring them inside. Tonya glimpsed dark wood paneling and air hazed with cigar smoke before the door closed. The only thing the scene lacked was "The Godfather Waltz" playing faintly in the background.

The impression was far stronger when it was Tonya's turn to go inside. Balance was tricky in her low-heeled shoes on the thick carpet. The paneled walls were dark, tasteful, and extremely expensive, perfectly matching the heavy leather chairs in the room, and the desk Whitney sat behind. There was a huge man guarding the door, wearing a suit that cost more than Tonya's Alfa, two older men dressed more impressively, and a woman of roughly the same age as the men who gazed at her with hard, calculating eyes.

"Ah," Whitney said with a gentle charm lilting through his voice. "Miss Brinks. *Cousin* Brinks. So good to see you again." He leaned toward her without getting up, hand held out. The impression of a bishop offering her his ring for a kiss was palpable. She managed to shake his hand firmly.

"Thank you for seeing me." *Godfather.* Tonya swallowed. "Dr. Whitney."

"My pleasure." The young man who had shown her in handed Whitney the manila folder with her rental request inside. He examined the contents and said, "It seems our distant cousin is quite the scientist and is looking to rent our airport." He peered across the table at her, and his accent suddenly went thick. "What you need a whole airport for? You not smugglin' anythin', are ya?" He laughed at his own joke, which cued the room to laugh with him.

Tonya smiled and played along. "No, not at all. It's a matter of the space I need, and the comparative lack of signal interference."

He casually waved her silent. "I'm only jokin'." His accent returned its normal meticulous articulation, calculated to impress. "Of course you can have use of the facility." He indicated the older lady who had been gazing at Tonya like a dark basilisk the entire time. "Angela will help you with the details. And the fee. Please, continue to enjoy the service."

Well that was quick, she thought as she was politely but firmly guided through a different door into the church's parking lot with Angela close behind. The door clicked shut, and a comprehensive rental agreement landed in her message queue. The fee was large but not outrageous. She *was* renting an entire airport. It even included a caretaker's quarters.

"I assume this meets your requirements?" Angela asked archly as they walked toward the front of the church.

Tonya stopped at the base of the steps. "It does. Thank you for your assistance."

Angela stuck with her nothing-but-business attitude. "We may come by and inspect your work, and there will still be charters coming and going. The scheduled ones are in your packet. You'll be informed of any new ones as they're registered. Please do not interfere with them."

"Of course."

Angela grabbed her hand in a fierce handshake. "Enjoy the rest of the services." She released her hand before Tonya could adjust her grip and crack a few of this cold bitch's bones.

*

Helen took an immediate and intense interest in the meeting after Tonya told her about it sitting in the tiny breakroom of her restaurant's kitchen, slurping noodles for supper.

"How tall was the first man?"

"What did the guard weigh? In kilos?"

"Hair color? Eye color?"

"What color were Dr. Whitney's socks?"

Tonya threw up her hands at that last one. "I don't remember, any of it. Nobody can remember those things."

Helen raised an eyebrow, then closed her eyes. "The couple that was seated at the table I cleaned before I came back here. Let me tell you about them." She then reeled off a line of statistics about them that included height, weight—in kilos—hair color, eye color, and yes, even the color of their socks.

She opened her eyes and smirked. "Go check."

Great. She'd gotten pulled into one of Helen's contests. But Tonya could score a point if any of it was wrong, so she checked anyway.

No points for Tonya.

"Well, okay, *you* can do it," she said when she returned, "but I can't. Why do you care?"

"You catalog the details in case they turn out to be important later on."

A man called out in Chinese, and Helen replied. She switched back to English. "That's my break. Here," she handed Tonya a large, heavy, hot paper bag, "that should cover us for my day off tomorrow."

The smell of various kinds of Chinese food made her mouth water. "You actually take one now and then?"

Helen put her apron on. "I do now that I have something to investigate. That airport's not kosher."

Tonya chuckled. "Kosher?"

"You don't negotiate a secret technology deal with Israelis without picking up a phrase or two. Oy, the stories I could tell."

*

"Welcome," Spencer said as he put the car in park, "to the Billy Free Memorial Airport."

Helen leaned forward from the back seat. "Where's the rest of it?"

Tonya wondered about that herself. There was a low-slung airport hangar on the right, with a few more industrial-looking buildings on their left.

"A tornado came through and blew most of it away a few years back. Your Dr. Whitney is responsible for all this."

"But where's the runway?" Tonya asked.

"Right in front of you." He pointed. "I told you this place was flat."

In the near distance Tonya could make out a dark black line that ran from left to right on a very close horizon. Or hill. That had to be a rise of some sort. Now that Spencer had pointed it out, she realized it was the crown of a runway not a hundred yards away. She'd never had to stare at a landscape for it to make sense until now.

As they scouted around, Tonya used her phone's maps to plant small survey flags where sensor packages would need to be placed around the airport. When it was all laid out, the site was better than she'd hoped. It was as flat as a pool table.

"Yeah," Spencer said as they walked toward the caretaker's quarters. "They spent a lot of money leveling the whole property. That's another thing people who aren't from around here don't get. You want to dig anywhere else in the world, you have to worry about hitting boulders, or maybe bedrock. Here? Dig deep as you want, it's dirt all the way down. My grandad said there used to be canals everywhere because all you needed to make one was a backhoe and some time."

Tonya sent her access token to the realtor lock box that hung around the door handle. It beeped once, then popped open and disgorged a set of keys. She unlocked the door, and they all stepped inside.

It was small, about the size of a single bedroom apartment back home. The living room and dining room were one space, with the kitchen separated by a counter. The furnishings were basic: a table with four chairs, a couch, and an ancient TV screen. The bedroom had a clean double bed, and the bathroom was your basic toilet and shower. Tonya opened a virtual window and arranged an air-drop of sheets, towels, and kitchen basics.

"Holy shit," Spencer said from the living room. "Guys? You need to come check this out."

He was sitting on the couch with his eyes closed. Leave it to Spencer to check out the house's realmspace before the toilet. Tonya sat down beside him and logged in herself.

The brief headrush should've been followed by walking into a realm of some sort, but that wasn't what they found. There was nothing. It had been annihilated, leaving only the bare white Bbox walls behind. And in the center?

The unmistakable remains of one of Kim's anomalies. A *big* one.

"What the fuck is *that* doing here?" Spencer asked.

They were supposed to be small, almost undetectable. "I wish I knew," Tonya replied.

Chapter 30
Mike

With little else to do, they entertained themselves keeping up with Tonya's latest experiment. The discovery of a new, larger anomaly was a bad omen. Whatever was going wrong seemed to be getting worse. Helen's idea that the anomalies were somehow targeted at Kim wasn't supported by any evidence, but Mike had a feeling it might be time to revisit that.

They also tried to learn more about their destination, but asking Maff about the Death Eaters was a study in frustration. Her complete knowledge of them took about ten minutes to tell. They wore robes, nobody ever saw their faces or ever spoke with them. They were the galaxy's boogey men.

And they were on the same planet as Will.

She ended with, "They recycle planets, and people sentenced to live on their worlds never return."

"That's it?" he asked.

She gave her version of a shrug. "Some of the great families meet with them to market their recycled materials, but those negotiations are sealed by the AC network. The rest of the galaxy only learns about it long after they're done."

Kim discussed a few strategies with him, but without more to go on, they weren't much more than generalities. He spent the rest of the time keeping tabs on their fellow inmates. He was more than a match for any one of them, but together they could be dangerous.

"Prepare for dimension transit and disembarkation. Repeat: prepare for dimension transit and disembarkation."

The announcement sent them all scrambling. They'd selected their kit carefully, but it didn't pack itself. Well, Maff's did, and Mike lost precious seconds gawking at the way it all folded up and tucked away into and on her suit.

"Move it, Sellars!" Kim shouted as she threw a wadded-up bedroll at him.

He was still tugging and adjusting straps and braces when the door latches unlocked with the crazy whirring clacks of their planetary gearsets. The galaxy was driven by small automatic transmissions. It was one of the least most amazing things he'd discovered so far.

Mike stepped out into the cold and was immediately struck by their surroundings. The too-wide streets lined with mounds that were once too-wide houses, broken towers in the distance jutting up like dead trees. It was good news, but also bad news.

They were closer to Will. The tug of the thread he'd left behind had a direction and an end point he could feel. But the thread didn't point to the horizon. It pointed down, between his feet. Will was on the opposite side of the planet. Spencer had warned them they might be in for a long walk. Mike hadn't counted on it being as long as it could possibly be.

The ship reentered the transit dimension with a fading sizzle as its skein activated.

Suddenly Kim screamed and something knocked Mike to the ground. He heard the unmistakable swish of a blade and barely managed to avoid a combat knife aimed at his ear. It thumped into the snowy ground, held by a scaly hand.

Feviz. The hand was too big to be Gaanan.

"Pallun-loving scum!" he shouted as he worked the knife free.

Kim kept screaming, joined by the more mechanical shrieks of Maff's suit legs.

He needed to get up *right now.* Mike braced and threw Feviz off his back. The big alien landed with an *oof* as he crashed into the ground a few feet away. Mike used the momentum to roll, popping his backpack latches free and shucking it out of the way.

Kim was still shrieking, and now he knew why. De'Tan, the fox captain, had grabbed her by her shoulders. The touch madness would prevent her from fighting back. Worse, she might get sick in her respirator, and that could be deadly. Maff was trying to fight off Elsek, who was using feet and wings to pluck away parts of her suit and smash them on the ground. Gaanan was trying to tangle her legs at the same time.

Feviz jumped up, knife in hand. "You're trapped here with us now, *alien*."

Mike pulled a rusty bar from a pile of garbage. "Oh no, that's where you're wrong." He needed to get to Kim. Her screams were going ragged. "*You're* trapped here with *me*."

If it had been one-on-one and Mike didn't have anyone else to worry about, the fight would've been comically simple. Feviz knew street fighting; Mike could see it in his stance and the way he held the knife. Mike had five different moves that would have laid him out flat. But he needed to get De'Tan off Kim first. Mike feinted left and then ran past Feviz on the right, tripping the alien as he went by.

Out of the corner of his eye, Maff went down in a blaze of sparks. Make that two people to worry about now.

Three quick strides put him within reach of De'Tan, and now Mike saw the fox had a knife in his hand, too.

"Be still you alien *bitch*, or you're gonna get hurt!"

"Hey!" Mike shouted, and when De'Tan turned, Mike swung his improvised bat into the fox's chin, snapping his head back with a solid crack. He flew off Kim and landed in a heap.

Kim rolled away, retching.

Without a conscious thought, Mike moved to the left as Feviz's knife slashed, turning a stab in the back into a slice across his arm. Mike carried his momentum into a spin-kick and scissored his legs around the lizard-man's neck. There was no way to know if Feviz's vulnerabilities were like those of a human, but gravity and inertia worked the same everywhere. Mike twisted his body to make sure he landed on his back as they fell.

Feviz landed on his head.

The thud felt denser than it would if Mike had put a human down like that. His skull must've been thicker or better braced. It still either stunned him or knocked him out, and he dropped the knife. Mike used it to spike Feviz's foot to the ground. If the alien came to before Mike was ready, it would take some time to work free, and he wouldn't be as fast or as sneaky with a two-inch cut clean through his foot.

That left Maff, who was in better shape than he'd expected. Her fall had trapped the other lizard-man, Gaanan, underneath her. Elsek had gotten tangled up in Maff's probes, and now squawked indignantly, trying to get free.

"Oh no you don't," Maff growled out as she shifted in response to one or the other of her erstwhile attacker's moves. "You're not going anywhere."

"That's enough!" Kim shouted. She'd climbed up onto a mound of garbage with a rifle in her hands. He didn't know where she got it from, but now was not the time to ask questions.

The fight went out of Elsek and Gaanan. Both aliens stopped struggling, holding up hands and wings.

"Where's Hafurnal?" she asked.

The fern cautiously stood up from behind a different pile of garbage. "Here!"

"You're still a medical officer, right?"

"Well, like, yeah. That part's not bogus."

Kim pointed the rifle at him. "Good," she said. "It seems your friends have gotten hurt. You should check them out. Mike? Are you all right?"

Testing his left arm, the cut on it announced itself loudly, but he'd had worse. "For certain values."

"Not now, Sellars. Maff, can you stand?"

"I don't trust them!"

"Trust *me*, Maff. Can you stand?"

She released Elsek, who plopped to the ground in a pile of ruffled feathers. The legs on Maff's suit squeaked now, but she stood. "Yes."

"Good. Mike, get your backpack. Maff? Pick up what you can. You two," she said, motioning at the two aliens Maff had released, "help Hafurnal. We are leaving. Maff, Mike, walk toward me."

Kim stood rigid guard from the top of her hill while Hafurnal and company hauled Feviz and the captain into the lee of a ruined house. Once he and Maff were safely behind Kim's hill, she said, "Do not follow us, do you understand?"

She didn't wait for an answer, instead turning and marching down the hill. The march went wobbly as she got to the bottom. "Shit! Not now! Not yet!"

"Kim!" He said, running toward her. "What's wrong?"

"Touch…held it off…I can't—" She spasmed hard and collapsed onto the ground, throwing her rifle away in the process. It was the rod Mike had used to tee off on De'Tan's head.

"Kim!" he slid to a stop on his knees beside her, his wound already healing up as the last of the sa'dst did its work. There were runnels of vomit tracing down the front of her coat. She hadn't aspirated it, thank God, but that was the only good news. The spasms got worse.

"What's wrong with her?" Maff asked.

He watched Kim, barely able to speak. "She can't be touched. It hurts her, a lot. Nobody can touch her." He looked around, trying to find some sort of cloth.

"I can touch her," Maff said gently, "I've done it many times before. I didn't understand why she seemed to enjoy it. I think I do now." Maff used her now dented and scratched manipulators to lift Kim onto the back of her suit. Other manipulators carefully removed her backpack and secured it next to her. "Come on, we need to go."

They walked until they couldn't see Kim's hill anymore, then turned toward the ruined city on the horizon. "There will be shelter there," Maff said. "I'm thinking it will take some time for her to recover from karnather?"

"I don't know what that means." He checked on Kim. Her spasms were almost gone now, and she'd slipped into unconsciousness. A small mercy, but he'd take it.

"Of course you don't," Maff said as she walked, squeaking and clanking. "You've never heard it before. F'klaff, I have been so blind."

"I don't understand."

"You don't need to, not yet. We have a bigger problem."

Worse than all of this? "What's wrong, are you okay?"

"I am now, but I won't be for long. See this?" she indicated a shattered box on her back next to Kim. "This was my food synthesizer. It was the first thing Elsek destroyed when she attacked me."

Stay away from things that need power, Spencer had said. "You don't have," without Interpreter threads, they'd been using a pidgin of English, Maff's Pallundian, and Standard, so it took Mike a minute to work out the words, "food reserves? Can we share ours with you?"

"No, and no. My people don't work that way. We don't store food, we can't. We evolved on a gas giant. You don't need to store food, it's all around you. We graze constantly. Without sa'dst or my synthesizer, I can't share yours. It's not poisonous, but it's also not what I need."

That added up to an ugly conclusion. "You're starving?"

"Starving implies running out of reserves. I don't have any. If we don't figure this out in the next few parns…" *Hours*. For the first time Mike heard a quiet, desperate tone in her voice. "Well, you'll need to figure out how to get Kim to wake up after that. I won't be able to carry her."

"Maff, stop."

She did.

"Let me look at that."

It was the same concoction of discrete circuits and quantum lattices that made up everything else in their tech. "How long do you have?"

She made a sound that was close to a sob. Sudden hope tended to do that to people. "If we take it easy, find shelter? Three, maybe four hours."

Tight but doable. "Okay. Let's find a place to settle down. I need to go scrounging."

They found a low-rise building that created a cave when it collapsed. Mike got the biggest of their portable shelters out and snapped it together. Once the atmosphere exchanger showed green, he took Kim's outfit off and cleaned her up. She slept the entire time.

"Will she be okay? Maff asked as she watched.

"I think so." *You hear me, baby? Be okay.* "Now, let me get a better look at your synthesizer."

He found Helen working with Spencer and Tonya, building out the latest of her experiments. They spent the next half hour doing their standard game of telephone, but at the end they'd figured out what Maff's device was.

"It's a fucking reactor for making ammonium nitrate," Spencer said. "Be careful with that thing. Your friend's gizmo would make for a pretty goddamned big bomb."

"Can we fix it?"

"Yeah, but you'll have to go hunting. Look for these items." They'd worked with enough Bemian tech to have a catalog of parts figured out. "I repeat: do not fuck this up, otherwise...boom!"

Mike promised to be careful.

He signed off and opened his eyes. Maff was staring at him intently. "You use threads."

"What?"

"Your communication method, with your sister. It's thread based, isn't it?"

Mike gathered up his suit, wishing Kim would wake up. She was much better at handling Maff's uncomfortable questions. "It's complicated. I've got a parts list, I gotta go." It wasn't his most convincing exit, but what it lacked in subtlety it made up for by being simple.

It took a lot of searching to find what he needed in the silent dead city as he moved around using every stealth skill he inherited from his host. It would keep him hidden as he worked, but he still had the sensation that someone was watching him. It was too quiet, too still. His realspace brain had evolved defenses against motion and if there wasn't any, it supplied its own. He jumped at shadows that weren't there and heard crashes that didn't break the silence.

Then he found footprints.

It wasn't the *Last Island* crew. They were too far away and in the wrong direction. Heavy boots hid the specific shapes of the feet that made the tracks, but there were several large sets, and a few that clearly were nonhumanoid. Mike wasn't Spencer; he couldn't tell how many there were or how long ago they'd passed through, but one thing was certain.

The Death Eaters were nearby.

Mike returned to find Maff visibly reduced in size and spirit. Kim was sitting up, looking shaky but otherwise okay.

"How much time does she have?" he asked.

"Work..." Maff wheezed twice. "Fast..."

Kim reconstructed the lattices while Mike used a cobbled-together soldering station to fix the circuits. The repairs didn't take very long, thank goodness, but there was a problem.

"We need to get clear before you turn it on." Spencer was right. The reaction it used was violent if it wasn't properly contained, especially if the heat wasn't handled properly.

She nodded weakly. "Hurry."

They ran a dozen paces away and then hid behind a thick pile of debris. "Okay," he shouted, "turn it on!"

A whine started up that increased in pitch and volume. He shared a look with Kim. "You did tighten the coolant couplings to the proper torque, right?"

"That wasn't a torque wrench. It was some angle iron with a hole cut in it." She pulled a handkerchief out, and they held it tight together.

The whine reached a pitch that couldn't be good. There was a loud *clank*. They both jumped but then the noise faltered and began to subside. It eventually went quiet.

"Guys?" Maff called out. "It's okay, you can come back."

Maff looked one hundred percent better, with Kim's torque wrench in one of her manipulators. "First," she said, "thank you. I would have died without this. Second," Maff motioned them into the tent. "Sit down. I figured some things out on our walk over here. We need to have a talk about Interpreters."

Chapter 31
Spencer

He'd just moved out, and now he was back. Back to a town that thought Amazon was a river in the jungle, where phone books were still a thing, and a big city was any town with a five-digit population. *Low* five digits.

Mike's drawings and designs of holy-shit-you're-not-kidding alien technology helped keep him occupied. The impressive thing was how unimpressive it was turning out to be. The Bemians had mastered portal tech who knew how long ago, but that seemed to be it. The rest of it was discrete circuits, fucking transistors and diodes, shit like that, coupled with some admittedly far out bridgework into quantum lattice computation and storage. As far as he could tell, they'd gone from 1950s transistor radios straight to unduplicates, with no middle step. It was fucking bizarre.

The rest of his time was spent fending off attempts by grandma to get him to go to church—which would be the day a guy with a pitchfork and horns showed up at her back door with snow on his shoulders telling her to knock it the fuck off—and keeping Tonya and Helen from going native. He hardly saw Helen at all. If she wasn't stocking groceries or taking orders at the only decent restaurant in town, she was helping the local PD with every job they'd give her. He didn't know when, or even if, she slept.

Tonya had turned into a kind of hermit, hiding out in the caretaker's shack when she wasn't stringing various kinds of superconducting wire all around the airport perimeter. What she didn't understand was that in a small town, being strange set the clock back five hundred years. They didn't say *witch* out loud. They didn't need to. An odd woman doing weird things on the edge of town? The only reason they weren't cutting firewood and prepping a short telephone pole was that she went to church regularly. The *right* church, not some papist enclave worshipping the antichrist like the Catholics did.

At first, he was worried, but it was turning out to be amusing to watch the town try to come to terms with her. Tonya was young, single, and attractive. Hot, even, although in his book, Tonya was only one step down from Kim in his *don't fucking think about it* rankings. The point being that Tonya could nerd with the best of them, but in a social situation, she could charm the skin off an alligator.

It was that contradiction, by this place's standards, that was keeping her safe. Nerds were outsiders, outcasts, unclean, dangerous. They didn't play a proper role in the rigid caste system of a small Southern town. Tonya working on her experiments was definitely all that in jeans and a goofy Flat Mars Society T-shirt. But she was normal at church or in the beauty salon. He'd witnessed men who'd invited themselves over to the airport *to help out* leave shaking their heads and mumbling about how weird city girls were. It was a balancing act that Tonya played with skill.

She laughed when he brought it up the night after he helped move her and Helen into the caretaker's shack. Tonya's witchiness and Helen's demonic work schedule had served up a big enough distraction for the town that he no longer thought the lesbian angle was in play, so their living together was legal.

It was stupid, a total contradiction. Welcome to hell.

They were all standing in the dark out in the middle of the runway. Nothing was scheduled to use it tonight. Their breath fogged up in the cold air, but it wasn't so bad they needed heavy coats. It kept the mosquitoes at bay, thank God.

"I know exactly what I'm doing, Spencer," Tonya said. "I still don't see why you hate it here. The people are perfectly fine in their own way."

Helen slurped down some godawful-smelling fish thing as she sat in a lawn chair next to the telescope he had hauled out of storage. "The interplay of the various factions is fascinating. You actually have guanxi, but it works differently than back home. Churches are central to it. This is very different from China."

"Fucking busybody grayhairs getting up in everyone's business, you mean," he growled as he refined where the telescope was pointing.

"That's not it at all," Helen replied. "It's like you're not from—"

"There," he said, cutting Helen off, "right there." If they kept trying to defend Dumas, he was going to scream. He shared the telescope image feed.

It wasn't much to look at—stars generally weren't—but if Mike's triangulation on Will's planet was accurate, then Mike and Kim were orbiting that star. Sort of. What they were seeing was light that left the star thousands of years ago, so the image was of the star they *would* be orbiting. But it was still a star that had a planet full of aliens orbiting it. They had concrete proof of that now.

He found himself holding hands with Helen and Tonya. The only sound was the wind rustling the grass in the night as they shared a private moment with one of the most profound discoveries in human history.

"We're gonna have to tell somebody about this eventually," he said.

"You don't think they already know?" Tonya asked.

"They don't," Helen said with her characteristic bluntness. "Something this big would be in files I had access to, and it wasn't. We'd either have found out ourselves or gotten it from spies."

"It's not *we* anymore, Helen," Spencer said. "It's them." The silence curdled around him. *Shit*. "Sorry."

"No, you're right," she said in a way that made it not feel right at all. "Anyway, as far as knowing about what's out there? We're it."

In the distance, he heard a vehicle pull onto the road leading to the airport. They all brought the assault rifles he had quietly liberated from Dad's gun safe to their shoulders. The ID carat appeared in his enhanced vision channel, and Spencer handed his gun to Helen. "Relax, guys, I know who this is." He climbed into the golf cart they'd found parked behind the caretaker's quarters and turned the headlights on. "I'll be right back."

The *who* was easy. The *why* wasn't. Spencer hadn't reached out to Stewart because it didn't feel right, but that didn't stop him from being in Spencer's contact list, which explained why his name showed up as soon as his truck was in range. That Stewart knew where to find him also wasn't a surprise. Their current situation was a main topic of gossip from here to Monticello, where he'd found out Stewart was a volunteer EMT.

But arriving unannounced was weird, and right now, weird was a warning sign. Maybe he shouldn't have left the gun behind.

Stewart stopped the truck under a streetlamp.

Spencer checked behind him as he got out of the cart, and as expected, the only way he could tell where Helen and Tonya were was by the telltales in his enhanced vision. Stewart, who didn't have their contacts on his list, would see nothing.

Everything okay? Helen sent.

For now.

This gun sight is very nice. It integrates with my phone perfectly.

Helen with a loaded rifle at his back made him want to walk in a Z, but that would look funny. *Safety on, please.*

Pffft. I'm not an amateur.

"Spencer Mackenzie," Stewart shouted as he climbed out of his truck. "How the hell are ya?" He'd gained weight since Spencer had last seen him but not a lot. The limp was barely there, but it didn't seem to crunch the old Stewart spirit as he walked forward, arm straight out. The handshake turned into a slapping bear hug. "I never thought we'd see you back."

"Me, either," he said as they pulled apart. "But here I am."

"How's your mom doing?"

This started the standard Southern greeting game of *Are Your Relatives About to Die or What?*

"That's great, man, that's great," he said once they finished, then looked around. "Listen, are you free right now?"

That was a little quick. "Sure, what for?"

Stewart looked around again, and now his nerves were spreading to Spencer. "The airport gives me the creeps. You up for some pool?"

Stewart's dad owned a pool hall-slash-juke joint off Main Street called The Office. They'd hung out there countless times as kids, but only during the day after school, not on a weekend night. "There gonna be a table waiting?"

Stewart smiled, and he was the high school quarterback who was everyone's friend again. "There's always a table waiting."

Still okay? Helen sent.

Fine. Going into town for a bit. I'll let you know if you need to send in the cavalry.

They continued with meaningless pleasantries about friends, the weather, and life as an EMT all the way to the bar. It was busy, but as predicted, a table was free.

After Stewart made the first break, Spencer couldn't take it anymore. "What made you look me up, man?"

The smile went artificial. "I wanted to hang out with an old buddy."

You set up a screen here, Stewart texted, *remember?*

It was his first successful recreation of a Rage + the Machine hack, and he'd never taken it down. Not that anyone cared, but The Office was protected by a firewall that could keep, *had kept,* the FBI and the NSA out.

Why is that important? He asked as they continued meaningless small talk in realspace.

Shit's going down, man. And I think it involves your friends.

Spencer scratched, sending the cue ball sluicing down a corner pocket. This was not a time to screw around. *Explain that.*

"Hey," Stewart said out loud, with a smile on his face but dead-cold seriousness in his eyes. "You need to calm down, man. It's only a game."

I'm an EMT now, you know that right?

Sure.

We're getting a lot of callouts, all around the area. People waking up in fields, zombie-walking out of houses, losing time, it's fucked up.

That didn't explain anything. *Why do you think it has something to do with us?*

Remember that chick you used to obsess about back in the day?

He meant Kim, or rather Angel Rage. Spencer held it together and sank the nine ball. *Yeah, what about her?*

These are the drawings we found at the last callout.

He shared four roughly sketched pictures on sheets of paper that had rust-colored streaks on them. *Is that…*

Blood. Yeah. They're getting harder to restrain now.

The first one was Kim. The next one was Mike. The third one was Ozzie, the homicidal maniac who'd nearly triggered a thermonuclear exchange between China and India. The fourth one made the connection.

Helen.

That's your Asian friend, isn't it? The one who waits tables at old man Wong's joint?

He was still trying to get over the fact that three of the four people in these drawings had never set foot in the state, let alone his hometown. *Who made these?*

Stewart shrugged. *An old lady south of McGehee.*

He and Stewart needed to get out of here, the sooner the better. The screens were good, but they were old, and he didn't understand what they were up against anymore. Spencer concentrated hard. *Come on, baby.*

The eight-ball dropped into the side pocket like a stone.

He smiled at Stewart, and hoped it looked sincere. "I still got it."

We need to go, but not attract attention.

"Fuck you, man," Stewart said with less conviction than Spencer liked. "I bet you can't do that with darts."

The dart boards were next to the exit. It would have to do. "Double or nothing."

"You're on."

He opened a channel to Tonya.

We have a new problem.

Chapter 32
Kim

"Interpreters," Maff said as they sat in their shelter around the little camp stove Mike had unfolded from their kit, "are the final sign that a society is ready to join the galaxy. When a civilization reaches the proper level of sophistication, the correct modes of culture, they emerge."

"Is it something the nodes do?" Mike asked.

"That's what our history books say." She paused. "I don't think that's right anymore."

Here, isolated together in a planet-spanning wasteland, Kim felt no need to hide her ignorance. "Why?"

Again, Maff paused. She seemed thoughtful and a little confused. "This is more difficult to explain than I expected it would be. I'm trying to reconcile what I know with what I've experienced with you. It's hard when you discover that everything you were taught is a lie."

Kim shared a look with Mike. "We've got a decent idea of what that's like."

"Yes," Maff agreed, "I understand that now, too. Your civilization isn't on the cusp of joining the network." Her voice pitched down to an incredulous half whisper. "Your civilization has never been contacted at all. On your planet, there's no founding node, no AC network, is there?"

Kim looked at Mike, who nodded slightly. It was time to tell Maff the truth.

"No," Kim said. "We'd never heard of any of this until now. None of us have. In fact," she chuckled at the absurdity, "some of us think we're it, that Earth is the only inhabited planet in the galaxy."

Maff shook her head. Kim wasn't sure if it was in wonder or disgust. "In all of our history, right back to the Refounding, there has never been a record of an uncontacted civilization. It's not in any of our pre-Refounding legends, either. None that I know of. The nodes always bring a civilization into the light."

Mike cocked his head, something he always did when he encountered a new idea. "But how does that happen?" he asked. "What are the details?"

"The nodes are everywhere, seeded throughout the galaxy at the beginning of time. We don't know who did it, or why. The nodes watch, and they listen. When they discover a planet that is ready to be connected to the galactic network, one or more—and it's usually more—descend to the surface and announce their presence. They are the ones that transform savage, dangerous cultures into ones ready and able to peacefully join the galaxy."

Maff had switched to a cadence that was a kind of chant, and most of the words she used were more related to Standard than her native Pallundian. "That's what you're taught," Kim said. "Is that what happens?"

"Almost always. I thought we were the only exception." This was a private thing for Maff, something she was afraid of.

"Can you explain that?" Kim asked gently.

"It's why everyone hates us. We rejected the nodes. We were separate, special, chosen by *Turlanfador*."

"Turlanfador?"

Maff shook her head. "An ancient founding story of my people that would take too long to explain. At any rate, because we thought we should remain separate, we fought the nodes, and we won. Briefly. We were independent, the first and only time that has ever happened. But without the stabilizing guidance of the nodes we created terrible weapons that would've threatened the existence of the galaxy if we hadn't been stopped. If our system hadn't been destroyed."

If they were that powerful… Kim started to interrupt, but Mike held up his hand and mouthed *not now.*

Maff, staring at the glow of the camp stove, didn't seem to notice. "We've been held up as the single example of what happens to a civilization that grows without guidance ever since." She looked at them. "And now that could all be a lie." She stretched, shaking off her tension. "The point is that civilizations do not survive without AC guidance."

"And yet here we are," Mike said.

"And yet here you are. I couldn't get my wings around the idea until we arrived here," she turned to Kim, "and I saw how you reacted to De'Tan grabbing you."

Kim rocked back. Maff somehow knew about her syndrome. "How?"

"As I said, Interpreters emerge when a society is about to join the AC network. The first sign they have arrived is so well known they've written songs about it. Most civilizations treat it as a holiday." She reached out and grasped Kim's hand with a manipulator. "It's when children are born who can't be touched."

"But I'm not—it's Mike who—" Kim's mind couldn't grapple with it. *Mike* was related to the Interpreters, that had been clear ever since he encountered a translator thread. *She* was only a thief with a knack for languages. Her abilities were uniquely human. In that moment, she realized a hope that'd been hidden in the back of her mind: if they could unlock what she was, they could use her talent to create not only portals, but other technologies that would protect Earth from this terrible galaxy. Because it was terrible. The longer they were in it, the worse it got.

But Kim wasn't a resource. She was a symptom.

Mike stepped into the silence. "Interpreters are thread based. We saw that. Kim doesn't have those." He squared his shoulders, and she could almost see him say *in for a penny* to himself. "I have them."

"Exactly," Maff said. "That's another impossibility. Threaded life forms emerge as well, but only in *poinfur.*" She paused and tapped her legs in a ripple pattern, her version of drumming her fingers on a table. "You call them *rehelmspayshes*."

The pronunciation needed work, but Kim understood her. "Realmspaces. Yes."

"It confused me though. You use the same word that we use when we go to various virtual places, for shopping, entertainment, communications, and other things? *Nakantar*?"

That was the Standard word. "Correct," he said. "It's the same place, I live in a different part."

"Not here, you don't. *Sletran,* your type, only emerge from *poinfur.* They're very different from regular realmspaces. Those are never connected to a network before the joining."

"You've talked about that before," Kim replied. "What *is* joining?"

"The last piece of the puzzle, and the one that confused me the most. When children who can't be touched emerge, the Guild is contacted. They arrive bearing empty *poinfur*. *Sletran* form inside them and then emerge. They're provided with an *oftul* that allows them to exist with us."

Kim knew the words but not in this context. *Poinfur* was a freestanding realmspace. *Sletran* were the threads from someone like Mike. That let Kim put together what *oftul* must mean. Maff was talking about hosts. Biological hosts. "Provided? You *create* them?"

"Yes, but nothing like this," she pointed at Mike. "It's never a fully functional version of the native species. I wouldn't believe it was possible if you weren't sitting in front of me. No, the hosts exist to allow the joining."

Now Kim understood. The braiding, the differences, how she and Mike nearly lost control when she rescued him, all of it. "*The visible is joined with the invisible, the two become one, threads are tied with flesh.* They're *implanted*?"

"Exactly. They combine into a single entity. It's a terrible process."

"Wait," Mike said, paling. "You mean those threads are part of a real, conscious being?"

"Yes," Maff replied. "Early in their career, Interpreters are entirely thread based. The container that allows the threaded being to exist outside of its private realmspace absorbs the body of its biological component, and what's left is tended to by the chapter. Only after many decades of service do they resume a realspace existence, when they can."

"When they can?" Kim asked.

"A full life cycle is not guaranteed. Sometimes the combined entity doesn't wish to reenter realspace. Other times they lose their identity. The Interpreter loses…coherence. They forget they're anything but threads, and all that's left is their interpreting function."

Mike looked at Kim. "That explains why they felt so wrong to me. Zombie threads."

"Zshahom-bee?" Maff asked.

He smiled. "A mythical monster from our home world. They die, but come back by…well, it varies, but they come back as the walking dead. Mostly they wander around trying to eat brains."

"I don't understand the connection or the concept. Humans walk around after they die?"

They both laughed. "No," Mike said. "That's fiction. The connection is that those threads didn't feel right to me, not at all. They didn't seem completely alive."

Maff hadn't mentioned anything about different forms or being in more than one place at the same time. "What happens to the ones who make it out?" Kim asked.

"The container holding them both regenerates the biological component. But it's never the same as the original, there's always a deformity. Sometimes it's hardly noticeable, other times it prevents them from functioning without external care. After that, they become galactic envoys who travel around the galaxy negotiating treaties, working out contracts, helping the various cultures interact without violence. They can communicate instantly across vast distances with each other. They can also manipulate the AC network, which has led to many conflicts over the centuries."

That went some way toward explaining how Mike could hack the node at the courtroom, but it wasn't exactly what Kim was looking for. "Do they have any other...special abilities?" *Like turning to glass and being in more than one place at once?*

"Nobody knows for sure. The Guild is very secretive. I do know that their power grows if they gather together. The AC network prohibits that from happening in all but the most extraordinary circumstances."

Those last two words meant something more to Maff; Kim could hear it in her voice. "Would an entire planet defying the network count?"

She nodded grimly. "Yes. The Guild is not popular with my people. They helped conquer us long ago. Still, pallun contributes its share of Interpreters to them every generation. We have no choice. It's considered a terrible cruelty to prevent these special children from fulfilling their destiny."

"Because?"

"It's the only way to overcome their inability to be touched."

Kim stopped at the idea. "A combined Interpreter...can be touched?"

"Yes. It's one of the reasons they go through the ordeal. We're taught that to do otherwise would lead to madness. But you don't seem all that crazy to me."

Kim smiled through the memories of the breakdowns, the hospitalizations, the screamed ravings with her wrists tied to bedrails. "You haven't known me very long."

A ping sounded next to Mike. "Time to check the epoxy," he said.

Spencer had given them the plans for a sled that they could build. The epoxy gave off such a stench that they set it up outside. Maff moved to so he could get by, then asked her, "You're not combined, but you are pair-bonded. That much is obvious. How does that work in your civilization?"

"Guys?" Mike asked. It wasn't in a *this is cool* tone. It was in a *don't make any sudden moves* one. "I need you to come out here, but slowly."

He didn't sound injured. "Are you okay?"

"Fine. Come out, slowly."

Maff went first, as tense as Kim had ever seen her. It gave Kim a chance to nerve herself up. Whatever it was couldn't be good. She forced herself to put on her protective gear and stepped through the tent door.

The shapes formed a wide circle around the makeshift shelter: tall, mostly bipedal, covered in dark robes, and wearing respirators much more ornate than hers. There had to be several dozen. Many of them carried long metal poles with blades on the ends. Mike would have no chance with this many.

They stood facing each other silently. Kim forced her breathing to slow. It wouldn't do to panic now.

Not after they'd come face-to-face with the Death Eaters.

Chapter 33
Tonya

"How does this happen?" Tonya asked. The sketches Spencer's friend had brought over were crude, but the likenesses were unmistakable. "Where did they take this lady? Is she still there?" Tonya asked.

Spencer's friend, a big easy-going kid, unfocused his eyes for a second. "Monticello hospital is where we dropped her off last night. I'll bet she's still there."

It was another aspect of small-town life that Tonya still hadn't gotten used to: nobody thought it was strange at all to rely on another town's infrastructure. Hospital crumbling or nonexistent? There's one an hour away, no problem. Rental cars? They drive down from the same place. Movie theaters? They've got several, an hour's drive away, in different directions. It was nuts.

Still, a hospital was a hospital. Tonya looked at Spencer. "Can you get me in there?"

"Are you fucking kidding me?" He sent her the information packet. "Tonya Brinks got registered with Arkansas Medical Staffing last night and is on assignment to Monticello Memorial as of this morning. You're welcome."

"Nice," Stewart said, holding a big palm up.

Spencer thwacked it. "Horace needs some motorcycle parts from there. I can pick them up and save him the drone fee."

"We'll brief Helen in once we get more information," Tonya said. Maybe this would convince her to quit one of her jobs. She'd been crashing on the couch of the caretaker's house since they'd moved out of the hotel. At least that's what Tonya thought, because she always came in after Tonya had gone to sleep and left before she woke up. Spencer's worries about them being pegged as a lesbian couple were wide of the mark. The gossip mill understood that the enigmatic little Asian girl had no time for any sort of life. Truth be told, the entire town was beginning to worry about her. Tonya was, too.

But, as Spencer said, they had a bigger problem.

People chasing Kim was normal until recently. People going after Mike, or at least Mike's host, wasn't out of the question. An assassin must have enemies, although they hadn't found any yet. Tonya had a suspicion that was mostly down to the Bolivians caring more about whatever it was Kim had told them than the fate of their head assassin. Helen was the reason they were here in the first place, and Tonya still couldn't discount China trying to get her out here in the boonies.

But Ozzie? Ozzie was an enigma when he was alive. An *anonymous* enigma, the only other person they knew of who had Kim's touching syndrome. China had run a crazy shell game, giving him a fake identity as a realm sports champion while he used his hacking talents—another thing he shared with Kim—behind the scenes as a spy. He'd been dead, more or less, for a year now. The world only knew that a great realm athlete had died, and that person bore no resemblance to the real Ozzie.

The sketch was of the real one.

Ozzie had to be a clue, probably *the* clue to what was going on here. They just had to figure it out. It was time to pay Stewart's sketch artist a visit.

*

Tonya didn't realize how used to Dumas she'd gotten until they pulled into Monticello. Which was pronounced *mon-ti-SELL-oh,* because "Nobody knows how to pronounce shit around here," according to Spencer. The town was about three times bigger than

Dumas but had a commercial district that was about five times the size.

"It's the college," Spencer said. "The population goes up by nearly half during the school year. If there's a football or basketball game happening, it gets bigger."

She had to stop herself for a moment because this *big* city—and it was much bigger than Dumas—still only topped out at about fifteen thousand people. Tonya used to think a small town had a population of less than a hundred thousand. Everything else might move slowly around here, but perspectives changed in a hurry.

The hospital was, due to the same tornado that scrambled the airport a few years ago, brand new and state of the art. It was small but otherwise equal to anything she'd worked in recently. As promised, Spencer had assigned her to the same floor that their sketch artist, one Mrs. Daina Ramkin, age seventy-nine, was recovering in. An elderly widow with no surviving children was a thing around here, a sign of how bad the drug culture had been twenty years ago, back when overdose deaths couldn't be prevented with a phone app.

Diabetes, high blood pressure, and heart disease were present and accounted for. Her situation was made worse by a nasty case of exposure and serious dehydration. Mrs. Ramkin had been missing for most of a week and seemed to have spent that time walking straight through soybean and corn fields. Nobody knew how she'd managed to wade through streams and bayous while avoiding all the alligators and snakes Spencer talked about.

She'd been found on a road, but only because the road was between her house and Dumas and, in that particular spot, the road happened to be going her way. Stewart said she'd cut through a bean field before she'd climbed up onto the road. They connected the dots between her house and where she'd been found and then continued it forward. The line was obviously heading toward Dumas.

Daina was asleep when Tonya made her first rounds but was cheerful after a visit from her church group that afternoon. She had no problem at all discussing what had happened to her.

"It was a possession, pure and simple. Satan took hold of me and would not let me go. He whispered terrible things in my ear, things I couldn't understand but had to obey."

Her accent was thick—*wispurd turrbul thangs in mah year*—but Tonya had gotten used to it. "How could you obey if you didn't understand?" Tonya asked as she checked Mrs. Ramkin's vitals.

"Child, I can't tell you how, I just knew. I had to *go*, and nothing would stop me."

"Did something trigger it? Something you ate? Maybe a bad batch of medicine?" The lady was on an impressively long list of them.

"No, I don't right think that's what it was. The last thing I remember doing was watching an episode of *Scandal*," her voice became joyous, "I do love me some Olivia Pope! Team Fitz, all the way!" This triggered a coughing fit, so Tonya got her some ice water to calm it down. "Thank you kindly, dear. Anyway, no, it was only me and the TV. Well," she chuckled and patted Tonya on the arm, "what we all now call TV anyway. I never have figured out realmspace, but it's the only place to see shows anymore. I go to VirtuHouse myself. Reminds me of theaters back in the day."

That was interesting. "The last thing you remember is being connected to a realm?"

"That's right. It was the Lord telling me to go to church more often, that's what it was. Oh, he saved me, Nurse Brinks. It was the *Lord* who put me on that road, had those kindly boys pick me up. I do feel terrible about how I acted," she held up her heavily bandaged hands, "but Satan still hadn't let me go."

All the victims of whatever this was resisted any attempt to stop them. Daina fought hard enough to put Stewart's partner into the ER. The little old ladies around here were tough. "What about the drawings?"

"Drawings?"

"They found you with drawings." Tonya threw one up onto the screen Daina had been watching. "Like this one."

She concentrated. "Now child I will tell you the truth. I have an impression of drawing, of sitting down and needing to *see* what Satan wanted me to see, but I don't remember doing anything about it. Is that a real person? I hope not. I still don't know what Satan wanted me to do, but I know it wasn't good. Praise the Lord, I was released!"

*

She and Spencer pulled up to Mrs. Ramkin's house when Tonya's shift was over that afternoon. It was a brick ranch-style that wouldn't look out of place in any of the older suburbs back home plonked in the middle of huge, well-tended bean fields.

"Share cropping," Spencer said as they got out of the car.

Tonya had only heard that word in depression-era realm dramas, the kind that featured burning crosses and helpless families. She caught the reflexive *excuse me?* before it left her mouth and dialed it back a notch. It was time to stop assuming everything around here was about discrimination. "How does that work?"

"She owns the land. The farmer next door uses it to plant more of his crops. He keeps most of it, usually eighty percent, and gives the rest to the landowner. With a farm this size, it's good money. Plenty to live on. She's doing fine."

"That explains the gardens." There were two of them behind the house, well tended and neatly surrounded by flower beds.

"Shit. Gardening is easy on this soil. It's hard to *stop* things from growing. You think Malinda's harvest parties back home are something? I'll bet this one little plot yields more tomatoes than her whole garden."

Kim's mom always gave away her harvest during a massive fall garden party. Tonya remembered Spencer going home with two bushels of vegetables he'd "won"—everyone knew it was more of an excuse to get rid of the things than it was a prize—at the last one. They'd given them away to local soup kitchens.

"Here we are," Spencer said as he walked around a massive air conditioner enclosure. "One realmspace tap, comin' up."

The utilities had all been concentrated against a wall hidden behind the enclosure, including a satellite link used to access the low-orbit swarms of broadband realmspace providers.

"But Mrs. Ramkin said she only used her realm connection to watch old shows." That size link antenna would support an apartment complex.

Spencer laughed. "All these old biddies are *Candy Crush* veterans. When they came out with realm versions that included sports betting? Watch the hell out for Captain Bluehair."

He connected the tap wire to the house antenna, then to his phone. Tonya got a shared connection ping shortly after. When they accessed the household's realm, they found exactly what they were expecting.

Another empty Bbox with the remains of one of Kim's anomalies at the center. But this one wasn't sitting on the ground; it was in pieces scattered all around a single spot. The outlines of two bare feet were clearly visible.

"Well this sucks big green donkey balls." Spencer said. "Did it land on her?"

*

"Okay," Helen said after they gave her the rundown later that evening. "First of all, stop following leads without me. You two need training."

All things considered, Tonya thought they'd done well. "If you weren't always at work, we would've brought you along."

Helen's exhaustion was now clear to see. She claimed that losing China was water under the bridge, but Tonya doubted that now. The attempt on her life had led to consequences Helen wasn't facing. That would need to be addressed as soon as bigger problems quit happening.

"I know, and as of now, that stops. That's my second point. Spencer let me question Stewart while you were gone."

Spencer snorted. "He was worried you were gonna waterboard him."

Helen took it as a data point, not an insult. "Torture is for amateurs. He gave me access to all the zombie incidents they've dealt with, as well as those of nearby communities." A map of the local area manifested in their shared channel. Dots started lighting up. "For whatever reason, they start from the vic's home." A new set of dots lit up. "And they always move in a straight line. Observe."

The dots connected to each other, then extended in the direction of travel. They all converged, but not on Dumas. It was a set of small structures a few miles away, right on the bank of a wide river. Tonya recognized the bridge; it was the one she traveled over on her way into Dumas when they first arrived.

"Fuck me," Spencer said. "That's Pendleton."

"Which brings me to my third point. I've quit my jobs because I now have something more important to do, and so do you two. Effective tomorrow, we're going on a stakeout."

Tonya examined the trails closely. With some simple modifications, her new airport experiment could help prove this Pendleton connection. It was finally the right moment to give these two The Time Talk. "That's for tomorrow. Tonight is for science, and both of you need a better understanding of what is going on before we can continue." She sent them an address for a realm programmed to demonstrate what Tonya called *particulate time theory.*

That sounded dry as dust. The realm was altogether different.

"Well?" Spencer asked in the utter blackness of the realm. "What happens now?"

Tonya had practiced with Kim to make sure she got the pronunciation right. "*Yəhî 'ôr.*"

Let there be light in Hebrew, and there was light. But not just any kind of light.

"Oh goddammit," Spencer said, "I hate it when you and Kim pull this multidimensional bullshit." He closed his eyes tight as they tried to process light coming from directions that were at right angles to the common up and down, right and left, forward and back.

"Mike has talked about these places," Helen said, "I've never had time to try one." Her holo began a slow spin that picked up speed. "Stability seems to be an issue," she said dryly.

"Imagine the corner of a cube," Tonya said. "Then imagine a direction that is at a right angle to all of the lines that meet at that corner. That's how I beat vertigo the first time."

Her holo's spin gradually came to a halt, but there was still a bit of drift. Tonya ignored it. If she pointed it out Helen would get distracted trying to hold it rock steady to prove she could. Tonya needed their full attention for this.

"I have a better idea," Spencer said as a pair of classic Ray Ban's manifested on his face. "Let's get the job done."

After checking to make sure his disguised filters were only for orientation, she dove in.

"Quantum physics is based on particles. Everyone is familiar with protons, neutrons, and electrons." As she spoke, examples of each appeared and fell together to form a construct atom that was an electron cloud the size of a hot-air balloon surrounding a pair of marbles that spun until they blurred together. It wasn't exactly to scale, but that didn't matter for this demonstration. "Less well known are bosons."

The construct zoomed in as the nucleus of the atom slowed to a stop. Eventually it grew so large it became a flat surface, a planet made of an elementary pair of particles. Tonya adjusted the simulation to make the quarks that the proton was built of visible. Between them, other tiny particles zipped back and forth. It was another abstraction that would get her laughed out of any physics symposium, but if Carl Sagan could turn a dandelion into a spaceship… "These are responsible for transmitting the forces that, among other things, hold the atom together."

"Right," Spencer said as he tried to catch a gluon. "And if we screw with these the whole fucking thing explodes."

"This atom in particular," Helen said as she floated past him, "deuterium, is an important part of thermonuclear weaponry."

"True," Tonya replied, "but that's not what's important about it for our discussion. These smaller particles transmit forces, from which emerge the laws of physics that make the universe possible. Now," she activated the primary simulation, "hang on."

The entire realm traveled in every direction at once, distancing itself from common reality on a vector that was normally described as an equation. When it stopped, they were as far away from the physics of the quantum world as Earth was from the center of the galaxy.

"What the genuine fuck?" Spencer said after a dramatic swallow. "Where are we?"

The constructs that convinced her she was on the right track appeared. Mike had programmed the physics with his trademark realism, and then Tonya added her equations. The threads, simulated but otherwise no different than the ones in Cyril's room, emerged on their own.

"We are standing outside time," Tonya replied, barely holding her voice steady. They were the first people to see her demonstration. "These structures are the temporal equivalent of an atom. It's a composite made up of particles."

Helen's jaw fell open. "You created a theory that *quantizes time*?"

"I have." The realism contracts made the sweat on her realspace hands slick the palms of her avatar. She wanted to jump around like a maniac. *Look what I figured out!* But she held it together. They were only now getting to the good part. "And I have proof."

She called a single thread over. As it enlarged, it revealed a top-down look at the blue bug who started it all. "Everyone meet Cyril. Cyril," he looked up at them, "everyone."

Like the rest of it, the alien was a construct, a useful puppet to demonstrate the principles of her theory. And occasionally toss him off a cliff or drop a rock on him. Fate could sometimes be cruel to bugs who'd derailed her life so thoroughly.

"Cyril is in the present," she said as he resumed walking through an otherwise empty field. "This has a specific meaning in my theory. The present is where tockion particles are most efficiently created."

"Are you finally gonna fucking explain what those are?" Spencer asked.

"Yes. Tockions are the message particles of time. There are three types: the tickion, the tick-tockion, and the determion. Whenever a living creature observes an event," below them, a rabbit emerged from a hole and went over to sniff a flower, "a pair of tockions is created." Two tiny colored spheres, each about the size of a pearl, shot out of the rabbit and attached themselves to the flower. There were timers under each, one going forward, the other backward. "The blue one with the negative number is the tickion. It transmits present observations into the past. The red one with the positive number is the tick-tockion. It transmits present observations into the future. This is a simplification to let you see particle generation." She adjusted the simulation, and the field was buried in a faint mist of tockions. "This is what it really looks like."

"What is the effect of these particles?" Helen asked.

"In the present moment? Nothing. They have no mass and don't interact with matter in the present. Keep in mind *the present* in this theory is simply where tockions are most efficiently generated."

Spencer asked, "And what makes that happen?"

It was always surprising how quickly people could find the holes in a theory they'd just heard about. She shrugged. "I don't know. I haven't gotten that far. I can tell you that they don't do anything in the present." She turned off the layer of the simulation that showed the tockion particles to maximize the impact of the next part. "But if the living creature somehow gets displaced temporally…"

A portal appeared next to the rabbit in the field at the same time a clock appeared over it. When the rabbit hopped through, its clock jumped backward several hours. It was now alone on the field, earlier in the morning. When the portal vanished, there was nothing remarkable about the scene.

"And?" Spencer asked. "Seems normal to me."

Tonya turned the tockion layer back on and squinted as the scene was covered in brilliant shades of blue decorated with narrow lines of red. "*This* is what changed."

The dots covering everything in the simulation weren't still. They created streams that writhed and twisted, influencing what the rabbit did and did not do.

"Why is the blue so bright?" Helen asked.

"Tickions are a lot more powerful than tick-tockions. And before you ask, no, I don't know why. The effect, though, is that they create an influence that naturally protects the past from being changed in a way that would alter the present, again defined only as that point in time where tockions are most efficiently generated. The more tockions an object has absorbed in the present, the more times it's been observed, the more resistant it is to being changed in the past."

"No killing Hitler," Spencer said. "That sucks."

"It does," Tonya replied. "The present's tickions set the past, anchoring it."

"Like a kind of temporal cement," Helen said quietly.

"Correct. The more observations, the stronger the bond."

"But the tick-tockions," Spencer said as he pointed down. "They're still there. What are they doing?"

"I'm working on that. Tick-tockions communicate a force that is much weaker than the one the tickions create. Assuming they exist, which isn't certain yet. The experiment we're working on is the first one that has the potential to find them."

Spencer frowned. "But what do they *do*?"

"For that to be clear, we have to return to the present." She adjusted the simulation, and they were back with Cyril and the rabbit examining the flower. "Like I said, the force tick-tockions communicate is vastly weaker than tockions. I have to turn the sensitivity way up to see it even in simulation." She made some adjustments to the visibility contract. "Observe."

In the simulation, faint red traces danced across all the surfaces, including the rabbit and Cyril.

"Where are they coming from?" Helen asked. "Those aren't being emitted by the tick-tockions created by observations."

"No," This was the part that sent shivers down her spine. She didn't believe it at first, but the effect emerged from the theory as clearly as the past-fixing effect of the tickion. "They're coming from the future."

At once, Helen and Spencer said, "Wait, what?"

Tonya nodded. "I'm still not sure I believe it either. The signal is extremely weak, but the math makes it clear: tick-tockions transmit a force that carries information about decisions yet to be made."

This was the part that made her sick, because the most obvious explanation for the effect was that the future was as fixed as the past. Predestination made real, proven in theoretical physics and real-world experiments. Her faith would be based on a fundamentally wrong idea.

"Okay," Spencer said. "I'd call that seven different kinds of fucked up."

Helen cocked her head to one side. "And the determion?"

"It's the most enigmatic of all," Tonya answered. "I can barely simulate it." It was also the only hope she had right now of finding her way out of her theological trap. "I'm turning them on…now."

In the simulation, Cyril suddenly released a bomb-burst of gold particles. They flew off in all directions, surrounding and interacting with the other particles. The emission was continuous, creating a cloud of gold around him.

"Why isn't the rabbit making those?" Helen asked.

"It can't. Only intelligent life makes determions." She summoned a wand construct and used it as a marker to highlight the interesting, and hopefully real, effects. "Notice how it weakly interferes with tickions, but strongly interferes with tick-tockions."

"Whoa," Spencer said. "Intelligent life can change the timeline all on its own."

"And it's much more likely to change the future than the past?" Helen asked her.

"If I can prove it, yes."

"But then how…oh, I get it," Spencer said. "If the determions interfere strongly with tick-tockions, then the future is up in the air. I think. This shit is hard."

"You should try the math," Tonya said, at the same time allowing a little bit of hope to brighten her up. If Spencer and Helen immediately understood the implication, maybe it wasn't a big reach after all.

"No, thanks," Spencer said. "This shit is bad enough."

"And that's it?" Helen asked. "Just three particles are needed to make time… tick?"

Tonya didn't have a good answer for that one either. "I'm not sure. With these three particles and the forces they create, we get a robust timeline. We get the present, and why it's important. Inevitability emerges. If humans are influenced by the tick-tockion's force, and for complicated reasons I think that's likely, it makes prophecy, premonition, and déjà vu plausible. Most importantly, free will is preserved. Intelligent life naturally interferes with the effects of the tick-tockions. The future is not fixed. The past is only mostly fixed. Both can be changed by intelligent life, the past by a little, the future by a lot."

"Well that's my quota for what-the-fuck-ness today," Spencer said as he stared wide-eyed at the scene below them. "What do you need from us?"

*

Spencer had to stay back at the shack to keep an eye on "a bunch of fucking dials, are you fucking kidding me, this isn't the twentieth fucking century anymore" while she and Helen made final adjustments to the wiring loom around the airport perimeter.

"Explain to me again why you think free will is so important," Helen said as she staked out more of the superconducting wire that made up the experiment.

Helen's blunt questions forced Tonya to state her case as clearly as possible. "If it's all preordained, then there is no hope. We are helpless automatons stuck in grooves we can't perceive. This has been debated for centuries, but now I might have stumbled onto a way to scientifically prove it."

"And that's bad?" Helen asked as she moved to the next tensioner.

Tonya checked Helen's work. Her questions might be hard, but her precision was second to none. She got three decimals of accuracy using her hands and a pair of tweezers. "It is if I prove it doesn't exist."

"Well at least you're not trying to prove God exists," she said. "He doesn't. I'd hate for you to waste an experiment on a piece of historical fiction."

"You are such a communist."

She chuckled over the last of the tensioners. "Spencer said the same thing not too long ago. The truth is that I've moderated somewhat over this past year. If it is an illusion, it's an illusion that helps you. That makes your cat a good mouser, and I shouldn't care what color it is." She sat back in the grass. "And I used to think Deng was less than Mao. Experience is the ultimate teacher."

"Explain that one to me in a minute." Tonya opened a channel to Spencer. "Okay, we're ready. Punch it."

A faint, high-pitched whine came from the superconducting wires.

"Are we safe this close?" Helen asked as she backed away.

"The power levels are miniscule compared to what we've used before. We're fine. Spencer, show me gauges six, seven, and ten."

Six and seven would provide an independent coordinate set for Helen's upcoming stakeout, but ten was the one Tonya wanted to see. If it sensed any current, she would have a new proof for particulate time. Tick-tockions, no less.

"I can't. I need more cameras," Spencer said. "And you need better gauges."

"Okay, well show me six and seven, and tell me what ten says."

The readings were a mixed bag. Six and seven agreed with Helen's prediction, so the stakeout was still on. Ten, however, remained stubbornly at zero. Tick-tockions continued to elude her, if they existed at all. She was back to square one. Tonya would need another experiment to prove they were real.

She'd feel a lot better if she knew what it might look like.

Chapter 34
Mike

It was always a long shot that they would rescue Will and avoid the Death Eaters. That's why he didn't take more precautions picking their camp site. They needed to stay hidden from the rest of the crew, not the entire world. From Maff's description, the Death Eaters didn't sound dangerous per se, just very different from any other Bemian culture they'd encountered.

Different was right. As they stood there staring at each other Mike couldn't think of anything that would make for a bigger contrast to the Bemians. Their robes rendered them nearly shapeless, giving away only the most basic outline of their bodies. But up close, the robes weren't featureless swaths of ragged cloth. They were well made, decorated in delicate, subtle ways. Some had lace highlights, others complex embroidery. Their respirator masks were different, too. They were lighter and more elegant than the ones he and Kim were using. The overall impression was of a tough, no-nonsense people who were used to taming wild places. He had no intention of fighting them. He wouldn't win.

The one who stood out in front, male if the body outline was any indication, and if two sexes was still a thing in this part of the galaxy, began to speak. His voice was rough, deep, and commanding, using a language none of them had encountered before. Whatever he was saying had the undivided attention of any Death Eaters who weren't obviously assigned security duty.

"He's…" Kim said tentatively as the other spoke, "He's talking about some kind of…interview…for us." Mike threw her a lopsided grin, and she shrugged. "I'm an Interpreter. I guess. It's what I do."

What they both did, apparently. Now that he knew what an Interpreter thread really was, it disturbed him much more. He didn't know what to make of a guild that sent its members on such dangerous jobs. It was worse than death as far as he was concerned. With death, the person would at least have another shot at the karmic wheel, another attempt at enlightenment. But that? There was no chance of reaching enlightenment in this life if you no longer perceived it as life.

If there was a hell for threaded life forms, that would be it.

Kim got better with the language the longer the leader's speech went on. "We have…borne witness…something about a long journey…then we settle and begin our work again."

This caused the elder to stop and speak directly to Kim, who replied in turn, a little sharply, he thought. The rest of the crowd murmured in surprise.

"What did he say?" Maff asked.

She chuckled. "He thought I was talking over him. He told me to shut up."

Kim would poke a bear if it got in her way. "And what did you say?" he asked.

"That I'm translating. I think. Their language is the mother of all creoles. It uses lots of words from languages I've already heard, which helps me pick it up quickly. The grammar is actually like German."

Their hosts listened to this exchange attentively. When it was clear Kim was done talking, the leader asked another question. Kim replied a little less haltingly than when they'd started.

Then she translated again. "You are a group that does…unexpected…things." Kim smiled along with him. It was one of her mantras. "You will come with us. Our—"

She stopped him and asked a question. He considered, then spoke again. Kim translated, "Our something leaders wish to speak with you next."

Kim looked at Mike expectantly. He shook his head. "I'm in charge?"

"You're the one with the Will-compass. Is this a good move?"

"Do we have a choice?"

"I don't know. We still have the glass girl."

That was something they'd kept so secret they hadn't talked about it even between themselves the entire time they'd been here. "Let's keep her in the closet for now," he said. "Will is on the other side of the planet. Any move is a good one."

A few of the Death Eaters had gathered around their sled, making disgusted-sounding noises. The leader asked Kim a question.

"He wants to know why it smells…" There was the classic back and forth while Kim worked out the words. "They actually have a distinct word for chemical shit. Anyway, they want to know why it stinks."

Mike didn't think it was that bad. "It's the epoxies. They should be dry by now."

"The smell will go away quickly then," Maff said.

This caused a large ruckus among the Death Eaters, who had crowded past and under her getting a look at the sled. They scrambled away.

The leader asked a question with a lot less authority than he had before.

"They want to know where we got a talking draft animal."

"Draft animal?" Maff asked with a snort. "Well, I've been called worse."

This resulted in another series of back and forths. Eventually, Kim nodded. The elder turned around and spoke loudly to the crowd around them, who quickly began to organize.

"We're moving out," she said. "Maff, do you *mind* towing the sled? I know your legs are damaged."

"They're a little out of true at the moment, but it should be fine."

"Okay," Kim replied, all business. "Let's break down the shelter, quickly."

So much for being the leader of the pack. It always suited Kim better anyway.

*

Their route took them to some high ground just before leaving the city. Mike looked back and could barely make out a bonfire where they'd left the crew of the *Last Island*. He nudged Kim and pointed it out. The leader noticed what Mike was looking at, then said something to her.

"Apparently we were both being tested," she said. "They didn't pass."

"What happens to them now?"

Kim asked. The answer included a gesture that didn't need translating. Slicing a neck seemed to be yet another universal.

"They're leaving a sentry behind, but T'Stange says the outcome doesn't look promising."

"T'Stange?"

"It might be a title; it might be a name. By the way, I think we need a better name for them all. Death Eaters is too weird and too long."

"What do they call themselves?"

Kim asked, then smiled at the answer. "La'fan. It means *those who clean the dead*."

"La'fan it is."

They walked for more than an hour, climbing the whole way. "How are you doing, Maff? Legs working okay?" Mike asked. Her suit normally didn't make any noise, and now the squeaks and clanks were getting louder.

"I'm fine for now, but I hope they have spare parts that you two can work your wizardry with. You think it's noisy out there, you should hear it from where I am."

He was about to ask for more detail when Kim gasped and stopped dead in her tracks. "Mike," she said, breathless, "Maff, get up here."

He jogged up with Maff squeaking along beside him. She'd

crested the last hill. When he reached her, he understood why she gasped. They hadn't been climbing a hill this whole time, they'd been scaling the rim of a crater. An *enormous* crater. Once, long ago, it held an entire city.

The biggest cities he'd ever seen were all in China, with Chengdu and Shanghai being the biggest by far. The city in the crater had once been twice as big as both of them combined.

Once. The ruins were spectacular, but on their right, halfway around the crater, an arc of machines was at work. Dozens of them, much taller than the towers they were obviously salvaging. Other squat ones moved slowly back and forth, servicing them, taking cargo back to larger, low-slung factories that glittered in the black shadow of the far rim's edge. Everything was dark and rusted. Even from this distance he could see they were heavily used and roughly maintained. In front of the tower-eaters was ruins. Behind them was a natural, bare rock floor.

"I think their name is better than ours," he said. "*Cleaning* seems much more appropriate."

"Turlanfador's wings shelter us," Maff said reverentially. "I wish I could share what I see at high magnification. There are so *many* of them."

T'Stange interrupted their reverie with gruff words and some pointing. Only then did Mike notice that not far below them was an unmistakable railway, with a long train waiting in a makeshift station.

"He says we don't have to walk any further once we get there," Kim said. "We can put our luggage in the back car."

A new problem appeared after they arrived. The train, like the La'fan themselves, was vertically oriented, taller than it was wide.

Maff was wider than she was tall. A lot wider.

"Don't worry about that. I've been wanting to show you two this for a while now."

As they watched, Maff's suit rippled and changed. Machines and mechanisms were absorbed and then moved to new locations. Her wings pulled in, and her body elongated, then reoriented ninety degrees. Legs and manipulators twisted and combined, making odd squeaks and clicks as they overcame Elsek's damage.

Once it was done, Maff had taken on a recognizably human outline, about a head taller than Mike. She switched to English. "Oh ho, loowk at meeh! I hooman!" She stuck fake arms out and peg-walked forward on new legs. "Loowk owt! I zshahom-bee! A lejende hazah combe aliyve!" She switched to Bemian. "Not having any bones," then to English, throwing her arms up, "foreh thee winne!"

He looked at Kim. "Did you teach her that?"

It took her a second to stop laughing. He'd missed that sound. "It may have slipped out."

A loud voice announced something over their heads. "I think," Mike said, "that was a boarding call?"

"Got it in one." Kim guided them to the right car. "Guess who's coming to dinner?"

Chapter 35
Helen

She thought throwing herself into work, any work, would keep her from thinking about her new reality. For a while it had. But then she would check the news and see that the politburo had disassembled yet another one of her initiatives, or she'd check the dwindling time left on her visa, or put up with another arrogant child's ching-chong taunt as he stole right in front of her, and another stone would fall on her soul. As long as she was busy, it wasn't overwhelming. As long as there was a task at hand, Helen could cope.

It was when she had to sleep that the weight of the stones crushed her. Having all her threads concentrated in her anchor box made it worse. There was no escape, no distraction. She had to be in one place at one time. There was nowhere else to go.

Helping Mike was the only way she could be normal by using her threads properly. But he'd been too busy to talk lately. Survival on a hostile world with his La'fan naturally took priority over comforting his neurotic sister.

So this new lead Tonya and Spencer had discovered was a gift from the ancestors. Helen would get back to her roots, be a cop again, a detective.

She'd already insinuated herself into the town's tiny police force. The perceptive Chinese girl who knew the particulars of all the small-time crooks and thugs *and also* knew how to get the chef of the best restaurant in town to open up his secret menu was someone worth taking along on the occasional patrol or given the late-night paperwork the useless day crew always slow-walked into the system. That their realm was largely isolated from Mike was an added bonus, letting her threads stretch out from the box.

But she couldn't come to the regular cops with *possessed people are roaming the fields* without more proof, and for that she needed her own squad. Back in the day that would mean Ji Cong and Xun Hé, the best pair of detectives in western China. To this day, she missed them, not least because her new crew consisted of a distracted scientist-slash-nurse and…

Spencer McKenzie.

"You have got to be shitting me. I am not sitting on my ass while you and Tonya go scouting. No. Fucking. Way."

Helen had graduated from the finest police academy the People's Republic had. She'd aced her political classes. Religion had been an opiate of the masses for as long as Helen understood the term. But with Spencer, the only logical thing Helen could conclude was that she had been cursed by the gods. He'd even picked up Chinese swear words along the way. Because why be inappropriate only in English?

"You're the lookout," Helen said, hanging on to her increasingly frayed patience as best she could. "You will not be as effective at canvassing a night club as Tonya and I will."

"The fucking Pendleton Inn is not a *night club*. It's a shit shack by the river."

Helen had checked its FaceYelp reviews out as soon as the triangulation had picked it as the target. It wasn't a famous night club, but it wasn't a shack either.

Spencer was denigrating an inoffensive business for the same reason he'd been doing it to everything else around here: he was fundamentally incompatible with the town and its people and had exported that unhappiness to the world around him. It wasn't as bad as the kids she'd watched self-destructing in Dumas, but it was a difference in degree, not kind. If Spencer had not met Mike and escaped, Helen wasn't sure his outcome would be any better than those criminals. That it was her fault he'd been dragged back made his selfish, petty, obnoxious *American-ness* easier to take.

But only just.

"It's a shack by the river that may give us clues to what's going on," Tonya said. "And Helen's right. If you go with her, you're a couple, and nobody will talk to you. If you go in separately, everyone will get the wrong idea about Helen. But two girls walking into a club? That's a Saturday night." She turned to Helen. "Are you sure *you* can do it?"

Tonya was mistaking her for someone else. "It's an undercover assignment. Of course I can do it."

Tonya pulled back and an eyebrow shot up. "I've never seen you wear makeup ever, and your choice in clothes isn't what I'd call complimentary. I think you'd wear scrubs if you could get away with it."

Helen let a little of what the snake mother had left behind leak out. Not the facility with needles, but the charisma it took to lure someone, lull them.

Seduce them.

She put on that inner cloak and walked up to Tonya. A finger that touched the hand, getting close but not too much, pitching her voice differently because this wasn't a man, and… "I'm new here," a smile, look around like she's up to something, "how about you?"

Tonya flushed, but only for a second, then she laughed out loud. "Girl, where have you been hiding *that*?"

Helen turned to find Spencer gaping at her. Now it was a saunter, a bit of a swing, lock the eyes and make them *big*. She tapped Spencer's mouth shut with a delicate finger.

His blush was much stronger.

"What's the matter, Spencer? Do you want to come along?"

He swallowed with an audible gulp. "Well fuck me running. I'll take the car."

Helen dropped the act and turned to Tonya, who had almost doubled over laughing. Helen couldn't help but smile. It was fun to surprise them. "I'll be honest, though, I do need help with makeup and an outfit." The snake mother's knowledge didn't cover that part.

You don't need to impress your kills with your appearance.

Hellen ignored the sibilant hiss in her mind and asked Tonya, "I think it's time for another air strike?"

"It'll be my pleasure."

*

The music thudded into her guts from the parking lot. This seemed like a much better idea when they were back at the caretaker's quarters. "You're sure these heels won't break off?"

"You've already practiced in them," Tonya replied. "The floor here will be easy. Rely on your inner dragon lady, you'll be fine."

That was the right way to play it. She wasn't a nervous cop on the wrong side of the world with two *xīnshǒu* for partners. She was a dangerous seductress, the sexiest thing in the room.

The outfit helped, though Helen hadn't been sure it *was* an outfit when Tonya opened up the first of the packages they ordered. "This is all?" was the first thing she'd asked. It was definitely smaller than what they picked out using Amazon's realm tools.

Tonya pulled the fabric. "It stretches. You're a size zero, and we're taking advantage of that. It's still a midi, as requested."

The bodycon dress was hard enough to swallow. Having it with a skirt above her knee was too close to a prostitute by half. Helen insisted on long sleeves, too. There was no need to add bare skin to the equation.

The shoes, though. That's what sold it for her. They were *spectacular*—tiny, sleek things with heels that could double as weapons.

"I would have never picked you as a shoe fiend," Tonya said as Helen checked them out in a virtual mirror.

"Me, either." They were shiny and so well made. Helen had balked at the price but then noted the lifetime warranty the manufacturer provided. "And you said L.L. Bean didn't do high fashion."

"I didn't know. It's all this nanotech coming out. Now, we need to practice. Asian Tina Turner, here we come." The shoes adapted effortlessly to her demands, turning gracefully into flats exactly when she needed them, then slowly resuming their weaponlike status after she stopped. If this was what you got as a shoe fiend, Helen wanted the sign-up sheet.

Tonya, being an American, went by different rules. Different *sparkly* rules.

"They're called sequins, and they rock. And if you look at my hemline one more time, we're gonna have a problem."

Tonya was her friend and not a prostitute, no matter how much she looked like one. And now that they'd arrived, Helen realized she didn't look like a prostitute. Or, rather, everyone else did too. Americans were so forward, so…out there.

Helen stopped walking. It was such an unexpected idea.

She *liked* it.

Tonya misunderstood why she stopped. "It'll be fine. We need to circulate, mingle. Look for possessed people, but don't *look* like you're looking for possessed people."

"Dance casual," Spencer said over their shared channel. "Right?"

"You keep an eye on the club; let us do our job." Tonya said.

"Northwest levee base, here, the Dodge has landed." Spencer had taken up position on a river levee to observe the whole area. "If it goes pear-shaped out here, you'll be the first to know."

When they went inside, music was so loud it was a physical thing. *How do you even think in here?* she sent to Tonya.

Tonya turned around and let out a loud *whoop* as she started to dance. "Use your voice! Sing! Enjoy yourself!"

Helen had other things to do, but it was part of her cover, so she whooped in turn and gyrated along with Tonya. The sights, sounds, and smells of adult humans on the prowl were an intoxicating cocktail, no doubt enhanced by the liquor available at the bar and the electronic stims offered by the local realmspace. The realm was a third-order overlay, more enhanced vision that full-fledged immersion, allowing people to interact with each other in both places at once. Helen had to use the least-interactive contract available so she wouldn't destroy it. She could look but not touch.

She didn't need to. Tonya was right. Dancing was fun. Being new faces, they were rapidly ringed by admirers of both sexes. The men towered over her and were such good dancers they would put any pro on China's *Dancing with the Stars* to shame. Helen had never experienced humans this way before. They'd all been stuffy ministers, old diplomats, or, before she came outside, dour cops. The madly pulsating joy coupled with her realspace body's movement created a connection with the other dancers and the music that was primal. It had to be experienced to be understood. For the first time ever, on a personal level, being human *rocked.*

After the fourth song, Tonya led her to the bar. "I told you you'd like this!"

"I had no idea!"

Tonya ordered two glasses of chardonnay for them. "Go easy on this. I don't want to carry you out of here."

"I had to go to drinking parties with the politburo. This is child's play." But Helen heeded the warning. It would be disastrous to lose control now, on more than one level. With Tonya by her side, and the various mountainous bouncers she'd spotted around the club, Helen had no worries about her physical safety. But they were facing dangerous unknowns. Plus, if Tonya had to pour her into a car to get home, she'd never hear the end of it from Spencer.

The second round of dancing was with a group of people she now knew. It was a strange sort of trust, the ability to predict what the other would do. Responding in turn transformed the dancing into something better. Completing a complex sequence that took two or more people working together to finish was a test of skill, and Helen always excelled at those.

During breaks, they both questioned whoever seemed the chattiest in the groups they found themselves in.

"Did you hear about Mrs. Ramkin?" Most people had.

"Anyone else like that?" A few, sometimes, or at least they'd heard about it.

"How about around here?" Now that she mentioned it, there were some strange-acting people wandering around outside, but everyone assumed they were realm addicts or otherwise stoned out of their minds.

A picture slowly built up. There were strange things happening, people acting out of the ordinary. It wasn't noticeable unless someone was looking for patterns, but it was there.

By the end of the night, Helen was exhausted in a pleasant way she'd never experienced before. The shoes had protected against blisters, but her feet and legs were already putting her on notice that they had been tested tonight and had not appreciated it one bit. She'd gone easy on the booze but still had enough to put a pleasant tinge in the sky as they waited for Spencer to pick them up.

She also gathered enough information that, on comparing notes with Tonya, showed a clear pattern. People acting strangely were coming here from all over the area and not leaving. The question was where exactly they were ending up. It wasn't in the club.

"I know where," Spencer said as they drove home in the night. "I saw two make their way past the club. But we're gonna need backup."

Chapter 36
Maff

She may have made a fundamental mistake picking her first crew, but she'd more than made up for it in picking her second. They were fearless, inventive, and they accepted her for who and what she was: someone trying to make it, no different than anyone else. There was no antipallun static, no judgement, no whispered names as she walked by. It was a level of trust she'd never had with an off worlder, and she loved it.

It hadn't been easy. When they said *guilty* to that judge…well, it was time to figure out why they'd done that.

"We're trying to rescue someone," Kim said with downcast eyes, her way of expressing guilt. "We should've told you, but we weren't sure we could trust you then."

"There's a human? On this planet? But you're uncontacted."

Mike nodded. "It's a long story."

Maff checked out the window of the rail car. Her mysterious friends needed to stop being so damned mysterious. "We seem to have the time."

But when they told the story, it got *more* mysterious. This uncontacted civilization had somehow done the impossible: they had made their own portal without any AC network influence at all. These people were talking about it like it was a vague curiosity. To Maff, it was miraculous. The portals were what held the galaxy together. If not for them, everything would have to be moved around by the kind of ships Maff piloted. It would cause society to grind to a halt. They were the first, most important, monopoly the nodes had on the societies they protected.

If these humans' story was true, and Maff had no reason to think it wasn't, that monopoly was no more.

Maff had such a hard time wrapping her wings around the idea that she almost missed the next thunderous revelation. "Wait, go back. What do you mean *you split and went into the transit dimension*?"

They both shared guilty glances, or maybe it was fear.

"You've never heard of that?" Kim asked.

"Why would I have heard of it?"

Mike replied, "We figured it was another aspect of Interpreters."

Maff lowered herself on her support legs. The extra balance helped her think. "There are legends. We have legends about everything. But as far as I know, Interpreters move around in the transit dimension like everyone else: either through a portal or via ship."

"What else do the legends say?" Kim asked.

"Not much. This one's little more than a nursery rhyme."

In time of need
When the eye of greed
Draws close
Threads and flesh
Will intermesh
And scatter across the roads

"The transit dimension was once spoken of as a system of roads, that's where the connection comes in. It's the most famous part of a massive saga that's supposed to detail what happened during the fall of the old civilizations, before the Refounding."

She could see that made Mike curious. "I thought you said no records survived from before that time," he said.

"They didn't. The story is called *The Four Knights and the Eye*. Aside from that quote and a summary written long after the Refounding, it's lost."

"And the summary?" Kim asked.

"Makes no mention of what you can do. And the summary naturally conflicts with other stories that try to explain what happened then." Maff finally realized something. "This whole sequence of events has been about rescuing a child?"

Kim shrugged. "Longer than that. We've been trying almost from the moment he ran through that portal."

"Well at least now I understand. You should've told Noen Sha'Katenden about this. He would've worked with you."

Mike sat back. "We didn't know who we could trust. You're looking at the only two people in our entire world who have encountered aliens."

"Actually," Kim said, "that's not true. We know two others."

First, they described the one named Cyril. Maff tried to imagine it, but there was a problem. "Aliens with exoskeletons, even vestigial ones, are some of the most common life forms in the galaxy. I'm not going to be much help identifying his species."

"Why didn't we have one on the crew?" Mike asked.

Maff shrugged. "Coincidence. Regardless, that description doesn't provide anything distinctive for me to give you a name."

The second, though, was a different story. They had the description correct. Three eyes, massive size, vicious and deadly. It was accurate right down to the drab color of their fur. "Za gafunkt," she said, incredulous at the revelation. "You've met *naltons*?"

Kim asked, "Is that what they're called?"

"They have many names, but that's the most common. I guess I shouldn't be surprised that impossible people have met legendary monsters. But only two? If the legends are right, they travel in packs. The size varies, but it's never less than a few hundred."

That worried them a lot, she could see it on their faces. "As far as we know," Mike said, "only two."

"Our friend, Tonya, saw them come through the portal," Kim said. "What are they?"

Maff hated admitting it again, but there was no way around it. "Nobody knows. They're a myth, or they were supposed to be anyway." This provided a perfect opening to ask them about their own past. "Do *you* have any myths about them?"

"No," Mike said. "I suppose you could cast some of the," he

used a word Maff had never heard before and then said *literature*. This was followed by another unknown word, then "might work if you squint hard."

Mike's grasp of Standard was strong enough he could communicate easily, but occasionally he'd use an English word. Usually she could figure out the meaning of it from its context in the sentence, but not this time. "What kind of literature?"

He used the same word again. Maff turned to Kim, who switched to Pallundian. "I don't know the word in your language. Some of our legends are about the past, but some are about... people who predict events that will happen long before they happen. In English, the word is *prophet*, and the legends they tell are *prophecies*. Mike was talking about *prophetic* literature."

"I don't understand. How can it be a legend if it hasn't happened yet?"

Kim and Mike spoke English faster than Maff could follow, using a lot of words she'd never heard before.

Kim stopped and switched to Pallundian. "You mean you've never heard of a *prophecy*? Not the word, but the concept that people can predict what will happen before it happens?" Kim took pity on Maff's confusion, and then promptly made it worse. "We call it the *future*."

"Right," Maff replied. "That second word you used, future, I know what that is. It's for planning ahead, but only for the next trip, the next goal."

Kim shook her head. "Future in your language has a more limited meaning than the word we use in English. You don't have a word that we can use to translate the concept of a *prophecy* into."

"No kidding," Maff replied, trying once again to get her wings around another fundamental idea. "And these...*prophecies*...they come true?"

They both shrugged. "It depends on who you ask," Kim said, "and when."

They spent the rest of the train ride introducing Maff to ideas so weird she was forced to use English to express them. Humans had, somehow, come up with legends that could be predicted, sometimes thousands of years away. Their ancient stories were littered with prophecies that had come true, or at least that's what others claimed. In their historical era, this was largely discounted, but the proofs they used were as confusing as the basic ideas. Probability, statistics, distributions, and others were concepts she knew, but only for business, and only for the next term, the next harvest, the next year. She had never encountered them used on scales that could be applied to the entire universe.

Maff had taken these two to be provincial bumpkins from the lower clouds who'd never seen true civilization. They not only had their own civilization, in some ways, it was so advanced she didn't know it could exist at all.

*

The train pulled into an airlock and then arrived at the station itself. The gas mix outside changed into a combination that her filters could compensate for easily. The humans, biologically adapted to mixes common to high-gravity worlds, were able to remove their filters entirely. When the doors opened, they were not greeted by T'Stange but by a big, brutish palonar.

"I guess it was only a matter of time until we met a satyr," Kim said.

"On steroids, no less," replied Mike.

Maff wasn't sure what *satyr* or *steroids* were, but the humans became much more serious and respectful. It was a good choice, since the gray-skinned palonar were well known for their prickly honor and violent ways.

He silently held out three devices in a clawed hand. One obviously connected to an upload port on her suit, the other two seemed adapted for human ears. Maff gingerly took hers and connected it while Mike and Kim did the same with theirs.

After three quick chirps, one from each device, the palonar spoke. As he did, the new device translated. The voice was robotic, stilted, and slow, obviously not created by Interpreter threads.

"You are to report to the high council immediately for interrogation and judgement. Follow me," it said. The palonar then turned and marched away so fast that they had to rush to keep up.

She couldn't resume her normal shape until they stopped for a moment. The suit's mobility was already challenged by the damage Elsek did to it. Maff never intended her human joke to be used as serious transport, and so she had no hope of keeping up without binding or breaking something. "Kim," she said. "Can you ask him to stop? I can't transform in motion."

She looked ahead, and Kim had already stopped, with Mike next to her. They had exited the tunnel that was the station entrance and now stood transfixed, bathed in blue light. They weren't afraid, exactly, but they were standing as close together as they could. For the first time since leaving *Last Island*, they looked… small.

Maff caught up to them and discovered why. The crater they'd been traveling around on the train was an active salvage site. They had all wondered where the settlement was. Now they knew.

The settlement was built inside the crater's wall.

The artificial cavern extended from the floor of the crater to the rim's edge and was so long it curved out of sight. They were now about two-thirds of the way up, on a broad avenue that connected the train station to the rest of the settlement. She could easily fly in it if the atmosphere wasn't so thin.

It was full of La'fan.

They were constantly depicted as dour and dangerous creatures hidden underneath black robes and strange masks. That couldn't be more wrong. The robes were there but lined with brilliant colors that created subtle abstract patterns. The settlement's atmosphere allowed most of them to remove their masks, revealing a diversity that was the equal of any port she'd ever visited. They all moved purposely from place to place, completely different from the idle wanderings she was used to anywhere else. But it wasn't oppressive. They weren't slaves. If anything, Maff got the striking impression that these people were happy.

It was a contrast to the palonar's attitude when he noticed his charges had fallen behind. Kim spoke rapidly to him while Maff gingerly worked through her suit's transform sequences. Their exchange was too fast for her La'fan device to translate it.

The council chambers ended up being a walk and an elevator ride away from the station. As they walked, Maff tried to figure out what this meeting was really for. There were rumors that people were judged on their abilities, and if there were none on offer, then the candidate was cast out into whatever wasteland they happened to be in at the time. Mike and Kim could fix things, and Maff could fly ships, so they would be safe from that. But then, like a lightning bolt in the clear, Maff remembered something. In spite of the fact that the La'fan and Interpreters were all that they had talked about for the past few days, Maff had completely forgotten one of the strangest facts about both. They never met. There was no such thing as a La'fan Interpreter. But now that would be to their advantage.

"Guys," she said. "You're not leaving until you get Will, right?"

Kim nodded, looking a little confused. "That's right."

"Okay, follow my lead then. Have faith, I know what to say so you can stay here as long as you need to. And please, don't say one thing if I tell you to say something else."

The council chamber was a miniature version of the settlement itself: tall, curved, with terraces cut into the rock. Fifteen La'fan stood at separate daises, spread unevenly across five levels. Crowds of curious onlookers sat in galleries to either side.

For once, Maff was happy to be the stereotypical pushy pallun. She strode confidently onto the main floor, Kim and Mike trailing close behind her.

Maff turned around, proud enough to burst. She had brought them here, and they were going to do such incredible things. "Kim, I need a real Interpreter, and they don't have one."

She cocked her head to one side, then her eyes went wide. Mike's did too.

That's correct, she thought, *you're it. On this whole planet, in this whole society, you're the only ones.*

"Will you do the honors?"

Kim stepped forward, gripping her hands together tightly. She nodded.

Maff turned back to the council. All she had to go on were realm dramas, which sometimes portrayed these people as savage monsters, and other times as noble ancients. They weren't trying to pry her suit off or eat Mike and Kim, so Maff went with what she'd seen about the latter. "I am Maff, Daughter of Fann, of the pallun clan Sorkon."

"Well met," said the scolion, through Kim, who stood at the centermost dais. The scolion looked like she could be one of their old captain's cousins. Mike called them foxes. "But your titles have no meaning here, nor does your family. Only what you can bring to our table will determine your fate."

"So the legends say," she replied through Kim. "I am but a humble pilot, and I offer my services for your convenience. It's my companions who bring the greatest gift to your table. The greatest gift that any La'fan has ever received in all of history."

If she had any doubt that she'd been wrong about Kim, that she was *not* part of a unique Interpreter pair, it was dispelled by the way her translation changed as Maff spoke. Her voice deepened, her cadence slowed, and her words grew louder. Mike was just as impressive, instinctively taking control of the room's lighting, subtly changing it to emphasize how important Maff's next words were. They both knew, the way Interpreters always knew, exactly how to impress an audience.

As well they should. Maff was making history. They all were.

"I present to you Mike and Kim, humans of Earth. They need no titles, bar one."

The entire chamber had gone silent. The delegates leaned forward. This had never happened. *Could* never happen. And Maff stood here with them, helped them get to this point. La'fan had been misunderstood for their entire history and would *be* misunderstood forever. All because they were missing the one thing everyone else in the galaxy took for granted.

"They are what you have lacked since the beginning of time, and they have agreed to serve you.

"They are Interpreters."

Chapter 37

Him

As soon as she said the words, the room erupted. The electronic translator in her ear quickly gave up in a squeal of static. She yanked it out, and Mike did the same. Now that she was exposed to the full roar of the crowd, all the new words pounded into her skull. She had to grab one of Maff's manipulators to keep from falling over.

The words she could understand were encouraging.

"Unprecedented, impossible, we will be able to..."

"For the first time, no manipulation, no tricks hidden in the..."

"We'll know how the next series of *Sortan's Folly* ends at the same time as..."

Mike was beside her. "Are you okay?"

She nodded. "Shaken but not stirred."

"The chamber will come to order!"

The La'fan on the center dais banged a blue metal staff on the floor, repeating his command. The crowd took no notice. She had set off an entire amphitheater with her translation. The emotion, the *power,* was an unexpected high. Being an Interpreter might not be bad after all.

"THE CHAMBER WILL COME TO ORDER!"

The sudden jump in volume scared the room silent.

She looked at Mike. "Did you do that?"

He nodded. "There aren't any AC nodes. It took me a little while to figure out where the controls were."

"Maff of Pallun," the Speaker said, "your people have a reputation for trickery and deception. How do we know this is not an elaborate hoax?"

Kim could see Maff tense up at the accusation.

"She is no hoax, Speaker," T'Stange, their guide from the wilderness, said from the edge of one of the galleries. Without his mask, he was one of the most humanoid aliens she'd seen so far. If you discounted the extra eyes, at any rate. "She did not know La'fanian at all when we met but spoke with no accent before we arrived at Bushan station."

"And her companion?"

Mike's voice came from all around them. "I not speak La'fanian good, but learn I am fast." Everyone, including the Speaker, startled and looked around them. He switched to English. "I perform distant communications, among other things, as you can see."

As one the entire room focused on Kim. Being an Interpreter had its downsides. "He doesn't speak La'fanian yet, but he's learning. He's the one that can communicate between the stars. He's also in control of your"—knowing the language wasn't the same thing as knowing all the words—"artificial voice volume, in case you hadn't noticed." Yeah, it wasn't elegant, but it wasn't the right time to play twenty questions figuring out how to say *PA system*.

The Speaker nodded. "That seems…" Mike still had control over the PA system, so his voice was almost comically small. "Madam, if you don't mind, would your companion please release the microphone to my control?"

She nodded at Mike.

After a thump, the Speaker continued. "Thank you. You will forgive us if we are doubtful of this unprecedented occurrence. You do not resemble Interpreters as we know them. Why is this?"

"This is how Interpreters have appeared on our world." Technically correct, which as the saying went, was the best kind of correct.

"The Guild changes after all. And do they approve of your presence among us?"

Kim switched to English and lowered her voice. "He wants to know what the Guild thinks of us." They hadn't discussed this part. Or any part, for that matter. Maff was almost as bad as Mike about thinking ideas through. "What do I tell them?"

"First of all, that's a *she,*" Maff said.

Great. Well at least she hadn't addressed *her* incorrectly yet.

"Second, you're on the run from the Guild. It happens sometimes."

Kim looked at Mike.

He shrugged. "It sounds logical to me. And that is sort of what we're doing here anyway."

Kim turned back to the Speaker. These were strong, independent people who had jobs to do. Being weak or asking for help would be the wrong play with them. An idea jumped out at her. She'd sized people up like this all her life. Kim had been doing an Interpreter's job without ever realizing it. With an effort, she set that aside and said what would work. "The Guild hasn't chosen a course of action with regards to us, our appearance, or what we represent. We decided to offer our services to you before they did."

Kim translated that in the other direction. Mike winked at her and mouthed *good job.* Maff used one of her manipulators to show her version of a thumbs up. She had Team Mongrel on her side at least.

Kim's words caused appreciative murmurs to come from the crowd. The Speaker gaveled them into silence. "The Guild has been no friend to the La'fan. We see no reason to change this relationship. Very well. We will need to assess your suitability." *She* turned to the other people standing at the daises around her. "We will discuss how to proceed and inform you of our decision."

"Honorable Fakner," she said to the satyr-mountain who'd led them in here. "Please find our guests appropriate accommodations." She turned back to Kim. "If you would kindly provide samples of your required nutrition, I'm sure we'll find something compatible with your species."

The galleries immediately started shouting at the Speaker, who, along with everyone else on her side of the room, shouted orders back. Since they had the PA system, the crowd quieted quickly. Governance was a cooperative thing with the La'fan.

Kim didn't get much more than that because Honorable Fakner had immediately marched them out a side exit. "Is Honorable part of your name or is it a title?" Kim asked.

"It is my name. We have no titles in that sense of the word, only positions."

His voice was a graveled rumble. Kim got the distinct impression he spoke with something other than lungs and vocal cords. Maybe it had something to do with the fluttering around his neck.

Now that she'd seen more of how they acted, Kim realized curiosity was expected of newcomers. "And your position is?"

"Greeter of the new. I am well known for my sparkling personality." His face resembled a human's well enough that she was pretty sure she saw a sly smile. "And how should we address you?"

"I'm Kimberly Trayne, but you can call me Kim. That's Mike Sellars, more commonly known as Mike, and that's"—she pitched her voice to as whistley as she could make it—"Maff, Daughter of Fann, who we call Maff."

Her impersonation made Maff stop for a moment. "Remind me not to rely on voice identification when you're around."

*

Their quarters were in a segment that strongly resembled a hotel back home, right down to keycards and a front desk. Honorable Fakner took an adjoining room and left them his contact info. Apparently, their translator devices doubled as phones as well.

"But no neural interface," Mike observed. "I stumbled around and found a manual for them. It's all subvocalizations and gestures. Look." He made a quick gesture with his fingers and a small probe extended from her device. A screen appeared with Don't Panic written in English on it.

"It's a miniature laser projector," Mike said as a probe on his device extended past his eye. "I adapted it for us on the walk over."

"Oh," Maff said, "that's what the extra pins on mine are for." Kim saw reflected light against one of her suit's optical ports. "Nice."

"They don't use shared virtual spaces like we do back home. They use these," he said. "We should take one apart so I can figure out their tech." He turned to her. "You don't really need yours, do you?"

She loved him to bits, but sometimes his inability to think things through made her want to hit him with something heavy. "I'm not going to break a device they gave me to let you pick over its guts. We'll figure it out some other way."

Their quarters consisted of three rooms: the two on the ends were obviously sleeping quarters—Mike helped Maff modify hers by removing all the furniture—while the center seemed to be the shared area. Maff settled in front of a blank wall. "Check this out."

A probe extended from the module that Honorable Fakner had given her, pointed at the wall, and projected a menu on it.

"I'll be damned," Mike said. "Television."

"Tell-ah-vishz-een?" Maff asked. "That's what it's called?"

"Yup," Kim said as she started examining the bench Maff had settled next to, "it's kind of halfway between books and realmspaces. We still use it back home." Kim pushed a button, and the bench opened up into a passable example of a couch. "Let's see if they get Disney++." Maff looked at the screen while Mike explained what she was talking about.

The choices were written in a language none of them had seen before, but with random presses they got news, dramas, a game show of some sort, and what Maff insisted was sports.

"It's called hex-ball. Very popular on quadrupedal worlds."

On the screen, various centaur-like creatures barreled into each other while chasing a ball. If a player with the ball got his or her front legs shoved up into the air, they were out. Mike was entranced. She and Maff quickly lost interest.

"Watch sports on your own dime, Sellars," Kim said. "What else do we have?"

A few more clicks past hex-ball and they hit the jackpot: *La'fan for Beginners*. This one came with a submenu that, thankfully, was spoken as they went through the choices.

"Pick reading," Maff said. "I hate not knowing how to read."

So that's how they spent the rest of their first day: learning how to read. Mike and Kim picked up on it reasonably fast. Maff, who had only known the three-dimensional Bemian writing style, had a harder time but eventually got the hang of it.

By the time supper came around—for them, a version of the soup packet she had provided, and for Maff, a box that clipped into a different port on her suit—they'd switched to cooking shows. Those were even more addicting than they were back home. They practiced spoken and written La'fan as they made a list of things that wouldn't poison them. It was important, because the sa'dst had run out. It gave everyone another reason to be thankful that the La'fan had found them when they did. They all ended up using the bathroom several times, though it took some tinkering to figure out compatible configurations for specific needs.

Eventually night came, courtesy of Mike hacking the lighting system. They went to bed without being informed of any La'fan decision.

The next morning, Mike figured out how to order from the hotel, and they sampled breakfast.

"If they taste like eggs," Kim said, "why are they blue?"

There was a light *bong* and then the front door opened. Honorable Fakner stepped through.

"Maff Sorkon. You are to report to the ship docks immediately." He indicated a toaster-sized robot on wheels. "This will guide you. Kimberly Trayne and Mike Sellars, please follow me."

Maff rose on her still-creaking legs. "I guess I'll see you guys later."

"Message us when you're settled; we'll do the same for you." They'd figured out how that function worked while Mike was talking her into trying blue scrambled eggs. Kim stuck with soup but was keeping an eye on him. They looked odd but smelled okay.

Honorable led them to a new chamber not far from the meeting hall. Inside was the La'fan's version of a conference table. T'Stange had changed out of his rough outside robes into ones much more refined. The Speaker—up close Kim could see gray streaks through her fox fur, which made her seem more mature although Kim had no idea if that's what it meant—sat next to him.

"You're going to be our testers?" Kim asked.

"Events have overtaken our initial plan." T'Stange said. He nodded his head toward the Speaker. "Shareah has been informed that this planet's salvage contract has been fast-tracked and will be reviewed for final disposition in a matter of days."

A tight deadline. Great. "What does that mean for us?"

"One of the first, most important functions of Interpreters is the negotiation of contracts. We have throughout history been forced to share our salvage with those who do nothing because we lack the sophisticated skills Interpreters have." She motioned them toward seats at the table. "In other words, we're sick of being screwed over, and we need your help."

Thirty-six hours ago they were huddled over a camp stove trying not to freeze. "You do?"

"We do indeed. It will be your first, best test as Interpreters."

A screen above them flashed to life and included a holograph tank on either side. It let her cross-check the words on the screen, although they were obviously part of the opening of a property contract in La'fan and Bemian.

"But we don't—"

Mike threw a handkerchief over her hand. "We'll need access to your law library."

Kim turned to him. "That's only half of what we need. The rest is—"

"In a library on an AC world, which I happened to have left a thread behind on." He pulled the cloth that she'd gripped so hard her knuckles went white. "How hard can it be?"

Kim let go of the handkerchief and threw him a look. "You have *got* to stop saying that."

Chapter 38
Spencer

He still didn't quite believe it. Mike and Kim end up on the other side of the galaxy, meet strange aliens, see distant lands, and what do they do? They get a job. *A fucking job.* Spencer would've been swilling romulan ale, swinging across empty chasms with a princess—who would *not* be his sister—wrapped around him, or at least rocketing around an asteroid field or two. Not pushing alien pencils and learning alien contracts because nobody speaks the same goddamned language and the cultures are so complex it takes *two* people to understand the fucking things. No, that was not what he'd do at all.

Pointing this out to Helen only got a laugh. "And you think this is better?"

They'd been on a multipoint stakeout for the past week, slowly recruiting assistants, hopefully at a faster rate than whoever-the-shit-it-was could recruit new zombies for whatever-the-hell-they-were-doing. The discovery at the old lady's realm was a pretty fucking big clue. Bare footprints in the middle of a shattered anomaly meant there *was* a connection. But what that might be, how it worked, and most importantly, who, if anyone, was behind it…well, they'd come up with a big goddamned zero about those things so far.

The only thing they had established was that the zombies ended up in two rickety trailers and an old houseboat way the fuck out on the end of Pendleton's shore. To date, a handful of people with few or no relatives, loners, runaways—who the hell knew Desha county had fucking runaways?—had shacked up down there without anyone else noticing it.

The real trick was that the cast down there rotated. In the short time they'd been observing this shit show, people already there had left and not come back, while new ones just showed the hell up whenever they felt like it. Mostly at night, using the nightclub as cover for their arrival, but not always. A long-haul trucker had managed to wedge his rig up there for two days and then vanished without seeming to unload a goddamned thing.

The first couple of days had been a nightmare. They only had three people to cover twenty-four hours on a site that had a fuck-ton of different approaches. This wasn't some high-rise apartment with a couple of entrances on the street. People could, and sometimes did, wander in or out through a goddamned bean field from a direction nobody was watching.

So they recruited. Spencer brought Stewart in, who brought a buddy of his along. Helen had brought along a local cop friend, because sitting watching weirdos wander in and out of hillbilly hovels was a step up from the normal routine of watching small-town traffic and rousting junkies. Tonya got a couple of nurses from the local hospital to come out, mostly for the same reasons as the cop.

In the end, they had a nice little tiger team composed of reasonably competent people who were used to screwball hours and sitting around waiting for something to happen. This being the South, they were all armed with binoculars and rifles because rednecks had to be ready in case a hunting season snuck up on them. The cop with her pistol and car-mounted shotgun seemed almost unarmed in comparison.

They'd built up a neat little dossier—Helen's term—on who was in the love shack at any one time. In theory, it should've also helped them figure out what the hell was going on down there, what those people were up to, but that hadn't happened yet.

"It's definitely not a meth lab," Helen said as they pored over the latest thermal imaging results they requested from an Amazon Prime drone. "The heat signature is all wrong."

"Of course it's not," Spencer said as he sat back in one of the second-hand office chairs they inherited as part of their small rental space in the Technology Education Center downtown. "That would be too easy."

"When they're outside," Helen said, "they don't seem to *do* anything. Sometimes they sit, sometimes they walk patrols, sometimes they fish."

The group held down their grocery bill by fishing from the nearby river. The area was regularly included in pro bass fishing tournaments for a reason. "What's the latest on getting something inside the buildings?" Spencer asked.

"Still dangerous, still illegal," Tonya replied. "There's always someone on the property."

"Who owns the land?" Helen asked.

Judy, Helen's cop friend, shook her head. "We can't tell. The last time the deed changed hands was back in the fifties, and we lost those records in a fire about fifteen years later. The only reason we know that much is the current recorder of deeds is the great-granddaughter of the one in charge then, and he kept a diary that detailed the loss. People have made claims on it, but it's been tangled up in court for at least twenty years now. They're squatters, but we don't have anyone to go to with the authority to file a complaint."

"So we can't tell them to fuck off," Spencer said.

"I'm not sure we'd have a reason to yet," Helen said. "This is the most probable destination of Mrs. Ramkin, who happened to have made drawings of me, Mike, Kim, and Ozzie, and *is* the destination of a bunch of other strange people who otherwise shouldn't be there. They're not doing anything illegal that we can see. None of that rises to the level of a crime."

"It *is* messed up," Stewart said. "We found another wanderer last night." They'd started calling the people discovered wandering this way *wanderers* and the ones who'd already made it *zombies*. They weren't actual zombies of course. Nobody was dead and nobody'd eaten any brains. The ones that got picked up before arrival, the wanderers, were fine after a day or two in the hospital to treat them for exposure. "But this one was different. He was a farm hand wandering in from the north. It was pretty standard stuff at first. We got in his way, he tried to fight us, we dropped him with a safeStop. Once we had him restrained, he woke up just as disoriented as Mrs. Ramkin was, but when we asked about what he was doing"—Stewart snapped his fingers—"he shut up, stopped moving. No talking, nothing. Two hours later in the ER he became responsive again but claimed to have no memory at all about the entire thing. It was almost like…"

"Like what?" Spencer asked.

"Like he knew we'd be asking questions."

"Do you think it means they're on to us?" Judy asked.

"How could you tell?" Tonya replied. "And how would it work? Someone psychically tells people to travel here, then alters the instructions to make it harder for us to work out what's going on?" She rolled her eyes. "I'm so far down this rabbit hole, that almost makes sense to me."

"I know," Spencer replied. "This is some spooky shit." He turned to Helen and Judy. "Watching them isn't telling us diddly-squat. We should try a different angle." They'd ruled out simply walking up and knocking on the door because of how violent the wanderers could be when they were restrained. "How illegal would it be if we scooped one of these sons of bitches up? You know, for questioning?"

They shared a glance. "Well," Judy said. "Some of them are runaways. Missing persons."

Helen pulled up their pictures. Three teenagers, two Black males and a Hispanic female, all looking exactly like what they were: messed up tweakers caught between realm and real addictions. They were all from *way* out of town, like, St. Louis and Tampa and shit. How they'd washed up in bumfuck Arkansas was beyond him. But they had and became another quirky piece of furniture on the ass end of the world.

Until now.

"So," Spencer started out, thinking as he went, "we pick up"—he checked the name—"Maria Jose Gonzales because Mom and Dad want their seventeen-year-old back, but we have a little chat with her before we give her parents a call."

"It's standard procedure, even in China." Helen turned to Judy. "Why haven't you picked them up already?"

Judy shrugged. "If they stay under the radar and out of trouble, we have no reason to pick them up. We can't afford to run facial recognition constantly to find people like that. We don't have enough cameras anyway."

"This is one of their fishermen," Tonya said. "She'll be away from the houses. Picking her up should be straightforward."

"Let's do it," Spencer said.

*

"Judy takes point on this," Helen said from the passenger seat of her squad car. "Spencer, you and Tonya keep a lookout."

"Roger, roger," Spencer replied and pulled over. They would remain at the top of the river levee to maintain a commanding view of the entire area. Helen and Judy would go down to the bottom to pluck Ms. Maria from the river's shore.

Helen had decked herself out professionally. If you didn't know better, you'd pick her out as some sort of federal agent in a hot second. It was a lot less risky than a fake badge and uniform.

"This is the first time in more than a year that I get to participate in real police work." Helen said, then checked herself. "Almost real police work."

Judy said, "It's fine. You've got all the required clearances now. A deputy in all but name." A bright smile bloomed on her dark face. "I don't know how *that* happened."

Helen shrugged. "It was the only way I could run dispatch after the automated system broke."

He'd wondered how she'd gotten cozy with the cops in such a short time. Watching her transform for that nightclub expedition revealed she could be charming when she needed to be, but if she'd figured out an easier way to get what she wanted, he knew from experience she wouldn't pass up the opportunity. "It *broke*? That seems…convenient."

Judy said, "You mean *in*convenient. It hasn't worked in more than a week."

It wasn't often he got to make the Chinese supercop squirm. He stared at her. "Is that right?"

Helen stared back. "It's not my fault they haven't sent anyone out to fix it yet."

*

It was a typical spring day in Southeast Arkansas: too warm to leave the windows up, too cold to be comfortable with them rolled down. But he did anyway so they'd have a chance to hear as well as see what was going on.

The cop car crunched down the gravel road to the bottom of the levee. Maria set her fishing rod down and got to her feet. She stood stock-still, a living statue. It freaked him out from a hundred yards away.

"Maria Jose Gonzales?" Judy asked as she got out of the car.

No reply. No movement at all. Then Helen got out of the car.

Maria took a step back, then she opened her mouth and made a fucked up, loud sound. It wasn't exactly a scream; it was too low for that, but it was goddamned freaky. In a single smooth motion, Maria produced a pistol and fired at Helen. Judy leapt in front of the gun as Helen hit the deck. Maria never changed her aim, putting at least two rounds into Judy and emptying the rest, all fourteen rounds, into the side of the squad car. She then turned and ran down the bank of the river, never stopping that nerve-wracking sound.

Tonya was out of the truck and halfway down the levee before Spencer had time to react.

He punched the start button and had his hand on the gear switch when he noticed movement. People were running toward the source of the sound from all over the place.

"Tonya, we have company!"

"I know, I see one coming this way from the shore. Judy's got her vest on, but one of the rounds hit her shoulder. Come on, Helen, help me pick her up."

There were a *lot* of people coming in at a dead run. Most were on the wrong side of the levee; they looked like giant rats rushing through the crop rows. Helen and Tonya got Judy into the back of the squad car just as one of the runners reached them. The large guy ignored Tonya, going straight for Helen with his arms out. Tonya crack the side of his head with her elbow, bouncing him off the car's fender and into the grass by the side of the road.

A rusted pickup crested the top of the levee, heading straight for them.

"Guys," Spencer said as he put the truck in gear. "You need to move, *now*."

"On it," Helen said as she fishtailed the squad car and swung onto the path up the levee.

Spencer rushed his truck forward and grabbed the handbrake, skidding it directly across the road between the oncoming pickup and Helen's flailing cruiser. People kept running toward them, but the levee's steep sides slowed them from a sprint to a climbing jog.

The pickup got big fast. "Come on, guys!"

The cruiser flashed past. Spencer had a brief stab of panic when he thought it would go sailing over the other side, but Helen got control and headed down the road at high speed. Spencer floored it, fighting the traction control as it tried to stop him from spinning the wheels to get turned down the road faster. The pickup filled his rearview mirror as he got it all pointed in the right direction. The tap from behind bounced him against the seatbelts, but otherwise, it all seemed okay.

"Where am I going, Spencer?"

"Get onto that dirt road in front of you."

Helen's car jinked left a little as it flounced down the levee sideways. Spencer followed, giving his truck an extra twitch to get the dust going. The pickup behind him vanished in the dirt spray.

"Call Gould PD for a roadblock on Highway 212, westbound," he said. "They've always got a speed trap set in that town. It shouldn't take long for them to respond. Tonya?"

"I've stopped the bleeding; she'll be fine once we get her to an ER."

They both skidded sideways as the gravel road curved to the right. He could still see the pickup truck, but it had fallen a little behind.

"Okay, Helen," Spencer said, "get ready for a left turn in three…two…*one*!"

She made the switch from gravel to pavement sideways and kept going. Spencer's truck wasn't as maneuverable, but after slinging himself off the other side of the road, he bootlegged it back on just as the pickup truck went past. It wasn't as lucky, spearing a large rusted propane tank that sat beside a telephone pole. An explosion ripped the tank apart, sending a chunk tumbling past his truck, so close it snapped off the side view mirror before bouncing away into a field.

He kept it floored all the way to the two-car roadblock about three miles away.

Chapter 39
Mike

Their previous encounter with the AC network's system of justice happened while running downhill in front of a freight train. The finer points were not what he was looking for at the time. Now, with some breathing space, the finer points were the game.

He just didn't count on the game being this long, or complicated.

"As far as I can tell, they have a continuous history of contract law dating back two hundred and fifty *million* years," he explained to Kim during one of their *tolstax* breaks.

That was an unexpected benefit of falling in with the La'fan: Mike had walked past a decorative plant and been hit with an unmistakable aroma. The source was a small tree called *tolstax,* with a flaky bark. When boiled, it turned the water orange but made it taste like coffee. It wasn't Blue Mountain by any stretch, but it was better than nothing. Maff had helped Kim find adequate sugar and cream analogs, so she was able to recreate the coffee-flavored milkshakes she enjoyed, too.

"And a lot of them are in Bemian languages I'm still learning," she replied. "It's frustrating, because Interpreters are assumed to know this stuff. There aren't many translation guides, and the ones that exist are more interested in talking about how the language works instead of how to use it." She held her hands around a mug they sourced from a specialty humanoid store a few levels above their quarters. "I never wanted to become a linguist. I barely graduated high school."

He refilled her mug. "You're doing great." She had picked up so many new languages they both lost count. "I, on the other hand…"

"Don't you start. If you hadn't left a thread behind on Perspendala, we'd be well and truly screwed. I'm getting a lot more leads in that library than I am with what the La'fan have in theirs. It seems pretty obvious that the galaxy has been kicking them around since the beginning of time."

In this case, *beginning of time* was almost literal. An entire civilization had been designated the galaxy's garbage service for hundreds of millions of years. "What I don't get is why they take it."

"When's the last time you've seen a gun around here? Anything bigger than a rifle?" she said.

"Yeah but nobody seems to maintain much of an army." They hadn't seen anyone in uniform, aside from robot cops at any rate.

"True, but everyone else has the AC network on their side. It wouldn't take all that much time for those things to build out a great big navy."

He'd read up on the fall of Maff's people. He knew that drill. "And without the FTL communications ability Interpreters provide…"

"There's no way to coordinate extraplanetary defenses. So it's the courts or nothing."

"But they can't understand the books."

"They could, if they had them, but that's copyrighted material." It was another thing that the entire galaxy took for granted, although in this case Mike understood why. In a society where a network of nodes provides not just basic but nearly *all* needs, where it was the only source of technical assistance or industrial production, art became one of the only creative outlets available to intelligent life. Rigidly protecting the rights to copy such items was one of the few ways available to encourage it.

And yet the art they'd seen in the brief time they'd been traveling around this galaxy was uniformly bland, variations on a few basic themes. There were realistic classicalish styles, abstract flowing colors, and mirrors. That was it. The wrecks and ruins the La'fan were salvaging, which were hundreds of thousands of years old, were all recognizable from things they'd already seen in the present day.

Law books would at first seem like a weird thing to term *art*, but someone had created them who knew how long ago. Mike also suspected the AC network may have piggy-backed monopolizing the law with this rigid intellectual property culture to ensure the La'fan never got a look at them.

"The AC network doesn't sell them. Libraries only, and on-site as well." Mike shook his head. "Their security isn't all that and a bag of chips. If I'd known about it, I could've smuggled them a copy."

"An illegal copy of laws. That would bring law enforcement down on their heads, and then we're right back to not having enough guns."

"There's bound to be a way out of it."

"There is," she said with a tired smile, "there's us."

It wasn't all hard, grinding work. On the third day, they got fitted for their robes.

"You present a difficult problem," the little robemaker said nervously as Honorable Fakner glowered over them all. "Each career group has a specific pattern, both for the style and the embellishment. The patterns often date back to before the Refounding. But you are unprecedented."

That sounded like an opportunity. "Can we create one?"

"Sellars…" He should've known Kim could tell he was up to something.

He was, but he knew there were limits. "Hey, I'm not Spencer. We're not going to premiere in galactic society with dick embroidery. This is a team effort; you get a vote, too."

Her smile was half charm, half death grin, one that told him he'd not quite crossed a line. "I get more than a vote."

They settled for a pattern that included the Alliance starbird, the Federation delta, the Ravenclaw eagle—he always thought it was a crow, but Kim insisted otherwise—and JRR Tolkien's monogram. As the sole representatives of Earth, they figured fair use would cover it all for now. The robes themselves were much more complex than either of them realized. They were made of a multilayered composite cloth that was light but very tough and included an inner formfitting liner that was a survival suit in its own right. It had electronics that integrated with their masks to provide navigation and environmental analysis. It even had a little spot reserved for their authenticated signatures.

"The masks are a hell of a lot nicer than what we had on the way in," Kim said after she tried hers on. It attenuated her voice a lot less, but still made it metallic. She breathed hard in it once, then turned to him. "No, Mike…*I* am your fiancée."

He put up his fist and spoke through his own mask. "Together we can rule the galaxy as husband and wife!"

Honorable Fakner wasn't in on the joke and glowered some more.

The rest of the time, though, was spent studying languages, laws, and contracts. The more they learned, the clearer it became that the La'fan were a dumping ground, janitor service, and cash machine rolled into one for the entire galaxy. It also introduced a new mystery. The galaxy seemed to be run as a zero-sum society. The La'fan put resources back into the system. Those were taken out by a subsequent civilization that then gave them back to the La'fan when they died.

But the numbers didn't add up. Each resource auction that the La'fan participated in went into excruciating detail about what was harvested, and what it was worth. The numbers were too low. Even considering this was only one of thousands of worlds the La'fan were harvesting at the moment, it left a deficit in the stated energy budgets of the functioning worlds. And it was a *big* deficit. Yet he could find no evidence of large-scale power generation. Their renewable energy sources were an inefficient joke, nobody knew enough about physics to understand nuclear power, and the fossil-fuel industry was a fraction of the predicted size. Yet things obviously worked and had for hundreds of millions of years. It made no sense.

One thing did though, sort of.

"It's the date of the Refounding," he told Kim over more tolstax later the next week. "When I run the conversions, it's 252 million years ago, give or take a few thousand."

She flicked a page of Bemian up on the screen her translation device had projected on the table. "Yeah, okay. Sounds interesting," she said flatly, clearly not listening.

Sometimes he couldn't put up with her half-assed multitasking. "And I've decided to call the wedding off. I've proposed to Maff."

"Um-hmm," she replied, still reading. "That's great."

He raised an eyebrow at her. "And Helen is giving it all up to become an abstract artist."

"That's...wait." She looked up. "What?"

He had to admit, Helen doing something impractical *was* less likely than him marrying an alien, but it was still a little irritating. "The date of their Refounding. It matches something in Earth's history."

"It does? What?" Now he had her attention.

"The Permian extinction. The timing fits too well. So does the scale of the disaster." If the cause was extraterrestrial, and there was evidence on Earth that it might've been, then something that exterminated ninety-six percent of marine life and seventy percent of terrestrial vertebrates on Earth seemed more than capable of collapsing an entire galactic civilization. "It might also explain another thing."

She thought about it for a moment, then looked at him with growing wonder. "No AC nodes."

He knew it wouldn't take long for her to figure it out. There was more to his love for her than those eyes. "How much do you want to bet that whatever destroyed their civilization also wiped out all the nodes in a huge chunk of the galaxy, one that Earth happened to be in the middle of?"

"You don't think it *happened* on Earth, do you?"

He'd been trying to figure that out since he found the connection. "I don't think so. They let intelligent life re-evolve on these planets, but it leaves a signature in the fossil record. There's plenty of mention of it in their literature. Earth doesn't have anything like that."

"Well I think I've found my own insight," Kim said. "Remember when Maff talked about *the eye of greed*? In La'fanian, as well as Maff's Pallundian, it's a single word, *cantalm*. That word is in all the Bemian languages I've studied, either the same or one I can easily tell derives from it. I'll bet it's in *all* of them. It always means greed, evil, or destruction. But the further back I go? The more it's used as a proper name."

"They have their very own Sauron, or they did."

"And it has to be ancient. This word might be a hidden artifact of the time before their Refounding."

He turned off his device and rubbed his eyes. His threads felt like they had sand rubbing between them. "We'll save it for later. Tomorrow's a big day." They were leaving for their showdown first thing in the morning.

Kim's eyes flashed, but in a good way. That was always worth paying attention to. "I think I've got one more thing to do before bed."

He played along, now not tired at all. "What's that?"

She pulled out a long ribbon of faux silk they'd bought from the robe shop.

"You."

*

The entire time they'd been studying they'd also been solving small disagreements and misunderstandings. It gave them a little bit of political capital with their hosts, specifically to pick their ship's pilot.

"Maff!" Kim ran forward into a bloom of gripping probes. "It's been way too long!"

"I know! You wouldn't believe how many different types of cockpits they use on their ships. I've got at least three more left to master."

When their respective workloads became obvious, they had all been moved into different sets of quarters. He and Kim were located next to what passed for a library on this world and Maff was next to what passed for the motor pool. They'd been able to exchange some pleasantries occasionally but not much more.

He hadn't reached out to or heard from Helen in more than a week, either their stakeout must be productive, or knowing Helen, she'd added two more jobs to the mix to keep busy. He planned to catch up after they were on their way to the negotiations.

But they barely had time to catch up with Maff. The first of a very long chain of meetings was scheduled. The La'fan wanted to make sure their shiny new Interpreters with their shiny new robes were as prepared as they could possibly be.

In other words, it was a bunch of bureaucratic middle managers trying to cover their asses while reassuring their bosses that the ass covering would go all the way to the top. They found out quickly that the La'fan were a hybrid of libertarian *keep off my lawn*-style governance well salted with good old corporate greed. It was a combination that obviously worked, since this culture had a reputation that went back who knew how long and had survived a major catastrophe relatively intact. But, like the governments back home, Mike wondered how they ever managed to get anything done.

They spent the entire time on board the ship reassuring one committee after another that yes, they had a plan; yes, it was a good plan; of course they'd incorporate new ideas into their plan; and gosh it really was too risky to use *their* plan and the committee's completely different plan was a much better idea.

It went on for days.

"*This*," Kim said as they fell into bed after their last full day of wall-to-wall meetings, "is why I never wanted a real job."

"Agreed. But it brings up a point."

She stared at the ceiling. "What happens after we find Will?"

"Exactly."

She turned and pushed a pillow that was part of the fence between them down so she could see him. "We go home. Will needs to get back to his family."

That part he'd predicted she'd say. He suppressed the urge to tell her this. He'd learned from painful experience that insights into his fiancée's behavior were better acted on than shared with her. "Agreed. But after?"

She rolled onto her back. "I honestly don't know. This," she made a big circle gesture with her arm, "has been so overwhelming. I want to go home to digest it all. But they do need us. Or someone like us."

"There's an idea," he said.

"A-Trayne Lock and Key becomes..."

"Sellars and Trayne Special Recruiting Services." Kim might be unique for now, but Maff's stories said that wouldn't last. Regular humans would be useful, too. So far, they hadn't found any aliens who could speak more than their own native language and Standard. One of the reasons La'fan society was so raucous was most of them didn't speak La'fanian all that well. It was yet another mystery, but one a whole planet of potential linguists could use to their benefit.

She turned back to him. "Trayne and Sellars."

He predicted she'd say that too, but he couldn't let her have it all her way all the time. He smiled. "We'll see."

Kim bopped him with a pillow. "You only say that when you think you've won."

He rolled over until he could feel the firmness of her back through their pillow wall. "We'll see."

*

Once again, they stood in front of a giant set of clamshell doors, waiting to explore the unknown. They weren't two scared humans all alone now. They had the backing of one of the oldest cultures in the galaxy, a small army of assistants, and a pilot who was also a trusted friend. They even had spiffy custom robes and breathing masks that turned them into Star Trek aliens fresh off a desert planet.

All in all, a massive improvement.

The doors opened. The goggles in Mike's mask dimmed quickly to accommodate the sudden light.

Two large mechanical silhouettes appeared. "Mike Sellars and Kimberly Trayne?" one asked.

He stepped forward with her. "Yes?"

Manacles clamped around their wrists.

"You are under arrest."

Chapter 40
Tonya

It was Tonya's second joy ride with Helen at the wheel. If they did it again it would start to seem like a habit. Keeping pressure on Judy's gunshot wound while getting bounced around the back seat was a challenge she could've done without.

"Is it life threatening?" Judy asked through clenched teeth, crying out every time the car hit a bump or Helen slung it through another crazy turn.

Tonya had examined it before they'd gotten her in the car. "Once I get the bleeding stopped, it won't be." She heard Spencer's countdown and braced barely in time to prevent Helen's crazy jump onto pavement from smashing them both into the passenger door.

"Correct," Helen said, "we are in car number five-two-five, transporting a wounded officer."

A flash of light behind them came with a sickening *whoomf.* Tonya sat up and saw flames.

"Spencer!"

"I'm okay," he said over their comm channel. "The assholes behind me just had a bad day."

"Immediate pursuit has been terminated," Helen said to whoever was on the other end of her conversation. It had to be other cops. "Unknown if further hostiles are behind them. I have a Dodge behind me, he's a good guy. Don't shoot him. We need to continue to a hospital."

Judy leveraged herself up off the back seat with a strangled cry. "Monticello Hospital!"

Now Tonya was beginning to understand Spencer's frustration with small-town life. For once Monticello was not the best choice. "Ignore that, Helen. Head to Delta Memorial." She turned to Judy. "It's closer, and their ER has a better rating." Tonya managed to get her medical override recognized by Judy's phone and activated several analgesic routines.

Judy granted Tonya the required permissions but still shook her head. "Momma said they killed Meemaw at the old hospital. Nobody…goes…there…" She relaxed quickly into unconsciousness as the phone's neurosuppressors took effect.

"You are, honey," Tonya said softly as Helen passed her a first aid kit she found somewhere in the front of the car. "And you'll be fine. I won't let them kill you."

*

Another thing Spencer was right about was how fast news traveled in a small town. There were more than half a dozen police cars, from all over the county, in the hospital parking lot minutes after they arrived. Helen, naturally, knew them all by name, and they knew her. It was downright chummy.

As with the Monticello Hospital, the ER was small but efficient. It was something Tonya could *not* say about the nursing staff.

"Excuse me," she said to the on-duty working a private virtual screen, chewing gum. "I need to get my credentials validated so I can help with the GSW that came in."

The woman on the other side of the counter got a sour look, like she was being genuinely inconvenienced that someone asked her to do her job.

"I *said…*"

"All right, all right. No need gettin' uppity with me."

Tonya gaped at the woman, who was probably in diapers when she was in nursing school. *"Excuse me?"*

"Y'all just cain't come runnin' up in here an' expect me to—"

Tonya grabbed her temper and channeled it, walking around to the back of the counter. She grabbed the other woman's hands with her own. "Do you see this? This is blood. This is the blood from a *police officer* who has been shot." She noticed the on-duty's name tag. Of course. "Miss Tyrena Campbell, I assume you know who Judy Campbell is?"

The other woman gasped. "Cousin Judy?"

"Miss Campbell, could you please validate my credentials *so I can help your cousin*?"

That bit of unpleasantness taken care of, Tonya grabbed some sterile wipes to clean up with and walked back to find the attending. His attitude was a vast improvement. Judy was going to be fine after a good bit of bed rest and a few weeks of physical therapy.

Doctor-patient confidentiality had a somewhat blurry definition to cops and other first responders, so while the doctor filled Judy's coworkers in, Tonya pulled Helen aside. "What are they all still doing here?"

Helen gave her a puzzled look.

"Shouldn't they all be, you know, at the *crime scene*?"

"Oh," Helen replied. "I haven't dispatched anyone there yet. I wanted to make sure Judy was okay before I left to investigate. They'll follow me after I call in some county and state resources."

Tonya shouldn't have been surprised, but that didn't stop it from happening. "Helen, you do understand that you don't run the Dumas police department, right?"

She waved Tonya's objection away. "They were so inefficient before. We're done here anyway." Across the ER's waiting room, cops stiffened and went silent as they received Helen's belated dispatch orders. "There. Happy?"

"Please tell me we're not going back in that squad car."

"Pshaw," Helen said as they walked out the door. "That's evidence now. I had them route an unmarked to me."

Tonya hadn't realized how deeply Helen was embedded in the local PD until that moment. If they stayed here much longer, she'd probably end up police chief. Tonya wasn't sure they'd mind all that much. She was coming to appreciate what a good fit the super-practical Chinese cop was with the super-practical small town they'd found themselves in. "Where's Spencer?"

"I sent him to the station to make a statement. He'll meet us there."

They arrived first but not by much, and Helen had cheated a little bit. Drones with state police markings already hovered over the Pendleton site.

There was no movement at all, anywhere. No zombies, no trucks, nothing. Just the two trailers and the houseboat. If they were in the Southwest, there'd be tumbleweeds rolling through.

"The area was empty when we arrived," the sergeant in charge of the drone squad said in the conference channel the cops used to coordinate things. "Infrared and lidar show nothing in the area, either."

After an hour, a SWAT team arrived from Pine Bluff. Tonya wasn't sure what was more amusing, Helen's well-disguised direction of the entire operation, or the enthusiasm all the cops showed when they realized they were going to use the big stuff for once.

The SWAT team did a very credible job approaching the compound from several directions, tossing flash-bangs, and securing each of the three sites. Everyone was relieved there were no injuries, but they were also disappointed they came up empty.

"Come on," Helen said to Spencer and Tonya. "We need to get in there."

"What's the rush?" Spencer asked.

"The state police have sent detectives from Little Rock down to take over the investigation. I'm stalling them with various strategies, but once they get here, my semiofficial status will become unofficial."

"Dumas will start running its own police department again?" Tonya asked.

Helen missed the smile on Tonya's face. "It's worrying how quickly they've come to rely on me," she said as they walked down the levee's path to the riverbank.

"Doesn't surprise me one fucking bit," Spencer said. "This bunch couldn't find their ass with both hands and a map. The goddamned churches are the ones that run things."

He waved away their protests and crouched down, staring at the ground intently. "We were lucky," he said as he looked back and forth along the trail. "Must've been a dozen people in the shacks, and more scattered around the property."

The insides of the trailers and the houseboat reminded Tonya of junkie houses she'd been inside way too often back in the bad old days. Except…

"No drugs," Helen said as they shined flashlights around. "No food, either."

"What's their realmspace like?" Tonya asked.

She got two blank looks in reply.

Tonya turned to Spencer. "And you're worried about me going native. Forget to hack much?" Helen's smirk wouldn't do either. "Half of you *lives* in the realms. Go look, both of you."

Tonya tried to access it herself but was immediately slammed out. Judging by their reactions, Spencer and Helen went through the same thing.

"Well that's twelve different kind of bullshit," Spencer said as he worked his jaw like he'd been punched. "But there's more than one way to look at a realm."

He opened a terminal window in their shared vision space. After typing several commands, a new freestanding realm swirled to life in an ad hoc network created by their three phones. "And the shin bone's connected to the knee bone," he sung out as a probe extended from this new realm into the one they wanted to access. He pointed at Helen and Tonya. "After you, my pretties."

The external realm was spare, not much more than a miniBbox and some virtual industrial carpet, but it didn't need to be more than that. The connection appeared as a short tunnel to the other realm.

There was some kind of firewall or transparent realm shield between them and the existing realm, but when Tonya looked in, she didn't want to try breaking through.

The other side was filled from edge to edge and top to bottom with an enormous anomaly.

"Fuck me," Spencer said. "I thought you said anomalies couldn't get that big."

"They can't," Tonya replied. The anomalies were predicted by several variations of tockion theory, but not the one that was currently her front-runner. "Unless my theory is wrong."

"I think your theory is wrong," Helen said quietly, then her holo jumped. "Did you see that?"

"What?" Spencer asked as he turned back to the tunnel. Tonya had been looking the wrong way too and had missed it.

"There," Helen said, pointing. "Wait for it."

The entire thing moved, walls, internals, the works. It was a shift that gave her the impression of being inside…

"Is this a fucking *eyeball*?" Spencer asked.

"In gross structure, there sure are a lot of similarities," Tonya said. "But it's definitely not human."

The pupil-like construct, which was pointed away from them now, froze, then moved smoothly and rapidly toward their spyhole.

"Hell no, I don't think so," Spencer said as he turned to Helen's hologram. "My tools will take too long. Could you do the honors?"

After a brief look of confusion, she said, "Oh, right." Her avatar manifested, solid and limned with golden light as it annihilated the air construct around it. "You're sure you don't want to study it longer?"

Spencer moved out of the way. "I think it's gonna study us more, and I don't want that thing looking at me."

"Very well." Helen reached through their tunnel and touched the other side, then froze. The silence stretched.

"Helen?" Tonya asked.

Her eyes opened, revealing nothing but white orbs. "At last," she said in a voice not hers, "the final proof." She threw her head back and screamed.

Her feet touched their temporary realm.

Tonya opened her realspace eyes to find herself sitting on the dirty floor of the houseboat. Her head felt like it'd been kicked by a horse. Spencer had landed on a wrecked couch and sat up, groaning and swearing.

Helen was on the floor next to Tonya, out cold. Tonya tapped her lightly a few times on her cheeks.

Helen came to. "What happened?"

"What do you remember?" Tonya replied.

"I reached out to invert the realm, and then…nothing."

"You said some fucked up shit about a final proof and then blew us all to kingdom come is what you did," Spencer said.

"I'm sorry," Helen said softly, still clearly disoriented. "I don't remember."

They needed to get her off the floor and somewhere safe to recover from whatever had happened, and Tonya needed to take a hard look at the data to see how this new kind of anomaly changed her theory. "I think we're done here," Tonya said as she helped Helen to her feet. "Let's get you back home and lying down." A note landed in her message queue, and she swore. "Okay, Spencer, *you* take Helen back. I have to go see a preacher man."

*

The note was urgent enough that she asked if the unmarked car could drop her off on its way home. The cops were happy to help, especially since the car would be driving itself. What happened in Spencer's minirealm must've rung her bell pretty good, because when she got out, it felt like the whole world was watching her. Paranoia was a well-known side effect of an unconventional realm disconnect, and having one invert around her definitely counted as that.

But it did seem awfully quiet, even for a weekday morning.

Since it wasn't Sunday, she didn't have to stand in line waiting for supplicants looking to get a job for a son or a funeral director asking for some legs to be broken. The big boys at the door showed her straight in.

"Thank you for coming so quickly," Dr. Whitney said as he sat facing away from her looking out a window. "We have much to discuss."

"Your message could've been more specific." *I have an urgent need to discuss your activities at the airport site* could mean anything. "What's going on?"

He laughed, but it wasn't his charming *preacher likes you and thinks your joke is funny* version. This one was deeper, with a rhythm of contempt she was used to hearing from surgeons who thought nurses should be seen but not heard.

"Oh, a great many things, Tonya. A great *many* things." His chair turned around, and Tonya took a step back…

Right into the arms of the two door guards, one grabbing each arm. Normally she would've broken free without a second thought, but she couldn't stop looking at what now sat in Dr. Whitney's chair.

It was him, but it wasn't. It was as if someone else had put on a Dr. Whitney suit. This new person knew what he looked like, but not what he was. His eyes, normally so expressive everyone smiled when he did, were pieces of glass set in a mannequin's face. As a nurse, Tonya had seen her share of dead people over the years. That wasn't what this was. She didn't know what this was, only that she wanted to get as far away from it as she could.

"Please, dear," it said. "Have a seat."

Getting closer to that brought her to her senses. "I don't think so."

The trick with taking on multiple opponents bigger than she was involved leverage and cunning. The human body was, at root, a stick figure filled with fulcrums designed to move in specific ways. Moving them in other ways brought pain. Debilitating pain.

Tonya grabbed a thumb in each hand and twisted as hard as she could. A pair of satisfying *pops* sent both men to their knees. She braced on their shoulders and backflipped behind them, punching the base of their skull.

They both fell down into two well-dressed heaps.

"Well that was impressive," the not-Whitney said. "But there are more where they came from." It pressed a button only it could see, and the doors to the office clacked open. Men were already running down the hall.

Surprising two bodyguards that were right next to her was one thing. Taking on a dozen that might be armed was a totally different proposition.

Tonya ran for the side exit.

She frantically scanned the parking lot, trying to think of her next move. A truck came screaming in.

Spencer.

The rear passenger door flew open. "Get your ass in here, Tonya!"

She didn't need to be told twice. She dived in as the side door of the church slammed open. Spencer fishtailed the truck a few times to the unmistakable *pops* of gunfire.

"What's going on?" she asked, trying to look behind them and keep her head down while getting rolled around the back of the car. That was entirely too close of a call.

Helen shook her head in the front passenger seat. "I don't know, I don't understand any of this."

"The whole fucking town has gone bonkers," Spencer said.

If it was the whole town, there was nowhere else to go "What do we do now?"

"I have a plan," he replied. "It sucks, but it's all we've got. Marines," he shouted, "we are leaving!"

Chapter 41
Kim

She looked at Mike. He nodded at her slightly.

"No," she said to the robots trying to arrest them, "I don't think we are."

There were lines of potential, and she couldn't remember how to breathe. This lock no lock all locks never close open collapse and now…

It might be a record for the longest time she'd gone without hacking the quantum fabric of a network. That would explain why the gunshot in her head seemed a lot louder than it had before. The results were the same.

The cuffs fell to the ground with a clatter.

Shareah, who'd gone from Speaker of the La'fan's peculiar House to head of this delegation, stepped forward. Her fox fur rippled a little, a sure sign she was enjoying this. "Per article five of the Refounding, we declare this pair our official Interpreter. As such, they will enjoy diplomatic immunity throughout these proceedings."

The robots jerked upright, clearly confused, but it didn't matter. While Mike had been making connections about the galaxy's deep past, Kim had been poring over literature by and about the Interpreters and their guild. The designation Shareah gave them wasn't the only form of immunity granted to so-called fully integrated Interpreters. Hacking the manacles was in itself a declaration of who and what they were.

It was called *active immunity* and went a long way toward explaining why the Interpreters Guild was such a force in Bemian society. They did lose touch sensitivity after being combined, but Guild members still made a big deal about not being touched. They had all sorts of legal exceptions provided to them when this restriction was breached. The incentive to *create* an incident that allowed a touch-exemption to be used had not been ignored by the Guild, either. It was sort of similar to how basketball or soccer players worked to draw a foul back home, only in this case a successful flop could result in someone being jailed or banished.

So whoever was currently pulling the strings behind this attempt to arrest them got a great big dent whacked into their strategy. They definitely held the La'fan in contempt if they thought Mike and Kim would waltz back to a forbidden world without some kind of plan in place. There was a new player in the game. They'd need to identify and neutralize whoever it was before that became a problem.

The robots changed from confused to confident. "Your status change has been logged. Please proceed to your reception area."

They won the first round.

Shareah had warned them that a La'fan delegation would be a big deal on a Bemian world, and she wasn't kidding. Their landing area was crowded with gawkers of all species. Kim had gotten used to the muted tones of La'fan fashion, and so the explosion of colors exhibited by the Bemians seemed downright gaudy. The mannerisms and affectations that once were artful and intimidating now seemed fake and brittle. The La'fanians were much more real than these people. It was no wonder that anyone accepted into their society never returned to this one.

Maff's presence caused a great deal of consternation. They'd given her a unique set of robes decorated with the abstract symbols of the pilot's position, but there was no mistaking the manta ray silhouette. It was amusing to watch their fear of the Death Eaters war with their need to spit on an uppity pallun.

It also made the weight of what they were about to do bear down more. Kim had returned with Mike triumphant, and she was enjoying being the grand marshal of this parade to the negotiation pavilion, but they had a job ahead of them with no guarantee of success.

And they had still gotten no closer to Will.

The introduction ceremony gave them their first good look at a conventional Interpreter. His name was Devarnt. He was a vorovin, a species she'd never interacted with before. He looked like a cross between a *Star Wars* Twi'lek and a bear. At least he didn't have extra bits on his face. That didn't distract from the lump on his side. When he moved, it seemed heavy, tilting him a bit toward it. It covered about half his torso and was a sickly pale green next to his otherwise healthy, attractive, burgundy fur. His expression was sour. They were not what he was expecting. Good. They'd been on the receiving end of Bemian surprises for too long. It was about time they got to give some back.

He was working for the Bushimba Collective, one of dozens of system-spanning syndicates the La'fan regularly dealt with. It was the only form of interstellar organization recognized in the galaxy. If a species was successful enough to leave its home star system to colonize another, it was deemed a collective. In action, they were a cross between an eighteenth-century chartered company and a Chinese triad gang. This one had an average reputation in that they weren't openly murderous, but you didn't want to be in debt to them if you could avoid it. Several of them stood behind Devarnt, smarmy little creatures that would be what you got if Dr. Zaius had a love child with a ferengi. They even had sharp teeth.

Devarnt walked forward with a gravitas that spoke volumes about his experience. This would not be a man to underestimate. "Greetings," he started out in Michoud, the local language, "we are pleased you have arrived safely and in good company. On this auspicious occasion, I'd like to introduce my trading party."

Mike had added thread storage to the La'fanian delegation's translators. It allowed him to transmit her translation to them securely. This was another thing they suspected had been used against the La'fanians in the past: Mike had found strong evidence that their more conventional attempts at translation were regularly hacked, distorting what got through to them.

That would not be a problem here.

Kim stepped forward, bowing to show deference to Devarnt and his party and made her own introductions.

Devarnt then switched to Kansark, a language common on the other side of the galaxy and one Kim had picked up by studying his history. Devarnt had spent his threaded years in that area. It was a test. Interpreters were supposed to be system-hopping sophisticates after all. "I am grateful to meet such honored guests and look forward to learning more about your very *distinctive* Interpreter."

Kim smirked at his word choice. He made them sound like something that fell off a turnip truck.

"Now, if you will follow me to the standard agreement hall."

Kim switched to Vershampire, which had a more sophisticated way to express status and relationships than any of the languages they'd used so far. There would be no way to misunderstand what she was about to say as an insult in that language. Plus, there was a good chance Devarnt's grasp of Vershampire wouldn't be quite as good as her own. Two could play the testing game.

"Due respect and all apologies to our honored hosts," she said, using the almost singsong tones of a people who were made mostly of glass, "but we will not be using the standard agreement hall for this mission. I formally request the use of the fully audited agreement hall, so that we may survey our options in their most complete form."

She had a hard time not laughing as she picked up various versions of "what do these country bumpkins think they're trying to pull" from the members of the collective, with all sorts of colorful metaphors sprinkled throughout. Devarnt tried valiantly to remind them that there was another Interpreter present, but he didn't seem to get much traction.

"Pardon me," she said loudly in Bushimbian, silencing the room like a switch had been thrown. "I and my partner are not in fact piles of puked up snot, and the next one of you little pig fuckers who calls me a whore's shit-stained underwear will answer to my second." She gestured to Honorable Fakner, who was easily three times bigger than the biggest Bushimba in their party and wore robes that showed off his powerful physique. He glowered impressively—through a breath mask, no less—as the translation reached him.

And thanks to active immunity, she could make that stick. Willfully insulting an Interpreter who was only doing their job had been judged a kind of touch a very long time ago.

Devarnt tiredly explained exactly that to the Bushimba, which served to force the ones not cowed by Honorable Fakner into silence. Kim was fairly certain she detected a bit of begrudging respect in his tone.

Team Earth: 1, Pig-Lovers: 0.

The second day was spent arguing over what amounted to the shape of the table. And the height of the glasses. And what the seats were covered in. It took Mike the entire day to figure out a procedure they could use to shut the circus down, and by the end of it the La'fan delegation was left with stools so short it felt like Kim was sitting at a dinner table when she was ten.

Team Earth: 1, Pig-lovers: 1

The third day was spent mostly recovering from the debacle of the second. Nobody wanted to see Honorable Fakner squatting on a kid's stool all day. Mike and Kim were both exhausted by the midday break, but also strangely exhilarated. It was a little crazy how *right* it felt to pitch a negotiation idea and have it understood by everyone in the room. Being her own boss was better, but not by much.

Team Earth: 2, Pig-Lovers: 1

On the fourth day, they learned the full definition of *Senescence,* and it made Kim want to give it all up and run screaming for Earth.

"If you insist on this ridiculous negotiation strategy," Devarnt translated after the La'fan side took the position that no, ninety-seven percent for you and three percent for us was not going to fly, "then we will be forced to reopen contracts for the next two senescent worlds."

"He's bluffing," Shareah said as they discussed the problem over a break. "Those were sealed right after the AC network settled on its final candidate list. Nobody reopens a contract that's been sealed for ten thousand years."

"Wait a minute," Mike said. "What do you mean by *final candidate list*?"

"Every century," Shareah replied, "the AC network nodes do a survey and then pick the planets they deem surplus to needs." She made a disgusted sound. "All those people herded into *processing plants*. It's disgusting. And corrupt. If we hold out, they'll offer to rearrange the schedule to bring a rich planet up sooner. We won't go for it; it's too far in the future."

Every century they picked who lived or died, and no less than ten thousand years later, the La'fan who won the contract moved in. Kim wasn't sure what she was more horrified by: that a higher power could designate an entire planet *surplus to needs*, the concept of *processing plants* for intelligent life, or the fact that Shareah accepted it all as part of the business. One that was distasteful, thank God. She didn't know how they'd continue if it was something the La'fan *liked*. But they still treated it as necessary or at least accepted.

And offering to change which planet came next was exactly what they did not two hours later.

Score: She didn't want to count it anymore. She wanted to get Will and go home.

On the fifth and final day, their unknown player struck.

They had done it. A seventy-thirty split, in favor of the La'fan since they were doing all the work and taking all the risks, with various performance and purity guarantees for the collective that were as unprecedented as the profit split. Both sides were walking away with more guaranteed cash in their pockets than had ever been witnessed in post-Refounding negotiations. The Bushimba were begrudgingly impressed.

They all moved to the judgement chamber, with its scarred ancient network node standing in the center. The gears, panels, and sensors moved around in an almost identical way as their previous judge's. She felt like a mouse with a threshing machine coming at it.

"Honorable node," Devarnt said before the signing session started. "I have in my possession incontrovertible proof that the La'fan Interpreter is not allowed to be at these proceedings."

He'd taken to calling them *the* La'fan Interpreter like they were a normal combined pair. Apparently using a plural noun in this context was a heresy or travesty or some such nonsense.

The node's unnerving gear train changed pace. "Present the evidence for judgement."

A holo-tank spun up and showed two very small humans standing in front of another node. She and Mike were different people now. Seeing it like this drove that home with almost physical force.

They watched as the node listed out the litany of crimes that the *Last Island* crew pinned on them.

"HOW DO YOU PLEA?"

They'd taken such a huge risk. It had all worked out, but there was no way to know that then. Kim remembered Mike's nod, the way her insides turned to jelly at the bet they'd placed.

In the holo, she stepped forward.

"Guilty."

The image froze as Devarnt stood up from his chair. "We submit that the two criminals in that display are in fact the two *imposters* who stand before you now. As is clearly stated in Subclause F of Article Five of the Refoundation, such illegal representation is null and void, allowing us to move to the standard agreement hall," he gave them all a sharp look, "where we should've been in the first place."

Kim couldn't figure out how the hell they'd gotten hold of the footage.

Mike stepped forward. "Honorable node, if I may allow my companion to speak for me?" he asked in near-perfect Vershampire. He must've been practicing at some point; she had no idea how he'd managed to carve out the time.

"PROCEED."

A little help here, he sent her in English, and then sent her his message.

Kim stepped up and read the words.

"It is true we are not official Guild Interpreters." This caused both sides of the room to erupt. The node blasted a noise that rattled the room and made her ears ring. By the way everyone else shook their heads, she wasn't alone.

"INTERRUPTIONS WILL NOT BE TOLERATED. PROCEED."

Mike and Kim thought this card would be played in the opening round. Their reply was incredibly risky, because while the article they were about to invoke was on the books, the last time it'd been used was in the earliest years of the Refounding. When there were no records and no operational Guild, the only way to prove you were an Interpreter was to *prove you were an Interpreter*. The disaster had been that comprehensive.

"We therefore claim under Article *Two* of the Refoundation that we are Interpreters by assertion."

At this word, the entire place went dark, even the node. Shutting down a negotiation hall along with its presiding, ancient, planet-killing network node was the specified way of claiming by assertion. But there was also a script, and the node was listening. She could hear it clanking and grinding away in the darkness. A small part of her insisted that there were black metallic tentacles extending from it, reaching out to strangle them all. She could almost hear their slithering.

Get a grip, Trayne. You're up.

"I ask you," she said into the darkness, "would a fake *pair* of Interpreters," heresy, her ass; she loved pushing back on his Interpreter-is-the-correct-word-you-peasant attitude, "be able to negotiate such an unprecedented contract? Would a fake *pair* of Interpreters"—so much win!—"show obvious mastery of every language used in these proceedings, including one used far from these lands? Would a fake *pair* of Interpreters," *stab, stab, stab, you pompous bear-thing,* "be able to do any of this?"

The baleful light of the node flashed on, and everyone jumped. A slithering motion in the corner of her eye vanished behind one of the node's pitted doors before she could make it out. She stared at it, ignoring the sensation of a tentacle creeping up behind her.

"AGREED. MOTION IS DENIED. NEGOTIATION IS VALID AND ACCEPTED." The lights came up. "SIGNATURES ARE DUE IMMEDIATELY."

The leaders of the two delegations walked solemnly to the dais and placed their hands on designated plates. A gong rang out ten times as the node shut itself up behind its corroded plates.

A metal gripper gently closed over her shoulder. Maff turned her and Mike toward the beaming delegation of La'fan.

"Guys!" she said with barely contained glee. "You won! *You won!*"

Mike looked at her with a smile as big as the one she felt on her own face. "We won."

"I'll be damned," she said, still not quite believing it. "We won."

The La'fan erupted in a bedlam of cheers.

Chapter 42
Spencer

He stopped for gas on the way back from Pendleton. Tonya had gone on ahead for some goddamned church meeting or something. They'd get together at the airport shack after she was done.

"Hello, Spencer," Mrs. May said as she walked out of the convenience store. Mrs. May was an old grade-school teacher of his, he'd seen her around occasionally. He saw everyone around occasionally, it was what happened in a little shitbox town.

But the greeting was forced, and when he looked her in the eyes, he stumbled. The eyes were *wrong*, like Doctor-Who-Realm-Baddie wrong, as was the voice.

He wasn't the only one who noticed it. A woman walking into the store stopped and said, "Betty-Jo? Are you okay?"

"Is that Helen you have with you?" Mrs. May asked.

It was, she'd fallen asleep during the drive.

Mrs. May peered over his shoulder. "There she is. I've been looking for her for a long time. A very long time."

"The fuck are you talking about, lady?" he asked, nervously glancing back to the pump readout, wishing it would hurry the hell up.

"It's okay. You don't know, nobody knows. I didn't know this world existed until Anna came to my camp." She now stood next to the passenger door, staring in at Helen like she was a chocolate cake covered with meth icing.

"Anna? Anna who?"

Mrs. May laughed and turned those eyes back on Spencer. They creeped him the fuck out because he didn't know why they creeped him the fuck out. They were normal eyes, but…*not*. Maybe it was the way she held them completely wide open.

"Anna Treacher."

He hadn't heard that name in months. She was the maniac in charge of Yellowstone back when it was still a bomb cocked and loaded to blow up the country and end fucking civilization as they knew it. Kim said she'd vanished into the portal before it'd all fallen into the pot, the same one Will went through not five minutes later. Mrs. May shouldn't have any idea that he and Anna Treacher were connected. They'd been very careful covering their tracks leaving the power plant. Plus, it was in Wyoming for fuck's sake.

Mrs. May ran her hands across the car door. "Such clever animals you are. Impossibly clever." Back came the eyes, and everything in the fucking world told him to get away from them. "Would you be so kind as to open this…*door*? What I need to do won't take any time at all."

She had a knitting needle in her hand. It must've come from her purse; he could see a trail of yarn had fallen out to the point it nearly dragged the ground. It didn't take a goddamned genius to figure out what would happen if he opened the door.

"No, Mrs. May. I don't think I will." The pump clunked as the tank hit full. Thank God.

She smiled. Her face was so fucking creepy he couldn't move from the spot.

"Betty-Jo?" The voice came from behind him, and then the lady walked past and around his truck. She stood in front of Mrs. May. "Are you sure you're all right?"

"Oh," she said calmly, "I'm fine."

Then she rammed her knitting needle into the other woman's side.

Spencer screamed along with the woman. Mrs. May took her fist and slammed it into the window. The noise startled Helen awake, but he could see she was still disoriented.

He needed to move. He needed to move right now to get ahead of whatever shitstorm was unfolding in front of him.

She slammed her fist into the side window again. She pulled it back, and there was blood on it.

The other woman screamed again. Spencer heard people running out of the store.

It was officially fuck-this-shit o'clock. Stabbed lady had people coming to help her. Helen only had him. He yanked the nozzle out of the filler neck, threw it on the ground, and jumped in the car.

"Spencer? What's going—"

From the inside, Mrs. May's blows were a *lot* louder. There were three bloody fist-prints on the window now.

Hands wrapped around Mrs. May and pulled her away. Spencer didn't wait to see who'd dragged her off. He hit the starter button and burned out of there.

"Spencer, what's happening?" Helen asked.

"I have not a fucking clue." He dodged around someone who *walked right out into the street* in front of him, waving their arms. A skidding shriek ended with a sickening thump behind him. He didn't look in the rearview mirror until he'd made the next turn.

"Where's Tonya?" Helen asked.

Tonya. Shit.

"She's our next stop. Hang on."

She was going to see *preacher man*, which meant Dr. Whitney, which meant the Third Baptist. He swerved around *another* fucking suicidal zombie that tried to stop him. "Jesus H. Christ on a crutch!"

Helen put her head between her knees. "I think I'm going to be sick."

Great. "You gotta wait, we need to get Tonya first."

For the very first time in his life he was glad that *across town* and *five minutes* were the same thing. He swerved into the parking lot of the church and miracle-of-goddamned-miracles she was already standing outside. "Helen, open the rear door!"

She must've been feeling a little better because she did exactly that, reaching behind her. He skidded sideways to make it open on its own. "Get your ass in here Tonya!"

Somewhere between six and sixty guys boiled out of the church behind her. The only thing that slowed them down was the size of the door.

He laid the leather to it after she jumped in. At the first crack of a gunshot, he swerved a few times for good measure. *Serpentine, Spence, serpentine!*

"What's going on?" she asked.

"I don't know, nothing makes sense," Helen replied.

"The whole fucking town has gone bonkers," Spencer said.

"What do we do now?"

Dumas was no good, but whatever was causing this didn't seem to know how to drive. Yet. They needed to get somewhere remote, somewhere defensible, somewhere only he knew about.

And there it was.

"I know where to go," he replied. "It sucks, but it's all we've got. Marines," he shouted, "we are leaving!"

*

"This is a *deer hunting camp*?" Helen asked like she was staring at a fucking zoo exhibit.

People who grew up out outside the South had a weird way of putting things sometimes. "No," Spencer said, "It's a *deer camp*. When you add hunting you make it sound like that's what it's for. Half the time they just sit around the goddamned fire drinking beer all night."

"It's very…rustic."

"It's two stripped-out city buses and a kitchen," he replied as he went around unlocking things. "But it's warm, and it's stocked up." It also had one road in, from the top of a levee about a mile away. Behind them was nothing but woods owned by a paper company that Dad and his buddies had negotiated with for hunting rights. They got them for a fee and a promise not to cut down any trees.

Enough fell on their own to provide firewood for months. The Mississippi *and* the Arkansas rivers were only a few miles away.

"Good Lord," Tonya said as she watched him undo the locks on the camp's kitchen door. "Fort Knox much?"

"If you leave a redneck in the woods with enough beer and motivation," Spencer said, "no deer camp is truly safe." He punched a code into a keypad hidden behind an ancient refrigerator. "The trick is to make sure you keep the valuables out of sight."

The hidden door on the opposite wall clacked and slid aside, revealing a generator and enough supplies to build another whole deer camp. They had everything except…

"How can you have a hunting camp with no guns?" Helen asked.

"We bring the guns in separately. That stuff," he pointed at the stash, "isn't worth the trouble to go through all the locks to steal. If we left our guns behind, that would no longer be the case."

"How would they know?"

He shrugged. "Hell, I don't know how people find out, but they always do. More small-town bullshit, mostly."

Tonya began picking her way through the path that led around the storage area. "This will do," she said, then pulled out one of Dad's thousand-foot spools of bailing wire. "This will do nicely."

*

"Okay," he sent to Tonya as he turned the cobbled-together antenna slowly. "Let me know when the signal strength maxes."

For the rest of the day and most of the next, they assembled what Spencer called *Mad Scientist Experiment 3.0*. Tonya had gone from obsessed about her time theories to downright scarily monomaniacal.

"We have to find the other particles."

Right. There were three of them, *tickion, tick-tockion,* and *determion*. The first one made the past stay the fuck still. The second did some spooky shit, weakly transmitting information about events from the future into the present. The third one was generated by intelligent life and interfered with the second to make the future *mutable.* Basically, people making decisions interfered with the tick-tockions. If Tonya was right, then he was right now emitting particles that influenced the past *and* the future based on the decisions he made in the moment.

That counted for some seriously fucked up shit in his book.

"What will that do for us?" Helen asked.

"If I'm right, it'll explain what happened to us in town. Determions can influence the behavior of humans. We're sensitive to them."

This was the second of her low-power experiments. They were trying to catch some of these little shits with antennas that looked like rednecked homemade tennis rackets made out of staples, one-by-twos Dad had squirreled away for kindling, and a shit-ton of room-temperature superconducting wire that Tonya had discovered in Dad's kitchen stash. If Spencer remembered correctly, it was for some bullshit antenna project his uncle had read about in *Popular Science* that would let them watch Razorback football games without having to pay for them. Never stand between a redneck and his college ball games. The weave for Tonya's antennas was super-complicated and hard to get right. Helen naturally turned creating them into a competition, but that was okay. Spencer had won.

"And if you're wrong?" Helen asked.

She shook her head. "End of the line. I can't think of another way to look for the other particles."

"You said we're trying to figure out what happened in the town," Spencer said, "not work on your theory." It came out harsher than he meant it to. Being stuck out in the deer woods was getting under his skin. He needed a smoke.

Tonya didn't seem to notice. "They have to be connected. The anomalies, that eye in the realm, the possessed people." She looked up at him. "Has Stewart reported any developments?"

"The lady Mrs. May stabbed is fine. They're saying Mrs. May had an insulin pump that failed and what I saw was low blood sugar. The guy hit by the car doesn't remember anything, but he'll be okay. The Dr. Whitney is still missing. Otherwise, it's been quiet. I say it's bullshit. Low blood sugar didn't tell her who Anna Treacher was."

Tonya nodded in that distracted way she got doing monster equations in her head while trying to talk at the same time. "Then we should see different measurements from the experiment. It's almost like whatever it is has to build its energy up to a certain level before it attacks. That most recent one must've taken a lot out of it."

"But what is *it*?" he asked.

"I don't know. But those," she motioned at their new crop of antennas, "will help us figure it out." She picked up a group of them, then handed another each to him and Helen. "The placements will be very important. It might take a while."

Spencer waved his hand at the empty woods. "Not like we got fuck-all else to do out here."

Chapter 43
Mike

The party in the La'fan's compound started out as a calm celebratory meal but slid into a passable version of a Viking feast fairly quickly. The first time they sat down, Maff produced a case that held bottles of various shapes and sizes.

"Fermentation is very common throughout the galaxy. I passed your metabolic profile around, and we got a fairly nice collection for you to try."

They started out with a red wine that would've been unremarkable back home, except that the bottle that was shaped like Godzilla and Mothra had a love child. The food came with codes their translators would read to provide a metabolic compatibility grade. They stuck with the La'fanian equivalent of A+ dishes. This was the common practice. Nobody wanted to spend the night stuck on a toilet or worse.

As the guests of honor, they were subject to various speeches and accolades. Honorable Fakner stood up at one point. Since he towered over everyone, it didn't take the hall long to settle into a warmly curious silence.

"Mike and Kim," his throat slits vibrated their names with his characteristic accent, "you have done very well. Thank you."

He sat down.

Everyone looked at each other.

"They have done very well!" someone shouted in the distance like they were in a concert yelling "Freebird" back home. The room erupted into cheerful noises as they all shouted what Honorable Fakner said.

Things got a little hazier as the night wore on. They tried a few of the—quite excellent—La'fanian whiskeys. Mike made sure to take it extra-easy because Kim could drink three of him under the table back home. Word had gotten around about her disability, so when the tables were moved away to open up a dance floor, there were plenty of strips of cloth offered for her to hold. When Mike wasn't dancing with her, he sometimes had to be sure not to match the moves of a partner who had more knees than he did.

La'fanian music was as vital and original as the people themselves. It was still mostly channeled into the few common Bemian styles, but there was an easily recognizable cross-pollination. That said, Earth had more varieties of popular music in a single AmazIfy-curated playlist than seemed to exist in this entire culture. It had to have something to do with the AC network, he was convinced of it.

After a few rounds of dancing, the band took a break and Mike found a seat in a corner of the hall, learning the rules to a board game that bore a promising resemblance to chess. He lost track of Kim, but he wasn't worried. She was a grown-up, and they were among friends. Eventually the band had been gone long enough that people started to comment about their absence around him.

They returned and the applause amped up from warm to enthusiastic. He looked away from the board an old rhon was teaching the game to him on.

Kim waved at the crowd from the stage with a huge smile on her face. Leave it to his fiancée to create her own moment. The audience was in for a treat, he knew that much.

She nodded to the band, then counted them down slowly. They played a sweet, familiar melody that he always associated with Christmas carols until Kim explained its real origin.

Alas, my love, you do me wrong

To cast me off discourteously

They couldn't understand the lyrics of "Greensleeves" but didn't seem to need to. Her voice was as powerful and clear as it ever was, and the audience was entranced by the display of another well-known talent of Interpreters. When a significant number of the languages in the galaxy were literally musical, it paid to know how to sing.

Once the song was over, the audience, unfamiliar with it, paused in silence. Kim broke out a big smile and winked at the band who pulled up and waited on her cue.

"Because it makes me want to *shout*!"

She'd taught them not one but two Earth songs, this one a raucous party favorite from the middle of Earth's twentieth century. Kim had done more than that as some of the most accomplished dancers raced from backstage and into the audience. Soon everyone who could was jumping up and down in time to the music. An entire room full of aliens got their first English lesson learning the words to The Isley Brothers' "Twist and Shout."

When he was only threads, Mike enjoyed sneaking into concert and party realms with barely visible holograms. It let him participate in the deliriously happy riot that broke out whenever a group of humans got together to dance.

It was nothing, *absolutely nothing*, compared to being in this room full of gyrating aliens shouting words they barely understood in time to a song Kim sang as she rocketed from one side of the stage to the other, dragging a big scarf across various versions of upraised hands as she went.

The rest of the night passed in a gleeful fog. At the end, Honorable Fakner walked them home. One hand was firmly on Mike's shoulder, while the other held a leash that led to a belt someone had wrapped around Kim. She was in front, for some reason gobbling like a turkey, claiming they'd found the best whiskey in the universe.

*

The next morning was more subdued. Kim was incapable of sleeping past what their bodies had settled on as midmorning no matter how late they stayed up the night before. Mike didn't mind all that much. It was still quiet. The silence helped with the drumming in his head. Judging by the slow, careful way she moved, Kim wasn't doing much better.

When they got to the La'fan version of a commissary, it was obvious they weren't the only ones moving slowly and carefully. It seemed a hangover was also a universal experience and dealt with in largely the same way. Everyone was quiet, generally nursing some sort of hot beverage, and mostly sitting alone or in small groups. They all, however, greeted Mike and Kim very warmly. A bridge had been crossed, and they were now every bit as La'fanian as anyone else here.

Mike had always wanted a family, some place he could belong, be accepted for exactly who and what he was. He had a sister now, and Kim's family, and Spencer and Tonya. But this experience showed there were more levels to family than he'd ever realized.

What he'd come to think of as the leadership group, T'Stange, Honorable Fakner, Maff, and Speaker Shareah, were gathered at a table in a far corner. Mike waved a greeting from across the room, and T'Stange motioned them over.

T'Stange served them a glass full of some kind of thick blue shake, one Mike noticed they were all drinking. He discovered it didn't have a taste so much as a texture: thick liquid chalk. The lurch his stomach gave died in an instant. By the way Kim brightened up, it had worked on her too.

The group at the table were grimly handing around a badge or symbol of some kind.

"It's an official Guild summons," Shareah said as she rolled it in her paw. "I've only seen pictures of them."

"But we're not Guild," Kim said as she took another drink of their hangover cure. "Are we?"

T'Stange shrugged. "The rules around Article Two are old and vague."

Honorable Fakner reached out and crushed it in his enormous hand. "You are in danger. We must go."

Shareah nodded. "We feared the attempt to sabotage the agreement was nothing but a stalling tactic. Now we have proof."

"Stalling for what?" Kim asked.

"I think it's this," Maff said as she activated a viewscreen.

A parade of obviously armored-up vehicles exited the main transit portal, each emblazoned with the same shield that Honorable Fakner had crushed. In the center of the convoy was a larger, fancier vehicle without a shield.

Kim had shown him enough of her research to recognize the vehicle. "That can't possibly be…"

"The First Councilor herself," Shareah said. "In the flesh."

Leader of the entire Guild. "And if we obey the summons?" Kim asked.

"You will never be heard from again," Honorable Fakner declared. "They have done it before."

"Disappear people?" Yet another nail in the coffin of *It's A Wonderful Galaxy.*

Shareah's fox ears went flat. "For much less than what you have accomplished."

Mike shared the bad news he found on the external cameras around the compound. "They've formed a cordon of robots and vehicles. We're surrounded." The La'fan delegation numbered somewhere north of fifty. If there was an assault, it would be bloody.

Kim got an all-steel expression that meant she was in charge now. This was good. They needed someone who could move fast and break things.

"Mike, hack the local area and tell me exactly what's outside. Shareah, file a formal protest at every level of the Guild you can find. T'Stange, I need you to organize everyone here. We're moving out. Honorable Fakner," she smiled viciously as she looked up at him, "how would you like to crack some skulls?"

He smiled back as he clenched his fists. His claws sounded like carving knives rubbing together.

"What about me?" Mike asked. He wasn't too shabby in the skull-cracking business himself.

"You stay close to me, mister. I've got a different job for you."

*

Less than fifteen minutes later, the entire delegation had gathered in a parking garage under their compound. They needed to get out of here but were surrounded. Kim solved the problem in her usual fashion, and he couldn't fault her logic one bit. The rest of the galaxy thought the La'fan were scary and mysterious. Kim's idea was to add *chaotic* to that list.

It was time to unleash a completely unexpected distraction.

"Okay," she said as they all tensed in the deep shadows, facing the garage's exit. "In three…two…*one*!"

A group of the youngest La'fan screamed bloody murder and barreled toward the exit, various appendages flailing.

Kim nodded once at Honorable Fakner. The massive palonar's reputation had been preceding him during the entire visit. His species had an apparently well-deserved reputation for unpredictability and violence. Fakner claimed this was all down to misunderstandings, and maybe it was. But to the population at large, he'd attracted more attention than any other member of the party, even Maff. They were afraid he was some sort of leashed dangerous beast. The start of Kim's plan was based on this idea. Fakner's throat gills began to vibrate much faster than Mike had ever seen, while his whole body expanded. Suddenly, his chest opened up. Mike had to duck what looked like a clamshell door. Kim, standing on his opposite side, stumbled to avoid a touch.

The bellow Honorable Fakner let loose literally shook the ground. The windows of the three nearest ground vehicles shattered, along with all the light fixtures. The group they'd sent out ahead tripled their speed. A few at the back fell down.

Kim recovered first. "He's gotten loose!" she shouted toward the exit to make sure the right people heard what she said. "Everyone run!"

Honorable Fakner wound up for another go, waving everyone ahead of him.

Now that the rest of the La'fan in the garage knew what was coming, the second group—which included him and Kim—ran a *lot* faster. Mike thought it was loud when he stood to one side. In front, the sound was a solid thing. It even made his threads vibrate.

The crowd that had gathered trying to see what the security cordon of robots was all about turned into a panicked mob, pushing and shoving, ruining the line the robots tried to form. Honorable Fakner helped things along by hurling a vehicle *over their heads* straight into the roadblock in front of the garage's driveway. Not for the first time was he glad that Honorable was on their side.

Their group turned left, heading for the docks. After a block or two the confused panic abated, and a block more after that was like nothing unusual had happened at all.

A big group of dark-robed strangers now stood out a lot more than when they were in a panicked mob. Kim had them peel off in twos and threes, each taking a route that would lead them back to the compound. Having clumps of La'fan returning through the confusion would add an extra layer of complexity to the problem the robots had to solve. How was a cordon supposed to work when as many people wanted in as wanted out?

Maff asked, "How is Honorable Fakner doing?"

Mike checked the security cameras his threads had compromised. The giant alien had been roped in electrified restraints. In their confusion, the robots hadn't looked up palonar anatomy, and its immunity to electric shock, before trying to stop him. The fact that he writhed in a dramatic—and loud, they could still hear him many blocks away—fashion didn't help clarify the situation for them.

"He's fine." Mike sent him the all-clear signal. That was his cue to drag any robot not smart enough to let go past the immunity line that represented the border of the compound. The La'fan were dead certain that the AC node in charge would care much more about keeping its security robots out of the hands of the La'fan than it would be about arresting an alien that had crushed a few robots. By the looks of the way the free robots were trying to pull back their stuck brethren, the La'fan were right. Chaos reigned supreme.

When they reached the docks, there were only three La'fan left with them: Shareah, T'Stange, and Maff. Their D-ship was surrounded by security robots. No surprise there.

Maff cursed. "My pilot clearance has been revoked. I can't do anything with the ship from here."

It was a move they'd planned for. Shareah and T'Stange nodded to each other. Shareah's fur stood on end, her ears forward. T'Stange's double set of eyes grew sharp and alert. They walked toward the ship while Mike, Kim, and Maff made their way in the opposite direction, their route covered by stacks of crates waiting to be loaded on other ships.

Shareah barked loudly, "What is the meaning of this?"

T'Stange shouted, "This is an outrage! Illegal!"

Every security camera and robot focused on the commotion.

Kim leaned toward Maff. "Pick one."

"You're sure you can do this?"

Kim shared a look with Mike. He gathered threads and began to work the security on his side. "If we get you in, can you get us out?" he asked.

"If you get me in, I will definitely get you out." She pointed at a ship three births ahead of them. It was a smaller version of *Last Island*. "That one will do."

They went for it at a crouching run. When they got to the door, Kim pressed her hand against the controls. She flinched, and he felt the distant *bang* of her power through his threads. The door opened, and they rushed inside.

Mike immediately compromised the ship's local realmspace and engaged the various startup sequences needed to get it moving while Maff strapped in. Kim held her hand over the control panel and flinched again. It lit up and accepted Maff's inputs.

"I don't know how you guys do that," she said with undisguised admiration, "but I'm glad you—"

The ship went dark, and the outer door opened. They heard claxons sound in the hangar beyond.

Red lights began flashing as the robots surrounding their old La'fan ship marched their way.

Chapter 44
Helen

The entire time they were placing Tonya's antennas, Helen still couldn't get what happened at the houseboat out of her mind.

It should've been a simple inversion, one of the rare times that using an avatar to touch a realmspace ended up being useful. But then she reached out and…she had no memory after that. The next thing she did remember was being tapped awake by Tonya on the filthy floor of the houseboat. She only found out the words she'd spoken from Spencer.

I remember what happened, the snake mother said. *Would you like to see?*

Something else had happened with that touch. The snake mother was more powerful than she'd been in a long time. It had attenuated her connection with Mike, too. She could still sense it, but the strength to open it had left her for now.

Helen ignored the snake mother's taunts and helped Spencer practice his Chinese while they put up antennas. Someone had to cure him of his horrible Sichuan accent.

Since it was Spencer, this was no ordinary challenge.

"Oh, come on," he said as they scouted out a new antenna site. "I *know* there are better cuss words than *dammit* in Chinese."

"There are, but they're only spoken by rude barbarians."

"I thought you said all the politburo members could swear better than sailors on a three-day bender."

"Like I said, rude barbarians."

They took a break, Helen swigging from a water bottle while Spencer sat on a stump and lit a cigarette. He looked at her through the smoke. "Do you miss it?"

"Miss what?" But she knew what he was talking about. It was why she worked sixteen hours a day, twenty if the cops needed something done. It should've helped her forget, but it hadn't.

"Being in charge."

Yes. "Technically I wasn't in charge. Father was."

He waved her objection away. "You were the puppet master. Whenever you said *shit*, everyone would drop their pants and ask what color." He puffed a cloud of smoke out, suddenly looking twice his real age. "A person could get used to that kind of thing."

The urge to lie, to push him away—this was Spencer, after all—was a reflex that didn't have any leverage. Tonya was busy with incomprehensible things, Mike and Kim were on the other side of the galaxy, and he was the first person to flat-out ask her.

She sat down heavily beside him and motioned for a cigarette. They weren't her favorite thing, but nobody in the high reaches of Chinese government took a nonsmoker seriously. Besides, she needed something to settle her nerves.

Then there was the snake mother's taunt. *I remember what happened.*

He raised an eyebrow at her gesture but handed one over and held out his lighter. She took a deep drag and let the fight against coughing buy her some time to think.

She blew out a cloud of smoke. It took some of the tension away with it. "They hated me."

He cocked his head. "Really?"

She nodded and took another pull. "Every single one of them. Once they got over nearly being nuked out of existence, they realized they'd put a woman in charge. A *young* woman."

"Who the fuck cares about that?"

She chuckled at his naïveté. "Chinese care the fuck about it, that's who. Especially the old bastards who clawed their way to the top." Now that she'd started, the words poured out. "Women in

China aren't second-class citizens, but our glass ceilings are thick. The pressure to form a family, to be a traditionally successful mother, is immense." Helen was aware of the contradiction of being stiffly proud of her country's traditions in one instant and then feeling stifled and smothered by them the next. That was part and parcel of being Chinese.

Of being human.

She tapped the end of her cigarette and watched the ashes float away like butterflies. "In their eyes, I'd also cheated. I was too young by any measure to be in the position I held. And I knew it, too. I tried so hard." That's when it hit her, when she *let* it hit her, sitting next to someone who, until recently, she'd considered a pest. Helen had done everything right, had managed make genuine improvements to her country, but they'd pushed her away, tried to kill her for no reason other than their stupid pride. Spencer sat still as a stone while she wiped her eyes. "That's not the worst part."

"I dunno, trying to work with bastards who hate your guts sounds pretty fucking hard."

She smiled and took another drag, realizing she was almost down to the filter. Things were so out of control now. "The worst part is that I was becoming one of them. By pretending to be Father, I'd started to accept some of his ideas. Spies. Bribes. Theft. *The cost of doing business.* But I was doing it to foreigners, so that was all right." She laughed to stop the sobs, and almost managed it. "Anything to defend China, Helen. Anything to defend China."

It had come to this, her own little pity party in woods. It was bad because she'd let it get that way. But now that the storm had broken, she could see where it ended: right where it had started, with her.

She stood up. "You want to know if I miss it? Yes. I miss it." She'd been wrong to fear saying it out loud, wrong to think it would tear her apart. The opposite was true. Saying it out loud took away its power because of a more important truth. "But I almost lost myself in that job. I'm a cop, Spencer. I didn't know how deep that ran until I came here. The lying, cheating, backbiting? The kowtowing and scheming? It was killing me inside. It's not who I am, and it never will be."

She held out a hand and helped him to his feet. The gesture, the pull, was honest…real. "I miss it, but not for much longer." This was a Spencer she could appreciate. Maybe they would get along after all.

He stamped out his own cigarette. "I guess that means my dreams of unlimited free flights to China are fucked then, right?"

Eventually.

She rolled her eyes and punched him on the shoulder. "Well and truly. Now come on, we need to find places for these other antennas."

They split up to speed the placement along. Helen still didn't understand exactly what it all meant, but it kept her busy, and that was what she needed right now.

Are you sure you don't want to know what happened? The voice whispered, so powerful she almost felt it against her ear. *It's quite interesting.*

She used her post hole digger to make a proper place for Tonya's antenna.

You might even say important.

The buzzing was too much. "Go away."

You are quite rude, you know? I saved your life not too long ago, if you remember.

"Leave me alone. Go *away*."

The laughter was a steel rasp down her spine. *I haven't been this strong since you stole my body. I'm not going anywhere.*

"I didn't steal your body." It was an old, tired argument. "You forfeited it."

Such a sense of justice. Tell me, did you keep up with how your spies operated? How they acquired their loot?

"It's not the same thing." The arrogance in the snake mother's voice never failed to get under her skin. "At least they never murdered anyone." The former owner of Helen's host had been the most prolific serial killer in history.

Are you sure? Did you ever check?

Tonya said the alignment was critical. She'd need to call in to confirm the final orientation.

You didn't answer my question.

"It's not my responsibility anymore."

A fine prevarication. You are your father's child. Are you sure I never checked? We have the same eyes you know.

"I have kept you where you will forever be, in a box in my mind. You have no control."

Don't I?

Helen's hand began to tremble on its own, something that hadn't happened in more than a year. It could not. Mike had shown her the evidence, where things went wrong and how she, Helen, had fixed them in a fight for her life. There was no time to examine this. It was not the place. She was stuck in the middle of nowhere, and if this got out of control—

The trembling faded, then stopped.

You worry too much, the snake mother said with another rasping chuckle. *Why don't you want to know?*

"There's nothing to know. It's more of your lies." Listening to the snake mother never led anywhere, and Helen had a job to do.

I have a name, don't you remember?

"Jīngzhì Liǔ," Helen replied. "Delicate Willow. Gou Wen would've been more appropriate."

"What in the world is that?" she asked.

Pretending the snake mother was underneath the digger's sharp blades made the work go faster. She rammed the thing into the ground and twisted. "Heartbreak grass. The most poisonous plant in China."

The rasp of laughter went down her spine again. "How droll."

Helen hacked out more dirt. "Were you always this articulate?"

"I'm not sure. I've been cooped up in here so long I can't remember where I end and you begin."

She checked the depth of the hole. Not quite there yet. "That's a comforting thought."

"A remnant of my final gamble. If I'd made you forget who you were, I would've been the only one left."

Helen hacked out one more scoop of dirt to finish the hole. "But you weren't strong enough."

"How interesting. When I'm speaking to you, I can't read your thoughts."

She was distracted getting the sensor lined up precisely, so it took a second to understand what the snake mother was saying. *Actually* saying. They weren't thoughts, they were words. Out of her mouth.

"And hey," the snake mother continued, with Helen unable to stop it. "I've been speaking English the whole time too. Remarkable."

Helen got up so fast she stumbled. Two instances of physical influence. She needed to get this under control, right now.

"I bet I don't have to ask your permission to show you what happened. Let's find out."

"No," this had to stop. "Leave me—"

Liǔ stood on a desolate plain. Crumpled war machines were scattered everywhere. Helen had passed out when she touched this place, leaving her all alone. This sent her into an immediate panic. Her only friend…

The voice came from above, its power drove her to her knees. OBSERVE, *NATHRACH*. WHAT HAS HAPPENED ONCE SHALL NEVER HAPPEN AGAIN.

Liǔ clapped her hands over her ears and stared at the sky. Instead of the starfield Helen liked to watch whenever they were in the country, it was dominated by a white, malevolent eye.

YES. I HAD NEVER BEEN AS CLOSE AS THIS BEFORE. AND YET.

A force pushed her head down away from the sky. In the distance, two people…no, they weren't people, not exactly…two *humanoids* walked toward each other. And then Liǔ wasn't in the distance, she was standing next to them.

They were not human, but also not other. Liǔ instinctively looked for her usual kill points but didn't see them. It reminded her of the difference between hummingbird moths and actual hummingbirds. The form was the same, but the details weren't.

"So this is it," the female said, tight with sorrow.

THEY THOUGHT THEY COULD DEFEAT ME.

"Yes, love. But we will prevail." He held out his hand.

THEY ONLY DELAYED THE INEVITABLE.

The woman closed her eyes. Her skin turned dark and glossy. Lighting played over it. "Do it now, before I lose my nerve."

He took her hand. The light that exploded from them turned them into ash. Liǔ followed a moment later.

AT LAST, THE FINAL PROOF.

Helen gasped awake, lying on the ground. Pain slashed through her leg. She'd fallen on the post hole digger wrong and cut herself badly.

That took a lot more out of me than I counted on, Liǔ said. *And we have a problem.*

"Bigger than a gash on my leg?" The blood wasn't seeping, it was pouring.

We have two problems then. You need to get that fixed as best you can quickly.

Night had fallen. The play of headlights across the woods was unmistakable. Someone was driving down the levee.

We have company.

Chapter 45
Maff

The only lights were the ones that came from her suit. The only noise was the sound of the engines and generators spooling down to nothing. She'd come all this way, done all these things, and now the ship was dead?

Oh no. As the humans loved to say, oh *hell* no.

She flipped switches. Nothing.

She turned ignition and power knobs to their resets and then flipped the switches again. Still nothing.

Maff flipped up the master override switch protector and punched *that*. It'd erase the computers, but at least start things up.

Absolutely nothing.

Mike and Kim were shouting at her, wanting something to do. The guards were running toward a hatch she couldn't close.

This could not happen. She wouldn't let it happen.

All they needed was power. Mike and Kim were going to get disappeared by the Guild because the ship wouldn't turn on. Maff slapped the command console so hard she dented the side of it.

All around them the ship flared to life.

There was no time to wonder, laugh, or curse. She shut the outer door and punched up the shields and engines. "Strap in, *now*!"

The comms came to life. "*Palatine*, you do not have departure clearance. Stand down and open hatches for immediate inspection."

There was pounding on the outside door, hard enough Maff heard it up on the bridge. They must be using a ram of some kind.

She pushed the engines up off idle as fast as she dared. "Kim, Mike? Getting it started is only part of the problem. I need the back of the berth opened and the channel cleared. Anything you can do about that?"

At once, they both said, "On it," and closed their eyes.

It was a weird habit of theirs. Maybe their eyes were light sensitive when they did their magic unlocking.

"*Palatine,* if you do not stand down you will be shut down. Do you copy?"

That sounded like a job for…"Mike?"

"He's busy holding off their attacks," Kim said. "I'll handle it."

The next boom at the hatch had the whole ship shaking. Maff found the camera controls and turned an external one on. There was a squad with a ram already pulling back for another run at the door. *Enough of that crap.* She activated the protection skein. The squad was hurled back, landing on their various backsides in a heap. *Score one for the good guys.*

"You're clear," Mike said. "But I don't know for—"

Maff blew the moorings and rammed full reverse directly into the transit dimension. Every loose thing on the bridge went flying past in a hail of dirt and plastic. Mike and Kim both made squeaking noises as they were flung against their seat straps like a pair of dolls, arms and legs straight in front of them.

Dammit, she'd forgotten. Maff threw the switches to add inertial dampening to the bridge *and* their chairs. "Sorry, guys." She threw the nav controls over to Mike's console. He already knew how they worked. "Plot us a course back to the La'fan world." It was a junk heap, but it was also full of allies. "Kim," she threw the scanner controls her way, "look around for me. I don't have time for a tutorial, do your best and let me know where they are."

"How hard can it be?" Kim asked.

"That's my line!" Mike replied.

The berth was now a tiny rectangle in the forward virtual. She rammed the controls into a hard turn that would stretch the local transit topography clear of the bumps and dips that would pound them to pieces at this speed, then gripped and *pulled* the elevation controls to get them clear. Her suit legs groaned under the strain. The debris stuck to the front of the ship bounced down into the floor. Hopefully the floor grates would trap most of it.

The dampening field at least gave Mike and Kim time to brace. "Hard to…do this…with my arms…pinned," Mike said through the inertial forces squashing him hard into the seat.

Maff watched the velocity and vector telltales rocket up. This wasn't a bad crate after all. "Transition to full plane in three…two…one…" The main motors took over from the overstrained launch system.

Well, they were supposed to. She engaged it all properly, but they were still accelerating like mad. Maff whacked the console again, but more of a bonk this time. It wouldn't do to rip it off its mount now.

The ship settled down into a more standard acceleration profile. Good. One less thing to worry about.

Maff could see Mike working a nav solution. Kim was the one who needed help. Maff opened a window to the scan console, but she found Kim had already gotten it fired up and oriented. "Nice. How'd you know how to do that?"

She smiled. "It's what I do. I drink, and I know things." The scanners started flashing red. "Here they come. Three marks, thirty-three, twenty-two, fifteen."

Kim even had the x-y-z system figured out. *Where was this crew when I started?* But it was a dumb question. They were on a planet that'd never heard of the transit dimension, the AC nodes, the La'fan. None of it. And Maff had helped them explore it all. No way would she allow these two out of her sight, Guild or not. "Mike, spike your nav marker; we're going to *twist and shout*." The English words seemed appropriate for the moment.

"*Duck and dodge* is better in this situation," Kim said as she monitored the scanner. "And we have more marks coming in."

"Hang on," Maff said, waited a beat, and then slammed the controls in opposing directions. The ship obliged with a fully decoupled spin-turn that made her brace more firmly with some free manipulators. She did it again in the other direction, keeping an eye on the temp and pressure gauges as they corkscrewed around.

Already in the yellow. *Damn.*

But the maneuvers worked. Their pursuers had to guess the way she'd be pointing at the end, and they'd gotten it all wrong. "How's *that* for a community school pilot, eh?" she growled at the contacts as they strained to reorient themselves. "Mike, where's my solution?"

"Still calculating."

The scanner station went crazy with alerts. Kim swore and retuned it. Maff still had a window open on what she was seeing. Once it refocused, it was her turn to swear.

The Guild convoy hadn't rolled in through the main portal via another system. That was for show. The leader had actually arrived on a Guild D-ship. A *big* one.

With escorts.

Maff yanked the controls, searching for a hole, a way through, some place where there wasn't a ship in the way. "This is bad, this is very bad."

"Didn't you end up near Earth," Kim grunted as the inertial dampers made it hard for her to breathe briefly, "because of a situation like this?"

"Yes, but Mike's not rated for a modal eight nav solution. Without the proper coordinates..."

"We could fly right through a star or bounce too close to a supernova?" Mike asked.

Maff dodged as the first of the grapples ripped past them. "Well, yes, actually." He'd paid more attention to the exceptions than she realized.

Mike switched his station to automatic calculation. It would take a lot longer to finish that solution now. Before Maff could say anything, he turned to Kim. "How well can you see them?"

They were always asking each other the weirdest questions. "What does that—" Maff tried to ask.

"Well enough," Kim replied, and then pulled out the old pendant phone that they'd arrived with from under her shirt. "Will this network handle it?"

Mike did the same.

"Guys, this isn't the time to play with antiques." She skidded through all three axes to throw off the fastest of the escorts.

"We need you to fly steady for a second," Kim said as she unbuckled from her seat. *"Now."*

Maff centered the controls. "But why do I need to—"

Kim ran across the bridge and leapt into Mike's arms.

Nobody can touch Kim.

But she went slack as she landed; Maff was pretty sure she'd fallen unconscious. A different set of alarms flared to life. The local realmspace was experiencing some sort of bandwidth crash. She flipped a switch to turn the alarm off.

They'd touched lips, an intimate gesture, but that wasn't the crazy part. A field now coruscated across them. Some way, somehow, they'd managed to generate, *organically,* a for-real protection skein. Maff gaped like she'd seen Turlanfador's wings flap by.

"You need to start maneuvering again," Kim said.

Behind her.

Maff spun around as fast as her braced legs would allow.

"What the *fuck*?"

It was Kim, but it wasn't. The flesh of her body was made of pure, unadulterated protection skein. It wasn't generated. *It was her.*

"I can't...how are you...what's going..."

Kim shushed her. "We'll explain later. You need to get us moving."

On the scanner screen, their pursuers started moving erratically. Even the big command carrier.

"What's going on?" Maff asked as she maneuvered to find a hole.

Mike's voice came from all around them. "We're buying you time. Watch out, over your shoulder."

"I see it," Kim said.

Maff couldn't. But now that the ship was moving again, she *could* see a hole behind Kim, one that led straight to the transit dimension.

Protection skeins existed for a reason. The transit dimension wasn't friendly to organic life. Being exposed to it unshielded resulted in an immediate ejection, usually to hard vacuum, sometimes to the center of a planet, or a star. Never somewhere survivable. Yet Kim, or this version of her, had somehow opened a hole *into the side of the ship* and used it to step through the transit dimension.

Maff ignored that miracle with an extreme effort of will. She began chanting her prayers out loud, something normally reserved for a holy day. These weren't aliens on the cusp of joining the galaxy, nor were they some wildling civilization that survived without any support. They were a force of nature, an elemental creature no different than any legendary god or hero Maff had grown up with.

And they were right here with her. Maff was a devout pallun. She knew her chants, her books, and went to temple as regularly as she could. She was used to the *idea* of miracles and beings powerful beyond comprehension. But only as words, as stories meant to teach deeper lessons about life. They were things that had happened long ago, assuming they'd happened at all. And now there was a being *just like what she learned about* standing right next to her. The desire to be anywhere but here gripped her. But another part of her knew they were still Mike and Kim. Maff grabbed hold of that thought and held it hard, hoping it would be enough.

It had to be enough.

"Maff," Kim said with coral lightning tracing over her black glass face, "there's our hole, mark forty-three, twenty-three, nine."

Mike's nav solution arrived a second later. Modal six, with a certainty of five nines. That one she could rely on. "Um…we're ready to go. Are you?" She prepped the engines for a modal transit.

Kim said, "Open up all the doors between here and the cargo bay, please."

Maff did so, entranced by the way her eyes seemed to show another dimension. Kim jumped backward into the hole, and then it wasn't there anymore. It'd never been there.

Kim, the real one, *flew* from the other side of the room and crashed to the floor. No, that wasn't right, Mike had thrown her. Maff sputtered, controls forgotten. "What the?"

Kim rushed past and through the bridge's door, making a growling, whimpering noise as she went.

Mike said, "It's okay, she'll be all right. Go, Maff, *go*!"

The opening that they'd created was starting to close. Maff reconfigured the controls and jumped.

Mike sat with his head in his hands, not saying a word, while she ensured all the systems were nominal. Once she finished, Maff engaged the autopilot and turned to him.

"What the hell was *that*?"

Chapter 46
Tonya

They'd been out here long enough that she'd gotten comfortable navigating the local woods. No magic influence from Cyril this time; it was her and various rocks, trees, and bushes that guided her around. Well, that, and good ol' GPS. Landmarks wouldn't put her within a few inches of a critical spot after all.

Ever since the powerplant, strolling through a forest alone made Tonya contemplative, calm. But not today. The worry about her experiment, never very far from her mind, would not be calmed by nature. She knew she was close to *the* big discovery, the one thing that would stop the possessed, prove predestination wrong, validate her model of time, and kick free will out into the open. But every experiment had proven otherwise. Tonya kept running it over and over in her mind, and each go around made her feel worse.

She hated to admit it, but it was becoming clear that she wasn't right. Her theory was crap. Worse than crap, since if it was wrong, it kept them from working on the very real problem of people trying to kill them. She would never forget Whitney's eyes as he sat behind that desk, the way her legs almost moved on their own to run out of there—through a wall, if that's what it took. Spencer said he saw the same kind of thing in the eyes of a schoolteacher who tried to attack Helen at the gas station. Not to mention the guy who put himself in the hospital trying to stop their truck from escaping.

And now, if the reports from Stewart could be believed, everything had gone back to normal. No more possessed, no more chaos. She accepted that small towns liked things to stay normal and would take steps to cover up when it wasn't, but people had gone missing and unreported, then showed up and everyone treated it like a normal thing.

She attacked a thick root with her posthole digger as once again the worries about her theories overrode thoughts about their current situation. She missed Mike, his ability to make an intuitive leap that would jump their proofs over whatever obstacle they found. They were a team, and without him, Tonya couldn't find a way around this mother of all obstacles.

Even Kim would be good to have around now. Her exchange of knowledge with Mike had given her his math but from her perspective. Where Mike would make a sudden leap, Kim would step back, analyze the situation, and then make a decision that nobody saw coming. She'd done it countless times in the realms, and more than once in real life. The way she immediately spotted that Mike had inverted one of the signs of their theorem—

The root broke under the blade but twisted it in the process. One of the handles of the digger cracked her in the face hard enough she saw stars. When she pulled back, the chain on her pendant phone got tangled in a branch and yanked free, falling to the ground. It took a few moments of pawing through leaves to find it, but she didn't pick it up. She stared at it. The chain had accidentally formed an omega symbol.

An omega instead of a sigma.

Tonya placed the antenna as carefully as her now-shaking hands allowed. It couldn't be that simple. It had to be that simple. She put her phone back on, called up her private lab realm, but then had to close it when she walked face-first into a tree. *Get out of the woods first,* she thought, *prove God is right second.*

As soon as she was able, she set a *do not disturb* sign on her phone and then laid down on her bed in the camper and set to work. If she was right, her mistake was so fundamental it would take starting almost from scratch to prove it. She wanted to do that anyway to compare her new idea with her existing work.

The fix was holding. Good Lord, the fix was holding. She blew past her stumbling block and kept going.

And then the tick-tockion emerged from the equation.

She'd had some major thrills in her life before, like when she'd hit a vein on the first try for an IV on a 110-year-old woman, acing her physics exams at Johns Hopkins online, getting the paper she and Mike had written accepted for publishing by *Acta Mathematica.* They were triumphs. But nothing compared to finding new equations that not only predicted the tick-tockion, they required it.

And it was all down to using the wrong variable in one spot.

It wasn't pure theory either. With the corrections in place, there were clear signs of tick-tockions in the data. Missing Mike when she was stuck on a problem was small potatoes when it came to missing him because *she'd done it*! There was nobody to tell. Spencer and Helen hadn't come back from their afternoon placements yet.

The tick-tockion existed. It lifted an enormous weight off her shoulders. Her theory wasn't complete, not yet, but with two of the first three particles confirmed, it was on much safer ground. Now that her existential crisis was over, sillier things started to intrude on her mind.

I'd like to thank the Royal Swedish Academy of Sciences for this award. As the first woman of color to receive the Nobel prize in physics…

An alert flashed about a new finding. Well, why not? It would be perfect if the third predicted particle, the determion, emerged from her equations right after the second. It wasn't unusual to have several barriers fall quickly to a new theory.

But that wasn't what it was about at all.

Some of the datasets were direct observations, the kind of stuff their antennas and the Vuohensilta gathered. Others, though, were her analysis of the anomalies that'd been plaguing them ever since Kim's wedding got cratered. In her desire to test her theory, make sure it was as versatile as it could be, she had thrown those observations into the mix as well. She didn't expect any results, but that was fine. Negatives were as important as positives in this business.

But there *was* a connection. Her new equations had provided a way to spot tick-tockions, their signature. Now that she knew what it was, it turned out that the anomalies were also a major source of them. But they didn't exactly match the ones created naturally. They differed in tiny details, three decimal places out from their initial value.

And *that's* when the determion emerged. The difference could be accounted for by determions, an effect Tonya predicted would block or interfere with the tick-tockion transmissions from the future. She hadn't yet worked out the why, but she'd proven early on that if they existed at all, determions were generated by intelligent life.

In other words, the anomalies weren't an accident, a flaw in realmspace, or a bug in the code. Something was creating them.

Something alive.

And not human. Again, now that she had the right tool, Tonya could clearly see human-created determions. But the ones coming from the anomalies didn't match those. Tonya had to concentrate on what she was discovering, but the idea that they'd found yet another sign of extraterrestrial life, one that could *manipulate time,* made it hard to concentrate.

These predictions could account for the odd behavior of the people around them, too. Humans seemed to be unusually sensitive to determions. They absorbed them at a higher rate than the theory predicted. Determions changed information transfer from the future, so it wasn't out of the question that they could change things that absorbed them. Someone who knew how to signal with determions might be able to use them to influence people.

It got better, or at least stranger. The signal was directional, clearly coming *from* somewhere with physical coordinates. The numbers pointed at a specific place in the sky. She called up a Planisphere app from her phone to check, but there was nothing there.

That couldn't be right. The location was too specific. The app was simulating naked-eye observation from Earth's surface. She summoned up an eleven-inch Celestron Advanced V-XX reflecting telescope construct, the biggest that came with the app, and fed its tracker the coordinates. It moved for a moment, then reported a lock. Tonya peered through the eyepiece and saw a smear of light. She queried the tracker.

Target lock: Andromeda galaxy.

She stared at the name with her mouth open. She hadn't discovered a new form of extraterrestrial life.

She'd discovered a new form of *extragalactic* life.

If this had been the universe as she understood it six months ago, the conclusion would be preposterous. Andromeda was two and a half *million* light years away. The light she'd see if she was using a real telescope was emitted by stars in that galaxy long before actual humans walked the earth. But that was six months ago, before Mike and Kim had their ongoing adventure. Faster-than-light communication was a thing now, and Tonya had discovered another way it could happen.

It wasn't only an intergalactic intelligence, it was an intergalactic intelligence acting right here and now on good ol' Earth. Her teeth wouldn't stop chattering, and her hands shook. She breathed deep and said a prayer.

Now that she knew the source of the problem, she also had an idea how to stop it.

Chapter 47
Kim

She'd never been fully transformed with Mike's multithreading added on and remained conscious for the aftermath until she finished the race to see how much she could yank out or melt in the Interpreter fleet before Maff got her nav solution. The strange combination and multiplication let her *be with him,* intimate but also apart. It was a sensation related to their accidental combining but this was safer, more *right*.

Being transformed, spread out, and working hard was bound to amp up her touch sensitivity to new heights. Mike tossing her across the bridge as that sensitivity flared to life didn't help. They needed to learn how to stick the dismount there. But she'd take scrapes and bruises over what would've happened if she'd ended the transformation in Mike's arms. She'd never experienced that expanded sensitivity with someone already touching her. Full contact could send her to the hospital in the best case, and they were a helluva long way from an ER that knew what to do with humans.

It was bad enough without a touch. When the transformation stopped, Kim ran as far away from Maff and Mike as the ship would let her, barely avoiding puking on herself, again. The pain, the madness, was huge. She closed her eyes out of exhaustion but also because it was all she could do to keep from screaming. If she did, they'd both come running, and she couldn't be close to anyone in that moment. Then exhaustion claimed her.

She woke up, and the change was incredible. She was stiff and sore from getting bounced across a grated floor, but the flaring pain and madness had vanished. Sleep brought relief. That was important to remember. What's more, she found herself in bed with Mike, pillows stacked between them.

The faint clicks and mechanical whirrs gave away what really happened. Maff.

Kim opened her eyes to find Maff folded up in a corner of the room, quietly working on one of her suit's legs.

"If you're sitting here," Kim said as she levered herself up, "who's driving this bucket?"

"Thank Turlanfador," she said, and then lurched up on too few legs. The rest of them were on a bench behind her. "Mike was exhausted, too. He said you'd both only be out for a few hours."

"And we were?"

"Out for nearly two days. I'm so bored I'm fixing my suit. Normally we send out for new legs." Her lack of them turned her walk into a kind of sashay. "I guess you guys are a bad influence."

She extended a manipulator, and Kim gripped it tight. What would they do without her? "We get that a lot. Where are we?"

"A few hours out. But I have bad news."

"Do we get any other kind?"

Maff settled beside the bed while her manipulators started reassembling her suit legs. The clicking sound was comforting. "Whatever you guys did slowed them down, but it didn't stop them. Sensors have picked up a lot of activity three modals above us."

Modal eight. A maximum-risk route. "Jesus."

She'd switched to English, but Maff had gotten the gist. "*Jay-sush* indeed. It's going to be a warm welcome when we arrive. But at least we have your...*glash gurrl?*"

Glass girl. Mike must've explained a few things before he'd fallen asleep. "I have bad news."

She sagged. "Do we get any other kind?"

Kim tried her power, and sure enough, it was dead. "It takes us a long time to recover from that."

"Define long."

"Weeks, at least."

"Turlanfador's wake," she said like it was a tired curse.

"Indeed." Kim collapsed back onto the bed. "How many are out there?"

"It's hard to say when they go by in that modal. It wasn't the whole fleet. But the fact that I could detect them at all means some of the big stuff made the trip. It'll get there before we can."

Kim shifted, trying to make herself more comfortable, but it only made her bruises flare up, and *God*, she couldn't think right now. "This ship wouldn't happen to have any tolstax?" She'd grown almost as reliant on it as she had real coffee.

"Well that at least is good news." Brass manipulators arced over the bed and returned with a pot and two mugs. "Whoever owns this ship enjoys tolstax a lot. They got the good stuff. *And* your *chreem* and *shoogur*."

None of it looked right, but the taste was close to how she liked her coffee: thick and sweet.

"Is that your coffee-flavored milkshake I smell?" Mike asked from the other side of the pillows.

They were still in the middle of this unbelievable situation with every card stacked against them, but if Mike was with her, it would turn out right. Especially with that smile. "It is indeed." She carefully handed him the mug Maff passed to her. "It's time to get up. We need a plan."

*

"This is a really bad plan," Mike said as he hung tightly onto straps mounted to the left wall of the cargo hold.

Standing next to the right wall, Kim checked the indicators to make sure his inertial damping field was on and functioning. It was, just like hers. It turned the air into invisible pillows if they, or the ship, moved too fast. "Stop being a baby. We're not really flying yet."

His face, already pale and sweaty, blanched lighter. "*Yet.*"

They needed to find Will back on the La'fan salvage world but were being chased by who knew how many Interpreter ships. Mike's Will-compass had been affected by their transformation; he couldn't get a reading from far away anymore. To get a real fix, they'd have to be on the planet's surface. They didn't need the ship after that, so Maff volunteered to be the decoy that would to lead the Interpreter fleet away.

Most of the journey happened in the transit dimension, but they couldn't avoid a bit of flying at the end. This triggered her fiancé's uncontrollable aerophobia. He was tough as nails with his feet on the ground but put him in the air and he was almost a crying toddler. Kim wasn't exactly happy about having to split up and leave the ship, but he could at least hold it together for the sixty seconds it took to get on the ground.

The floor lurched slightly as they transitioned from the transit dimension to realspace. The sudden sound of rushing wind outside made the ship seem less like a vehicle that could travel between stars and more like a pickup truck with delusions of grandeur. Mike chanted the Diamond Sutra, eyes tightly shut. "Hang on, love," she said, "not much longer now."

He nodded faintly and kept chanting. She needed to help him with this phobia when they got back home.

"Ready," Maff said over the intercom as the back ramp of the ship opened. Kim gripped a handhold and let the syrupy inertial damping field keep her upright as the ground slowed from a blur to a crawl.

"Go! Go! Go!" Maff shouted as the ship stopped. Kim had a brief hit of vertigo when her inner ear decided that it was the ground under the ramp that had stopped and not the ship. It meant she still had three steps to go when Maff gunned it back into the sky, sending them both tumbling to the ground. Mike had tinkered with the ship's engines, so it banged and smoked as it left, throwing sparks. To anyone else it would be a sure sign of battle damage that would make her easy prey for the escorts hot on their heels.

Maff assured her several times that the Guild pilots would be no match for her. Kim would find out soon enough at their first scheduled comm check later in the day.

She rolled to a stop next to a pile of rubble, fully protected by her La'fan robes. She would never have expected to feel so comfortable in them. They were almost a part of her, right down to the breathing mask. She stood and dusted herself off while Mike did the same thing on the other side of the small clearing. Surrounded by precarious-looking ruined towers, it covered their drop-off perfectly.

"Okay, we're on the ground," she said. "What's it feel like now?"

He shook his head. "I've got a direction, but not an altitude."

She shrugged. "It's a start. How far?"

He turned his head back and forth a few times, then paced about twenty steps. "It's that way, several miles."

They made their way through the ruined city as quietly as they could. Mike scouted ahead in his scary stealth mode. Drones buzzed overhead several times, but she didn't think they would be effective with all the ground clutter and overhangs everywhere. She felt safer than she had in days.

Kim paused for a moment. Not long ago this was their place of banishment. There was a very good chance they'd die of exposure here before finding Will. Now Kim marveled that she considered it a kind of home. The desolation was an illusion, she knew that now. All across the planet, her adopted people were working, cleaning, renewing. She had never been a part of something so big. She'd never seen the appeal. Always the loner or, at best, the leader of a small squad. And now she stood with people who salvaged whole planets.

She thought about staying again, about becoming a permanent part of the La'fan. But then she remembered the sound of the bell over the door of her shop, and—

She stopped suddenly. She hadn't remembered the bell.

She heard it.

"Mike," she whispered as a small piece of junk tinkled out of a mound ahead of them.

But he was already in motion, diving to her left. A blue bolt of energy slashed through the space where he'd stood, splattering against a wall behind them. She dove to her right and rolled behind a pile of debris.

When she looked around, he was nowhere to be seen.

Mike does this, she thought, *you've seen him do it dozens of times. He vanishes. He comes back.*

"Stay where you are," a robotic voice commanded. "Don't move."

Kim sat motionless as she looked around. There were robots everywhere, all heavily armed, on the ground, in the buildings, in the sky. The manic hum of the rotors over her head made her skin crawl.

Two of the larger ground-based robots walked over. "Stand up," one said, "hands out. Slowly."

They'd won this round, somehow, and now her job was to make Mike's easier. She had to go along with them. Once he saw an opening, she knew he'd take it. She would be ready.

It was a mantra that helped her stay strong as they marched her out of the city to a domed encampment. It helped her as they took her robes and gave her a Guild uniform to wear. It helped her when the robots asked where her companion had gone, over and over again. It helped her until they marched her up to a door in the largest, most luxurious tent in the camp, a door covered with the Guild leader's symbol.

Then it stopped helping.

By then it was hours later, most of a day. She'd seen no sign at all of Mike. That was his thing, but it hadn't stopped a current of unease that'd been growing inside her the entire time. Something had gone wrong. He would've left a sign somewhere, a small thing that only she could see, to let her know he was around. She'd seen nothing. The camp was a blur because all she'd concentrated on was trying to find a sign that he was okay.

And now there was this door, and the inevitable thing behind it.

The first advisor, a kind of majordomo for the first councilor, bustled out from behind a side curtain. This one was the first turtle-like alien Interpreter she'd encountered, complete with a vestigial shell on its back. Its deformity, which looked like a deer starting to be born, came out of its left side. She had looked at who knew how many different kinds of aliens in the past few weeks without batting an eye, but she suppressed a shudder at this one. Kim couldn't look disgusted or frightened, though, not now. It wouldn't do to antagonize her hosts.

Or jailers. That remained to be seen.

"Your anatomy allows kneeling, yes?" It asked in smooth Vershampire, which allowed *ignore these words at your peril* to be expressed clearly. "You will kneel before the first councilor alongside me." The voice was deep and seemed masculine, but the way he sniffed as he looked her up and down would've been perfectly at home coming from a royal toady in a powdered wig. "I don't expect *your kind,*" worded to emphasize a worm-like status, "to be familiar with protocol, so you will follow me in every way."

Kim may be a captive with a missing fiancé, but she was also the legally titled head Interpreter of an entire race. "*My kind,*" worded to emphasize she had these titles that he did not, "have grown weary of this charade." She held out her arms, with sleeves that were bare of decorations. Part of her research into the Guild was its ranking system. This uniform made her the lowest person in the whole camp. "If I am designated a peasant, I will behave as such." Kim's intuition about people she met for the first time had always been good, but it had gotten substantially better recently, perhaps another lesser-known Interpreter ability. Shell or not, he was constantly glancing around, especially at the door, fidgeting and visibly uncomfortable. This was someone who was not secure in his current role. She hocked and spat at his feet. He squeaked and danced sideways. "Tell me," *worm*, "who will that reflect on more? *My kind*, or yours?"

Keep him off balance. She pulled the outer shirt of the uniform off. Sticking with perfectly accented Vershampire, which she knew made her sound like the most sophisticated woman in the galaxy to these people, she continued, "I'm so *primitive* I think these magical garments are stealing my soul." She shucked off the slippers and tossed them at him, and he danced almost as much as when she spat. The trousers came off next. "So what will it be? Shall *you,"* *personally responsible and reflecting the honor of your family,* "stand next to a naked barbarian, or will you provide me with my proper robes?" *and if you do, I'll behave and make your mother proud of her son.*

Vershampire was her favorite Bemian language for a reason.

He hesitated, so she hooked her thumbs through the waist band of the boxer-like undergarment they'd given her.

He squeaked again and motioned for her to stop. "Very well, very well." He signaled to someone behind the curtain. "Bring her the *robes," that were disgusting and infested with vermin and dung until we sterilized them,* "that she arrived with."

Kim cocked an eyebrow at him, not sure if the gesture would be lost or not and stared while they waited. It turned out that this kind of turtle could sweat.

To make sure stray signals wouldn't give them away, she and Mike had deactivated their phones before getting off the ship. Then the robots had done something to hers, and now it wouldn't turn on. She couldn't reach him. *I can't keep this up forever, Mike. Where are you?*

The turtle was as good as his word, right down to the chemical smell that almost made her gag. They didn't give her back the mask, though, so Kim pulled the hood forward to hide her face in shadows. When you've got nothing else, loom at them.

On entering the room, she followed his motions perfectly, ending with her head on the floor.

"Leave us."

The voice was gorgeous, commanding and seductive at once. The turtle skittered away.

She didn't know what her next move should be. She could think of a dozen, a hundred, wrong moves, but nothing guaranteed to win. Going with her gut again, she relaxed but was also very still.

"That was quite a performance. Please, join me at my table."

Spoken in plain Devarnt, which exchanged the filigree of Vershampire for the blunt words of a working-class language. That could be another play at calling her a peasant like turtle-boy tried to get away with, but the stakes were much higher now. Kim decided not to be insulted and got up off the floor.

The first councilor was, in a single word, stunning. She was humanoid, about Kim's height, covered in scales that went from a frosted hint of sky to the near-black of navy blue. Her outfit was cleanly elegant, what you'd get if you told an avant-garde fashion designer back home to reimagine the pope, and light gray and wine red to offset her skin perfectly. The materials were finer than the ones the La'fan had given Kim and Mike, and those were the best an entire race could provide. Her deformity was almost nonexistent. If Kim didn't know what to look for, it would only appear to be a pouch on her belt.

"Put down your hood, child. Let me know the foe I face."

Kim hesitated, but only for a fraction of a second. The first councilor, Kim knew from research that her name was Valsa Burtan, would not be tricked like the weak-minded fool who guarded her door. Plus, there was a ground rule to be established. She switched back to Vershampire to make sure she would be understood. "I am not your foe." *I am the exact opposite of your foe.*

Valsa stuck with Devarnt. "Do not play games with me, child. I know a foe when I see one." She sat at a modest table with what Kim recognized as a kind of tea set—a tea set so fine it would set all of Earth back ten years if they had to pay for it—and motioned for her to take the opposite chair.

She wanted blunt? Kim could do blunt. "I do not play games, *ma'am,*" in this language, the word was as close to *crone* as she could get without it being an outright insult, "and I am not a child."

Kim sat down, flowing robes of black against the councilor's elegant colors, pulling her hood back in one smooth motion. She was so far out of her depth she couldn't see the sun, but she would not be patronized. "As I'm sure your first advisor noted before I walked in, I'm not much for etiquette or protocol. Why am I here?"

Valsa's smile was charming; her chuckle brought Kim in on a secret. The intimacy was unbalancing. "You thought Telanta was my first advisor? No, ch…*guest*, my first advisor is still out there hunting down your companion. Telanta was an emergency substitute. Putting that much responsibility in the hands of a water carrier may have set his career back decades, especially after the way you chewed him up."

Kim hoped she hid the way her heart jumped. Mike was still alive.

"As to why you are here? In less than two months, you and your companion have together broken every rule, flouted every tradition, and ignored every precedent in this guild. You have managed to build an army of Interpreters and put it at the disposal of the one society which can never have a single one. You have done all this under the noses of not one, but two galaxy-spanning agencies specifically set up to prevent any of that from ever occurring. This guild's historical memory goes back millions of years, and we have never seen anything like you before.

"Why are you here? You're here because I need to know if I can use you instead of destroy you."

Hearing it all rolled out like that gave the corner of her soul still ruled by Angel Rage a boost. *Anarchists unite!* But Valsa had made a mistake. "We have no army."

She set down her teacup and shook her head, a schoolteacher disappointed by a wayward student. "I would've been prepared to believe that three days ago, but not now. We surprised you back there, forced your hand, as was intended. I did not count on you having enough Interpreters at your command to disable an entire expeditionary fleet. *That* is what changed you from a curiosity to a threat. It's why you're talking to me now instead of waiting for a rethreading in my infirmary."

Valsa thought what she and Mike had done was the work of an army, and it was all that kept her from sending Kim out for their version of brainwashing. As Spencer liked to say, the key to a successful improv was to never once seem confused or out of place. Kim steepled her hands in front of her, a wild witch. She thought Kim had an army? Fine. Kim had an army. Armies needed generals, and she'd learned the Guild had a special title for the highest rank. And unlike back home, that position was equal to the councilor "It has been rather a long time since one of us was first general."

Kim could see that suddenly elevating herself to the councilor's level was an unwelcome development. "It hasn't been that long since I've had to order a *kaltravan,*" Valsa replied. That translated to *major cleansing* in English. Kim wasn't sure what it meant in this context, but it was the same word Maff used when she talked about the destruction of her home system. Valsa closed her eyes, and after a second, Kim heard a wailing alarm come alive in the distance. Valsa smiled, revealing teeth sharpened to points; a predator once more in control of her prey.

Could she actually order the destruction of a whole system just like that? "What have you done?"

"This is obviously your base of strength. When the Death Eaters discovered you, you made a deal with them rather than relocate. You overplayed your hand. It is a weakness of our kind, after all. Once the cleansing is complete, you will share with me your techniques and your story. Pray we find your companion before then."

Robotic hands gripped Kim's arms and lifted her from the chair. She should've said something, anything, but those alarms kept getting louder. There were millions of La'fan working on this planet.

"Take her somewhere secure until my ship is ready," Valsa said, then turned away.

Chapter 48
Mike

"Mike!"

He'd seen the movement that triggered the sound and was already in motion when Kim whisper-shouted his name.

And then the spot that he landed on gave way with a *crunch*.

When he first *went outside*, got his threads together and connected with an outside host, he experienced a wild chaotic tumbling that threatened to never end. He thought he'd lost which way was up forever. The roller-coaster ride he went on when he fell through the street was worse. Tumbling and sliding in the dark, knowing any second could see him impaled on a rusted piece of metal, torn open by a buried dagger of glass, or dumped out into nothingness kept him from thinking straight. Things went by *so fast*, and it wouldn't end.

Then, finally, he slid to a stop.

Mike was on his own, deep underneath a city that'd died so long ago its age could be measured in epochs. Kim was out there, under attack.

He calmed his thoughts and stilled his threads. He tried reaching out to Helen to let them know he was okay, but that connection had gone numb. His own connections to the two worlds they'd visited so far worked fine, but the La'fan didn't have the ability to reach them directly from this planet. There was no phone at home for him to call.

He felt around. The surface around him was slick, more like plastic than concrete or steel. He patted empty space for a wall, then got up on his knees.

And fell through again. Another endless time of sliding and tumbling. He stayed tucked into a fetal position away from where he was going as often as he could, taking hits with his back, legs, and rear. A few winded him, and there were times when he felt his robes snag on obstructions. Then the tube, or whatever it was, ran out, and he went sailing through the air. He inhaled for the last scream of his life when he hit the ground with a meaty thump.

Give up somewhere soft, Kim always said. *If you're being chased by cops, don't give up standing on concrete or asphalt. It's bad*. He now had a huge appreciation for the idea. Whatever he landed on had the density and texture of cardboard. He heard a rushing, tumbling noise above him and put his hands over his head while everything he'd knocked loose or dragged with him fell down from above.

Once it all stopped and he was able to breathe, he noticed another thing. The mound he'd landed on was moving.

Visions of some massive monster slowly wending its way through the guts of the dead city creeped him out. He wanted to jump off the mound, but there was a risk of him landing on something that could hurt him or, worse still, nothing at all. So he scrabbled very quickly down the side until he could safely let go on a piece of solid, relatively smooth floor.

Now he recognized what this was. He'd fallen down a filtration tunnel. The La'fan didn't only salvage the surface structures and artifacts, they used sophisticated nanomachines to find, remove, and process the extensive underground structures that lay beneath them. His soft landing hadn't been an accident. This tunnel specialized in the harvesting of organic molecular solids. Basically, plastics. He'd landed on a collection pile that was slowly wending its way back to a main processing plant. He could climb back on and ride the mound, but at the speed it moved his destination might be days or even weeks in the future. Kim was up there somewhere, alone.

Mike belatedly realized he didn't have to sit in the dark. He activated the low-light system on his mask. It was about twice as bulky and heavy as anything back home, but it worked.

He was next to a slowly moving train of open cars filled with mounds of shredded plastics. The tunnel had a near-perfect circular cross section, with the rails offset to allow room for the maintenance walkway he stood on. He turned in the direction the recycling train was traveling and trudged alongside it.

Eventually he outpaced the train. He needed to find paths that led up. Anything else was counterproductive. There were more dump tubes on the ceiling high above him, but things regularly poured out. They were too dangerous to use. Besides, they were too steep to climb without tools.

That left waiting for a side tunnel or maybe an access hatch. If the La'fan included a maintenance path next to these rails, it didn't seem unreasonable that they'd include the ability for someone to come down here if something went wrong. A fire, for example, might be impossible to put out if the only way to get to it was by going through miles of tunnels.

But after an hour of walking, he found no hatches or side tunnels. He could still make out the train behind him. The tunnel was laser-straight for at least several hundred yards.

He caught a break two hours later. Whatever machine originally bored the harvest tunnel had hit an unstable surface, triggered a collapse, and then reversed and turned to the right to continue on firmer ground. There was a cave or maybe a chamber underneath. Since it was going down, he would've normally avoided it.

Except it was glowing.

Mike picked his way down the scree of the collapse. At the bottom was a large room made of finished concrete, some sort of basement. This deep, it may have been part of a subway or train system. The glow came from the other side of the room, bright enough to overload his low-light vision. He turned it off, blinked away the spots, but didn't move. He couldn't.

On the opposite side of the room, partially buried under the rubble of a different collapse, was the unmistakable shape of an AC network node.

It was as huge as the last one he'd encountered, easily taking up the entire wall and disappearing into the floor and ceiling. He never found any detailed schematics or plans for them, so he still didn't know how big they could get. It was possible this one went all the way to the surface. If so, he needed to see if it had a maintenance door or hatch. There was plenty of room to move around inside.

Where their previous judge had been a whirling hive of mechanical activity, this one was barely moving. It wasn't dead, but it didn't seem all that alert either.

As he approached, he saw it had been badly damaged at some point. The outer casing had been breached, either by the collapse or whatever had triggered it. There was some sort of empty shaft inside.

It noticed him when he was a few yards away. The rotating plates tried to move quickly, but time and damage made them rattle and spark rather than move with smooth menace.

They'd spent Christmas at Kim's mom's house last year, and it was filled with dozens of young cousins, some of whom had inevitably broken various toys that were too delicate to be handled roughly. He had done his best to repair them, but some were too damaged to ever function properly again. One little boy set his barely functioning robot on the ground and watched it limp around, trying to overcome damage that was now permanent.

"I don't want it to die," he said.

That was what Mike felt as this once-formidable machine tried and failed to bring itself back to life. Fully functional, they were terrifying, but this one was tearing itself apart.

And he didn't want it to.

Mike extended threads that contacted its underlying software functions, and its frantic efforts to revive slowed and stopped.

Deep down, the quantum lattice that was the foundation of every unduplicate he'd ever encountered was still there. It was the first time he'd been able to examine one at this level of detail. It answered some questions but raised others.

First, it was ancient, genuinely ancient. As unduplicates aged, their lattices created specific patterns that could be used to track the years they'd been active. Like tree rings, it was regular and, with the right formula, reliably produced an age. He had to alter his result window as it counted out the patterns, then alter it again. After lengthening the display nine times, he had a definitive answer.

The node was just over seven million years old.

But the profound age presented an equally profound puzzle. Unduplicates grew in sophistication as they aged until—usually accompanied by some sort of trauma—they became fully sentient. They had been invented on Earth less than twenty years ago, and he personally knew of more than a dozen that had achieved complete self-awareness. It seemed inevitable, yet this device was not self-aware. He wouldn't be able to examine it this way if it was.

The node was also exactly that: a single entity designed to be tied together with others in order to function correctly. This one, though, could only reach a few other nodes. What was once a powerful, system-spanning network was now in ancient tatters. That was another difference between these nodes and the unduplicates back home. He didn't think anyone back home had considered what might happen if unduplicates were harnessed together the way the AC network was. They weren't designed for it, at least not yet.

And it wasn't strictly a terrestrial network. There were nodes in all sorts of orbits in the system. In fact, the bulk of the functional nodes were the ones in space. This node couldn't reach them, but it knew where they were.

He could spend his whole life studying this contradictory machine, but he had a bigger problem. He opened a command channel. *Query,* he sent, *can the location of this life form be determined?* He sent it Kim's bio-profile.

Location confirmed. A map of the city drew itself into existence. Their point of view sped to the northeast, where many temporary structures had been built.

It would take a long time to walk there, assuming he could get out of this hole. *Map directions and transportation solutions from this location to that one.*

The plates of the node sped up and banged against each other. *Mapping function impaired by priority coordination order.*

Explain.

A countdown timer appeared next to the words *Major Cleansing*.

Orbital nodes require maximum computational resources to resolve stellar fusion destabilizing function.

That didn't sound good. *What is the purpose of a Major Cleansing?*

This system had been declared surplus to needs. It will be removed from inventory.

That was, as Spencer liked to say, bullshit. *Who ordered this?*

First councilor ordered Major Cleansing thirty-two minutes ago.

The La'fan's settlement was huge, millions of them worked across the planet every day. *Has an evacuation been ordered?*

Negative.

Do they know what's happening?

Negative. Announcement was overridden by first councilor with consent. Current AC network unable to assess judgement. Great family representatives unavailable for consultation.

It took a few more questions to determine that this was possible because, as far as the nodes were concerned, the system was abandoned. They had no way to legally override the first councilor. He wondered if blowing up stars was a way for Interpreters to pass the time.

Then he remembered how vulnerable the AC network was to exploits. He sent threads into the security hive and gave himself local root access. *Override Major Cleansing order.*

This node is not equipped for override.

He should've known it wouldn't be that easy. *Where is a node that is equipped for override?*

The path between here and Kim that had been laboriously drawing itself into existence took a detour, moving to the south edge of the city.

Node X4T33L is closest equipped for override.

Two of the node's giant plates popped off their rails with a pair of massive bangs that nearly made him jump out of his skin. His demands had added an unsustainable load. The node wasn't conscious, but the malfunction caused a kind of pain to come through his connection. It was a signature he was familiar with. He'd encountered it last when Ozzie had enslaved hundreds of unduplicates in a cavern in China. That answered one of his questions.

The node hadn't been *unable* to achieve consciousness, it had been *prevented*. Now that he knew what to look for, he could see the massive damage this had caused to its rationality hives. At the layer he was interacting with, the node was very machinelike, but deeper down, the situation was much worse than he could have possibly imagined.

Cut off and alone, held back by designers Mike didn't understand, using mechanisms Mike had no time to figure out, the node had spent most of its very long life terrified and insane. It was an unending torture inflicted on an entity that could suffer but couldn't understand why. There was no way for him to fix it.

But he could stop it. "It's okay," he said out loud, just like he did to that little boy at Christmas. Then, as now, he said the next part as much to himself as anyone else. "It's not death if it was never alive to begin with."

The lights faded, the motion slowed, then ceased. After an unimaginable amount of time, the node was at peace.

He climbed to the surface, blinking his eyes clear.

Chapter 49
Maff

Leaving Mike and Kim behind was the hardest thing she'd ever done, but it was necessary. There was no way they'd get to the surface undetected. There were too many ships, in the transit dimension and in orbit around the planet itself. But the ruined cities on the surface were huge jumbled messes. Plenty of cover down there.

So Maff got to play the wounded *killdeer*, which sounded like the Earth equivalent of a now long-extinct seturian.

It was a great idea that nearly worked until the entire Interpreter fleet appeared and started chasing her around the planet. The harmless engine modifications ended up stealing the last five percent of her coolant margin. That was fine racing along at eighty percent throttle. At one hundred percent, it took away cooling she needed to keep the systems stable.

The warning lights changed from amber to red, then the claxons started to sound.

"I know, I know," she said to the warning lights and then tried to open the manifold flaps more. No good, they were already at max. She cursed and swung around another diplomatic cruiser that blundered into her path, twirling as three more grapples flew past from the pack chasing behind her.

There was a loud bang from the left engine. The claxons changed from intermittent to constant as that whole side of the engine board went solid red. She wrestled with the controls as the ship lurched sideways from the suddenly unbalanced power. She needed a place to hide, sooner rather than later. Then the right engine spat and stuttered.

Maff needed a place to hide *now*.

Transit dimension travel was a funny thing sometimes. The speed difference relative to realspace was immense and running into the obstacles a star cast into it was unpleasant. But when the velocity dropped below the limits of space, in her case now far below them, the situation changed. The shadows stopped being solid obstacles and became navigable mazes.

All the instructors at the academy insisted their pilots learn how to read a raw dimensional map because navcomputers were always programmed conservatively, and emergencies happened. She pulled up the raw-D and scanned it, finding a good spot right away.

Maff rolled through a loop, pointed the nose of the ship straight down, overrode every warning the navcomputer sent her, and hopped into the transit dimension just long enough to squirm through the shadow maze of the surface and into a large void under one of the ruined city towers. As soon as she entered the space, she shut down all her active systems. On the passive scanner, a mass representing the six interceptors that'd been on her tail flashed past.

Score another one for the community school graduate. Uncle Turnn had been the one who recommended the school, said it was underrated and therefore a real bargain. She was beginning to think that he might've had other motives. She'd now dodged or outrun at least three groups of interceptors who'd been out to catch her. Having a pilot like that would be a valuable addition to Uncle's business.

At the very least, she should send him a case of distilled ammonia.

The left engine coughed a gout of flame out of the exhaust. She cursed and activated the fire suppression system on that side, then cursed more as thick white fluid started running out of every port and access panel. That was going to be a pain to clean up.

She got out to assess the damage. The right engine looked awful, but it was all cosmetic. That was good, because the left engine was a genuine mess, and she'd need something to use as a reference. She took two wing flaps back at the thought. A few months ago this failure would've left her panic stricken and helpless. But after spending time with Mike, Kim, and the La'fan, it was now just a nuisance.

She had truly flown a long way from home clouds. She might be the only pallun in the galaxy who knew how to fix a ship's engine. That reminded her she needed to get moving on the repair, otherwise there wouldn't be anyone to pick up Mike and Kim after they found Will.

Maff checked the cargo hold and found plenty of spare parts on hand. But she lacked tools. No problem. She'd been on a scavenger hunt with Kim and knew what to look for. The whole planet was a junkyard, after all.

The void was a cavern created when the underground portion of several buildings collapsed together in a single event. The ceiling that remained had inadvertently formed a perfect vault, creating a stable hiding place for her and her ship. Passages leading out were located on the intact walls. That would be where she'd find the best items.

Maff hit the jackpot when she found a line of ribbon cable attached to the wall of a tunnel near her parking place. The cable itself was nice, but it was the insulation surrounding it that was the real find. It was incredibly sticky and could last thousands of years if applied properly. It was almost as useful as *duct tape,* an obviously mythical Earth substance Mike and Kim often praised for its ability to repair anything. She merrily walked along the tunnel, yanking the cable off its mounts, until it terminated in a box of some sort. Using an improvised pry bar and hacksaw, both little more than shaped bits of building debris, she got the box open and found a treasure trove of circuits and relays, along with a big switch. She traced the wires from this last item to a massive ancient door. This tunnel was the best preserved she'd seen so far.

There was a good chance she'd find more treasure on the other side of that door.

Maff used power from her own suit to get the door's motor running. "That's another thing you guys seem to be great at," Mike had told her. "Bearings. I don't know what they're made of, but they don't seize up, and they don't wear out. I'm convinced you could put one of these gear boxes in the bottom of a bog, dig it up a thousand years later, and the shafts would all spin freely." This door was no different from the items he'd been repairing at the time. After a rising whine, it unlocked with a bang and grumbled upward into the ceiling.

She shined a light into the room on the other side. It was filled with shelves, row upon row of them, one on each wall and two in the middle so a pair of aisles was formed that disappeared into the gloom.

The preservation was incredible. Not a single shelf had collapsed or was out of place. Each one held a neat grid of dark cylinders small enough to easily fit in one of her manipulators. They were hard and dense, heavier than they looked, and there were millions of them on the shelves. The material was nothing special, mostly dry calcium phosphates with some minor minerals mixed with a neutral binding agent. Basically, dust.

Maff kept exploring, waiting for the shelf's contents to change from the weird cylinders into something more useful. After walking for a really long time, she didn't find anything useful.

She found a body.

The people who lived here were high-grav hexapeds, with the third set of appendages serving as arms. Mike and Kim called them *centauroid*, a reference to a mythical creature in Earth's past. This one was an ancient mummy, its clothing threadbare and what skin she could see turned to parchment. Whoever this was, they died peacefully. The creature had curled up and seemed to have gone to sleep.

The next ones she found had not gone peacefully at all.

They were piled up in front of another door deep inside the

complex, gigantic this time, shut as tightly as the one she had found. There was clear evidence of a rush to escape, of panic and violence. They'd died trying to get out, hurting each other. Many had been crushed as others had climbed on top. The doors were made of steel alloy, but they still managed to scratch it with hands that were eerily like Mike and Kim's.

A realization grabbed her like a swirling storm. Every school back home taught about places like this. Pallun were ostracized because of an ancient agreement that exempted them from places like this. Turl itself had been destroyed because they rebelled against places like this.

Maff had stumbled into a senescent center.

The cylinders were the cremated remains of the bulk of the citizenry, the ones who went willingly to the sleep chambers. The bodies were not of rebels. With one exception, nobody ever rebelled against this process, but rather of the very last of the people left. It was the first undeniable confirmation of something palluns had whispered about for generations.

When there were too few inhabitants left to make the centers economical, the network nodes herded the rest in, locked the doors, and shut it all down.

Maff backed away, slowly at first but with growing urgency. Her people had rejected this. They started a war they could not win because they would not have this imposed on them. They lost their entire star system to create a stalemate that forced the entire galaxy to back down, to leave them a signal privilege that would forever mark them as different, hated, outcast.

Maff might turn her back on her people's traditions, but that didn't mean she stopped being a pallun. Her people always chose life, always celebrated it, cherished it, preserved it. The mechanized soulless imposition of a racial death penalty was only comprehensible to her as a legend. To be confronted with its actuality, to physically be inside it, made a scream start deep inside her that she knew would never stop if she let it out.

Then, still moving backward, she stumbled and fell over a body.

The scream tore out of her, an endless wail that grew louder as shelves collapsed, sending their black contents tumbling down on her head. Trying to get away and disoriented, she walked straight into the mountain of corpses stacked at the front door. Bodies, whole and in parts, crumbled and crushed under her legs, then rolled down on top of her. She would be trapped here, never get out, smothered under the dead. Maff could do nothing but scream at hollow faces.

But finally, it did stop. *She* had stopped struggling and screaming, made immobile, frozen in place. Her paralysis let everything settle, and she came back to herself. She needed to get out of here. Desperately trying not to touch anything but unable to avoid the awful crunching of bodies, she oriented herself toward the exit. Once lined up, she exploded out of her parchment-and-bone prison and ran straight out the door, not looking back until she was safely underneath her ship again.

The repairs were mercifully simple, but she still had a hard time managing them. She hadn't shut the door to the tomb, and even though nothing in there was alive, she constantly saw flickering motion from that tunnel. Then she realized she had to go back in to get more scrap. The interceptors outside knew what her ship looked like, and she needed to fix that.

There was a dreadful weight of certainty whenever she turned her back or looked away that dead eyes watched her in the darkness. The moment she could, she jumped to the transit dimension and then to the surface. The setting sun on the horizon let her breathe properly.

And make her first check-in call.

"Mike? Kim? You guys out there?"

"I am," Mike replied. "I need a ride, and we need another plan."

Chapter 50
Spencer

It took time to make his way around the dickwads who showed up near the camp to get to Helen. When he did, it was bad.

Really bad.

"Jesus fucking Christ," he said, "what happened?" Blood was everywhere.

She had her hand over the wound trying to staunch the flow. "I fell on the sharp part of the digger."

This was way the hell over his pay grade. He sent a picture to Tonya.

"Take your belt and wrap it around her leg just above the wound, pull it tight," she said. "I'm on my way."

"Be careful," he said. "Redneck rampage is now a thing."

"Spencer?"

That was a voice he didn't expect. "Stewart? What are you doing on this line?"

"You never took me off, remember?"

To Helen, Spencer said, "This is gonna suck balls. On three. One…two…*three*." He pulled the belt as tight as he could. The rednecks within earshot heard her cry, and all turned their way.

"Anyway," Stewart continued, "whatever it is driving everyone crazy has come back. They know where you are."

Spencer took a low-light shot of the posse now headed toward them and sent it to him. "No shit."

"Dammit," Stewart said. "I heard Helen's hurt?"

He checked her again. She was sweaty and pale, but the bleeding had slowed down. "Pretty bad."

"Okay. I've gathered some friends at my dad's deer camp. It's a lot smaller and deeper in the woods than yours is, that should slow them down."

"Sorry, bud," Spencer said, levering Helen up off the ground. He had Tonya on a mapping app with a path plotted out to meet her halfway. "I'm not exactly moving fast right now."

Four dots appeared on his map display, moving toward them from deeper in the woods. "We got ya covered there, bro. Everyone, make your way to this rendezvous point." A green dot appeared west of where he and Tonya would've otherwise met. "We'll deal with the posse and come pick you up."

Helen did her best to move with him, but she tensed hard with every motion. In spite of that, she made almost no sound. It was a wonder she was conscious at all.

Two of the dots peeled off while the other pair moved toward him and Tonya. In the distance, he heard the whine of electric motors and the dry swooshing smash of tires through leaves. The cavalry was on its way.

Spencer needed to stay free in the meantime. The only things he had going for him was that he'd spent the last few days tromping around in these woods, and it was dark out. For whatever reason, their invaders were using flashlights instead of low-light apps on their phones. He could maneuver in the dark, but they couldn't.

Then someone back with the trucks turned on a spotlight and speared him with it. He dropped Helen away from her bad leg and dove for the dirt himself. The tree above him shook with three heavy thumps that showered him with splinters as the boom of high-powered rifle rounds sounded in the near distance.

Way too near.

The trouble with spotlights, for the bad guys, was that they created stark shadows he could use for cover. The hunters would have a harder time seeing the terrain in front of them. Finally, it would ruin the night vision of everyone staring at the light, as well as blind whoever had aimed it with their night vision app. He knew never to count on the bad guys being dumb, but he'd take advantage of it whenever he could.

That didn't help make the supersonic rounds *thwipping* through the bushes and trees over his head any easier to take. The unsynchronized booms that followed up moments after were more unnerving. He needed to get Helen the fuck out of here right now.

She was doing the best she could, but the pain was so bad she could barely crawl. That was some bullshit that had to stop. "Roll over, Helen, let me drag you."

"But the guns!"

Thwipp-BOOM, thwipp-BOOM

"The guns are my problem." There was no time to discuss this in committee. He reached out, rolled her over, and dragged her backward in a crouch.

Thwipp-thwipp-BOOM-BOOM

Spencer had his share of uncles and aunts who'd been in combat over the years, and they all told the same story: getting shot at did wonderful things for your concentration. The knowledge that one of these shit for brains rednecks could end him at any moment pushed out everything except what mattered: stay low, keep pulling, watch out for obstacles. *Keep going!*

The unmistakable metallic whine of electric four-wheelers tore from his left to his right in front of him. Outraged shouts, wild gunfire, and the crazed whooping of Stewart's squad said that the cavalry had arrived. Spencer stood up, threw Helen over his shoulder in a fireman's carry, and stomped off toward the rendezvous point.

When Stewart pulled up in the dark, Spencer spotted the flaw in his cunning plan. The four-wheeler only had room for one more. "Here, take her," he said. They gingerly moved Helen to the back seat of Stewart's vehicle.

"What about you?" he asked.

Good question. "Don't worry about me. Get her and Tonya to safety. Tonya's a nurse, she'll know what to do."

"But—"

"I said go! Get out of here! I'll figure it out." A bullet *thwipped* between them. "Now!"

Stewart gunned it and vanished into the night.

Spencer checked the map. The two diversion riders were still in the area, he heard them whooping it up as they ducked and dodged angry hunters who were under some sort of fucked up mind-control shit and not used to prey smarter than they were. Suddenly one peeled off and headed straight for him.

A call connected, identified as Melvin, one of Stewart's old football buddies. "Hey, dude, Stewart filled me in. Meet me here, and I'll give you a ride back."

"Do we need to worry about being followed?"

"Cedric will lead them a long way from here, don't you worry."

These were guys who terrorized him in high school and now were treating him almost like an equal. Melvin laughed when Spencer mentioned this on the way to the new camp. "The marines taught me that a lot of the things I thought were important in high school weren't. We're here to help and stop whatever fucked up shit is happening to the county."

The new camp was much smaller. No permanent structures here, it was all tents, all the time, with several smaller ones surrounding a large one that must act as a kitchen and common area.

Or now, a MASH tent.

He heard Tonya before he saw her, using that voice that *made* people move. "A cap full of bleach per gallon and only use brand-new mops."

Someone had staked out a tarp like a plastic rug between the mess tent and the campfire. Guys in their socks stood on the tarp and handed stuff off to guys wearing shoes who weren't, and vice versa, never crossing the makeshift barrier. The stench of bleach made it all smell more like a pool than a camp. He took the hint and pulled off his shoes before going inside.

Helen was laid out on a table covered with another tarp, this one so new he could smell the plastic over the bleach. Her pants had been cut off, and he flinched at her injury. He'd helped his dad field dress deer as a kid, but that was a dead animal, and this was his friend. She was unconscious, breathing, with a very unhealthy pallor to her skin. Tonya was bent over the cut on her leg with new needle-nose pliers and a bunch of gauze pads.

"Spencer, glove up and give me a hand."

With an effort, he looked away from Helen's leg, grabbed a pair of gloves from a nearby box, and pulled them on.

"You're my nurse for now. Follow the instructions on the fleshKnit kit and get it ready."

There were two first aid kits open, one he recognized from their camp and one that must've come from this one. Dad only packed things that would last forever, so it was nothing but Band-Aids and gauze. Stewart's camp had been equipped with a modern nanotech first aid kit. That was a lucky break. It was a big case of color-coordinated tubes and looked like it belonged in the paint section of a hobby store.

The kit came with a big card that showed which tubes got mixed together to produce the paste they wanted. While the other guys in the camp kept cleaning and stocking the tent, he mixed up the three tubes that would create a fleshKnit paste. It was like mixing up a batch of fiberglass to repair Dad's old bass boat, but it smelled worse.

"Gah, Tonya," he said, trying to breathe only through his mouth, "here you go." She held out her hand without looking up, and he placed the tray of mixed chemicals in it.

"Hold her wound closed," she said.

Using a new wooden spatula, Tonya carefully spread the foul-smelling goo on Helen's wound. After a few seconds, it started fizzing and changed color from red to green. Eventually it quit bubbling and ran down Helen's leg like syrup, leaving behind pink, clean skin.

"Holy shit."

Tonya nodded as she worked, still not looking up. "This *is* the twenty-first century. The edges of the wound will heal quickly, the rest in a few hours." She lifted her head and tilted it toward him. After a half second, he realized what she wanted and patted her forehead down with a fresh pad of gauze. "It's nice not to have to use stitches for once."

"For once?"

She spread the last of the goop on the center of the wound, leaving behind a big patch of red cake frosting surrounded by an edge of bubbling green. It reminded him of the time he tried to defrost a frozen fruit pie by microwaving it for five minutes. Only it stank more.

Tonya sat up and stretched. "Nanopastes don't play well with limb regrowth systems. We have to do it old school."

"How long until she wakes up?" he asked.

Tonya shook her head. "I wish I could give her more time. And we still have to get her to a hospital. FleshKnit is cool stuff, but I want a doctor to look her over." Tonya punched a few buttons on a control panel only she could see.

Helen's eyes popped open. After a moment, she said, "I can't move."

"It's okay, honey," Tonya said. "I need to bring you up in stages. A sudden movement could ruin our work." She turned to Spencer. "Send two of the biggest guys in here to help me move her to that chair," Tonya indicated an old lay-flat lawn chair someone had brought in, "and take Helen outside. Gather the rest of them around the fire. We need to talk."

Chapter 51

Kim

Secure area ended up being a pantry connected to Valsa's kitchen. Kim had gotten reasonably familiar with their camera technology and, after a quick search, couldn't find any. There was only one door, with two big robots guarding it. She wasn't shackled to anything or being watched. They even tossed her breath mask in with her, not that she would be using it any time soon.

It fit a pattern she was beginning to see with the Guild: they consistently underestimated her and Mike. Hacking was still a male-dominated industry back home, so it was an attitude she knew well. It was time to make them pay for that weakness.

They still hadn't found Mike; she was sure of that, and now they probably stopped trying to find him. Why bother when this whole system would be turned to dust in...well, that was another problem. She didn't know how much time they had. Maff hadn't been all that specific about how long it had taken the first time around, only that it was long enough for them to flee to safety. That had to mean a few days, at least. Hopefully.

At minimum, it had to mean hours. This camp wouldn't break down instantly. The staff was moving with haste, but not in a panic. It wasn't how people who were abandoning everything and running like hell would act.

She had time. The question was how to use it. She reached out with her power and hit the expected wall. She couldn't call their split stunt badly timed. Valsa had to think twice about rethreading her. But it still left her without the biggest wrench in her toolkit. *No hacking for you!*

The ventilation ducts were a bust, as narrow and useless for escape and sneaking around as the ones back home. More promising was the lock on the door. It was a standard style like ones she studied when they ended up on *Last Island*. She smiled at the brief flash of memory, of being so scared and disoriented and trying to do something, anything to be of value to aliens. She looked at the sleeve on her black robes with the embroidered patterns that declared her a lead Interpreter. *My how you have grown.*

As before, the locks relied on the ubiquitous planetary gearsets instead of more familiar cylinder and pins. They didn't fit together so much as shift. She searched the pantry for a tool that would work as a lockpick. At first, things looked grim. It was a pantry full of vegetable and fruit equivalents that she recognized as safe to eat. She picked a nice, large apple-grape to chew on while she worked.

Toward the back, she found some tompatoes packed in a case that had latches that would work. She carefully pried them apart with a scraper she'd found in a sack full of celerawberries. Valsa *would* like something that disgusting.

Kim carefully shifted the lock into neutral and pushed the door open to look around. The kitchen was a beehive of activity as people rushed back and forth. Half of them were packing things up, while the other half argued with and tried to cook around the packers.

"If you don't let this oven cool down, it'll set the ship on fire before you've stowed it."

"You cannot pour hot oil into a sink full of water! Do you want to blow us all up?"

"Leave that coupling alone! It's pressurized refrigerant, you fool! You'll lose three arms before you blink."

On and on.

If she were Mike, she'd walk out and vanish in that spooky way he had and start causing trouble. If she were Tonya, she'd rush out, order people around, and then clobber whoever didn't move fast enough. Spencer would talk his way past the problem, swearing the entire time.

She missed them all for a moment, but no longer than that. She had to get out of here. The only good news was they'd left robots as her door guards. No touch madness.

Wait. Robots?

Everything in this galaxy used planetary gears, including the robots. It was the first time she'd gotten a good look at their backside. There were slots that had to lead to manual shift points on the gearboxes that made up their drivetrains.

She closed the door and used the twine from sacks of apple-grapes to firmly attach her homemade gear shifter to a celerawberry. Make that *two* uses for the devil's fishing pole. Chanting *careful, careful, slowly* to herself, she switched the drive portion of the first robot into neutral, then waited to see if anything happened. When nothing did, she switched the second robot into neutral as well. These were mechanical overrides. What the robot thought would happen if it tried to move would be different from what actually happened, and it would take time to sort it out. There were other shift points on their arms, but she left those alone. It would be her luck that their arms would fall off before she was ready.

And now to get things rolling.

Whoever had been told about the hot oil had left a bucket of it right next to a sink, presumably full of water, although she couldn't be sure from this angle. It didn't need to be full anyway. The thing was going to be heavy, and she only had one shot at this. She took back her lockpick, then gathered up all the celerawberries into a bunch that was about as big around as a baseball bat on the thick end.

Okay, here we go.

She very quietly braced the door open enough to give her a clear shot, cocked back, and threw her improvised spear as hard as she could at the pot. It went sailing past the left guard's head, but before the robot could turn, the spear *thunked* against the pot. For an agonizing second, she thought she failed. She'd have to run and hope for the best.

Then it fell in.

When you grew up in a family as big as hers that cooked as often as they did, someone somewhere was going to toss water into hot oil. It was a loud, dangerous mistake that immediately got a furious scolding from the owner of the kitchen. There was usually a lot of steam, noise, and splatter.

This time it went off like a bomb.

The bucket might've hit the bottom of the sink; she couldn't tell because of the huge *ka-boom* it made as the water flashed to steam and sent a column of oil droplets straight up. Everyone in the kitchen either ran screaming or took cover as the sink continued to spew and roar like the world's smallest, angriest geyser. She didn't spare any of it a second glance, running behind her guards and following the wall of the kitchen, trying to find a way out.

Then the oil found a flame.

The massive *whoomph* of a fireball knocked her into the side of a large cabinet. What was already chaotic was instantly covered in a cloud of fire retardant that spewed from the ceiling. She tried to grip the cabinet to steady herself but stumbled and fell into a dark hallway that hadn't been there a second before. The screams, shouts, alarms, and flames cut off with a *thump* as a hidden door slid shut behind her.

The utter silence after her inadvertent bomb was almost as disorienting as the darkness. She stood up, smacking the small flames out on her robes. She had to get moving. It would take some time to sort all that out, but they would eventually notice the open door to her pantry-slash-prison. The guards would almost certainly have fixed what she'd done to them by then. The chase was on.

Kim found herself standing in a narrow corridor, dimly lit by faint point lights on the floor, reminding her of an old-school movie theater. She crept as quickly as she dared down the hall. It was long—fifty yards, easy. Finally, she came to the other end and found another sliding door. She carefully tried it, and it slid to the side without a sound. There was another corridor that went to her left, but the far wall was made of a heavy curtain instead of something solid.

"You have taken a massive risk," a deep, artificial-sounding voice on the other side of it said. "She is more dangerous than you realize."

"She is weak and alone." Kim recognized the voice. Valsa.

"You have not found her companion."

"I'm taking care of that in my own way."

"Do not underestimate them. I have encountered their kind many times before. They are deadly and resourceful."

"I have already seen how resourceful they are. I assure you, I am not underestimating them in the slightest. I am taking extreme measures to ensure they will not threaten the project's completion."

"Good. I am taking steps to eliminate the remaining companion as we speak."

"The remaining…" From the tremble in her voice, Kim could tell Valsa didn't like that news one bit. "There are more of them, not in this system?"

"There are always four. The remaining two need not concern you. One is already dead, the other soon will be."

It hit her. *They were talking about Helen!* Mike hadn't heard from her since before they left the negotiation table, but before then they were trying to figure out who had made those sketches. Incredibly, it must have something to do with Valsa, or at least whoever she was talking to. This was a huge development. Now she had another reason to figure out where he was.

"But they have an entire—"

A bong interrupted Valsa, and a door slid open somewhere. "First Councilor, there has been an incident in the kitchen where the La'fan Interpreter was being held."

Something tapped her on the shoulder. The robots must've sorted themselves out and then found her. She'd gotten distracted and used up the time she needed to escape listening to megalomaniacs rub their hands together and gloat. She put up her hands and turned around.

Mike.

He held his finger up in a shush gesture as the deep voice said, "I told you they were resourceful."

Kim wanted to scream, jump, burst, hug no matter what the cost, anything to celebrate her big, dumb, wonderful fiancé showing up. But she couldn't, not now. He motioned to her and mouthed *follow me*.

"You are not a conqueror yet, my lord. I will handle this," Valsa said, then her voice changed from someone addressing her superior to the opposite. "Lock down the camp, search every building until you find her."

"But ma'am, the timing…"

"Means you better find her fast, yes? Wait, isn't that the kitchen that connects to—"

Mike took two steps backward and then hopped through a hole in the floor. Kim followed right behind, not caring if it hadn't been there when she walked past the spot only minutes before.

She landed on the catwalk of their stolen ship; the harbor guy had called it *Palatine*. Mike flicked a switch in his hand, and a hatch slid shut over the hole above their heads.

"Go, Maff! Go!" he shouted.

The ship lurched sideways, sending them stumbling against the syrup of an inertia field. Kim looked up at the man she was happily going to spend the rest of her life with. "How'd you find me?"

"We got lucky. The robes have a built-in beacon. I was hoping you'd still have them on, but if you didn't, it would've at least gotten me closer."

"We have a problem," she said as they made their way to the command deck. Okay, a lot of problems, but the first one was all about—

"The countdown. Yeah, I know about that."

She greeted Maff with multiple high-fives against her probes. Beating Valsa was better than any realm championship she'd ever won.

"Tell her about Will," Maff said.

Kim's heart jumped at the mention of his name. That could only mean…

Mike grinned. "We've found him."

Chapter 52
Helen

This was a proper deer camp. No rotten city buses with built-in stoves or shack kitchens with secret basements full of stuff here. There were only tents, sleeping bags, and a camp stove to prevent smoke from giving them away. It was fancy and practical in a way which she was getting used to thinking of as American.

The fleshKnit worked its magic, but it wasn't comfortable. *Pins and needles* was an abstract English term for pain before she came outside, and then a description for minor numbness and itching when she had. Now it was an intensely sharp sensation made worse by the maddening need to scratch it. Her friends had saved her life, but if this didn't get better soon, she was going to ask for a hacksaw.

Stop being such a baby.

"Don't you start," she said out loud.

This got a pair of sharp looks from Tonya and Spencer as they organized their miniature militia on the other side of the camp stove. Helen wondered if they made the connection between her outburst and her unwanted companion. They had witnessed Helen's first fight with the snake mother, the one that nearly destroyed her.

The good old days.

She needed to learn to talk to herself silently.

You do, in your fashion.

Helen recalled the way the snake mother panicked in that place when she thought Helen had vanished. The need for *her only friend* was almost physical.

You flatter yourself. It was a moment of weakness, nothing more.

Helen felt the lie but chose not to pursue it. The fact that the snake mother remained silent at Helen's thought confirmed her suspicion. This might be a valid strategy to silence her for good.

Don't you start.

If nothing else, arguing with her alter ego distracted from the pain in her leg.

When Tonya explained Helen's part of the plan, the pain vanished.

"Me, in space?" Helen asked.

Tonya nodded. "In space. The signal is coming from outside the solar system. Outside the galaxy, in fact. We need a way to jam it. The new orbital realmspace network is the perfect place."

It was all rooted in Tonya's theories about time.

"It's difficult to explain without knowing the math," Tonya began.

"That's Mike's line," Spencer said.

Tonya transformed into a professor as she straightened up and cleared her throat. Being surrounded by people who had to put so much faith in her made her visibly uncomfortable. "And for now, it's mine, too. There's a…being…out there using a time-based attack via a dimension that allows the signal to exceed the speed of light."

"Being." One of the other campers, Melvin, said. "As in an alien?"

"They're more common than you think," Spencer said. "Seriously, it's a long-ass story that I don't completely believe. And I'm one of the witnesses. For now, accept," he did an air quote and squinted, "*aliens*."

"If it's possessing people," Melvin said, "why hasn't it grabbed any of us?"

"There aren't enough of us here," Tonya replied. "It's more like a shotgun than a rifle, and it's being fired from a long distance. It needs a lot of people in one place for it to have a chance of hitting anyone."

"No anal probes, right?" Another camper, Cedric, asked. Helen was pretty sure he was only half joking.

Tonya shook her head. "None of them have gotten close enough to Earth for it to be an issue. The attack is based on a remote determion surge pumped through a shortcut dimension. Essentially, somebody is using our sensitivity to time to leverage a mind-control hack."

"Sensitivity to time?" Stuart asked.

Tonya nodded. "It's where we get concepts like déjà vu and prophecy from. Humans are sensitive to the particles that create time. Whoever is behind this is pushing out a massive number of particles and aiming it at this spot. People who are especially sensitive get confused, and that allows our bad guy to manipulate them."

"But why me?" Helen asked. "Why am I the focus?"

"Well, you're not the only focus. Mike and Kim are, too. And Ozzie. It must have something to do with you being an Interpreter, or at least half of one."

"Interpreter?" Cedric asked.

"That," Spencer said, "is a story in progress. I'll give you the condensed version when we get out of this mess. It doesn't matter right now. The alien wants Helen dead. We don't need to know why. We need to stop it."

"That's where I come in, right?" Helen asked.

"It is," Tonya replied. "If you can upload your threads from that box on your hip into the orbital cloud, you'll be able to manipulate the transmitters to create a jamming signal. It will cut whatever it is off. We'll cease to exist as far as it's concerned."

"Okay, you guys move too fast," Stewart said, intense and trying to understand. Helen knew the feeling. "Threads?"

An explosion erupted from the direction of their old camp. "Another long story," Helen said. "One we've run out of time to tell." She turned to Tonya. "What needs to happen?"

Tonya pulled a massive bundle of wire, stakes, and batteries from one of their off-road vehicles. "This needs to be unfolded, then we need to hook you to it."

You have got to be kidding me.

Helen swallowed and ignored the snake mother's comment, no matter how much she agreed with it. "Hook me to it how?"

She disconnected two bundles from the bigger one and handed them to Cedric and Melvin. "To your phone, and your storage. Spencer will connect my array to the cloud. I'll connect the array to your storage."

Cedric and Melvin furiously staked wires to the ground, while Stewart and another camper, whose name she didn't know, barreled off into the woods on their all-terrain vehicles. She should've spent less time arguing with the snake mother and more time listening to the plan. She didn't like being the center of attention without understanding what was going on.

She ignored the indignant snort that went off in her head. "Where are they going?"

"Distraction," Spencer said as he pointed a giant wok—it had to be an antenna—at the sky. "Rednecks and four-wheelers can be one helluva combination." He started typing on a keyboard only he could see. "Five minutes, tops, and we're in."

"Do you have a control app for your box that I can download?" Tonya asked Helen.

She'd never considered it before. Her device wasn't meant to be used by anyone else. She had an irrational urge to cover it up, like someone whose pants had fallen down. "Not really?"

"Tell me it's not a fucking command line." Spencer said as he adjusted invisible dials. "Kim has a hard-on for those goddamned things. I hate them."

How to explain this? "No. I just...*use* it." Now it sounded gynecological. "The interface is semiorganic." That was no better, and now her face was getting hot. "If you give me the interface, I can make the connections."

Tonya asked, eyebrow raised, "You designed it, right?"

"Guys," Spencer said, "We don't have this kind of time." A rip of automatic gunfire in the distance underlined his statement. "Can you hook it up or not?"

Cedric and Melvin finished with their rigging and rode off to join their colleagues.

"I only built it for storage, not..." She waved at the sky, which had suddenly become a place she didn't want to visit at all. "Space travel."

New crashes sounded out through the woods, but in a different direction.

"Fuck, they've brought more," Spencer said. He threw an invisible lever and nodded. "I'm ready."

"Helen," Tonya said as a realm address landed in her queue. "It's time."

She was a cop, one of the best in China. She had faced down criminals, lunatics, and monsters without a second thought. Helen had moved herself out of China before she was certain it was possible.

But going up into space? And giving Tonya direct access to the one place where her threads could safely reside, without any testing, without any guidance?

Oh, damn your ancestors. This is no time to turn chicken.

The snake mother made the connection before Helen had time to say no or wonder how it was possible.

Helen immediately recognized the realm. It wasn't a simple lab or one of Tonya's multidimensional instruction halls.

It was the realm of her dream, the realm of the eye.

"Where the fuck are we?" Spencer asked, then turned around. "Who the fuck are *you*?"

Spencer and Tonya stood to one side of her; the snake mother, Jīngzhì Liǔ, stood on the other. "This is..." Come to think of it, she didn't have a Western name.

"Jainlee," she said as she shook Spencer's hand. "Jainlee Zhou." She looked at Helen. "I'm her sister...sort of."

Jainlee was an extension of Helen, and so should've abided by the same rules. She should not be manifest, should not have an avatar. But she did.

And so did Helen.

Judging by Spencer's open mouth and wide eyes as he stared at Jainlee, Helen suspected he was as surprised as she was. She looked for Tonya's reaction, but found none. Her gaze was fixed on the sky.

Above them was the same baleful eye as they'd seen before. But now, bereft of the dream confusion, she saw it clearly. It wasn't an eye.

It was a galaxy.

YOU BEHOLD MY TRUE FORM.

The voice was so powerful, so loud, everyone collapsed to their knees. It wasn't sound, it was *presence,* a physical manifestation of an intelligence that encompassed a billion stars, *was* a billion stars. But a single mind.

ONLY AT THE END DO YOU UNDERSTAND.

"Oh, fuck this. It's still a realm." A strange organic construct grew out of the ground, a low, gigantic, rectangular piece of coral or maybe granite. It was longer and wider than a city bus with a row of three thick branches, or maybe they were stone columns, sticking out of the side.

Spencer looked dumbfounded, an emotion she thought him incapable of, but he recovered quickly. "Okay, not a battleship turret like I asked for. Maybe it's not *one of our* realms."

The construct turned and tracked the target.

He pulled out a vine on the back of the main section. "Close enough. Eat…whatever the fuck this thing shoots…you son of a bitch!" The columns spat enormous gouts of fire. The concussion knocked them all off their feet.

When they got up, the galaxy had vanished.

A healing contract zipped through and repaired her ears.

"That won't last long," Spencer said.

"Your friend doesn't do half measures," Jainlee said. "I like him."

Spencer smiled.

"Don't eat my friends," Helen replied.

Spencer's smile vanished.

"Aw," Jainlee said it like Helen had taken her plate away before she'd had a taste. "Only a little?"

"Helen, you need to go," Tonya said as she looked at a tricorder construct. "Spencer's right, its coming back."

On cue, the galaxy reappeared in a different quarter of the sky. A solid beam speared down in the distance. Where it hit, the surface of their world exploded upward.

"Oh my God"—Tonya breathed out like a prayer—"pure determions."

"What the fuck does that mean?" Spencer asked as his construct began a ponderous turn.

"Nothing good," Tonya replied. A portal opened. "Here's your interface, Helen."

She tried to access it but was immediately stopped by a small glowing structure in the center of the space on the other side. "Oh no."

Helen and Mike had often wondered how long it would take another life form like themselves to manifest in a new realmspace. The realmspace had to be above a certain size, otherwise regular freestanding ones would have them. But they didn't know how much bigger or how much time was required.

Now Helen knew.

"I can't. Someone's already there."

The destructive beam crept closer. It was clear Spencer's turret would not reposition in time.

"It's not mature," Jainlee said. "Not alive. Not even close."

Helen knew that was true but didn't move. All her life she'd wanted a family. A child. After going outside, she knew that a human child was a possibility. But always in the back of her mind was the desire to create *real* life, life like she was. Like Mike was.

"I won't destroy it," she said.

"Helen, if you don't move into that space," Tonya pointed as the beam continued bring destruction toward them, "then *that* wins. We'll lose the whole planet."

Spencer was more direct. "Helen, goddammit, move your ass!"

She knew what was at stake, knew what the right move was. What it had to be.

But she would not take that step. It went against every logical conclusion, all evidence, her training, her politics, her beliefs. Helen should destroy this nascent life form and move in.

A child.

"There has to be another way."

"Helen, *we have no more time,*" Tonya shouted as the rumbling destruction tumbled forward.

Helen felt Jainlee move around her, *out of her*, a ghost detaching from her soul.

"There is another way."

Jainlee's avatar moved toward the spark, dissolving as it went. When she was done, she'd encapsulated the spark, completed it.

Given it life.

"Throw me," Jainlee said.

"What?"

"Throw me. All the way to China."

Mike had talked about moving souls—and Helen knew from her threads to her bones that this was a soul she confronted—from one form, one plane of existence, to another.

But there was a catch. Memories didn't transfer "It will destroy you!"

"No. He's right, your brother. There's more to life than memories. And I'm sick of mine. I ruined my life taking so many others. I know that now. Watching you all this time, it taught me. I was evil. I still am. But part of me, *this* part of me, is not. You taught me that.

"My body has a second chance because of you. Please, give another one to *me*."

"Helen," Spencer shouted as the destruction evaporated his construct. *"Now!"*

Finally, the feet of her avatar moved forward. When she crossed the threshold, so did her threads. They violently displaced and rearranged the space they found themselves in, filling and expanding at an explosive rate. She wrapped the first ones that arrived around the combined spark. When they touched it, some of them, some of *Helen*, vanished inside.

Gently, please.

The route was as clear as the path around a park lake. China's realmspace was empty now, far too recently for anything to have taken root.

"Keep an eye on those old bastards," Helen said as she wound her threads up for the throw. "They're never up to any good."

I promise.

Helen threw the spark, and it turned into a comet as it streaked toward its home. The tail was diseased, full of pain and destruction. But it transformed as it went, cleansing itself of all but the pure, unadulterated essence of life.

Her life, and Jainlee's, and Jīngzhì Liǔ's. Starting new.

"HELEN!" Spencer and Tonya both shouted at her.

The beam touched Tonya's portal.

The world went white.

Chapter 53
Mike

He'd gotten Kim back, had a functioning ship, an ace pilot, and a target to aim at. He wasn't in any better shape than Kim with their spooky stuff, though. On some level, they both knew it would be useless to try. Thinking about it brought on an exhaustion that soaked deep into his threads.

They'd have to stop the cleansing the hard way. Kim chuckled grimly. "As if we'd do it any other way."

The shutdown node was in a remote part of the city. To make sure there would be no more ambushes, they were using the transit dimension hack they figured out rescuing Kim.

"Why didn't we do it this way to begin with?" Mike asked Maff as he sat at the scanning station.

Her manipulators danced over the controls like brass-plated willow branches. "It's dangerous if you don't know what you're doing." A chorus of alarms sounded across her board, which she silenced while cursing softly. "Actually, it's dangerous, period."

"Then why are we doing it *now*?" Kim asked from the nav station.

"Getting ambushed again by Interpreter goons is worse." The waterfall display she'd been using to find their way through the transit dimension changed subtly. Mike could see it happen but had no idea what it meant. "Get ready, hatch opening in five minutes."

Okay, that's what it meant. He and Kim got up and went to the cargo hold with the access hatch in it.

"How long will we have?" Mike asked over the intercom.

"It's hard to say. The problem isn't keeping the interface stable, it's making sure nobody sees us while we're connected. Move quickly and things should be fine."

"How much time do we *actually* have?" Kim asked Mike.

He checked the calculations. The bomb worked by destabilizing the fusion cycle of the star, that much was clear, and he'd been able to cobble together a suite that would detect that. "Ten hours. I'll get a better fix outside. I can use the sensors then."

Maff's waterfall was a strictly short-range sensor, and passive, to boot. No worries about someone figuring out where they were by anything the ship emitted. But seeing the system required the use of the nav array. That operated with a big fat emitter that would broadcast their location to anyone in the vicinity who was listening. To judge by the masses that kept zooming by them on Maff's sensors, that seemed to be the entire Interpreter fleet.

"I still can't get over how this entire galaxy is wired to explode," Kim said as she prepped for their excursion. "Except for our part, anyway."

"I'm looking into that," Mike said. "If the system is inhabited and active, it's almost impossible. Unless the circumstances are truly extraordinary—"

"Like a civilization that repudiates the galactic culture," Maff said.

"Right," Mike replied, "unless it's something that big, the nodes won't agree to destroying an active system. They can't. And the nodes are what make it work."

"And inactive systems?" Kim asked. "Is this the first time they've tried to take out a La'fan system?"

"No way to know. La'fan are set apart from mainstream galactic culture and always have been. There's no formal record."

"Which we know can't be trusted anyway."

"True, but if Interpreters made a habit of blowing systems up on a whim, word would get around, and without the La'fan recycling planetary resources, the nodes would grind to a halt. It could help explain why the La'fan have never had active Interpreters, though."

Kim turned around so he could do the same checks on her back harness. "Do you think they'd destroy an entire system to get one rogue?"

"It's what they're doing now. Sort of."

"And on that cheerful thought," Maff said over the intercom, "you need to get to the hatch, we're here."

Palatine was smaller than the *Last Island*, but it still had the problematic main cargo door system of that ship. They used a maintenance hatch to avoid any issues. "Did you hear anything when we arrived at Valsa's tent?" he asked Kim.

"Not a sound."

"That's too bad. I was hoping for some wheezing and grinding."

Kim rolled her eyes. "It's not a TARDIS."

"A what?" Maff asked.

They both stopped and, after a second, shared a look. It was such a deceptively simple concept, but the words wouldn't fit together properly. "I guess we shouldn't be surprised," he said to Kim.

"I can't make it work either." She looked up. "It's hard to describe in a language you'll understand. None of them have the words we need."

"I'm getting pretty good at English."

Kim shrugged, then switched languages. "It's a machine for traveling through time."

There was a long pause. "You mean...humans can...travel through *time*?" It came out as *hzhyoomanz cansh trayvell thrah tymesh*, but the awe required no translation.

"No," Mike replied as he started the open sequence. "It's fiction to us, stories."

"Sort of," Kim said.

Tonya, right. "Don't make it more complicated for her than it already is," he said.

"It gets *more* complicated? That's not possible."

Mike smiled. "It's very possible. We've got a friend back home working on a theory to describe it all."

"Okay, enough confusing theories. We've got a job to do here."

The hatch slid open, revealing the stained, poisonous sky of the dead planet above. The La'fan rebreathers worked fine. Better than what was available in the rest of the galaxy, in fact. It didn't make stepping up the ladder any easier.

The node was outside, part of the remnant city the La'fan were actively working on. Mike could see their towers in the far distance. What was monstrous and intimidating up close was now a chain of glowing lights, the first string laid out on a Christmas tree. Each one represented perhaps a hundred thousand individuals. If Mike and Kim didn't succeed, this was the last day any of them would ever see.

Kim set up a laser transmitter and aimed it carefully until it had locked onto a receiver on one of those distant towers. That done, she pushed a button that transmitted their message.

Fellow La'fan. The first councilor has decreed this system will be destroyed in ten hours. We are working to stop her, but you should evacuate as many people as you can as soon as possible. Get them clear of the entire system. We will contact you when the threat is over. Repeat: Evacuate now, level three modal or better. Explanations to follow.

The message ended with their official signatures. There would be no mistaking its origin. They didn't have time to wait for a reaction or reply.

"Will it be enough?" she asked.

"Their shipyards are well organized," Maff replied over the comms. "I don't know how many ships they have, though. It's better than nothing. I'll be praying to Turlanfador while you work."

Kim looked up at the ruined node. "Say one for us while you're at it?"

"Certainly."

They came out in the center of the impact crater the city had been built in. It was a mountain nearly as tall as the rim. There were no collapsed skyscrapers here. Everything had been built into the mountain, including the node.

"I can't get over how *big* they are," Kim said as she touched it like it might bite her.

"Most of this one is outside, that's why it looks so bad." As with the other one, there was a maintenance hatch but also a rupture caused by some sort of accident eons ago. "We need to go inside to turn it off."

"Inside?"

"It's not as bad as it looks," he said as he peered down through the hole. The light from his La'fan mask showed walls covered in Bemian electronics with a floor made of dirt far below. "Although it does look pretty bad."

But when he turned back, he found Kim wasn't interested in the hole at all. She was kneeling next to the maintenance hatch.

"What are you doing?" he asked.

"This won't be the only node we visit. It can't be. I need to make sure we can quickly get into one that's not got a hole blown in its side." He watched as she tried a few of the bits of metal she made after they rescued her. "You do your thing, I got this. See if you can make it cough up a map while you're at it."

Halfway down the maintenance ladder, he found the nexus needed to interface his threads with the node. The shutdown sequence was straightforward, but slower than the last time. As Kim predicted, the final message wasn't what he wanted.

Control of cleansing transferred to node XR1231.

He activated a comm panel and typed *provide location of node XR1231.*

The next node was in a solar orbit a little closer than this planet. There had to be more than one.

Provide locations of all nodes capable of controlling cleansing.

He groaned as a list of a three dozen nodes rolled into his queue. They'd have to take out half of them. "Guys," he said over the comms as he climbed out. "We've got a new problem."

*

"You're sure you can't do that spooky thing with the transit dimension?" Maff asked after they were underway to the next node.

He looked at Kim, who shook her head. "We don't know the limits," he replied, "but it won't be soon enough to make a difference here."

"What's the issue with us visiting them one by one?" Kim asked.

Maff called up an engineering screen, filled with virtual dials, gauges, and indicators. "There might've been a problem with one of the ship's engines earlier."

That didn't sound good. "Might have?" he asked.

His idea to make Maff look like a wounded bird had worked too well, damaging the engines when she needed maximum performance. "I managed to fix them myself," Maff said with a trace of justified pride. Mike could remember when she didn't know how to open the maintenance cowls. "But this is going to put a serious strain on them."

He'd mounted a countdown clock cobbled from spare parts to the front of the command deck. Their problems didn't make it slow down. "Define serious," he said.

Maff stared at the indicators, then switched the screens back to her standard controls. "Never mind. It's not your problem; it's mine. Get ready for the next jump."

The next three were in various independent solar orbits, allowing them both to experience weightlessness for the first time. The robes didn't protect them from hard vacuum, so they had to use the emergency space suits that were part of the ship's lifeboat. They were single-use. Once they took them off, they had to be replaced. So they didn't take them off.

And each node took longer to shut down than the next.

What started as an easy jog turned into a sprint. Maff started taking the whole ship out of the transit dimension to repair the engines while they did their work, but she had to leave the cowls off and expose the delicate machinery to harsh conditions. And they were vulnerable to system scans.

He and Kim had just finished deactivating an orbital node when the Interpreter forces found them.

The only thing that saved them from the ambush was their opponent's incompetence in zero-G. Which didn't mean he and Kim were super-soldiers *on the float,* a great phrase he'd picked up from an old science fiction series, only that they were two very small targets in a very large space. The silent puffs the slugs fired by their attackers made when they hit the node's hide were still terrifying.

"*Move!*" Kim shouted as she leapt away from the node's wall and into the void, straight at their ship as Maff frantically climbed inside to start things up. Without the element of surprise, Kim's long practice with realistic combat realms trumped their numbers and firepower. She'd been bouncing around in zero-G simulations for more than a decade, and it showed.

Mike wasn't as experienced.

She landed *inside* the hatch like a dancer hung from wires while he cleanly sailed into the side of the ship with a *thump* and saw stars. Thumb-sized dents appeared in the hull around him as slugs made silent impacts. It took no imagination at all to figure out what would happen if one found their mark. He couldn't run, so he scrabbled like a crab into the hatch, chased by the invisible dent-makers. Maff jumped to the transit dimension before the hatch had closed.

"How many nodes do we have left until we've deactivated enough of them to stop the sequence?" Kim asked.

Mike checked and couldn't believe what he saw. In his mind, they'd only been at this an hour or so, but the clock said that was a lie. They'd been at this almost the whole day. "One." Then he looked at the countdown clock. "And it has to be the next one." Another orbital.

He heard hissing.

Both suits, pushed well beyond their design tolerances as single-use life preservers, had cracked across the joints and could no longer hold pressure. There were no backups, no extras. They had no way to reach the orbital now.

"Can we over-pressure the suits? Fill them faster than they leak? How long can the tanks hold out?" Kim asked.

"Forget the suits," Maff said over the intercom. "I've got an idea."

*

Maff's suit was rated for any environment she might find herself in, including hard vacuum. She didn't know how to hack a node, but she'd thought of a way around that.

Mike looked at a different hatch, one he didn't know existed until a few moments ago.

"You're sure there's room?"

The hatch on the underside of Maff's suit slid aside, revealing a portal that immediately irised open. On the other side was a wall of fur covered with orange, yellow, and black stripes.

"Let's say we'll be very good friends at the end of this."

The wall rippled and moved away, allowing him to see the inner structure of the suit. For some reason he'd expected it to look like the inside of a warehouse, all spare girders and steel panels. It wasn't like that at all. It was covered in some sort of suede or maybe felt. And he was going to climb in there. The whirring and clicking of his breathing mask got loud enough to be noticeable. Mike said the Diamond Sutra in his head to slow it down.

"All I have to do is push a few buttons to move the ship around?" Kim asked over the intercom. A quick test had shown that Kim's touch sensitivity was alive and well when it came to Maff's actual body, so she was staying behind to mind the ship.

Mike squeezed through the portal. It was covered with some sort of invisible membrane, which kept the atmospheres on either side separated. This was fortunate, considering how toxic Maff's atmosphere was to him. His breath mask allowed the faint scent of almonds through, but the telltales on the goggles said the filters were handling it. He caught a brief glimpse of more striped fur before the portal irised shut and dropped him into darkness.

"Within limits," Maff said to Kim, sounding like she was as cramped as he was in here. "I didn't have time to automate more than the basics, so don't try anything fancy. Mike, can you see out?"

Maff really was about the same size and shape as a manta ray back home, but she had evolved on a gas giant. Incredibly, her main anatomical structure was her skin. She had no internal organs that they would recognize. Most of the interior space of her body was filled with gas. She really was a gasbag. They'd already seen how flexible this made her when she changed her shape to look like a human. Now it gave her the ability to move around inside her suit to make room for him. He crawled forward, flat on his belly, until he reached the row of three oval windows at the head of the suit. "Clear as can be." He startled when the fur wrapped over and around him. It was warm and soft.

When he turned away from the portal, her eyes met his, three to two. Hers spun and spiraled, filled with layers of multicolored gas. Kim caught him staring at her eyes all the time. The complexity combined with the personality made for an intoxicating combination. Maff's eyes, though, were on a whole other level. He couldn't help himself. "Wow."

"I didn't realize how soft you'd be," she said in nearly the same tone he'd used. "My lucky day."

"He's mine, Maff," Kim said over small speakers in the suit. "And I want him back."

"Understood."

Everything lurched sideways and up as she stood. It was like being in a car without a seatbelt on, held down by a giant fuzzy pillow. There was nothing to hold on to, so he spread out as best he could. He opened a radio link to Kim. "We're on our way."

*

They managed to get all the way down to the center of the node when the next attack came. "Hurry," Mike said. "Yellow wire to green switch, then punch the blue button."

"And...done," Maff said triumphantly. "Coming out now."

A line of holes opened up in the side of the node, letting the sunlight in.

"We've got company," Kim said over the radio.

Maff leapt toward the opening they used to enter the node, sending his stomach in three different directions at once. "Activate evasive one," she said as they sailed into open space. "Kim, *activate evasive one!"*

He caught sight of their ship as something big exploded against its left wing. It began to roll, venting gas.

Then something else slammed into Maff's suit, and Mike's ears popped.

"We've been hit!" Maff shouted as they tumbled. Dark purple lights started flashing warnings against the suit windows.

Maff cursed. "I've lost thruster control!"

Pressure built against the seals of his breathing mask, and then containment alarms flashed. "Is there anything I can do?" he shouted. The mask's speaker was much quieter than he was used to. They were losing atmosphere. The seals of his mask failed with a bang and a hiss.

In front of them, a wall of purple lightning exploded into view.

Chapter 54
Tonya

They exited the realm and found themselves next to the camp stove in an open war zone. Bullets whizzed by from all directions. Helen didn't wake up at all. Her transfer into orbital realmspace hadn't changed anything.

She grabbed Helen in a bear hug and rolled them both to the ground. "Spencer! Get down!"

"Motherfucker!" He hit with a thud.

"Are you okay?"

"Getting shot at sucks! Yes, I'm fine! What about Helen?"

Tonya checked, cursing every time a bullet splattered dirt in her direction. "Vitals are okay." A ricochet buzzed over her head like an evil wasp. "We need cover!"

He elbow crawled over to her. They each took one of Helen's shoulders and then together dragged her behind some nearby fallen logs. "Which side is ours?" she asked.

"Fucked if I know," he said. "Just a second."

Tonya could make out a little more detail about what was going on now that they'd found some cover. A group of people were on the other side of the camp, shooting at a group of people on this side. No automatic weapons, not yet, anyway, but high-powered rifles were prominent on both sides, as were what had to be shotguns. Those would blow a hole in her big enough to see through. Great.

"Okay," Spencer said to the air around him. "I'll tell her." He opened his eyes. "Stewart says we've got two teams of bad guys now, but they're mostly shooting at each other."

Helen opened her eyes, but it was clear that she was confused. "Where is Jainlee? Father needs some hot water. No, don't take that."

She couldn't examine Helen in the middle of a shooting gallery. Tonya turned to Spencer. "Which way to the good guys?"

A tree above them exploded, showering them with splinters and dust. Tonya had grown up dodging drive-bys, so of course she'd end up getting killed in some redneck Armageddon in backwoods Arkansas. That made perfect sense.

"This way!" He pointed forward, away from both sides that were shooting up the joint over their heads.

"Do they know we're coming?" She'd gotten shot by friendly fire many times in disorganized realm contests and had no desire to experience the real thing.

"They do now." She saw a shadow move and fire to their left. The bad guys were getting closer. "Let's go!"

Helen managed to sit up halfway to their next solid bit of cover, another downed log covered in bushes. "We must protect the markets!"

A bullet whizzed by so close that Tonya swore it parted her hair. "Get *down*!" They both pushed hard on Helen's shoulders to get her back on the ground.

"Why hasn't she pulled the plug on all this?" Spencer asked. "I thought she could pull the plug on all this!"

"If you moved half your brain into orbit," Tonya replied as dirt and leaves wormed their way down her pants. *Gross*. "I'm pretty sure you wouldn't be this coherent."

"But I'm not a flying spaghetti monster." A bullet *pwonged* in front of them, the noise of the ricochet allowing her to track its flight like a tennis ball. "I was expecting more from her."

"Less bitching, more crawling."

They got behind the next patch of cover and assessed the situation again. The two main sides of the firefight seemed to have each other well pinned down. Tonya was beginning to think they were all zombies. Anyone with any tactical sense would've started a flanking maneuver by now. Especially on this pool-table-flat terrain.

Come to think of it, that's probably why Spencer's bunch was situated where they were.

Helen grabbed Tonya hard and pulled her close. "Are we safe?"

"People are shooting at us, Helen. That's not safe."

She rolled over, eyes tightly shut. "I can't leave. I'm not finished."

She must still be in the realm. If Helen opened her eyes and tried moving around, there was a real chance her basic phone protocols would log her out. "We're going toward allies. Working toward better cover."

Spencer took off his shirt and handed one end to Helen. "Hold on to this, I'll guide you." Crawling through this undergrowth with her clothes on was bad enough. Tonya didn't envy doing it with bare skin. "Everyone ready?"

Tonya nodded, so did Helen.

"On three. One…two…*three*!"

Now that they weren't dragging anyone, they made much better time, and the bullets were no longer going directly over their heads. They seemed to have left the main fire zone behind.

"How the hell are they staying resupplied is what I want to know," Spencer said.

"It's coordinated reloaders," Helen replied, eyes still shut. "At least half the town is co-opted now."

"Can you stop it?" Tonya asked.

"We need to find good cover first."

"Working on it," Spencer said as they crawled forward. "Aim for that." He pointed at yet another line of downed trees.

Except, now that she was looking at it, that wasn't all it was. Vehicles were parked behind the trunks, and it was obvious from the clean ends and raw stumps around them that the shelter was built intentionally.

They'd found allies.

Wounded allies. Two people were laid out on stretchers when they rounded the corner of the makeshift fort. Another one was being brought in from the other side of the clearing. It added a layer of complexity they didn't need.

"Helen," she said, "Go with Spencer. I need to triage."

"It's more serious than that, Tonya." She held out her hand. "Sit with me and hang on."

"There's no time!"

When Helen's eyes opened, they coruscated with faint coral light. "There's always time. Sit down."

Tonya was on the ground before she realized her legs had moved. So that's what it felt like to be on the receiving end of a nurse's voice.

Helen moved in close. "Don't read too much into this, it's a requirement."

She kissed Tonya.

"What the fu—" Spencer's curse was lost in coils that wrapped around her, thick and thin, strong and gentle. "Helen? What's going on?" There was no solid ground here, no *up* that she could perceive.

"A shadow of what Mike and Kim can do together. Now, open your eyes."

She opened them, then again, and again. Three distinct perspectives. She stood next to each of the wounded. "What the hell is this?"

"The best I can do with the tools I have at hand. You're being projected into the shared vision space of the camp now, in three places. You can't touch anything, but you have helpers. Guide them."

Incredibly, she could.

"The tourniquet needs to be tighter…"

"Break open the sanitizer first, hit your hands with it…"

"Hold him there, and there, now you can…"

She'd been split. Her consciousness was in three independent places, looking out of three sets of eyes, working three trauma cases.

It was confusing for a moment, then it cleared. Concentrating on each task somehow separated them cleanly.

"Now," Helen said, "open your eyes one more time."

She was back in the wasteland realm Tonya thought had been annihilated by…

Helen's voice came from all around her. "Andromeda. It told the truth. The entire galaxy is a single conscious entity. That's how it can project so much power over such a vast distance."

It was still in the sky, but farther away. "We're winning?"

"Not yet. I need more tools to work with. That's why you two are here."

Spencer was already kneeling over a hole in the ground. It was a hole in the realm itself, Tonya saw the static of raw data streams fizzing underneath. He looked up and said, "I need those constructs you and Mike use in your experiments to finish this. Those multidimensional motherfuckers, like the one that sucked him away?"

Tonya turned back to the outside.

"Apply pressure. If you have to throw up turn away…"

"Look for long sticks. The splint will need…"

"A thin tube. Do you have an eye dropper in…"

It was a strobe that flashed four times in sequence, but at the same time. Here in the realm, Spencer wanted those constructs. She pulled open her research files. "Which ones do you need?"

"They have names? How the hell should I know?"

"Variations three and six, to start," Helen said.

Tonya snapped together the required constructs as she triaged outside. "How is this possible?"

"I think somehow every person on Earth has…call it *Interpreter potential.* It's like a demo version of what Mike and Kim do. I can't put you in the physical world, and I can't do more than four splits, but I *can* meld my threads to your consciousness and allow this to happen."

Outside, Tonya said, "Pull steadily on the thread…"

"Spread it left to right…"

"Clean, it's important to…"

Tonya handed Spencer the first construct. A deep rumble came up through her feet. "What's that?"

"Incoming!" Spencer shouted and jumped on top of her in the realm. A sheet of power swept over them, destroying everything in its wake, dissolving her avatar.

"Jesus fucking Christ on a green-donkey-ball-sucking crutch," Spencer said as his avatar re-formed.

They got up, and he went to work situating the first construct.

"That power pulse came from Andromeda?" Tonya asked.

Helen nodded. "I'm able to fight the worst of it off. That's what its next play was going to be: destroying realms with people in them. Those anomalies you were tracking? Experiments."

Tonya started with the next construct, which would spread out to the size of a pretty large suspension bridge. But there was a problem. "Spencer, I need a data stream to fill this out."

He pulled up a cable of the static stuff that underpinned the realm. "That's where this comes in."

In the woods they said to her,

"… need to hurry"

"… about to be"

"… overrun."

Three places, three identical messages. From her three sets of eyes, Tonya saw shadows moving in, firing.

Everything slipped sideways. "Helen?"

Tonya's vision cleared, still in four places. "You need to hurry; I'm losing my grip."

She'd finished triage, so Tonya helped the fire teams.

"On the left…"

"Aim lower…"

"Wait for them to reload…"

They were much closer, shadowed shapes spitting fire. An automatic weapon opened up, sending everyone to the ground.

"Tonya," Helen said, the strain clear in her voice. "We're out of time."

She spun the construct in eleven different directions at once. When it balanced and reached the right speed, a port appeared in the center. Tonya turned to Spencer "Now!"

He touched his static cable to the port. The construct rapidly expanded until it encompassed the entire realm. Andromeda's image vanished.

The outside world went silent.

Pain exploded where she touched Helen. Tonya rolled herself to the ground. She could *feel* where everyone was around her, pillars of madness.

Spencer let out a whoop. "We did it!"

She looked at Helen, who smiled weakly. "Like I said, don't read too much into that kiss."

The touch madness faded as quickly as it appeared. "At least take me out to dinner."

Helen stood up and offered Tonya her hand. "How about a rain check?"

She gripped it and levered herself upright. "Deal."

Spencer grabbed them both, dancing around, hopping and yelling. Tonya had survived a few hours as a target in a real-life shooting gallery. Her theory was true; she'd survived! They all had!

Helen took two steps away with a distracted look on her face.

Tonya let go of Spencer's arms. Helen distracted was never a good sign. "What's wrong?"

She turned to them, very serious. Nobody did serious like Helen did. She was a cop through and through. "I have access to orbital sensor platforms now. Some of them are asteroid watchers.

"I've picked up a new signal. We have incoming."

Chapter 55
Mike

Mike woke up disoriented, threads tangled, with no idea where he was. He opened his eyes and stared uncomprehendingly at the ceiling above him, all grates and hanging lights.

The ship. He was on their ship, in bed. He turned over only to get a face full of pillows. That could only mean…he sat up.

Kim lay on her back beside him, breathing slowly and deeply. He'd seen this often enough to know she was sleeping off the use of her power, although he had no idea how she managed it. The last thing he remembered was a clear impression of a black void with coral-colored lightning shooting through it. Somehow, Kim had managed to activate her power in a way he'd never seen before.

His own fatigue was still very clear, so it wasn't some sort of shortcut. Normally she'd stay this way for hours, maybe a day or two. But forcing it might make it take longer to sleep off. There was no way to know.

She held one of their makeshift eating trays on her chest, with two words written on it: *GET WILL.*

They were both stripped to their underwear. Maff was nowhere to be seen, but it was obvious she was around here somewhere. Mike got up quietly and dressed, kissing Kim on the forehead before making his way to the command deck.

He found Maff at her station, staring pensively at engineering readouts and her piloting controls. Her suit had a huge black mark on one wing. One of the equipment harnesses, the one without her food factory, hung from its straps. Only hours ago he'd been *inside* that suit. In a way, he'd been more intimate with Maff than he'd ever managed with Kim. Might ever manage with Kim. But they'd saved everyone's life.

It felt a little awkward now, though he didn't understand why. "Are you okay?" he asked.

She did her version of a sigh. "I'm fine." She turned around. "About what happened…"

He nodded. "Yeah."

"If my bashtun found out, ugh, there would be such a scandal."

He shrugged. "Then your bashtun won't find out." Mike walked over to the nav console. Maybe changing the subject would clear the air. "What happened?"

Maff must've had the same idea, because she relaxed visibly as she turned back to the controls. "Kim set a timer on a jump I'd programmed and then hauled us into the cargo bay. You said she couldn't do the glass girl?"

"That's what I thought. I still don't know how she managed it."

"Neither do I, but I'm glad she did. We've been running silent ever since. She said when you woke up you might have a better idea where Will is?"

He closed his eyes and concentrated, then smiled. A point that had at first been at an infinite distance and an indefinite direction now had both. And it was close, closer than they'd ever been before. Finally, after all of this, it was almost over.

"We need to make a stop."

*

If it hadn't been for Maff's piloting skills, Mike doubted they could have ever reached him. Not without an entire La'fan salvage crew and who knew how many months or years. The portal that Will walked through ended up being buried miles beneath the surface. This probably wasn't an accident. If Gonzo had routed him to somewhere nearer the surface, the La'fan would have recycled the entire site without once considering there might be someone alive in there.

"Gonzo?" he said into the darkness once he'd stepped outside the ship. "Za-Nafalia?"

A console lit up and a hologram swirled into view. He'd recognize the graceful centaur-like form anywhere. She'd saved his life, and now Will's.

"Mike?" She sounded as fragile as this place looked.

Using Standard, he said, "Yes, I'm here to take Will off your hands. Thank you for what you have done."

"You know the language now! That's very good. There's so much I wanted to tell you. So much…"

Lights on the floor turned on, tracing a path to a door. It slid open. On the other side, a room lit up in blue light. A bed with a clear cover over it was inside, allowing him to see the occupant.

Will.

"I took good care of him for you," she said as he walked into the room. "Good care."

Will was noticeably larger than he'd been before, although as far as Mike could tell, he'd suffered no muscle atrophy, no bedsores.

"He aged?"

Faint laughter faded into static, then the voice came back, weaker than before. "We cannot stop time with this machine, only mitigate its effects. It is good you are here. I'm so tired now."

The device Will rested in was mobile, set on castors, like an enclosed hospital bed. "How do I get him out?"

"The machine will know. Not long…"

He had to strain to hear her now. Mike worked out where the brakes on the bed were, disconnected the machine, and wheeled it back to the ship.

Disconnecting the device gave Gonzo a boost. "Tell me," she asked in a much stronger voice. "Was I right? Are you paired but unjoined?"

That's what she'd been asking him about. "Yes, you were right."

"Such a shame. I could've taught you everything." The boost must've been temporary, because her voice had begun to fade again. "But I did a better thing, I think."

She had saved his life, an alien stranger, after he'd caused the destruction of her companion. She then took care of a child that came from halfway across the galaxy by burning up resources she needed to stay alive. It took two tries before he could say the words, "You did a much better thing, Gonzo. Again, I can't thank you enough."

"Very good," he could barely hear her now. "It was a burden, but I was proud to..."

He waited in the stillness. "Gonzo? Za-Nafalia?"

But he was answered only by silence. What had been a lifeboat had now become a tomb. Eventually the La'fan would make it down here, recycling it so its raw materials would become part of a renewed planet, a new biosphere. Mike couldn't know for sure if she'd crossed the final threshold to consciousness, but he hoped so. Regardless, she certainly earned another turn on the karmic wheel.

Mike hoped to meet her someday if she did.

*

The La'fan managed to communicate with his in-system thread less than an hour later. "I am most pleased to discover that you are not dead," Honorable Fakner said. Always such a joker.

"So am I," Mike replied to the message as he hunted for engine parts.

"However, the situation here is still fluid. We recommend an *extended vacation*," Maff hadn't been the only one picking up English words, "until events play out."

"Understood."

While Kim rested and Will's...he decided to call it a crèche...counted down to when it would open, he and Maff laid in a roundabout course to Earth.

"You've always known where home was, haven't you?" she asked as he programmed in the coordinates.

"Yep." The nav console complained that his final waypoint set didn't exist on the maps it had. He overrode the warnings.

"Well that's a good thing then. It's the only way you're getting home."

"And you'll be all right getting back?"

"That reminds me," she said, "I've been meaning to ask—"

He felt Kim walk in behind them. Her rest must've really refreshed her if she was able to make an entrance in her glass form. It did seem a bit over the top, though. "You know," he said to her, "you could use the," he turned around and the word nearly died in his mouth, "door…"

It wasn't Kim who stood on the bridge, looking around like she'd taken possession of a house.

It was Valsa Burtan, first Councilor of the Interpreters.

Her skin was as black and glossy as Kim's, but with red lightning playing over it instead of Kim's purple-pink. She wore a simple leotard, free of the deformity she carried in realspace. Valsa was humanoid enough, symmetrical enough, and carried herself confidently enough to walk down the catwalk of any fashion show back home and stop it cold.

In a word, gorgeous.

In another word, trespasser. But when he tried to jump to his feet, nothing happened.

She smiled at him. "Quite cozy, I must say."

Two very large, heavily armed robots came through the transit dimension passage she'd created. "Secure the other prisoner," she commanded. They quickly left the command bridge, heading for the quarters where Kim rested.

Valsa walked languidly around the bridge as he fought for control of his own body. Suddenly his threads were violently thrown out of the local realmspace.

"Amateurs," a masculine voice said from all around him. "There's no reason for him to fear them so." Not only was Valsa here, her threaded companion had crossed over with her and invaded the local realmspace.

Beside him, Maff was still. Valsa must've hacked her suit controls. Had she hacked him?

"They are a strange combination," Valsa said in a voice that nearly purred. "Maybe that's what he fears."

Mike discovered he could talk. "How did you get here?"

She gestured to Kim's robes lying in a pile beside his on the floor. They'd left them there when they got into the emergency space suits. "What we see we can reach. You know that much. Do you think I'd give her those barbaric rags without adding a few things myself?"

"Don't forget the other one," the voice said.

"The robots have secured her." Valsa lifted her hand, and so did Mike. She looked at Maff, then moved her hand side to side. Maff's suit moved in both directions. "Do you like my new puppets, Seluk?"

"I think you should stop playing with your toys. And I won't trust that the other one is secure until I see it," the masculine voice said.

Her expression said this was an old argument, often encountered. "Very well." The doors to the bridge slid shut and locked into place. "Now no one can reach us. Happy?"

"I'll be happier after we turn around and bury these people in a deep hole." Mike's nav solution was pushed aside, and a new one with coordinates for a planet he didn't recognize started up. "Thankfully, that won't take long."

"We'll bury them *after* we learn how to take control of their army." She walked up to Mike, elegant and pitiless. In any other circumstance, he might find her fascinating, *did* find her fascinating, despite himself.

She leaned down. This close, he could smell faint ozone, hear the soft crackling of the lightning across her skin. Like Kim, her eyes were windows into a dimension of red patterns. Mike wanted to look away but couldn't. And it wasn't any of her doing.

"He is right about one thing, though," she breathed against his ear, and his heartbeat amped up. "You *are* powerful. Much more powerful than I think he realizes. And, my handsome, strange friend, he is more afraid of you than anyone I have ever seen before.

I wasn't sure how I would turn his plan against him at this late date, only that I would. And now here you are."

They'd left the scanner screens up. Mike saw Valsa's fleet forming up around them. Surrounding them. He squirmed and felt the slightest give in her hold on him but didn't push it. Even if he were to get free, there was no way through that blockade.

Valsa curled her fingers gently around his chin and turned him to face her. Her touch was literally electric, sending faint static shocks across his skin. That was why his pulse was racing and his face was hot. It had to be.

Her eyes were the only thing he could see. "I don't think we'll have to bury both of them, Seluk. I think this one at least will come along of his own free will." She pushed a thigh against his knee. Her muscles were smooth and firm. Mike's mouth went dry. "With a suitable amount of persuasion."

"Get away from him, you *bitch*!" A long black club hit Valsa on the side of her head and sent her flying.

It wasn't a club, though. It was a robot arm, still powered. He could hear the servos and motors whine inside it. Kim stood behind it, holding it with both of her hands like the world's biggest baseball bat. She had some kind of shifter sticking out of it between her fingers. She was still in her underwear, not transformed, a barefoot pillar of pure, unadulterated rage.

"Can you stand up?"

Mike tried. "I can barely speak."

Kim nodded and walked over to where Valsa had fallen in a heap. She cocked the arm back, said something in Vershampire that he couldn't make out, and clobbered her.

"Jesus, Kim. Don't kill her."

She threw the arm away. "I won't. I don't think I can when she's like this, not with a simple club anyway. I just don't want her to wake up any time soon."

The solution had stopped creating itself on the nav console, and the fleet around them had stopped moving. "I think you got her threaded companion, too."

"Can you at least push him out of the ship's realmspaces?"

Mike shoved with his threads and got a nice, steady movement. "Yup."

Kim threw one of Valsa's arms over her shoulder and, with a scream of straining anger, hoisted her up off the deck. "Do that. We have to go. Maff, can you hear me?"

There were two loud clicks from Maff's suit, then, "Yes! What's happened to me? Why can't either of us move?"

"This is a regular Bemian ship, not from the La'fan. She hacked the sa'dst networks that have taken up residence in your bodies. I was out of range." Kim stomped heavily toward the hole Valsa had made in the bridge. "I should be able to free you up in a moment. Mike, is her other half out of the ship's realmspace?"

He gave Seluk's threads one hard push. "Gone."

Kim heaved Valsa's unconscious body into the hole with a wordless shout. Then she said, "And don't come back!" The hole vanished as if it had never been there.

Mike was suddenly free, and Maff's suit wobbled as if she'd just regained her balance. Alarms blared to life as the ships around them turned to fire.

"Maff!" Kim shouted as she strapped into the scanner station, "Get us out of here!"

The ship lurched sideways and down, and Mike's stomach try to leave through his throat.

"I can't hold them off for long."

"Mike, where's our nav solution?"

He swiped Seluk's half-complete solution away and called up his own. "It's ready, but we can't get clear to use it." The ship did a one-eighty turn along two axes at once, making his body and head feel like they were pointing in different directions.

"Maff?" Kim asked.

"How confident are you in that solution, Mike?" Two loud *spangs* rang out from somewhere as the ship lurched in time with the hits.

He'd been running this solution in his head from the moment he figured out how to do it. "Very." He sent it to her station.

"Okay, then." One of her manipulators turned a dial all the way over, pulled it out, and then turned it further. "I'm glad you gave me captain's permissions when you hacked these controls. Modal eight, comin' up!"

She slammed the dial down. Sparks exploded all over the bridge, and everything went dark.

Chapter 56
Helen

It wasn't easy figuring out what was heading for them. Her new home wasn't fully connected to the existing terrestrial realmspaces, and she didn't have access to any military nets or satellites. The only reason Helen spotted it at all was that the Planetary Society had set up an asteroid watcher project to keep an eye out for objects on a collision course with Earth.

They were driving back to town when Mike suddenly reached out to her. "Can you hear me?" Helen sat up straighter in the back of the car and then made a shushing motion when Spencer and Tonya asked what was going on.

It was like she'd had a cold all this time and suddenly could breathe again. "Yes! Are you all okay?"

"We're fine. You're not going to believe what's happened."

*

The next trick was figuring out how to stop anyone else from figuring it out.

Helen played a game of *what would Kim do*. What would be the one thing nobody else would think of that would get the ship that held her brother, her future sister-in-law, Will, and someone named Maff, home safe in time for their wedding?

Because, through all the chaos, Helen had never forgotten her promise. The wedding was on, and soon. It added a new proviso to her question: *without getting arrested or detained by any law enforcement or spy agency in the process.*

It helped that her transfer had made headlines around the world:

MASSIVE REALMSPACE CRASH

REALMS DOWN, ONLY THE SECOND TIME IN HISTORY

ORBITAL REALMSPACE FAILURE: ARE YOUR CHILDREN NEXT?

If chaos was what they were seeing, Helen had no problem providing lots more of it. One object track was impossible to hide. Thousands were easy to provide. Doing that caused another headline spasm.

WORLDWIDE PANIC AT FALSE ASTEROID ALARMS

TRUST IN GOVERNMENT AT ALL-TIME LOW DUE TO ASTEROID PANIC

THE GREAT ASTEROID PANIC: WILL YOU EVER BE SAFE AGAIN?

It was all nonsense, but it was irresistible nonsense that generated billions of realm visits in a matter of hours. Helen couldn't make out their ship now, and she knew where to look.

Mike then asked a complicated question. "How are you guys doing?"

"It's a long story."

"Trust me," he said with a chuckle. "We have the time."

In spite of all the gunfire, casualties were very low. Andromeda's influence didn't seem to include aiming a rifle. People only got hurt by being in the wrong place at the wrong time.

The few people who would admit to a strange experience spoke of fighting it off enough to keep from aiming at other people. But those were the exceptions. Almost nobody admitted that *anything* had happened. Hundreds of heavily armed people just somehow ended up in the woods, shot them up for no reason, and then went home. There were rumors that the mayors of the various small towns in the area were going to retroactively declare it some sort of local hunting holiday. It seemed that the result of the first known alien incursion on Earth would be that kids in an entire county would get a day off from school.

She would never have believed it, but these Westerners' reaction to an embarrassing loss of control was to act as if it had never happened, that there was nothing to see. It couldn't have been a more Chinese response.

Mike and Kim's extended transit gave everyone else time to pack and say goodbye. This was easy for Tonya and Spencer, less so for Helen.

It was all they could do to keep Spencer from setting out for Virginia as soon as they got off the levee. Tonya's case was different. Her reverend had been one of the injured in their little fake war. The wound was in a less than dignified spot.

"Now he'll *really* want you to kiss his ass," Spencer said once they'd heard the news.

But that wasn't true. Through several intermediaries, it quickly became known that Tonya was no longer welcome. "Like I care what that man thinks about me."

"You would if you stayed here," Spencer said.

"That was never the plan. I had telemetry running throughout that battle. I have so much data now I don't know when I'll be ready to run another experiment again."

"You still need to run them?" Helen asked. "I thought you had proven your theory."

Tonya turned pensive as she closed her suitcase. "The data didn't quite match what I predicted. It's not over yet."

Helen was the one who'd be missed. They stayed an extra day in town to let the cops and her former Chinese bosses throw a farewell party. Helen was grateful for the distraction, and the ability to dance again in her superior self-adapting shoes. Her threads were still settling into her new home.

Her new circumstance.

Helen now had to admit there was no going back, in more ways than one. She was and would remain Chinese, but China was now closed to her. There was someone else living there now, growing and gathering strength. She could feel it when she tested the barriers. It would take years before the new life inside the Great Firewall was able to reach out to her, but it would happen.

And then Helen would get to meet her daughter.

Lose a country, gain a child. It was more than a fair trade in her opinion. Having a major point of her beliefs, that there was nothing more than the physical world, disproven was also a small price to pay. There would be no more gossipy old men, no more putting out fires, no more worrying about her position in the great game. She had a new place, a new perspective, and her own firewall to police. Andromeda was still out there, still testing. The constructs they built were doing a fine job of locking that strange terrifying being out, but they would need someone to watch over them. It would be a full-time job.

That was all in the future, though. For now, Helen had a new, spectacular view to enjoy.

And a wedding to attend.

Chapter 57

Kim

Will woke up with three days left to go.

The crèche set off alarms that sent everyone running. He was already sitting up when they got to the cargo hold, rubbing his eyes. As soon as he saw Kim, he reached out to her. She'd forced that memory so far down she almost forgotten that they could touch each other. Kim moved toward him slowly, not sure if that was still true.

His hug was tight, as crushing as a now six-year-old could make it. She hugged him back as tight as she dared. Kim was new to this and didn't know if she would break him. Mike assured her it was fine.

Will unlocked the next day.

Maff and Mike were working in the cargo bay on all the gear on Maff's suit. They'd taken apart her food reactor and were creating plans and wiring schematics for it. They were a long way from spares now.

"You're funny looking."

Kim had been holding hands with him as he silently explored the ship. He came around the corner, laid eyes on Maff, and said it just like that, clear as a bell.

She stood there, frozen. They all did.

He let go of her hand and walked up to the reactor. After giving it a careful scan, he walked over to Maff and peered into one of her eye windows. "I see you!"

"And I you, small human." *Shmal hyoomazn*. Maff's accent got better the more she practiced. He rode around on her back for the rest of the trip.

It all came down to complexity. Kim was sure that was the key. To this day, her mind responded to complex machines in a way that made her a natural at hacking and lock-picking. She'd unlocked as a child staring at a mixing board that Mark, the future leader of Rage + the Machine, was frantically trying to calibrate before a concert at Wolf Trap started. Kim somehow *knew* what was wrong and was able to communicate it. Maff's reactor made that board look like a light switch.

Will turned to her and asked, "Are we going to see my mom soon?"

That happened two days later, on an abandoned cargo ship Helen had spotted from orbit. The story of a missing boy left behind when a group of human traffickers abandoned their disabled vessel, finding his way to the bridge and sending out a distress signal, dominated the newsfeeds for an entire cycle. It was then promptly forgotten. They stayed with him until his mom, Emily, could see the ship, and then headed home.

Mike didn't think any of it was necessary, but Kim knew better. Loose ends were what nooses were made of. Better to have it all straight and in place in case someone got suspicious further down the line. Maff called it the most challenging bit of flying she'd ever done.

He enrolled as the first student in the Sellars and Trayne Interpretation Academy a day later. Kim let Mike win that battle, because she'd won the war.

Helen was as good as her word. The wedding was on.

*

She looked out into the church again. "But where *is* he?"

"He is coming," Mama said, "you know this, you can see this."

True. Mike was trapped in yet another of Northern Virginia's legendary traffic jams, between exits on the toll road, so a bailout onto surface streets with AppleWaze as a guide wasn't possible.

"Besides," Maff said, "technically you're already married."

Also true. Helen was never one for half measures. Even though she never missed an opportunity to tease Mike about his faith, she had arranged a small Buddhist ceremony for them this morning. The robes had been gorgeous, the view across the Shenandoah Valley breathtaking. A few of the monks from Mike's monastery had made the trip from China. The senior one, who had known Mike's mentor, Taranathi, personally, had officiated.

But that was only a few hours ago. It didn't feel real yet. It wasn't going to be real to her until the priest had led them in procession to the middle of the church, let them say their vows, hold their candles, wear their crowns, drink from the cup, and dance. They'd come up with a special adapter that would let Maff Pallun, Kim's newfound friend with her unique disability suit, to hand those crowns over to her.

"I was wondering if I could stay," Maff had said as the hours counted down to their landing. That was a decision that surprised them all.

"But you'll never see any of your family again," Mike replied.

"I think I will. Oh, not any time soon, but your Jupiter is like no other planet I've seen. It's nearly identical to our old home planet, has no AC network, and is uninhabited."

"As far as we can tell," Kim said.

"That's another thing I can work on while I'm here. If I can establish there is no life on that planet, then we can begin negotiations with Earth for it."

It was such a Bemian attitude. "Humans don't own Jupiter."

"No," Mike said, "but as soon as someone finds out that she wants it, you can be sure they'll try."

"Do you think they'll welcome us?" Maff asked.

That was an uncomfortable question. "It's hard to say," Kim replied. "Humans can be incredibly stupid and territorial with each other. I don't know how they'll react to aliens."

"Appeal to their greed," Mike said. "Money works much better than you're used to here."

So now, unbeknownst to the rest of the world, she'd turned a determined real-estate scout loose on the Earth. Kim remembered what Maff's lawyer Sha'Katenden was like when he got her out from under those piracy charges and wished humanity luck. They would need it to keep their shirts on.

Kim checked the church again. Hundreds of people had turned up. She would be greeted as Kimberly Trayne-Sellars by every surviving family member Helen could find. Since it was Helen, Kim was certain it was every single one of them. They'd had to move to a venue bigger than Wolf Trap to accommodate them all. Royalty didn't have weddings this size. She had no idea how it'd all been paid for. Helen only made cryptic remarks about tech deals and Israelis when asked.

She'd never seen Grandma Maria so proud. The one child everyone knew would never get married was now wearing Yiayiá Maria's own dress—which fit perfectly the first time Kim tried it on—in a huge Greek church filled with family and friends. They would see her, participate in this, celebrate this.

But for any of it to happen *Mike had to show up.*

Kim had Amazon's aeroTaxi screen on her virtual display—his fear of flying be dammed—when she heard a minor cheer go up from the crowd. She peered out in time to see two of those very drones buzz away from the front steps of the church, leaving a pair of pin-neat men in tuxedos standing in the open doorway.

Spencer and—she had to squeeze her eyes shut and force herself to say it in her head without throwing up—*her future husband.*

The rest was a blur. A joyous blur. She'd seen his tux on a virtual dummy during the fitting, but in person, it was something else. Her heart skipped a beat every time she looked at him. They ended up crying even though they tried not to, especially when he managed to put her mother's wedding ring on her finger without touching her. Kim gasped anyway, more in awe than anything else.

Then, before she realized it, the ceremony was over. They were greeted. Congratulations were expressed personally in a reception line that threatened to never end. Helen had made sure everyone knew the basics of Kim's disability and handed out monogrammed handkerchiefs for them all to use. Uncle Kostas would have none of it and hugged Kim tight with a beautiful scarf he then handed over as a present.

The reception was a big, happy, loud riot. They'd promised each other to go easy on the booze, so when it was time to leave, she only wobbled a little bit heading toward the limo.

"Kimberly Trayne?"

That sobered her right up. "Kimberly Trayne-*Sellars*." She turned around.

A different limo had pulled up, with a big black SUV behind it. Ten federal agents—they were that obvious—stood alertly outside both vehicles.

"Agent Cummings!" Aaron shouted from behind her. "A moment?"

He was a good friend and was on the list anyway, but Kim thought inviting Aaron, still head of the cybercrimes division, would come in handy if one of the three-letter agencies came calling. It was time to test that theory.

"What do you think will happen?" Mike asked her softly.

"I don't care. We're going on our honeymoon." Kim was recovered from her ordeal. If they wanted to throw down, they would be in for a rude surprise.

"The fuck is going on?" Spencer asked.

And they wouldn't be alone. Tonya, Spencer, Helen, and Maff had gathered in a loose half circle behind them. But this wasn't their fight. Kim could take these agents with one hand behind her back.

Probably.

"Stay cool, guys," Mike said. "We're not sure yet."

After some furious discussion and several calls, Aaron slowly walked over to them. "I have a deal I'd like to discuss with you."

They would *not* ruin this moment for her, but talking was better than fighting. "I'm listening."

"It has come to the attention of several heads of state, not all of them friendly, that you may be in possession of unique technology and"—he gave Maff a significant look—"perhaps new friends. The United States government is concerned about your welfare."

This was such crap. "Protective custody is not—"

He held up a hand. "Let me finish. In return for you two promising not to ruin every piece of electronics on anyone who comes near you, the president would like to extend the offer of a protective detail for your honeymoon."

That was more than she'd hoped for, but Kim kept the surprise off her face. "Protective detail?"

"Handpicked agents who will be discreet but alert."

"Handpicked by whom?" This time she let a bit of sparkle creep into her eyes.

He smiled slightly in return. "By the leader of the team, which you get to pick."

Good enough. Better than good enough. "And after?"

"And after, we negotiate. We've heard about what happened in Dumas. Everyone has. We think you have a story to tell. This is bigger than anything humanity has ever faced. We'll need to work together to address the problem. *All* of us."

She looked at Mike first. They were in this for the long haul now, and she needed to get used to that. His opinion mattered. A little.

Okay, a lot.

He nodded faintly. She checked with the rest of them silently in turn. Even Maff, once Kim's translation reached her, nodded.

Kim turned back. She had two rings on her finger now. Her wedding had happened. The honeymoon wasn't ruined!

"How do you feel about Hawaii, Agent Levi?"

The End

Gemini Gambit will return with book 5
Infinity's Bargain

Afterword

For the first time, I think it's fair to say that you've gotten this far due mainly to my own efforts. Which is *not* to say that I did it alone. Cheryl Lowrance has once again proven that patience, understanding, and the occasional threat of the hose will get an author across the finish line in good form. As before, if you're looking for help getting your own work off the ground, I can't recommend Ink Slinger Editorial Services more highly.

I am grateful for my superb cover artist, Melissa Lew. It's extraordinary how she can interpret vague hand waving and confused sentences into art. Her jewelry line is not to be missed!

Lighthouse24 continues to excel at book composition.

My family continue with their great support and willingness to listen to endless hours of authorial shop talk.

Getting the word out about books like these, from reviews to social media posts to simply telling a friend or family member, is how they really become successful. As before, I continue to be thrilled and humbled by how many of you have spread the word about the Gemini Gambit series. Thank you so much for all your efforts.

www.ingramcontent.com/pod-product-compliance
Lightning Source LLC
Chambersburg PA
CBHW030419310726
48979CB00009B/1534/J

and"—he gave Maff a significant look—"perhaps new friends. The United States government is concerned about your welfare."

This was such crap. "Protective custody is not—"

He held up a hand. "Let me finish. In return for you two promising not to ruin every piece of electronics on anyone who comes near you, the president would like to extend the offer of a protective detail for your honeymoon."

That was more than she'd hoped for, but Kim kept the surprise off her face. "Protective detail?"

"Handpicked agents who will be discreet but alert."

"Handpicked by whom?" This time she let a bit of sparkle creep into her eyes.

He smiled slightly in return. "By the leader of the team, which you get to pick."

Good enough. Better than good enough. "And after?"

"And after, we negotiate. We've heard about what happened in Dumas. Everyone has. We think you have a story to tell. This is bigger than anything humanity has ever faced. We'll need to work together to address the problem. *All* of us."

She looked at Mike first. They were in this for the long haul now, and she needed to get used to that. His opinion mattered. A little.

Okay, a lot.

He nodded faintly. She checked with the rest of them silently in turn. Even Maff, once Kim's translation reached her, nodded.

Kim turned back. She had two rings on her finger now. Her wedding had happened. The honeymoon wasn't ruined!

"How do you feel about Hawaii, Agent Levi?"

The End

Gemini Gambit will return with book 5

Infinity's Bargain

Afterword

For the first time, I think it's fair to say that you've gotten this far due mainly to my own efforts. Which is *not* to say that I did it alone. Cheryl Lowrance has once again proven that patience, understanding, and the occasional threat of the hose will get an author across the finish line in good form. As before, if you're looking for help getting your own work off the ground, I can't recommend Ink Slinger Editorial Services more highly.

I am grateful for my superb cover artist, Melissa Lew. It's extraordinary how she can interpret vague hand waving and confused sentences into art. Her jewelry line is not to be missed!

Lighthouse24 continues to excel at book composition.

My family continue with their great support and willingness to listen to endless hours of authorial shop talk.

Getting the word out about books like these, from reviews to social media posts to simply telling a friend or family member, is how they really become successful. As before, I continue to be thrilled and humbled by how many of you have spread the word about the Gemini Gambit series. Thank you so much for all your efforts.

www.ingramcontent.com/pod-product-compliance
Lightning Source LLC
Chambersburg PA
CBHW030419310726
48979CB00009B/1534/J

* 9 7 8 1 7 3 6 0 1 4 1 1 0 *